THE DUKE'S
Dangerous Kiss

ON HIS MAJESTY'S SECRET SERVICE

—————————— BOOK 2 ——————————

PATRICIA BARLETTA

patriciabarletta.com

Published Internationally by Patricia Barletta
Boston, MA
Copyright © 2019 Patricia Barletta

patriciabarletta.com

Exclusive cover © 2019 mightyunicorn.ca
Interior design by Tamara Cribley www.deliberatepage.com

PRINT ISBN 978-1-7324769-7-4
EBOOK ISBN 978-1-7324769-6-7

Editor: Joanna D'Angelo
Proofreader: Christine Knight

This is a work of fiction. Names, characters, places and incidents are either the product of the author's imagination or are used fictitiously, and any resemblance to any person or persons, living or dead, events or locales is entirely coincidental.

ACKNOWLEDGMENTS

Producing a novel from concept to publication takes many people. Once again, my tribe has come through for me: Joanna D'Angelo, my editor, who cajoled me into writing "funny"; Steve at mightyunicorn.ca, who created yet another gorgeous cover; Tamara and Christine at The Deliberate Page, who turned my manuscript pages into a beautiful book; and last, but certainly not least, my critique group—Wendy L., Linda, Wendy R. and DeAnna—I love you, ladies.

I would also like to acknowledge one book in particular that I used often for reference: *Georgette Heyer's Regency World* by Jennifer Kloester. Thank you Ms. Kloester, for producing a comprehensive guide to the Regency period as described in Ms. Heyer's novels.

ALSO AVAILABLE

Moon Dark
BOOK 1 AURIANO CURSE SERIES

Moon Shadow
BOOK 2 AURIANO CURSE SERIES

Coming Soon

Moon Bright
BOOK 3 AURIANO CURSE SERIES

Sign up for Patricia's newsletter at patriciabarletta.com.
Follow Patricia Barletta on BookBub.

CHAPTER 1

London, Early Spring, 1812

She'd had enough. Enough socializing, enough dancing, enough gossiping. Jillian St. Claire was done. Her cheeks ached from smiling. Her feet hurt from standing. The little chair stuck in a corner of the ballroom behind a tall clump of potted greenery was a welcome sight. With a sigh of pleasure, she sank onto the brocade seat. She pulled at the ribbon ties of her dancing slippers, kicked them off, and wiggled her toes. Long, open windows next to her let in a refreshing breeze and cooled her flushed cheeks.

From where she sat, she could see nearly the whole ballroom without being seen. Before her, the dancers flowed together and apart like the colored designs in a kaleidoscope. The music and conversation washed over her, ebbing and flowing like the ocean waves on a beach. She had not wanted a season in London with the balls, the dinners, the salons, the visiting, but realized it was the only way to free herself from *him*. *He* was her guardian, and *he* had insisted on presenting her to society to find a suitable husband. Besides, it was what her mother had wanted for her, he told her. And so, she obeyed.

Male voices came through the open windows next to her from the veranda. All evening she had seen people escape to it—couples trying for a few secluded moments, gentlemen wanting a quiet conversation or pinch of snuff, ladies needing to revive themselves from the heat and dancing. The voices which came to her now were low, intense, not a conversational tone. Several potted evergreens outside the window screened her from the speakers. She caught the words *secrets* and *smuggle*.

"…little time before the Americans lose their patience," she heard a deep, male voice say. "I'm aware of what a confrontation with them would mean. Parliament seems determined to aggravate them. We cannot afford to fight both the Americans and Napoleon. Tell me about America's naval strength. How many ships? How large? How many guns?" The voice rumbled the questions, deep and demanding. Its tone sent a tiny thrill down Jillian's spine.

"Their navy is small but fearless," another man answered. "You know, of course, of their victory over the Barbary pirates."

"A hollow victory, at best." There was a shrug of dismissal in the first man's voice, as if he might have done better himself, single-handedly. "They were still made to pay ransom for the prisoners and tribute money."

"Not such a hollow victory," the second man disagreed. "The pirates don't harass their shipping any longer. The pirates have no wish to anger them again and receive another whipping. The Americans are arrogant on the sea. They don't follow the orders passed by the Privy Council. They trade with whomever they wish and smuggle where they are legally barred, including with France and her allies. They are angered by the impressment of their sailors into our navy."

Jillian was riveted, both by the information and that first man's voice. Who were these men? The exchange sounded more significant than a casual political discussion between two gentlemen.

"This is an explosive situation. Parliament still thinks of the Americans as our colonies, despite winning their independence. Is there anyone in their government who is against a conflict with England?"

"I intercepted a letter from one of the senators from Massachusetts to a senator who lives in Tennessee. He was urging his colleague to patience. Here is a copy of it."

"Adrian!" a third man exclaimed, interrupting the conversation. "I was just telling Harry about the horse you have running in next week's race."

Jillian saw a hand shoot through the greenery and drop a tiny, tightly rolled piece of parchment. Instead of landing in the bush, it landed on the windowsill and bounced off into her shoe. It was smaller than her little finger and sealed with a bit of wax. Fascinated, she stared at it.

What secrets did it contain?

"Jillian St. Clare!" a voice hissed.

Wincing, Jillian tore her eyes away from the clandestine note and faced her chaperone.

"What are you doing here hiding by yourself? You should be mingling with the other young ladies and dancing with marriageable young men." The feather stuck in Lady Pennington's turban vibrated with indignation at finding her young charge shirking her social obligations. "Have you no gratitude, girl? Do you think his lordship spent that fortune at the modiste's for your new gowns to have you sit in a corner by yourself? And the time and energy I spent to teach you the proper behavior of a young woman entering society… Well, that is beside the point." Lady Pennington's glance fell on Jillian's unshod, stocking-covered toes. "Put on your shoes!" she gasped.

Jillian hurriedly stuck her feet back into her slippers and tied them. The tight little roll of parchment pressed beneath her toes. Ignoring the pain, she stood to avoid having the older woman's ample, violet-clad bosom in her face. "I'm sorry, Lady Pennington. I meant no harm," she said. "I only wanted to rest a few minutes."

"Hmph. Rest. Young people these days are so weak. Why, when I was your age—"

"Are you giving Lady Pennington trouble again, Jillian?" The hard voice of her guardian, the Earl of Rystoke, broke into the woman's tirade.

Jillian lowered her eyes to avoid looking into the cold, dark gaze of her guardian. "No, my lord, no trouble."

"Then why aren't you dancing? I did not bring you to London to hide behind the floral decorations." He flicked an offending leaf that had the audacity to brush the sleeve of his coat.

Jillian remained silent, wanting to disappear.

"Who is your partner for the next dance?" The earl raised an imperious brow.

Jillian panicked at the brusque request. She had no partner for the next dance.

"Partner?" she parroted to gain time to think. "I...ah...it's..."

Rystoke's mouth thinned into an angry line.

Jillian paled before his cruel gaze. She was in trouble now. When they returned to the earl's townhouse, he would berate her for being ungrateful, foolish, stupid, and a host of other terrible things. Lady Pennington would look on without a word, her mouth pursed in the middle of her moon face. Jillian hated the earl. She hated Lady Pennington. Most of all, she hated her season in London.

"Um, it was..." She searched her brain for the name of some young man she had met.

"Don't you remember in that empty head of yours what young blood had asked for the next dance?" Rystoke's eyes narrowed dangerously. "You did have a partner for the next dance, did you not?" The earl did not bother to disguise his sarcasm.

"I believe the next dance is mine," a deep voice said from just beyond the tall group of plants.

Jillian stifled a gasp and peeked around the ferns. *That voice!* The same deep, velvety voice she'd heard through the open window demanding the secret information—the one that had riveted her attention and sent delicious thrills down her spine.

She had imagined the owner of that voice to be handsome, suave, dashing, and perhaps just a bit dangerous. The man who stood on the other side of the plants certainly fulfilled her expectations but seeing him in the flesh left her speechless. He was tall. His dark hair was tousled fashionably. His black evening clothes hung perfectly on his graceful, male frame. But what took her breath away and made her want to duck back behind the potted ferns were his eyes. They were not brown or black, the normal shade to match the man's coloring. They were not even blue, which would have been startling enough. Instead, they were the color of topaz. Jillian was reminded of the eyes of a lion she had seen at the Exeter 'Change in the Strand.

The orchestra was beginning the opening strains of the next dance.

"You cannot dance with Miss St. Clare," her guardian declared.

Jillian was amazed to hear a touch of nervousness in the earl's voice.

"Oh? Why is that?" the dark stranger asked.

"Because it is a waltz and she has not received permission." The earl's tone was smug.

"How delightful," the dark stranger commented. He held out a hand to Jillian. "I do so enjoy the waltz. I'm sure no one will mind if I break the rule just this once."

Jillian knew that he was referring to the rule that young ladies like herself who were just entering society were not supposed to dance the waltz. Before they were allowed to indulge in that scandalous behavior, they were to receive permission from the seven women from Almack's who were the caretakers of social convention. Breaking that rule tarnished the young woman's reputation. She had not yet been to Almack's Assembly Rooms, that temple of the social elite of London. Therefore, she had not been granted permission to dance the waltz, and certainly not with this total stranger.

Rystoke stepped between Jillian and the stranger. "*I* do not give my permission, sir."

The stranger dropped his hand and raised a cool eyebrow. "Really? And who are you, sir, to deny the young lady a dance?"

Veins stood out at the earl's temple. "You know very well who I am, sir. I also happen to be this young lady's guardian."

Amusement lit the stranger's eyes. "I never thought of you as the paternal type, Rystoke. I'm not sure the role suits you. Let us not create a scene. I promise not to abscond with her, and I'm sure the young lady would like to dance the waltz." He held out his hand again and smiled at her over her guardian's shoulder.

Jillian studied his hand. It was large, with long slender fingers. Calluses marked the palm and revealed that its owner practiced often with the sword. She had the feeling that this man broke the rules whenever he felt like it.

Propriety demanded that a proper introduction be made between a gentleman and a young lady before they conversed. To dance with a complete stranger was scandalous, and to dance the waltz... Well, that would shock the members of the ton down to the tips of their well-clad toes.

Jillian wanted to shock them. Most of all, she wanted to defy the Earl of Rystoke and Lady Pennington. Throwing away all caution, Jillian stepped forward and placed her hand into the stranger's, allowing herself to be drawn onto the dance floor. His warmth through her glove was surprisingly comforting. As she slipped past her furious guardian and the scandalized Lady Pennington, she flashed them a quick smile of triumph. Stepping onto the dance floor, she immediately felt her gloating turn to apprehension at what she had done. That little bit of rolled parchment squeezing beneath her toes reminded her why this stranger had invited her to dance.

"If we are to dance, perhaps we should exchange names," she managed to croak.

He smiled. "Isn't it more exciting to be mysterious? We are two strangers who will dance together, then part, never to meet again."

His statement conjured up romantic visions of star-crossed lovers in her head. But this man was not her lover. She did not even know his name. He was involved in something clandestine, maybe even treacherous. Perhaps she had been too eager to escape her guardian.

The stranger's arm slipped around her waist, preventing her from fleeing. The heat and flex of his muscles through the sleeve of his coat made her much too aware of how dangerous he might be. Committed now to dance with this man, she placed one hand tentatively in his palm, and with the other she gathered up the small train of her gown. He pulled her closer into the embrace of the waltz, making her breath whoosh from her lungs. Although he held her lightly, as if she were a porcelain doll and quite breakable, his body exuded a restrained strength. As she dragged in a breath, she realized he smelled quite wonderful, like limes underscored by the scent of *him*. Shyly, she peeked up at him from beneath her lashes.

"I have never danced the waltz before, sir," she confessed breathlessly.

"It's quite easy," he said. "Count 1-2-3 in your head and follow my lead."

After a few experimental steps, Jillian found the dance was as easy as the handsome stranger said, even with her toes crowded by the tiny roll.

"I hope you won't think me too forward for agreeing to dance with you," she said.

"Not at all," the stranger reassured her. "If I were a young lady, I would have agreed to do almost anything to get away from Rystoke and that harridan of a chaperone. I despise the idea of parading young women about like race horses to match them up with a profitable husband."

Jillian's eyes flew to his face. "You heard through the windows," she gasped. It had not occurred to her that she could be overheard as well as the other way around. The amused glint in those startling topaz eyes made her lower her gaze. Staring straight at his snowy cravat, she said stiffly, "Thank you for your chivalrous gesture, sir, but you need not feel obligated to finish the dance. You have rescued the damsel in distress. As the knight-errant, you may now continue on your quest."

The stranger chuckled. "This knight-errant never leaves a damsel in the middle of a dance. Too many dangers lurk behind the potted plants."

"Such as conversations that are not supposed to be overheard?" Jillian asked rashly.

The stranger cocked his head in curiosity. "Such as?"

"Nothing," Jillian mumbled as she shook her head. She had said too much. Guessing that what she had heard and what now crowded her toes would somehow get her into trouble, she tried to break away from the man who held her. "Please excuse me," she began. "I must—"

"The dance is not over," the stranger said. His arm tightened about her waist. "Surely you would not embarrass me by leaving me in the middle of the dance floor?"

"I... No, of course not." Confounded and just a little frightened, Jillian fell silent and prayed the music would end quickly. The man's hold on her threatened her equilibrium. Her knees were shaking. Her head felt as though it were floating above the rest of her body. She never should have accepted his invitation to dance. Why was she so impulsive? It always got her into trouble.

"I seem to have lost something that I really must retrieve," the stranger said. "Perhaps you know of its whereabouts?" He gazed down at her with an intent expression.

Unnerved by the question, Jillian stumbled a bit and murmured an apology. Recovering the rhythm of the dance gave her a moment to think. Innocently, she asked, "What exactly did you lose, sir?"

"Nothing of much value to anyone else." He shrugged. "A bit of parchment."

"A note from a lover, perhaps?" she teased, pretending innocence. "Really, sir, if I were that lady, I would be most incensed upon hearing that you lost my gentle sentiments."

As he opened his mouth to respond, she heard the last strains of music. Not allowing the stranger to question her any further, she nimbly pulled free of his embrace, forcing him to escort her from the dance floor. But she could not escape that easily. His fingers curled about her elbow and held her fast.

"Keeping things that do not belong to you could prove to be very dangerous," he murmured.

Without answering, she broke away from him and sought refuge in the crowd. She avoided Pennington who glared at her from the other side of the room, and with relief, saw no sign of Rystoke. She sought out her friend, Phoebe Southwood, another young woman enduring her first season in London. She found the short, curvy brunette at the buffet table, about to select a cream puff from a tray of decadent pastries. Without apology, Jillian snatched the delicacy from Phoebe's fingers, and placed it on a corner of the table.

"What are doing?" Phoebe demanded. "That was to be my one indulgence this evening."

"Sorry," Jillian mumbled, knowing how much Phoebe liked sweets, then grabbed her friend's arm and dragged her toward the sweeping staircase which led to a gallery overlooking the ballroom. Phoebe sputtered her protest, but Jillian threw a pleading glance at her over her shoulder. Her friend tagged along in silence.

When they stood at the balustrade of the gallery, Phoebe turned to her with a confused frown. "Whatever is the matter with you?"

"I just danced the waltz," Jillian announced breathlessly.

Phoebe's hazel eyes grew wide. "You did? Who was your partner?"

Jillian pointed to the tall, dark man who was leading a strikingly beautiful, pale blonde woman onto the dance floor. "Him."

Phoebe gasped. "*Him*? You danced the *waltz* with *him*?" She glanced from Jillian to the dance floor and back again. "Do you know who that is?"

8

Jillian shook her head as a hollow feeling opened in her stomach.

Phoebe grabbed Jillian and pulled her close. "That," she whispered dramatically, "is the Duke of Dunbary."

Jillian stared blankly at her friend.

"Haven't you heard of him?" Phoebe demanded. "He's only *the* most eligible bachelor in England. He's rich as Croesus. He might even be involved in smuggling. I've heard he goes through mistresses like that." Phoebe snapped her fingers to demonstrate. "He's been mentioned in connection with an *actress*." Her eyes widened at the scandalous idea. Then she turned to watch the dancers. "He hardly ever comes to these horribly crowded affairs. I wonder what he's doing here?"

Gathering secrets and being overheard, Jillian thought.

Phoebe gazed speculatively at Jillian. "I wonder why he asked you to dance?"

Jillian grinned at the unintended insult. "Why, because I am the most ravishing woman here." She tossed her head and imperiously stuck her nose in the air. She could not tell anyone, even Phoebe, why the duke had really asked her to dance.

Phoebe giggled. "Oh, Jill, I'm sorry. I didn't mean that. You are quite lovely, really. It's just that the duke has a mistress, and he usually takes to older women, like Lady Avingdon." She indicated the spot on the dance floor where the duke was dancing with the platinum blonde.

Jillian watched them. A sense of foreboding surged through her. If what Phoebe said were true, then she had to be careful. The duke had only danced with her to retrieve his secret correspondence. He was involved in something clandestine, and that made him dangerous. She did not think he would give up easily. He would pursue her until he had recovered what he thought was his. But that conversation she had heard through the window made her wary about returning the note to him. What if he was plotting something treacherous? What should she do?

Phoebe nudged her. "There's the Viscomte Pelham," she said, using her fan to point at a young man who was dancing with a lady who appeared to be his mother. "Isn't he just bang up to the mark?"

Distracted from her conundrum, Jillian focused on the dancers below and listened to Phoebe recount the viscomte's qualities. Later, she would decide what to do with the little note that had fallen into her shoe. And the disturbing, handsome man who seemed determined to retrieve it.

Adrian Bennett, Duke of Dunbary, effortlessly followed the intricate patterns of the quadrille he was dancing with Diana, his mistress, who also happened to be one of his spies. She had arranged the meeting with his agent on the veranda, who had botched passing him the secret information. Diana usually held his complete attention, but at that moment, his thoughts were on the lovely young woman with whom he had just waltzed.

As the steps in the dance brought him beside Diana, her shrewd blue eyes gleamed. "Your mind is miles away, Adrian," she reproached. "Are you thinking about that bewitching girl you just danced with?"

"How could I think of anyone except you, Diana? You're more than enough woman for me," Adrian answered smoothly.

Diana gave a tiny sniff of disbelief. "I know you are getting bored with our arrangement, just as I am. Besides, it has always been dangerous for us to be intimate. If you wish to break off with me, just say so." The dance forced them apart.

When they came together again, he murmured, "The young lady in question is Rystoke's ward. I'm certain she has the information from my agent in her possession."

Diana drew in a breath as they moved away from each other once more. When they drew together again, she whispered, "Do you think she will pass the note along to Rystoke? He's a very strong supporter of the Orders in Council."

Adrian only had time for a discreet shrug before the dance ended, but he was more concerned than he'd let on. Rystoke had been his adversary for a very long time, and if the older man discovered what was contained in the secret correspondence, England's future could be threatened.

As he led Diana from the dance floor, Rystoke stepped in front of them, as if Adrian's thoughts had beckoned him.

Without even a perfunctory greeting, Rystoke said stiffly, "I will have you know, Dunbary, that I am very displeased with your conduct concerning my ward. I absolutely forbid you to have anything else to do with her. She is an innocent, and should not be subjected to the advances of men like yourself."

Adrian's brow lifted and a dangerous smile played about his lips. "Are you insulting me, Rystoke? If so, I shall have to call you out."

A flash of fear widened the man's eyes before it was replaced with icy disdain. "I have no wish to meet you on the field of honor," he said haughtily, "but be warned that I will make a suitable match for my ward despite any intrusion on your part."

"My dear Rystoke, I would never dream of intruding on your plans of marrying off your ward for whatever gains you are after." Bowing slightly, Adrian murmured his excuses and led Diana in the direction of the dining room.

"What an unpleasant man," she observed as they approached the buffet table.

"He has always been a disagreeable thorn in my side. It's a shame he is guardian to that lovely young lady."

Diana gave a throaty chuckle. "So she *did* make an impression on you."

Adrian smiled down into her twinkling blue eyes. "Mixing business with pleasure is never a hardship."

"I knew you would find someone to amuse you," Diana said with a grin.

As Adrian guided her to a small supper table, he realized that Rystoke's ward more than amused him. Her defiance of both her guardian and society's rules intrigued him. Her quick wit charmed him. Her gray eyes bewitched him. Her golden hair made him want to remove the pins to let it flow across his fingers. And her lithe body made his pulse race. He hoped he could coax her into returning the note. She had no way of knowing just how important the message was—how dangerously crucial to peace. He would have to keep things light the next time he saw her. And once the note was in his possession, he could indulge in the wicked pleasure of dancing with her again. The thought made him smile.

The Earl of Rystoke watched his nemesis stroll away through the crowd with the blonde hussy on his arm. His hands clenched into fists as rage boiled up in him. He would not allow Dunbary to foil his plans. Even if he had to marry Jillian off sooner than he wished, he would not allow that devil near her. What the chit did after she said her vows was her own affair. But for now, her reputation would be as pure as snow. He would see to it, even if he had to lock her up.

He sent Pennington off in search of Jillian. It was time they left. The girl was not performing as she should tonight anyway. Annoyance surged through him. How was she going to make an impression on prospective husbands by hiding behind potted ferns?

Finally, they were in his coach and rolling down the drive. He turned his attention to his ward, who was huddled in the far corner of the seat across from him.

"Well, girl," he started, keeping his anger in check for the moment. "What have you to say for yourself?"

"I'm sorry, my lord." Jillian ducked her head.

"Yes, yes." He waved away her automatic apology. "But do you understand what you have done?"

Jillian gave a silent shake of her head.

"A disaster," Lady Pennington intoned.

With a glance of exasperation at the woman, he turned back to the girl across from him. "There is to be no duplication of tonight's events in the future. Do I make myself clear?" Without waiting for her to respond, he went on, "Besides the fact that you openly defied me, you completely ignored the proper decorum for a young woman by dancing the waltz. I should beat you for your insolence." He leveled a hard gaze on her. To keep her on edge and pondering the error of her ways, he went on more mildly, "We will discuss this further at the house. Pennington will advise you on your mistakes before you retire for the night. That way, you will be able to think about them before you fall asleep and wake up in the morning with a renewed sense of propriety. Tomorrow evening we will be visiting Almack's, and God save you if you should make a *faux pas* there. As it is, I will have to do some very fast maneuvering to get those seven witches who control the place to forget tonight's events."

"Yes, my lord." Jillian's response was barely audible.

Rystoke turned from her and stared out the carriage window. If he had known the girl was going to be this much trouble, he never would have allowed her mother to talk him into becoming her guardian. In all the years that he had supported both the girl and her mother, he had not had very much contact with the chit. Occasional glimpses as she grew up had proved that her looks were acceptable enough, but he had no idea she was so rebellious. Only the promise of a profitable match for her kept him from tossing her into the street. Even that damnable paper her mother had tricked him into signing would not have kept him to the task of finding the girl a husband if he did not think the benefits would be satisfactory.

His anger seeped away and a smile played about his lips. The benefits would be more than merely satisfactory. When the Laird of Ayton discovered what he was doing, it would destroy that pesky Scot. And that would be one less enemy he would have to worry about.

Jillian lay in bed and stared up at the dark canopy above her. The faint lines of the reverse side of the damask swam before her eyes. A sliver of moonlight cut between the drapes, across the small expanse of rug, and reflected in the cheval mirror on the far side of the room, lighting the space to dusk. It was a comfortable room, and she had been surprised when it had been assigned to her upon arriving in London. She had expected to be put in a tiny room under the eaves, although she supposed her guardian had to at least appear to be somewhat generous.

She had escaped another tongue-lashing from him, but had been forced to suffer through Lady Pennington's harangue about how irresponsibly she had acted this evening. The resulting gossip would turn her reputation from a pristine white to gray. Jillian did not care, except that she might have a bit more trouble finding a suitable husband and escaping from the earl. In fact, she had enjoyed dancing the waltz. What had made the experience disconcerting had been her partner.

She squirmed, not sure if her discomfort came from her rash behavior or the man who had guided her in the dance. The relaxed strength of the hand that had supported hers belied the restrained power of the arm about her waist. Instinct told her the Duke of Dunbary could be ruthless in getting what he wanted, that he was not a man to cross. And she had definitely crossed him this evening. Although he had been polite, his last words of warning had sent a chill chasing down her spine.

She lit the candle on the bedside table and pulled the secret message from beneath her pillow. Should she read it? What secrets did it contain?

She rolled the tiny bit of parchment between her fingers. The wax was not stamped with a seal, but marked only by a series of anonymous crosses. She slipped her thumbnail along the edge of the wax. No one would know if she took a peek. She unrolled the secret letter and began to read.

The writing was extremely tiny and filled the paper edge to edge, top to bottom. As she had overheard through the open window, the letter was an appeal to patience concerning the English Orders in Council. That was all it was. Nothing about war, nothing treasonous. Perhaps she had missed something.

She held the parchment closer to the candle flame and reread the letter. She gasped when she saw other writing appear, its lines running perpendicular to those already visible. She quickly pulled the paper away from the flame and waved it in the air to cool. But the parchment had not been damaged and the other writing remained, trailing off into invisibility. She realized the heat from the candle flame had revealed the secret writing. Carefully, she held the paper up to the flame again and passed it slowly back and forth. More writing appeared.

It was a message to the duke from his spy. The Americans were angry about the impressment of their sailors by the British and the Orders in Council, which required neutral ships to stop in an

English port before trading with France or her colonies. Some northern Americans wanted to attack Canada to drive the English off the continent. Others in the south thought that taking over Spanish Florida would help because Spain was England's ally. A bargain was being discussed between the northerners and southerners to help each other with the plan.

Jillian's hand shook as she set the note down. This could only mean that America was very close to declaring war on England. The final sentence gave one ray of hope: that immediate concessions by Parliament concerning the Orders in Council could prevent war and the loss of England's American territories. She held the future of England in her hands. But what was she to do? Should she give the letter to Rystoke, whom she did not trust? Or Dunbary, whom she did not know?

Her mother had taught her to trust few men. As the earl's ward, she had come to value that lesson. Jillian intended to hoard her information until she knew what to do with it. She had little knowledge of politics and less of spies. She'd grown up in relative seclusion on her guardian's estate in Northumberland, far from London where one could become well informed about national and international affairs. Now, she chafed at her ignorance. But she did know that England was already involved in a war with France, and becoming involved in another war would be disastrous.

Rising from her bed, she went to her writing desk and carefully rolled the piece of parchment up as tightly as before, sealed it with her own wax and stuck the original wax on top. She needed to hide the note. Her gaze fell on a rag doll her mother had made for her fourth birthday. Besides her clothes, it had been the only personal possession she had brought to London from the country. If she sewed the secret letter inside, no one would ever suspect its hiding place. She collected her sewing basket and set to work, snipping at the seam down the doll's back, stuffing the note inside, and then skillfully resewing the seam. Turning the doll over, she smoothed back its red-woolen locks.

A tear slipped from her eye. She would turn nineteen tomorrow, her first birthday since her mother's death ten months earlier. She swiped the tear away. The day would be hard to live through with no little birthday surprises from her mother, no special meal or sweetmeats. All she had to look forward to was a visit to a solicitor to receive one last message from her mother. And an evening at Almack's Assembly Rooms with her guardian.

Jillian wondered if the Duke of Dunbary with his wild reputation was accepted by the seven lady patronesses who ruled Almack's invitation list. She fervently hoped he was not. She did not want him asking in that smooth, deep voice what she had heard through the window. She did not want to reveal to him that she had his secret letter. He was dangerous and made her feel strange. Those topaz eyes seemed to bore into her. As much as she wanted to irritate her guardian, even she would not be foolish enough to be seen again with a man such as the Duke of Dunbary. Yet, she had to admit to herself, that one dance had been very exciting.

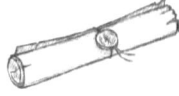

CHAPTER 2

The next night, Jillian sat with Lady Pennington at Almack's and watched the artifice of London's elite society gossip and strut. She had made it past the seven social guardians with only a few raised eyebrows and one restrained reprimand for dancing the waltz the night before. Relieved at those mild reactions from the lady patronesses, she suspected she would not be allowed to dance the waltz again for a very long time, if ever again. But at least they had allowed her through the sacred portal of Almack's.

Phoebe, who had managed to get her chaperone to settle next to Lady Pennington, sat beside her. Jillian sipped her tepid lemonade to cover a yawn of boredom, and her gaze met Phoebe's, who held a hand before her mouth to cover her own yawn. They shared a giggle, then snapped their spines straight at a combined harrumph from each of their chaperones.

Jillian's fingers drifted to her mother's brooch pinned to the neckline of her requisite white gown. She had received it that afternoon at the offices of Mr. Oliver Whittlesby, her mother's solicitor. It was a beautiful piece, shaped like a stalk of heather and encrusted with diamonds and amethysts. Jillian had sat in shock, holding it in her hand as Mr. Whittlesby had also revealed that her mother had bequeathed an estate to her. She was an heiress.

The solicitor had explained that the house and land had been neglected for many years, but they were still quite valuable and would be a handsome enticement to any prospective suitor. Jillian wondered if her guardian knew of her inheritance.

As she pondered her new-found wealth, a riffle of excitement ran through the crowd. Phoebe nudged her with her elbow.

"Look who just walked in," her friend whispered.

At first, Jillian could not see anyone who might stir up the ladies. Then she caught a glimpse of a dark head and broad shoulders. When the man turned to greet Lady Sefton, one of the lady patronesses, her stomach did a little somersault. The Duke of Dunbary had arrived. She wanted to get up, hide behind the nearest potted fern, but she could not make her body move. She closed her eyes, gulped some air, and prayed that he would not see her.

"Why, Jillian, you look positively ashen," Lady Pennington said. "I did tell you to eat a bit of supper."

Jillian opened her eyes. "I must be excused. Please."

She shoved her cup of lemonade at Lady Pennington and stood glancing around for a pillar or plant to hide behind, turning her back to the crowded ballroom. She saw Phoebe's eyes widen and her chaperone's cheeks flush a bright red. Her stomach plummeted at the disaster that was about to descend on her.

"Oh, Elenora, here you are." Jillian heard Lady Sefton's voice float over her shoulder as she approached Lady Pennington. "I'm sure you already know the Duke of Dunbary," Lady Sefton gushed. "He has asked permission to dance the waltz with Miss St. Clare."

She was well and truly caught. Jillian slowly turned to watch the man bowing politely before her chaperone. He was the epitome of grace. A whimper of distress escaped her.

Lady Pennington shot her a glare before she addressed Lady Sefton and the duke. "That is very flattering, your grace, but as I am sure you are aware, Lord Rystoke has forbidden Miss St. Clare to dance the waltz."

His deep chuckle sent a traitorous shiver of anticipation through Jillian.

"Has he? That is rather tardy of him, since the young lady has already danced the waltz with me," the duke said.

Jillian's cheeks burned with embarrassment and anger. He did not have to announce it to the whole world. Slowly, she turned to face Lady Sefton and the duke.

Lady Sefton rapped him on the arm with her fan. "I heard of your mischief last evening. You are a very naughty boy for doing such a thing without permission. Do you know that could get you excluded from the invitations list?"

"Then I shall have to break your rules more often," he said.

"Oh, you do tease so," Lady Sefton admonished.

Spying the glint in his eye, Jillian suspected that being barred from Almack's would not depress him in the least.

"Well, Miss St. Clare?" the duke asked as he held out his hand to her. "May I have the honor of the next waltz?"

Jillian once again found herself staring at the man's hand before she met his gaze. His eyes bored into her. His request vibrated in the air between them. As if her hand had a will of its own, she reached out and rested her fingers lightly on his.

"Well, I really don't think —" Lady Pennington began.

Before the woman could finish, the duke swept Jillian onto the dance floor. His arm slipped about her waist, and like before, she felt lightheaded, as if his large body used up all the air. She was intensely aware of every inch of him that touched her — the hard, muscular arm and the calloused hand. Getting a grip on herself, she took a deep breath — and breathed in the delicious scent of him. No, she could not fall under this man's intoxicating spell. Undaunted, she met his gaze.

"You are a very persistent man. I really should not be dancing with you," she blurted.

He lifted a brow. "Then why did you come so readily?"

Flustered for a moment, Jillian glanced away and saw her chaperone furiously fanning herself. "Because I enjoy aggravating Lady Pennington."

The duke threw his head back and laughed.

Jillian's brows drew together. "I don't see where that is so funny... your grace." The use of the man's proper form of address was an afterthought. She had better not make him angry.

Grinning, the duke told her, "But, you see, it is quite amusing. I have never had a woman agree to dance with me only because she wishes to escape from her chaperone. You have done it twice. I find it charming."

Jillian did not believe the reason this man had asked her to dance the waltz was because of her charm.

He tipped his head. "You do not think I am telling the truth," he observed. "Miss St. Clare, if I were in the market for a wife, I would seriously consider you a candidate."

Heat crept into Jillian's cheeks. "You are toying with me. Why would a man like yourself even glance at someone like me?"

"Why not?" he countered. "You are beautiful and available. I would put you at the top of my list of candidates."

"I'm not beautiful. And you know nothing about me," she protested.

"On the contrary, I know a great deal about you. I know that you are just entering society, that you are the ward of the Earl of Rystoke. I know that you do not always follow the rules of society, that you learn quickly, and are graceful when you dance. And you *are* beautiful. Your hair is the color of spun gold, and your eyes are as gray as a stormy sky. Your lashes are so thick they sometimes turn your eyes black." His voice dropped to a low, intimate murmur. "And I know that you smell like wildflowers."

Stunned, Jillian's mouth fell open, and she stared up at him with wide eyes. His compliments made her giddy, and the seductive timbre of his voice spun a magical web about them, excluding all the noise and movement in the room.

Chuckling, he told her, "You'd better not look at me like that, Miss St. Clare. People will begin to spread a rumor that we are lovers."

Jillian snapped her mouth closed and lowered her eyes. "You certainly know how to get a lady's attention, your grace. Is there nothing you don't already know about me?"

"I think you have the answer to that question, Miss St. Clare." The duke's tone turned serious. "You should not keep secrets which are not yours to keep."

Jillian felt her stomach begin to jig again. Hiding her fear, she bluffed, "I don't know what you are speaking of. I have no secrets. I am merely a simple young woman who has come to London for her first season."

"Perhaps. But behind those lovely gray eyes I think there is a mind that is as deep as the North Sea. There are some matters we should discuss. For instance, that item I mentioned last evening which I seemed to have misplaced."

Jillian forced a little laugh. "I really don't know what you are talking about, your grace. If you are in the habit of losing things, you must learn to be more careful of your possessions." With relief, she heard the orchestra play the last measures of the tune. "Please escort me back to Lady Pennington. I am sure she is quite vexed that I danced the waltz with you again. She can be so tiresome when she is angry."

The duke acceded to her with a small bow. "As you wish, Miss St. Clare." He politely brought her back to the spot where Lady Pennington waited. Just before he let her go, he murmured, "Don't think this is the last we shall see each other, Jillian. I mean to retrieve what is mine."

The implied threat and the use of her given name made Jillian's knees turn to porridge. Sinking down onto the chair, she watched him saunter away through the crowd. She felt little relief at seeing him go. Instead, a sense of foreboding and a large lump of anxiety settled in her middle. The man could charm the shoes off a beggar, and if she were not careful, she would find herself telling him all she had heard and handing over the little roll of parchment.

How did she know where his loyalties lay? What if he meant to use the note to commit treason, to foment war with America for his own gain? She had no way of knowing. What she had read in the note was much too important to hand over to someone who might use it in the wrong way. Through a quirk of fate, she had landed in the middle of an espionage ring.

She had started her season in London with little more thought than navigating through society's rules without a blunder, and perhaps finding a nice young man who might be kind enough to pretend to fall in love with her, for she was not quite ready to marry. She had never expected to become entangled in a quagmire of subterfuge. She could turn the note over to the authorities, but they would come calling with questions and Rystoke would learn of the note's existence. She would never give it to her guardian, for she did not trust him. And she did not know Dunbary. She needed to learn more about the situation. And about him.

Just the thought of Dunbary sent a delicious tingle up her spine. Which had nothing to do with his deep voice, topaz eyes, or muscular body, she told herself.

Adrian, Duke of Dunbary, made his excuses to the lady patronesses of Almack's, collected his evening cape, and left. As he stood on the front step of the establishment and waited for his coach, he breathed deeply of the night air. It was good to be outside, away from the crowd and stuffiness of the assembly rooms. He hated the place. He tried to avoid it as much as possible, but tonight he'd had little choice. Having discovered that Miss St. Clare would be a guest there, he'd had to go. And now he wished he had not.

Irritated, he slapped his gloves against his thigh. Not only had he endured the inane chatter of members of the ton, but he also hadn't made any headway with Miss St. Clare. She'd been extremely difficult. Why couldn't the girl see that he was trying to keep her out of a potentially dangerous situation? She was too naïve to be caught up in what he was doing.

His irritation seeped away. But Jillian St. Clare was enchanting. A quick and clever mind clicked behind those stormy gray eyes. And yet she was an innocent. His attempt at seduction during their dance had not been difficult, and he had enjoyed seeing the blush on her cheeks and the shock in her eyes.

Despite her prim manner, he imagined the secretly rebellious Miss St. Clare would look magnificent when aroused. Wild. Delicious. There was an earthy, sensual quality about her that appealed to him. She moved with an unconscious grace, unashamed of her feminine curves. He sincerely hoped whomever she finally wed would have the sense to nurture that passionate nature and not abuse it.

God's blood! What was he thinking? He had no interest in the young lady except to retrieve his secret correspondence. And he had less interest in whom Miss St. Clare finally married. And yet, he was surprised by the surge of jealousy at the thought of another man sharing her bed. Conceit made him consider seducing her and being her first lover. Damn. The idea was far too tempting. And foolish. He had no wish to marry, and he certainly could not make the innocent Miss St. Clare his mistress.

As his coach slowed before him, his footman jumped down and had the door open before it came to a complete stop. Absently giving an address, Adrian climbed in and settled back against the leather seat, but his thoughts still lingered on Jillian St. Clare.

She was going to be more trouble than he had first anticipated. Tonight he had realized she was more than just a young woman who had come to London for her first season. The young lady was not one of the shallow, flighty, husband-hunting females who were so common during the London season. She was clever and mysterious, two attributes that usually intrigued him. With Miss St. Clare, he found them confounding and frustrating.

He did not know how close she was to Rystoke. Had she told her guardian what she'd overheard the night before, or worse, had she given him the letter? If she had, then all the work he had done in the past months would be for nothing.

Her refusal to acknowledge she had the secret correspondence worried him. Twice now, he had tried to be a gentleman about asking her. If he danced the waltz with her one more time, then the gossip-mongers would have his name linked romantically with hers, and that would not do. He could not become entangled with an innocent like Jillian St. Clare, no matter how sensually appealing she was. Yet, besides being an absolute cad, he could see no other way to get her to talk to him.

What a bloody mess. If only his agent had not panicked and dropped the letter into the shrubbery, then he would not be in this situation. He should not have let Diana talk him into meeting his agent at that infernal ball last night.

Sighing, he stared out at the passing street. He had wanted to meet his agent in Cornwall, but that had been impossible. He had to be seen about London, to defuse accusations that he was being less than diligent on the government's behalf and also to squelch the absurd rumor that he was running contraband from France. The only option open to him had been to arrange the meeting with his agent in some public place. So, he had gone to the ball.

He would make one last discreet attempt to retrieve the note from Miss St. Clare. After she returned it—if she returned it—he would never have to see her again. Her reputation would be safe, and she could continue her search for a suitable husband. He frowned at that gloomy thought as he continued to gaze out into the night.

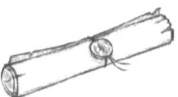

CHAPTER 3

Early the next morning, Jillian breathed in the crisp morning air and sighed with pleasure, as she turned her horse down Rotten Row, the path that wound through Hyde Park. The sun had barely cleared the treetops and the mist still clung to the grass in a filmy layer. It wasn't a fashionable hour to be riding through Hyde Park. Later that afternoon, society's members would emerge from behind the elegant comfort of their townhouses with their stone facades and damask draperies to promenade through the park, to see and be seen by those who mattered. But at this early hour, the meandering paths and lanes were deserted.

She had escaped a confrontation with the earl after last night's second encounter with the Duke of Dunbary by pleading a headache and leaving Almack's early with Pennington. By the time the earl had arrived home, she was safely in bed. This morning, she had slipped out of the house with only a groom to accompany her. She knew she would incur the earl's wrath for this small defiance, but she needed the time to herself to sort out her thoughts.

What was she going to do about the duke? And what was she going to do with the bit of parchment that had fallen into her shoe? Despite the fact that her guardian was active in Parliament when it suited his needs, she would never turn the note over to him. He seemed to dislike Dunbary immensely, and that sentiment appeared to be returned by the duke. She could sympathize with anyone who shared her feelings about Rystoke, even Dunbary. But right now, she could not let that sway her. She needed to discover how Dunbary planned to use the information. For good or for ill?

The duke was a very charming man. Last night, as she danced with him, she could feel herself falling under his spell. His low voice seemed to swirl about her, making every other sound disappear. When he laughed, an unexpected warm spot of pleasure expanded in her chest. But she could not let his seductive words and alluring laugh sway her decision. She had been able to distract him last night, but how long could she keep him at bay while she tried to find out more about him? How long before he demanded outright that she give him the note?

She was deep in thought when a strange sound wafted through the trees. It was halfway between a drone and a wail, and an incongruous noise in the park. Jillian stopped her horse and listened, realizing the haunting chords came from a bagpipe. Some deep, forgotten memory of her childhood tugged at her. She set out across the grass to find the source of the music.

At the far end of the park, she came upon a man, dressed in a kilt with his plaid slung over his shoulder. He strode back and forth at the crest of a small rise in time to the music. Enthralled, Jillian watched and listened. A thrill of excitement and a sense of familiarity washed through her at the bagpipe's music. The man turned to her when he finished his song.

"I hope I'm not intruding," she called out to him, "but I had to discover who was playing the pipes so beautifully."

Gravely, the man appraised her. Bowing low, he accepted her compliment. "'Tis a fair lass that kens the pipes," he said. His burr softened his syllables and made his voice warm and mellow. "There are na' many here who feel as you do."

"Have you just arrived in London, sir? I haven't heard you playing here before."

"Aye, na' many days ago." He sauntered down the rise until he stood at the same level as Jillian, seated on her horse. She saw he was not much older than herself. "'Tis a sad place that does not ken the pipes," he said. "How does a lass like yourself know them?"

Jillian blinked. "I really don't know," she said. "They just sounded familiar."

"Ah," he nodded solemnly, but his gray eyes twinkled with mischief. "Perhaps you were a Scot in another life."

Laughing, Jillian agreed. "Perhaps." The sun gave his dark brown hair bright highlights. He was quite handsome, with a straight nose and well-defined jaw and chin. The groom who had accompanied her cleared his throat. Jillian knew he was anxious to get back before the earl rose for the day. "I must be going," Jillian said. "Maybe we will meet again. Perhaps you can play the pipes for me."

The man bowed. "'Twould be a joy to play for a bonny lass like yourself."

With a smile, Jillian turned her horse and cantered off. Behind her, she heard the bagpipe's magical melody. At least her morning had started out well, for now she had to return to her guardian's house and most likely a sharp reprimand.

As soon as Jillian stepped across the threshold, Williams, the butler, informed her that his lordship was waiting for her in the dining room. Biting back a groan, she walked down the hall, knocked and entered. Her guardian was just finishing breakfast and reading the *Times*. The *Spectator* lay in a messy heap on the floor beside his chair. Without looking up, he motioned for her to sit.

Jillian perched on the edge of a chair. Williams offered the teapot, and she nodded her thanks as she nervously waited for her guardian to finish reading the newspaper. She was about to get a dressing down for the night before. When the earl raised his chilly, dark brown eyes, Jillian steeled herself.

"So, Jillian," he said mildly, tossing aside the last few pages of the newspaper. "You were not feeling well last night. I see you have recovered enough to sneak out this morning and go for a ride. Did you enjoy the morning air?"

"Yes, my lord." Jillian was careful not to volunteer anything. His mild manner was merely a deception, hiding his anger.

"Good." A cold smile curled the earl's lips. "There will be no further early morning rides until I decide otherwise."

"But –"

"Shut your mouth, girl." His eyes flashed with ire. "I had forbidden you to dance with that devil Dunbary, but you defiantly went against my wishes and danced the waltz again with him last evening. What are you trying to do, girl?"

"Nothing, my lord," Jillian murmured. She sipped her tea and wished she could disappear.

The earl went on as if she had not spoken. "Already the gossip links you with him." He indicated the pile of newspapers on the floor. "The man is a rogue, and will ruin your chances of finding a decent husband. Don't you understand that? Are you so stupid that you have learned nothing from Pennington? Why do you continue to dance with him?"

Jillian blinked, attempting a show of innocence. "Because he asks me, my lord."

"That is no reason and you know it." He scowled. "There are ways a woman can refuse a dance partner. There is something else going on here."

"No, my lord." Jillian shook her head. "There is nothing else. He only wishes to dance with me." She poured more tea and hoped he believed her lie.

"Has he made indecent advances?"

"No!"

His eyes narrowed. "Has he asked about my affairs?"

"Your affairs?" Jillian's eyes widened at the thought and contemplated using that as the reason Dunbary wanted to waltz with her. Then she realized using that excuse would get her mired more deeply in her lies. She shook her head again. "No."

He studied her with a thoughtful gaze. "He does not pursue innocents," he said. "What does he want of you?"

Jillian's need to keep her secret made her snap, "How should I know what he wants?"

The earl's face turned stony. In the blink of an eye he backhanded her across the mouth.

Shocked, Jillian cried out. Her hand flew to her cheek. She tasted blood where her lip had scraped against her teeth. Her lip throbbed, and she could feel it swelling. While Rystoke had never been kind, he had never struck her before. She glared at her guardian. "Do not ever touch me again. I don't have to remain with you. I can leave here whenever I wish. My mother bequeathed an estate to me."

The earl leaned back in his chair and barked out a laugh. "Ah, yes. The estate in Lancashire? Evidently that fool Whittlesby told you all about it yesterday. Did he also tell you that it remains in trust until you are wed?"

Jillian frowned in her confusion.

He laughed again. "That's right, girl. Not until you are wed." He shrugged. "So, you see, you will have to rely on me for a while longer yet before you get your estate. And I have complete power over who and when you will marry. You could be a very old woman before I decide the time is right for you to go to a man's bed. By that time, who would want you?"

Jillian's fists clenched in her lap. "You are vile. How could my mother ever have allowed herself—" She halted, unable to voice the rest of her thought.

"—to become my mistress?" the earl finished. His eyes narrowed and he leaned forward on the table. "Your mother got everything she ever wanted from me. Everything. Don't fool yourself into believing your mother was a romantic fool. She knew exactly what she was doing when she ran from your father and came to me."

"My father?" Questions swirled in her head. "You knew my father?"

The earl's smile was cold. "Of course. Why do you think your mother came to me? Why do you think I put up with the demanding bitch for all those years? Why do you think I agreed to launch her disobedient, sly, little whelp into society? If it were not for the distinct pleasure I get out of knowing that I'm causing your father pain, I would not put myself through all the bother of dealing with you. You are almost more trouble than you are worth. *Almost.*"

Overwhelmed, bewildered, Jillian tried to make sense of what her guardian was saying. She had always thought her father was dead, but Rystoke spoke of him as if he were still alive. What was the truth? Why had her mother led her to believe a lie? She had been a very little girl when they had arrived at Rystoke's door and did not understand why they had left their home. She had only a vague recollection of her father, a large, gentle man who would carry her about on his shoulders. But that was all. She did not know his name, nor where they had lived. Her mother had never wanted to talk about him.

Obviously, the earl disliked her father. Jillian wondered if the enmity had been — was — returned. What terrible thing had happened between her mother and father that had forced her to run to an enemy, that had made her concede to him the future well-being of her daughter?

In silence she stared at this cold, cruel man who had control over her life. She vowed she would extract herself from his clutches as soon as she could and try to find her father. But before that could happen, she had to pretend to be obedient. Meekly, she bowed her head. Out of the corner of her eye, she watched him relax and lean back in his chair.

Rystoke studied her. Her mother had been a sly enchantress, knowing instinctively how to bend a man to her will. But the daughter did not know all the mother's wiles. Or did she?

"Now, tell me," he said mildly. "What have you done to attract Dunbary's attention?"

"Nothing." She dabbed at her lip with the napkin.

He was not quite sure he believed her denial, nor her show of meekness. She was a pretty piece. Perhaps Dunbary was in the market for a wife. Having this baggage wed to him could be profitable and advantageous. He and Dunbary had been on opposite sides in Parliament since the boy's maiden speech. She could be a useful spy in his adversary's camp. He would have to give that more thought.

Idly, he wondered how interested the duke was in her. Perhaps marriage was too permanent. Perhaps some relationship a little less binding would better suit everyone's needs. Since the girl's mother was dead, no one would complain if he did not fulfill his end of their agreement to the letter. Circumstances could be arranged that would force the girl into doing what he wanted.

He waved his hand in dismissal. "Go have that lip looked after." As Jillian reached the doorway, he said, "There will be no more dancing with the Duke of Dunbary, or I will find you some tottering, old, shriveled-up fool for a husband."

He watched with satisfaction as the girl scurried from the room. All he had to do was keep her obedient for a few more months. With any luck, she would be wed by the end of the season. And he could revel in his revenge.

Jillian was shaking as she rushed up the stairs to her room. She pushed her guardian's threats out of her mind for now. But the revelations about her mother had shocked her. What did the earl mean when he said her mother had gotten *everything* from him she had ever wanted? He was stingy in the extreme. Had her mother sapped all his wealth from him? No, that could not be possible. Her mother had never been an extravagant woman. She and her mother had been comfortable in their little stone cottage on Rystoke's estate, but they had by no means lived lavishly. Jillian had found no hidden stash of jewels or gold when she had packed up her mother's clothes and belongings after her mother died. And the earl certainly didn't seem to be wanting for anything. She strolled to the window, and pushing aside the pale blue silk panel, gazed out at the bustling street of Mayfair.

She knew nothing about her father, not even who he was. Her mother had told her only that she had loved him. But why had she run to Rystoke? Her mother had never loved him. Even when Jillian had been very young, she had sensed that. Her mother's relationship with the earl had been much more complicated. As Jillian had grown older, her mother's visits to the big house trickled to a stop, but she and her mother were allowed to remain in the small cottage at the edge of the earl's property. Despite that, Jillian felt that there was some animosity between her mother and the earl, as if the two were playing a sort of hostile cat and mouse game. And then a week after her mother's death, Rystoke summoned her, looked her over much like he would a horse he was considering to buy, and informed her that she would have a season in London. And so the lessons and the fittings began. But something about the situation raised Jillian's suspicions.

Before she could give that much more thought, the door to her bedroom flew open and Lady Pennington swooped in. Jillian reminded herself to lock her door next time.

"We will not be visiting today, Jillian," Lady Pennington announced. "Lord Bertram has invited us to his country estate. We must go through your entire wardrobe and pack only the most flattering gowns. Otherwise, you will not catch — " Lady Pennington's mouth dropped open. "Good lord girl, whatever happened to your lip?"

Jillian touched the bruise where the earl had slapped her and winced. The corner of her bottom lip felt twice its normal size. "I tripped as I dismounted from my horse," she lied. She did not feel comfortable confiding in Pennington.

"Well, that was certainly clumsy of you. Do go put some parsley on it. You look like you have been in a brawl. No young gentleman will want to be seen with you looking like that."

Jillian sighed and made her way down to the kitchens to ask the cook to prepare a poultice for her lip. She would have to puzzle over her guardian's words later.

By the time they reached the country estate in the late afternoon, Jillian's lip had nearly returned to normal. She was looking forward to a few days out of the city, for that meant she would not have to worry about Dunbary. Surely, he would not be invited to the same event as her guardian, since they traveled in different sets.

As Jillian stepped from the coach, she was awed by the size of the house. The only other estate house she had ever seen was the one belonging to Rystoke, and that was a converted medieval castle, much smaller than the structure before her, with its four stories of windows, sweeping entry staircase and grand portico.

They were greeted by their host, Lord Bertram, a middle-aged, portly widower, who eyed Jillian with more than a polite stare. By the time they had settled in and changed their clothes, it was time for dinner. Not all the guests had arrived yet, so the gathering this night would be small. But Jillian counted at least twenty people in the salon where they met for sherry before dinner.

Just as dinner was announced, Lord Bertram approached her. "May I have the honor of escorting you in to dinner, my dear?" he asked, offering his arm.

Lady Pennington beamed and nodded encouragement. Politely, Jillian pasted a smile on her face.

"Of course, my lord," she said. "You honor me by such a request." Gingerly, she placed her hand on his arm. She had not liked the way he had stared at her when they first arrived, like a fox eyeing a hen.

As they passed from the salon to the dining room, a young man was coming down the stairs to join the group. Jillian bit back a gasp when she recognized the Scottish gentleman she had met that morning in Hyde Park. Instead of his plaid kilt, he was fashionably dressed in coat and pantaloons. Although he looked quite handsome, Jillian decided she liked him better in his native dress. She wondered who he was, but she could not ask her host, for he was bragging that the venison they would be partaking for dinner was from a stag he had bagged on a morning hunt. She decided she would eat only vegetables.

Jillian was seated to the right of Lord Bertram, and her guardian was seated directly across the table from her. There would be no chance during dinner for her to quiz Lord Bertram about the identity of the young man, who was sitting a few seats down on the opposite side of the table from her, too far away to converse, but close enough to study him.

He smiled at her as he took his seat. A warm little glow erupted within her. Perhaps this weekend would turn into an enjoyable experience, rather than just an escape from the Duke of Dunbary.

Unfortunately, she had to get through dinner first. She was forced to listen to her host's hunting exploits, smile, and exclaim at the appropriate moments, all the while having her guardian's judgmental gaze on her. Hunting did not interest her in the least, but she knew if she did not perform well, Rystoke would no doubt lecture and admonish her once more. After their confrontation that morning, she wanted to avoid that.

Occasionally, she allowed her gaze to wander down the table and rest on the young Scottish gentleman. In polite conversation with the lady beside him, his gray eyes twinkled and his smile was warm.

Jillian was struck by the same feeling she'd had when she heard him playing the bagpipes that morning—a strange sense of familiarity. But she was sure she would have remembered meeting him, and besides, she had never been to Scotland where he obviously made his home.

"I say, have you heard the latest about what those Americans have done?" The question caught her attention. It came from Lord Winslow, who sat to her right. He was of about the same age as Lord Bertram, but the similarity ended there. Where Bertram appeared to care little about fashion or a neat appearance, Winslow was fastidious in his dress, but that refinement obviously did not spill over into his conversation. Politics and world affairs were not proper dinner conversation. Those topics were reserved for the gentlemen and their brandy after the ladies left the table. Given the circumstances over the past few days, Jillian's interest was arrested, while she feigned a concentration on the peas on her plate.

"They've struck again," Lord Winslow announced. "Confiscated my ship loaded with cotton. Said it was in violation of their policy of non-intercourse with England."

"Damned if they haven't!" Lord Bertram exclaimed from her left. "Begging your pardon, Miss St. Clare."

Jillian cast a forgiving smile at Bertram and took a sip of wine. But in truth, she was so riveted by the conversation, she barely noticed the profanity.

"A bloody mess is what it is." Lord Winslow shook his head mournfully. "I was waiting for that load of cotton to sell to the weavers in Yorkshire. Now, I will never get it."

"Really, Winslow, how common of you to engage in trade," Rystoke sniffed.

Lord Winslow shrugged. "Perhaps, but it helps to keep my cellar stocked with French brandy."

"Still smuggling, old boy?" Bertram winked. "I should think the revenue officers would have caught you by now."

Grinning, Lord Winslow said, "They are too busy trying to watch for Napoleon's invasion to worry about me."

Jillian had heard that some of the extravagant items for sale in the fashionable shops in London were contraband, but she was shocked to hear one of the guests so blatantly admit to smuggling.

"If we go to war with America, the authorities will have even more to worry about. Too bad it has come to this now, but those colonies need to be put in their place. I say, 'Once an Englishman, always an Englishman.' They should abide by English laws." Lord Bertram pounded his fist on the table.

"Damned right," Winslow agreed. "Who do they think they are? God's teeth, they should have been taught a lesson when we occupied the accursed place years ago."

Rystoke interjected mildly, "I believe teaching them a lesson was the purpose of the latest Orders in Council. The Orders prohibit the Americans from trading directly with France or any of her allies."

"Yes, yes. Their ships are supposed to stop first at an English port. But have they been obeying them?" Lord Bertram asked.

"No, damned if they haven't!" Lord Winslow exclaimed. "We should make the Orders even stricter, even if it means war with those bloody colonists."

Jillian blurted, "Maybe some of the Americans don't want to go to war."

Immediate silence fell and everyone stared at her. She could feel their eyes on her like a chill blanket. Heat blossomed in her cheeks. Young ladies were not supposed to be interested in politics, and they certainly were not to voice an opinion. Her guardian raised a disdainful eyebrow at her, his eyes icy with his disapproval. Dropping her gaze to the table, she made a point of adjusting the napkin draped across her lap. She could think of nothing to say to correct her *faux pas*. Reaching for her wine glass, she caught a supportive wink from the Scottish gentleman. Her shame faded a little.

The silence was broken by the lady two seats away, who laughed with forced gaiety and said, "Bertie, what wonderful entertainments have you planned for us this weekend? Are we to ride to the hounds tomorrow morning? I do so love your hunts."

As Bertram answered her with enthusiasm, conversation resumed around Jillian. Miserably, she picked at the rest of her meal. How could she have said something so stupid and so revealing? She would be questioned by the earl when he had her in private. He would want to know how she formed such an opinion. She would never tell him that it came from a secret letter and an overheard conversation in which the Duke of Dunbary was involved. She would have to improvise and dissemble, for she couldn't afford to raise Rystoke's suspicions.

Dinner finally ended, and Jillian escaped from the table and her embarrassment. Everyone adjourned back to the salon where tables had been set up for games of Whist. A few people gathered about the pianoforte as one of the ladies played. Jillian found a quiet window seat where she could be part of the gathering, while keeping a safe distance, for draperies partly obscured her perch.

As she tried to be inconspicuous, she heard a deep male voice ask, "Is this window seat reserved, or may anyone sit here?"

She peeked around the drape and saw the Scottish gentleman. Her lips quirked up in a smile. "Anyone may sit here who has the courage to be seen with me."

"It does not take courage to be seen with someone as lovely as yourself," he said as he sat. "Are you always so outspoken about your political views?"

Jillian's cheeks burned once more. "I'm sorry. I should not voice such outrageous thoughts."

The man grinned, and she immediately felt better. "Don't apologize. I think it's refreshing to hear a woman give an opinion about something besides her friend's new frock."

Giggling, Jillian said, "I give my opinion about that, too." She held out her hand and introduced herself.

The man gently shook her hand. "It is an honor, Miss St. Clare. I am Kenric Payton Bryce Phillip Giles—Kip, to my friends."

"Then you may call me Jillian," she said, feeling quite at ease with this man.

"The name suits you." He smiled. "I would be quite interested to hear why you think the Americans would not want to go to war."

She blushed again and ducked her head. "My views are not that interesting. I just don't believe that everyone in America would want a war."

"Why is that?" he asked.

Suspicious, Jillian wondered why he should be so interested in her opinion. She forced a little laugh. "I don't know. It was only a suggestion. Not everyone cares for war." She changed the subject.

"Your accent has changed. You sound as if you have lived in London all your life, not at all like this morning."

He shrugged. "I find it easier to get along if I speak like everyone else." Then his lips curved up mischievously. "But a bonny lass like yourself shouldna' mind how a laddie speaks," he said, switching to his brogue. "That is quite a beautiful brooch you are wearing. I noticed it when we met this morning."

Jillian smiled as she allowed him to change the subject. "My mother left it to me in her will. I was told that someone very special gave it to her." Jillian placed her hand protectively over the stalk of heather rendered in gold, amethysts and diamonds. She had worn it ever since Mr. Whittlesby had placed it in her hands the day before. She liked to think that perhaps it had been a gift from her father.

"Whoever gave it to your mother must have been very fond of her. It is quite a valuable piece of jewelry." Kip tipped his head thoughtfully. "I believe I have seen a piece rather similar to it."

Jillian's eyes widened as she felt a rush of excitement. Perhaps he knew something about her father. "Do you remember where?"

Before he could answer, a commotion in the entry hall distracted him. Other guests had arrived and passed by the door to the salon. Jillian felt the blood drain from her face. The woman was Lady Avingdon, and behind her was the Duke of Dunbary. She leaned back, so that she was behind the draperies.

"Jillian?" Kip asked. "Are you ill?"

She forced a smile. "No, I'm quite all right."

Kip inclined his head at the new arrivals. "Do you know that couple?"

She worried her lip as she wondered how much she should tell him. "I only know the gentleman a little." She was not about to confess anything more, so she stood and shook out her skirt. "Please excuse me. I believe I will retire for the night."

Kip also stood. "I will escort you."

As she hesitated, Kip extended his arm to her.

Jillian glanced around the salon. Her watchdogs were both occupied. Her guardian was deep in a game of Whist, and Lady Pennington was snoozing before the fire. With a smile, she placed her hand on Kip's arm. Allowing him to escort her even to the base of the long, winding staircase, without a proper chaperone was rather brazen of her, but she liked him, and for some reason, she felt safe with him. Besides, she did not want to be alone if she met up with the duke in the candle-lit hallway. Throwing away propriety for caution, she allowed him to escort her up the stairs.

Jillian felt the play of strong muscles in Kip's arm where her hand rested and could not help comparing him to the duke. She would be hard pressed to tell which man would be the winner in a match of strength, for each of them was tall and broad-shouldered. She wondered why she was making such a comparison. The two men had no reason to be adversaries.

When they reached the top of the stairs, Kip took her hand. "There. We have reached the safety of no man's land, where no man should tread without good reason."

Jillian laughed at his quip as he shook her hand.

"I bid you good-night, Jillian," he murmured.

"Retiring so soon, Miss St. Clare?" a familiar voice asked.

Jillian's head jerked up and she found herself staring into those disconcerting topaz eyes. A merciless smile curved the lips of the duke.

"It is late, your grace," she said coolly. "I do not frolic the night away until dawn."

"No?" An odd light of anger heated Dunbary's eyes as his gaze flicked to Kip then back to her. "A pity. I thought I might prevail upon the lady at the pianoforte to play a waltz and entice you to dance with me."

Jillian gasped. "Really, your grace!"

Kip stepped between them. "Your manner towards Miss St. Clare is insulting, sir. Unless you refrain from such forward behavior, I shall need to make you retract your words."

The duke gave a small chuckle, but his eyes sparked with anger. "I have no intention of dueling with you, sir. I thought it was common knowledge that Miss St. Clare dances the waltz without permission. Forgive me if I spoke out of turn." Bowing, he sauntered past them and on down the stairs.

Jillian shook with rage. "That horrible man!"

"He is a disagreeable fellow," Kip agreed.

"You must think me quite wicked, now that you have heard of my indiscretion." Jillian could not bear to see censure in the eyes of her new friend.

"Not at all," Kip reassured her. "It was that rake who was in the wrong." He glared after the duke and patted her hand. "If you ever need someone to help you, I will be glad for the honor. Good night, Jillian." With a smile and a bow, he turned and left.

Kip's gallantry warmed her as she undressed for the night. His defense of her before the duke proved how kind he was. In contrast, Dunbary's words chilled her. He was obviously getting impatient at her refusal to admit she had his secret correspondence, for he was using innuendo to coerce. How much farther would he go with his sly words to insinuate she was less than proper?

A note slipped beneath the door and interrupted her musings. When she opened it, her insides froze. It was from the duke.

My dear Miss St. Clare,

I believe we have much to discuss concerning a missing bit of parchment. Please meet me in the trophy room tomorrow at the hour before tea, and please come alone. I am sure you would not wish either your chaperone or your guardian to become aware of what you have in your possession, for you have taken this indiscretion a bit too far for a proper young lady. I look forward to a mutual, agreeable settling of this matter. I remain

Your Servant,
Dunbary

In a rage, Jillian crumpled the note and flung it across the room. The audacity of the man! He was contemptible. She did not care if the feel of his arm about her waist made the breath leave her lungs. Nor did she care that his voice made everything else around her fade to nothing. He was unbearable. And she would tell him so.

His invitation was bold and presumptuous. Jillian had no intention of returning his bit of parchment, not until she could discern if he were working on behalf of the English government or against it.

His conflicting behavior—one moment rescuing her from Rystoke and the next insulting her honor—told her only that he was eager to retrieve what he had lost. Jillian's lips flattened and her eyes narrowed thoughtfully. What would her mother have done?

Lilith St. Clare had been able to handle the horrid Earl of Rystoke all those years. Her daughter should have little trouble keeping the Duke of Dunbary at bay. She began to make a plan.

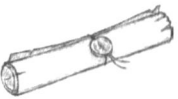

CHAPTER 4

Jillian awoke the next morning to barking hounds and the light-hearted chatter of the guests gathering for the hunt. Rubbing the sleep from her eyes, she flung the coverlet back and padded to the window over-looking the drive. Peeking through the curtains she watched the activity in the courtyard. The morning was still dim, for the sun had yet not risen, but there was enough light for her to make out the figures of the guests, some still milling about on foot, some already mounted on horseback.

The Duke of Dunbary looked at ease upon a huge white stallion. Beside him, on a dainty bay filly, sat Lady Avingdon. Her bright green riding outfit complimented the red of the duke's coat. She said something to the duke and he laughingly answered her. Jillian's chest tightened at the exchange. Lady Avingdon was a beautiful woman. She was poised and experienced, having already been married and widowed. Of course the sophisticated Duke of Dunbary would take her for his mistress. Jillian told herself she should be unconcerned about where Dunbary focused his attention. She should be glad that Lady Avingdon distracted him, for that meant he would not concentrate on her. But she could not rid herself of that strange feeling in her chest.

Several servants offered trays of steaming stirrup cups to the hunters. The duke took his cup, and raising it in a toast to the lady at his side, murmured something. The lady's laughter floated up to Jillian. Their flirtation was evident for all to see, even from Jillian's window.

The duke took a sip from the cup and glanced up. Jillian gasped as their eyes met. He had the audacity to wink at her! She stepped back, not wanting him to see her in dishabille, but she saw his lips curve in a cocksure smile. Her cheeks aflame, she scrambled back into bed. He was conceited enough to believe that he could have one woman as a mistress while he attempted to charm another into making a fool of herself. Jillian refused to be that fool. She would teach him that lesson when she met him in the trophy room.

With a little huff she plumped her pillows and pulled up the coverlet. She wondered what the duke's reaction might be if she told him she had passed the secret letter to the Earl of Rystoke. She had not done that, of course, for she trusted her guardian even less than the duke. No, her decision was made. She would not let the note out of her possession until she could find out more about the duke. She smiled. The meeting with Dunbary that afternoon would be quite interesting.

Later that morning, Jillian joined the guests gathered in the dining room for the hunt breakfast. The chase was discussed amid much laughter and gaiety. Several of the riders had been thrown from their horses, but no one had been seriously injured. She listened to the taunts and quips as she strolled to the sideboard and filled her plate with fluffy eggs, ham, spring onions in cream sauce, warm bread, and marmalade. Jillian enjoyed a good ride through the countryside, but her aversion to the pitiful end of the fox had kept her from joining the hunt. She could not abide watching the ferocious dogs corner the poor creature, nor the final shot that brought its life to an end. She especially did not enjoy the tradition of cutting off the fox's tail as a token of victory. She wondered who had won that trophy.

As if her thought had traveled through the room, Lord Bertram said loudly, "Winslow, show us your trophy."

Lord Winslow triumphantly held up the luxurious, bushy tail of a red fox. After everyone had admired it, he admitted, "This should really go to Dunbary. If his horse had not gone lame at the last, he would have bagged the prize."

Jillian missed Dunbary's comment when Kip murmured beside her, "The duke is an exceptional horseman."

Distaste twisted her lips. "I'm not surprised he was first to the quarry. After all, who better to outwit a fox than a viper?"

Kip smiled down at her. "You are still upset over what he said last night."

"He was quite impolite." She frowned down at her plate.

"Yes, he was," Kip said, "but this morning I found him rather personable. He apologized to me and explained that he was rather too quick to speak since he has had such unfriendly relations with your guardian."

"Certainly you were not charmed by him? I find his explanation a poor excuse," Jillian scoffed. "The man is insufferable. What gentleman lays the attributes of a guardian upon the ward?"

"What gentleman, indeed?" a voice spoke from her other side.

She turned and saw the duke smiling down at her. He bowed a greeting. "Your sparkling wit was missing on the hunt, Miss St. Clare."

"I am sure you were well enough occupied, your grace, not to have been too bored. After all, you almost won the trophy." Jillian raised a cool eyebrow, but her insides fluttered nervously. Even with Kip next to her, the presence of this man unsettled her. It was a dangerous game she played with him.

"Almost winning in the hunt is never as satisfying as catching the fox. Wouldn't you agree Miss St. Clare?" His words were casual, but Jillian caught a gleam in his eye.

"Yet, allowing someone else the thrill of victory is good sportsmanship," Kip put in. "Did your horse truly go lame on moss and soft earth?"

The duke shrugged. "These things happen."

Jillian glanced from one man to the other. She was bewildered by Kip's civility towards the man. Was he trying to say that the duke had purposely given up the trophy to another man? If that were so, then perhaps the arrogant Duke of Dunbary had one redeeming quality after all.

Lady Avingdon strolled up beside the duke. "Dunbary, introduce me to your new friends," she demanded sweetly.

He performed the honors. Jillian was surprised by the warmth in the lady's smile.

"I saw you dancing with Dunbary at the ball the other evening," she said to Jillian. "You are very graceful. Had you danced the waltz before?"

Jillian blushed. "No, my lady." Her answer came out in an embarrassed whisper.

Lady Avingdon frowned at the duke. "Adrian, have you been up to your old tricks again? Have you been charming this young lady into being naughty?"

The duke placed his hand on his chest in a show of injured innocence. "I would never do something as dastardly as that. Miss St. Clare can vouch for the fact that I was a perfect gentleman that evening." He turned his topaz eyes on Jillian. "Come now, Miss St. Clare, absolve me from such an accusation."

Jillian played his game for now, and flashed him a brittle smile. "The duke speaks the truth," she said. "My guardian was present when his grace asked me to dance, and Dunbary escorted me from the dance floor when the music ended." Which was true. Up to a point.

"There, you see?" he crowed triumphantly to Lady Avingdon. "A perfect gentleman." His gaze slid back to Jillian, and he gave her a quick wink of shared conspiracy.

Jillian gritted her teeth at the duke's brazen attempt to charm her. That "perfect gentleman" was hiding something and possibly embroiled in treachery. She raised her eyebrow, glanced away, and met the cold gaze of her guardian. She bit down on a groan.

After a barely civil greeting to the others, the earl said brusquely, "Jillian, Lord Bertram wishes a word with you."

Jillian hid her dismay behind a polite smile, excused herself, and followed her guardian. As they threaded their way through clusters of guests, he said in a low tone, "Lord Bertram is very keen on you, girl. If you are pleasant to him, it will be to your advantage."

Jillian's dismay turned to anxiety. Lord Bertram wished to court her. Before she could come up with some excuse, their host stood before her. He greeted her warmly and bent over her hand.

"I hope you had a restful night, Miss St. Clare," he said.

Jillian gave a polite nod. "Yes, thank you."

"And your room? Is it to your liking?" he asked.

"It is very nice, my lord." Jillian wished she could be hiding in that very nice little room.

Lord Bertram shifted from one foot to the other. "Miss St. Clare, would you honor me by joining me for a ride into the village this afternoon?"

The last thing Jillian wanted was to spend the afternoon alone with Lord Bertram. She threw a quick glance at Rystoke and caught his chilly stare. If she declined their host's invitation, she would reap her guardian's wrath. Trapped, forcing a stiff smile to her lips, she replied, "A ride into the village would be lovely, my lord." As he beamed at her acceptance, an inspired thought popped into her head. "Perhaps some of the other guests would care to come along. We could have a most diverting outing."

Disappointment flashed across his face, but he recovered quickly. "What a splendid idea. I shall ask them immediately." He brightened. "Perhaps you would care to see my trophy room."

Again, Jillian was trapped. With her guardian looking on, she had no polite way to tell their host that she was not in the least interested. "I'd be delighted," she murmured.

His smile became even brighter. "Splendid!"

As he held out his arm, her gaze darted around in the hope of finding someone to save her. No one seemed to notice. Pasting a smile on her lips, she allowed Lord Bertram to lead her from the room. At least now she would now be able to find the trophy room quicker that afternoon when she was to meet with the Duke of Dunbary.

Jillian gaped in awe as they entered the room. Stag heads stared down at her. Large fish glared with their glassy eyes. A clump of fox tails trailed down beside one of the windows. A stuffed boar stood ready to charge the furniture. Above the hearth, several guns were mounted.

"Oh, my," Jillian said as they entered. Awestruck at the number of dead carcasses, she could only stare, speechless, and try not to look revolted.

Lord Bertram smiled widely. "It is quite a splendid sight, isn't it?"

It was not *splendid* at all, but that seemed to be Bertram's favorite word. As he led her proudly about the room, he gave a detailed and graphic account of how each animal had been killed. By the time they reached the far end of the room, Jillian was trying to keep her breakfast in her stomach. She sank gratefully into a chair near a large window that looked out over the grounds. All she wanted was to escape to the rolling lawn and trees.

"Please, allow me a few moments to sit," she said, not wishing to insult her host. "Your stories overwhelm me, my lord," she said. "Your bravery makes me absolutely dizzy."

"Oh, my dear, I did not mean to frighten you." Lord Bertram went down on one knee and took hold of her hand. "Please forgive me for being so insensitive."

Jillian smiled wanly and tried to free her hand, but he would not let go.

"You know, my dear," her host said hesitantly, "you are quite beautiful sitting in that chair with that rack of antlers above your head."

Jillian forced herself not to jump up. She imagined the animal's hot breath on her neck.

He stroked her fingers. "This house is very lonely since my devoted wife, Anna, passed away five years ago." He wiped the corner of his eye.

Jillian yearned to take back her hand, but he still held on too tightly. She had the inappropriate thought that his wife must have died of boredom or horror.

Lord Bertram bowed his head, and Jillian was amazed to see a pale flush spread across the bald spot on the top of his head. "I would be quite honored if you could see your way to –"

He was interrupted by a voice saying, "See, Diana, here it is. I knew I could find the trophy room."

The Duke of Dunbary and Lady Avingdon entered the room. Relief flooded Jillian. Lord Bertram climbed quickly to his feet, and Jillian jumped from her chair. Their movement drew the duke's attention.

"I didn't realize this room would be occupied," he said. "Forgive us if we interrupted a private moment." He bowed slightly to Lord Bertram, but his gaze landed speculatively on Jillian.

"Not at all, not at all," Lord Bertram blustered. Jillian noticed he was looking a tiny bit annoyed. "Miss St. Clare was feeling a bit faint, that is all."

"How unfortunate," Lady Avingdon murmured as she approached. "Then we arrived just in time." She placed a comforting hand on Jillian's arm. "You do look a bit piqued. Would you like me to call for assistance?"

The last thing Jillian needed was to draw the attention of her guardian by summoning help. Frantically, she shook her head. "No, thank you. I just need a cool compress and to lie down. Please, excuse me." Sidestepping around the lady, she brushed past the duke and hurried out of the room.

With relief, Jillian reached the safety of her room without crossing paths with anyone. She leaned against the closed door and drew a deep breath. She had narrowly escaped a proposal of marriage from their host. Although Lord Bertram might be a very nice gentleman, she had no wish to marry him.

A sharp rap on the door startled her. She barely opened it a crack when her guardian pushed it wide and strode in.

"Close the door, girl," he ordered brusquely, "or do you wish the rest of the guests to hear what I have to say to you?"

With a sinking heart, Jillian closed it. The earl was furious. His eyes snapped and his lips were tight. She watched him pace across the room several times before he stopped and faced her.

"Are you completely stupid, girl, or are you purposely trying to destroy me?" he demanded.

"My lord?" Jillian asked innocently.

He scowled. "Don't deny it, girl. You had that black-hearted knave, Dunbary, follow you to the trophy room."

Jillian shook her head in denial.

"Do you think I'm an idiot?" Those chilly eyes glinted in anger. "Don't you know why Bertram wanted to show you his trophies? He was going to ask for your hand in marriage, you stupid baggage."

Bravely, Jillian raised her chin. "I am very aware of what he was about to do, my lord. And I had nothing to do with the Duke of Dunbary coming to the trophy room. Surely, I cannot be held accountable for coincidences beyond my control."

The earl's eyes narrowed, and he took a step towards her. Jillian was sure he was about to hit her again. He glared a moment, then he took a breath. His anger seemed to leave him. He reached out and pushed a strand of hair away from her face. Jillian felt more threatened by the gentle gesture than if he had raised his fist to her.

"Of course not," he agreed. "We cannot avoid coincidences."

His fingers traced across her cheek and down her neck. He rested his hand on her shoulder. Jillian wanted to duck away, but was afraid to move.

His tone was calm as he went on. "But you will rectify the situation. You will write a note to Lord Bertram and invite him to ride with you tomorrow. You will accept any offer he makes to you." His hand squeezed her shoulder. "Is my meaning clear, girl? *Any* offer."

Jillian was not so naïve that she did not realize what her guardian was saying to her. Appalled, her words tumbled out. "But, my lord, I thought marriage… I mean, I thought you wanted…" Her voice trailed off before the cold light in his eyes,

"What did you think, girl?" His voice turned hard as flint. "Why should the daughter of a whore mind so much about selling her charms to the highest bidder?"

Heat flooded Jillian's face. "My mother was no whore."

The earl laughed coldly. "You know so little about her."

His eyes fell to his hand on her shoulder. He loosened his grip and began to stroke the skin beneath his fingers. His hand moved to the back of her neck. Jillian was shocked into immobility.

His lips curled in a cruel smile. "If I did not need the wealth you can bring me, I might consider keeping you for myself."

Sickened, Jillian tried to pull out of his grasp. He caught her hair.

"No, you can't run away," he said. "Let me tell you exactly what I want from you."

"I know what you want." Jillian tried desperately to keep her voice steady. "I would sooner be a beggar on the street."

The earl tightened his hand in her hair. "If you don't do as I tell you, you soon will be. Have no fear of that." He gave her a shove toward the little writing desk in the far corner of the room. "Now, sit down and write what I tell you."

Fearful of the consequences if she did not do as he said, Jillian obediently wrote what her guardian dictated. The note was short, asking if Lord Bertram would consider escorting her on a ride the following morning. The implication was that they would be alone, and Lord Bertram could infer anything he wished from that. After she sealed the note, her guardian swept it from her hand.

"Don't look so downcast, girl," he said with a smile. "If things go well, you could soon be the mistress of this house."

Jillian sat frozen as he left. She did not want to be mistress of this house. Nor did she wish to become her guardian's mistress. Her only option was to find another suitor who would be acceptable to her guardian. But who? Topaz eyes flashed in her mind. Definitely not him. Her thoughts flitted to a pair of kind, twinkling gray eyes. Kip. The thought of his warm smile calmed her. Perhaps he would be interested in asking for her hand. He was kind and seemed to genuinely like her. They could get along very well. They didn't have to love each other.

Dunbary's striking eyes glimmered in her mind once more. She pushed that handsome visage out of her thoughts and began to pace. Think! She had to plan how to get Kip to ask for her hand, she had to avoid Lord Bertram, and she had to contrive to be in the trophy room just before teatime to meet with Dunbary about that blasted secret message.

Jillian composed another note to Lord Bertram begging to be excused from the outing that afternoon. After directing a maid to deliver it, she spent the remainder of the afternoon in her room, taking no chances she might cross paths with Rystoke. She stared out the window as she planned how to deal with Dunbary. She would need to be on her toes if she were to outsmart him. And it was crucial that she did.

That afternoon, Jillian stopped before the closed door of the trophy room. This part of the house was quiet, for most of the guests had gone to the village with their host. Nervously, she smoothed her skirt. She had worn an afternoon dress of white lawn embroidered with vivid green leaves about the hem and neckline. The dress was a bit lightweight for the cool weather, but the neckline was cut quite low, a distraction to divert the attention of the duke from the true purpose of this meeting. To ward off some of the chill, she had draped a filmy shawl over her arms. She had pinned her mother's brooch to the dress for luck. Sending up a silent prayer for help, she pushed open the door and walked in.

The room was empty. As she walked its length, she gave the trophy heads on the walls a furtive glance and the stuffed boar a wide berth. She thought that Dunbary would be here already. Anxious, she stopped by the chair where Lord Bertram had tried to propose. The seconds ticked by. Each moment seemed like an eternity. She stared out at the overgrown garden beyond the window and plucked at a worn spot on the back of the chair.

"So you decided to come after all."

Startled, Jillian swung around. She had heard no one enter, had heard no footfalls cross the carpet. The duke stood in the middle of the room. A smile curved his mouth, and the light from the window turned his eyes bronze.

"I was afraid you would not honor my invitation," he went on, "that you would be too timid. But I should have known that the unconventional Miss St. Clare would laugh in the face of convention."

Jillian said nothing, still trying to gather herself after being startled by his silent approach.

He sauntered a few steps closer. "I hope I did not interrupt anything of a serious nature this morning between you and Bertie."

Jillian finally regained her voice. "That is none of your concern." Then she added, "Your grace."

"You are quite right, of course," the duke agreed. "But all the same, I did want to apologize."

He wandered nearer. Quite a bit nearer. Because he was so close, Jillian had to tilt her head up to look at him. That odd sensation of having little air to breathe assaulted her once again. Her stomach started its crazy dance. All thoughts about punishing him for his ill-mannered behavior fled from her brain. He was so very handsome. His features were chiseled perfection, yet she noticed he had a tiny scar at one corner of his mouth, something she had not seen before. She wondered how he'd acquired the scar. The small imperfection only made the rest of him seem more devastating. She was tempted to ask him, but thought better of it. He would think her even more brazen than he already did, and that could prove dangerous indeed.

A wry smile curled one corner of his mouth. "Since I am apologizing, I should ask your forgiveness for last evening's rudeness. It was uncalled for, since I know so little about you."

"I beg to differ. You seem to know a great deal about me," Jillian said. "You told me yourself when we danced the waltz at Almack's." The memory of that dance brought a rush of heat to her cheeks.

Dunbary's smile reached his eyes. "Ah, yes. At the time, I thought I knew a great deal about you, Miss St. Clare, but I have since come to realize I know very little. I do not know, for instance, if you enjoy riding, or playing the pianoforte, if you have many friends or few, if you like children…" His voice dropped to an intimate murmur. "I do not know what you look like when you sleep. I do not know how you kiss."

Stunned, Jillian's eyes widened and she gasped. Perhaps she had made a mistake wearing a dress with such a revealing décolletage. "Your grace! You defy good manners." She pulled her shawl closer about her shoulders.

He grinned like a school boy. "I seem to do that quite often." He cocked an eyebrow in curiosity. "Have you never been kissed, Miss St. Clare?"

"Of course I have," Jillian huffed, trying to ignore how his eyes twinkled when he smiled. "Not that it's any of your business," she added for good measure. She looked away, trying to hide the telltale blush in her cheeks, only to have her gaze land on the stuffed boar. She grimaced with distaste.

"Prove it," he demanded.

"I beg your pardon?" Jillian's gaze flew back to his in surprise.

"Prove to me that you have been kissed." His topaz eyes seemed to challenge her with silky seduction.

Involuntarily, her gaze fell on his mouth. She wondered what it would feel like to have those chiseled lips touch her own. Shaking her head both to rid her mind of such scandalous thoughts and to answer his outrageous demand, she squeezed back against the chair and shut her eyes.

"Don't you want to kiss me, Miss St. Clare?" the duke murmured. "I want to kiss you."

A shiver ran down her spine. "No." The word—the lie—came out in a whisper.

"A pity."

Jillian felt the light touch of his fingers trace down her bare arm. Her eyes flew open. He was standing only inches away from her. That mouth, *his* mouth, was coming ever so close.

"Are you sure you do not wish to kiss me?" His words sighed into her mind like sea fog pushed ashore by the breeze.

Mesmerized by his intoxicating nearness and the subtle charm of his words, Jillian stared up at him without moving. She ran her tongue over dry lips. She should not want this man to kiss her, but she did. She wanted it so badly that if he did not, she would surely kiss him. And hang the consequences.

And then it happened. At the first hint of his lips on hers, her lids fluttered closed. Although she barely felt his touch, a ripple of excitement coursed through her, so powerful she placed her hands on his chest for support.

When he pulled back, she opened her eyes in disappointment. "No," she whispered, not realizing she had spoken.

His lips curved up once more. "No what, Miss St. Clare? No kissing? Or no stopping?"

He taunted like the Devil himself. Jillian swallowed and closed her eyes. She could not bring herself to answer him with words. What she was doing was too wicked to admit aloud. But it was so exciting.

She felt his arms close around her and his hand cradle the back of her head just before his lips came down on hers once more. This time, the propriety imposed on him by being in public was gone, unlike when they had danced the waltz, when he had held her away from him. His embrace was firm, encompassing, unrelenting. She was pressed against the length of his hard, muscular frame.

Jillian was aware of this only in the periphery of her mind, for she was entirely focused on what this man was doing to her mouth. Slowly, back and forth, his lips grazed hers, now nibbling, now soothing. Then, ever so gradually, the pressure increased, until finally, her lips parted, inviting him in, her tongue dueling with his, and making her feel more alive than she had ever felt, as she clung, helpless, to him. Waves of pleasure cascaded through her.

The breath was squeezed from her body, but she wanted this kiss never to end. All thought ceased and her mind was aware only of sensation.

When she was dizzy from his kiss, when she had to lean into him for support, slowly, he pulled away. She sucked in a breath and reluctantly opened her eyes. Reality was a vague intruder into her brain. One part of her registered that his eyes had turned dark and that his lips curved in a soft smile.

"Aren't you glad you kissed me, Miss St. Clare?" he asked as he punctuated his question with a tiny peck at the corner of her mouth.

Jillian, still too shaken to speak, merely nodded.

"I am very glad I kissed you, Miss St. Clare," he went on, with another tiny kiss to her lips.

Jillian could only blink.

"You see," he said, "now that we have kissed, we are friends. And friends should not hide secrets from each other. Don't you agree?"

Again, Jillian nodded.

"Since you agree, perhaps you will share your secret with me."

With her mind still dazed, Jillian frowned up at him in confusion. "What secret?"

He smiled. "Why, the secret letter, of course."

His words were like a splash of cold water on her face. She could not have been more disgusted with herself than if she had landed in a pigsty. This man wanted only one thing from her—that bloody secret letter. He had not really wanted to kiss her. He was not interested in whether she liked to ride or to play the pianoforte. He cared little if she liked children. He wanted what he wanted and would use any means to get it.

It hurt. It truly did. For a moment she'd lost herself into believing that he wanted to kiss her because he was attracted to her. She had been stupid and naïve.

"You cad!" She gave him a mighty shove and stepped away. As she did, her brooch caught in a buttonhole of his coat. With a sharp rending sound, her dress ripped several inches down the front.

She gasped. "Oh, look what you have done! How could you?" Horrified, humiliated, she pulled the edges of the gap together.

"But I didn't—" he began.

"You vile man! You deliberately seduced me and now you have torn my dress!" Tears of frustration and embarrassment filled her eyes. "I hate you!"

"What is going on here?" an angry voice asked from the doorway.

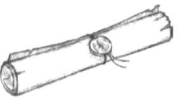

CHAPTER 5

Jillian's head snapped around at the question and she saw Kip strid-ing into the room. She clutched her torn dress together and tried to cover the rip with her shawl, but his expression said he had already seen the damage.

"What is the meaning of this, sir?" Kip demanded angrily. He turned to Jillian without waiting for an answer. "Are you all right? Has he dishonored you?"

Mortified at the same time she was relieved at the sight of Kip, all Jillian could do was shake her head.

"You are no gentleman, sir," Kip declared to Dunbary.

"Really?" the duke drawled. "If I am not a gentleman, what does that make you, sir, for barging in where you were not invited?"

"If I had not 'barged in', as you say, God knows how far you would have gone with your debauchery," Kip returned.

"Debauchery?" Dunbary's eyes took on a feral gleam. "What are you accusing me of, sir?"

Kip took a step toward him. "You know what I am accusing you of. In the name of Miss St. Clare, I demand satisfaction."

The duke gave a curt nod. "You shall have it. When and where?"

In growing horror, Jillian watched the heated exchange. The pos-sibility of a duel between these two men terrified her. She vividly remembered the hand of the duke, with its marks of frequent sword practice, and his restrained strength as they danced. And she remem-bered Kip's hard muscles beneath her hand as he escorted her up the stairs the night before. If these two men dueled, they might both die.

She jumped between them. "No. Please, no duel." There was silence from the men as they glanced at her, then glared at each other. She sensed that they were about to disregard her interruption. Again, she pleaded, "Please, no duel. There is no reason. I want no bloodshed on account of me."

After a long moment, Dunbary said to Kip, "It would seem the lady does not feel her honor is in question."

"Although I have great respect for the lady, I disagree," Kip answered. "I feel her honor should be upheld."

"No," Jillian repeated. "No bloodshed. Please, Kip."

"It seems the lady does not wish your blood to be spilled," the duke observed. "I find that very touching." He smiled coldly. "Since Miss St. Clare does not want us to duel, I see no reason to inconvenience myself by standing in the damp chill of dawn with you." Bowing to Jillian, he said, "I hope to see you again very soon, Miss St. Clare. I apologize for any insult or inconvenience I may have caused you." Pushing past Kip, he stalked across the room.

The raised voices had drawn some of the other guests who had just returned from the outing to the village. Three ladies and two gentlemen stood in the doorway absorbing the scene, their avid gazes clearly relishing the prospect of spreading juicy gossip. When Dunbary approached them, they hesitated a moment, reluctant to let the subject of their social tattling escape through the door. Then, beneath his withering glance, they shuffled out of his way.

As he passed by them, he said dryly, "The performance is over, ladies and gentlemen. I believe tea is being served elsewhere."

Properly chastised, the guests drifted away. Someone discreetly closed the door.

Jillian swung away from Kip's gaze. All she wanted was to disappear, to hide away in her shame. What must Kip think of her?

"Please, leave me alone," she begged in a strained whisper.

Kip came up behind her. She felt his coat placed about her shoulders. Gratefully, she held its warmth to her.

"I will not leave you alone," he said. "Especially now, when that man refuses to stand up against me. If you'll allow me, I'll take you to your room." He held out an arm to her.

"It's not what you think." She sniffled. "My torn dress. It was an accident."

"Of course it was," Kip agreed a bit too readily, as if he only meant to placate her. "Even so, the man is a cad and should be taught some manners."

"Yes, I suppose he should," she agreed vaguely. Her thoughts had turned to his kiss, and the new, wild sensations it had aroused in her. With a shiver, she blocked them from her mind. "Please, excuse me," she said, slipped past him and out of the trophy room. In her embarrassment, she couldn't even bear Kip's comforting presence. She needed to be alone to sort out her thoughts.

She was relieved that she did not meet either her guardian or Pennington as she hurried through hallways, getting lost once, and finally up the stairs. She was relieved she only met one maid. The news of what had taken place would soon reach the guests. It was too juicy not to be passed along with additions and embellishments.

When she reached her room, she dropped Kip's coat from her shoulders, then pulled off the lovely gown with its accusing rip and stuffed it into the bottom of one of her valises. She never wanted to see the rag again. She could not even bear to wear her mother's brooch.

She placed the treasured piece of jewelry on the dressing table, her finger tracing its delicate contours. "Oh, mama, what have you done to me?" she whispered brokenly. There was no answer in the fine, filigree gold nor the bright stones as they glistened back at her.

Tears of loneliness clouded her eyes, but she resolutely sniffed them away. Sifting through the colorful gowns hanging in the armoire, she pulled out the most modest dress she had brought with her. Donning the long-sleeved, pale violet frock of soft wool, she felt more secure. Perhaps, the incident in the trophy room could have a positive result. The gossip would surely spread and Lord Bertram would find her unacceptable as a suitable wife. She would not have to worry about finding a way out of the proposed union.

With a sigh, she sank onto the chair before the dressing table and pulled the pins from her hair. She studied her face in the mirror. Her lips still showed signs of the passionate kiss she had shared with the duke, and her cheeks were a bit pale. Other than that, she still looked the same. Yet inside, she felt very different from the person who had arrived at this manor house only the day before. Yesterday, she had been Lord Rystoke's timid pawn in some terrible game of chess. But pawns sometimes won the gambit. He would be furious at the social blunder she had committed, but she was not going to let him ruin her life because of one mistake, one stupid kiss. Her mother's brooch winked up approvingly at her from the table.

As she picked up the brush, she could still feel the duke's strong fingers tangled in her hair. His warm lips on hers. His breath mingling with hers as their tongues dueled. Was the kiss so very wrong? The memory of her body pressed up against his made her squirm in her chair. Had he felt the same surge of feelings when their lips touched? She had felt wonderful. Alive. Staggered.

She sighed as she ran the brush through her hair. She was not supposed to feel such excitement with a man who was involved in some sort of treachery. What had she been thinking to allow him to kiss her? And now, because of that one kiss, disaster hovered over her like a storm cloud about to unleash a torrent of rain.

A knock came at her door. Reluctantly, she rose to answer it. She had been waiting for this knock. She knew it was Rystoke who had come to berate her for her mistake. But she was surprised to see Lord Bertram.

"Harrumph. Miss St. Clare." He nodded brusquely. "I wanted a word with you. Please. In private."

Silently, Jillian swung the door wide and let him in. He had no doubt come to tell her that whatever he had been about to say that morning had been a mistake. He wanted nothing more to do with her. She would not have to refuse his proposal after all.

Lord Bertram cleared his throat. "Miss St. Clare, this morning — ah — this morning —" He halted and stared at her. "I say, you have beautiful hair." His eyes gleamed as he gazed at her." Like gold silk."

Self-conscious, a bit uneasy, Jillian pushed her loose hair back from her face. She never should have answered his knock. "Thank you, my lord. I was just freshening up before tea."

"Tea, yes, well, I should make this quick then, although I can't abide the stuff myself. Prefer a good Scotch whiskey, you know, or even a bit of gin." He grinned and winked slyly. When Jillian said nothing, he sobered and went on, "Well, as I was saying... Damn if this isn't dashed hard!"

"What is so hard to say, my lord?" Jillian asked, knowing that he was going to tell her that no marriage proposal would be coming from him.

Bertram shifted from foot to foot. "I heard about that ruckus in the trophy room. I know that Dunbary is a bloody good-looking gent and, well, I understand, and I don't hold it against you. Blast, I suppose if I were a woman and all, and young, I suppose I would... well, never mind. You see, my offer still stands."

"What offer, my lord?" Jillian held her breath, hoping his offer was not about marriage.

"Why, to marry me, of course!" Lord Bertram's chuckle sounded nervous. "That's what I was trying to say this morning. What do you say, girl? Eh? Want to give it a whirl with old Bertie?" He winked suggestively.

Dismay made Jillian's stomach plunge. She managed a smile. "That's very kind of you, my lord, but, you see, I will have to think it over, and, of course, my guardian will have to give his approval."

Lord Bertram waved away her arguments. "That's no problem. Rystoke already gave me the go-ahead. So. It's settled then."

"Well—"

Before Jillian could get out another word, he stepped close and touched her hair. "Soft," he said. "I knew it would be. You are a beauty, girl. Rystoke will probably clean me out in the marriage contract."

"But, my lord," Jillian protested. She edged away from him. "This is all so sudden. Please, I must have time to think about it."

"Um. Of course. No matter. You'll come around." He ran his hand down the length of her hair again. "So soft."

"The baggage isn't yours yet, Bertie," Rystoke said from the doorway.

Lord Bertram dropped his hand and jumped away from her as nimbly as his pudginess allowed. Jillian was torn between relief at the interruption and dread at her guardian's appearance. He sauntered into the room. His cool demeanor hid what she knew to be a rage of overwhelming proportions.

"So," he said to Bertram, "you still find my ward an attractive catch?"

"Harrumph. She is a beauty, Rystoke." Lord Bertram self-consciously stuck his hands in his pockets and would not meet Rystoke's piercing gaze.

"Yes, she is," the earl agreed as he turned a cold smile on Jillian. "If you still want her, she will not come cheaply, despite her lack of morals."

Jillian gasped at her guardian's barb.

"Now, see here, Rystoke," Lord Bertram began in her defense.

"She is what she is, Bertie," her guardian said flatly. "If you wish to make an offer for her, you may come to me in London." He walked to the door and held it open for Bertram. "Now, if you will excuse us, my ward has some packing to do, for we must return to the city."

Despite being intimidated by the earl, Lord Bertram was brave enough to bow over Jillian's hand. "Until we meet again, Miss St. Clare," he said, then he hurried away.

As soon as he had gone, Jillian began to pull her valises from the armoire.

Rystoke grabbed her arm and swung her about to face him. "Let the servants do that," he snarled. "You and I have some matters to discuss."

Jillian tried to twist out of his grasp. "I have nothing to discuss with you. I have done nothing wrong."

"Nothing?" He shook her. "You have ruined any chances you might have had for a profitable match."

"Lord Bertram seems to still find me attractive," she argued.

"That ninny? He was never a real contender for your hand, you stupid girl. He isn't wealthy enough, doesn't have the right connections. I merely wanted to string him along so others would have to make their offers higher. I had great plans for you. But with one stupid meeting with that whoremonger Dunbary, you have become soiled goods. God knows what I'll be able to get for you now." His grip on her arm tightened as he shook her again.

For some reason, Jillian felt compelled to defend the man who had kissed her. "The Duke of Dunbary is not a whoremonger," she declared. "What happened was an accident."

He hissed through his teeth. "Every birth can be accounted as an accident. It was fortunate you were interrupted. You could have been found on your back with your legs spread."

"How dare you!" She itched to slap him. Fear kept her hand at her side, but her fingers clutched at the woolen fabric of her gown.

He slammed her up against the armoire. "I dare, you slut, because I own you. I own that lovely body and that malicious soul inside it. You're just like your mother. Until I turn you over to some other man as his wife or mistress, you are mine." He flung her away with such force that she tripped and sprawled across the carpet. "Now, get the maid in here and get packed. I want to be on the road to London before dark."

Jillian watched him stalk out of the room and slam the door behind him. After catching her breath a moment, she climbed shakily to her knees. She was trembling too much to stand, so she sat where she was and leaned against the armoire. Since her mother's death, she had always felt a vague fear in her guardian's presence. Now, she understood why. He was a violent man, a man who did not hesitate to prove his power over weaker individuals. Why had her mother given herself to such a man?

The door opened and Lady Pennington peeked in. "Oh, my dear," she clucked and hurried over. "Dear, dear." Her hands fluttered over Jillian's shoulders and arms. "Are there any broken bones? Any bruises?"

Jillian shook her head. Her chaperone's sudden compassion put a strain on her emotional defenses. An overwhelming urge to bury her face in the woman's shoulder and weep swept through her. She had to swallow several times before she could trust herself to speak.

"We must hurry and pack," she said. "Lord Rystoke—"

"I know what Rystoke wants," Lady Pennington interrupted with a sniff. "But if he cannot refrain from being a brute, he will just have to wait until we have collected our composure."

In surprise, Jillian stared at her chaperone. The woman had always bowed to what the Earl of Rystoke wanted. After all, he was her only means of support.

"I don't want to get you in trouble, Lady Pennington," Jillian told her. "All this is my fault."

Lady Pennington lowered her plump bottom onto the floor and sighed. Jillian nearly giggled at the sight.

"What you did was very naughty," the woman told her gently. "But Dunbary is a handsome rogue. I was young once, and thought I was madly in love with a man who was quite unacceptable to my parents. He traveled with the wrong crowd, you know." She smiled at the memory. "He was terribly handsome and one night, we met at Vauxhall Gardens on the Dark Walk."

Jillian bit her lip to hide a smile. The Dark Walk was a path through Vauxhall Gardens that was poorly lit and gave young men and women a chance to meet secretly. Somehow, she could not picture the proper Lady Pennington sneaking away for a secret assignation with a beau.

Lady Pennington continued "My father came after me and dragged me away just as this young man was about to kiss me. I was devastated. The next day, my father announced my betrothal to Lord Pennington, and here I am, the widow of Pennington after thirty years of a happy marriage."

Fascinated by her chaperone's story, Jillian asked, "What became of the young man?"

"Oh, he lost all his money gambling and killed someone in a duel. I think he fled to Spain." Pennington turned serious eyes on her young charge. "So, you see, the wild, handsome ones are not the best choices for husbands."

"Yes, I see," Jillian murmured. She did not want to explain that she had no intention of marrying the Duke of Dunbary. But Lady Pennington's story did make her feel better. She scrambled to her feet and then helped the woman up.

"I think we should start to pack," Jillian suggested. "I'll ring for the maid."

Perhaps she had found an ally in Lady Pennington. Her future did not look quite so dim.

Adrian stood at his window and gazed out at the gathering dusk. He was undecided about whether he should return to London that night and run the risk of being accosted by outlaws on the road, or wait until morning. He knew his chances of seeing Jillian again here in the country were nonexistent. He had been stupid and had miscalculated her response to his kiss. Her sense of betrayal when he asked for the letter revealed how innocent she was. Remorse at his ruthless seduction twinged. He tried to assuage his conscience by reminding himself that the letter was quite important. He was only trying to keep Miss St. Clare out of danger. He would have to find some other way to convince her to hand it over.

Kissing her had been an unexpected, exciting experience. She had been soft and warm and beguiling. He'd kissed other soft and warm women, but something about her drew him, fascinated him, made his pulse race. He had expended a great deal of effort to keep his head. The young lady was very desirable.

Absently, he tapped his fingers against the sill as he mulled over recent events. Diana had broken off their arrangement. While she still would work as one of his agents and remain his friend, she had announced she would no longer be his mistress. She needed to find herself a husband. He suspected that was not the only reason she had broken it off. He had not been as attentive as he should, especially in the last few days since he had lost that letter and crossed paths with Miss St. Clare.

He sighed. Miss St. Clare was definitely a distraction. He could not decide if that was good or bad.

The sound of a coach on the drive below drew his attention. Two women, cloaked and hooded, emerged from the house. The plumper one had her arm protectively about the other, whose shoulders drooped dejectedly. As soon as they had climbed into the coach, a man strode out of the house. He angrily jerked on his gloves. A thread of guilt ran through Adrian as he recognized Jillian, her chaperone, and her displeased guardian.

He watched the disappearing coach lamps as the vehicle drove off. Soon after, a horse was brought around. A young man swung up into the saddle and galloped away. Mr. Giles followed the young lady to London. Adrian frowned, annoyed at the man's gallantry. Then he caught himself up short. Was he jealous? No. Impossible. He only wanted the letter. He dropped into a chair and stretched out his legs.

He had botched the whole affair, from the minute his agent had panicked and threw the letter in the bush. Not only had he lost valuable information, he had also ruined a beautiful young woman's reputation. He wondered if the girl would be able to marry anyone at all now.

He jumped out of the chair and paced. Dash it all, she was so bloody stubborn. All he wanted was the damned letter. She probably had no idea of its importance. She probably thought keeping the letter was like playing a game. Except it was not a game. What he was involved in was deadly serious. Lord Castlereagh, England's Foreign Minister, needed that letter to convince the Prime Minister that America was angry enough to declare war. England could not afford another war. The country was already engaged in one with Napoleon.

Adrian ran his hand through his hair. He had been stupid. He had allowed his feelings to get in the way of his responsibilities. He had arranged to meet Jillian to retrieve the letter, but he also wanted to get her alone. He had not planned to kiss her, but he had not entirely ruled out the possibility either. Jillian attracted him. She was intelligent. She was clever. She was beautiful. The more she eluded him, the more fascinated he became. He did not want to hurt her, but he had. She was in disgrace. If only that nosey Scot had kept clear…

He brought his fist down on the back of a chair. He should have accepted the Scot's challenge despite Jillian's protest. There was no question about the outcome of the duel. Jillian would be better off without that interfering Scotsman.

And without that interfering Scotsman, he could…what? Offer to wed her? No. Marriage was out of the question. He had decided long ago he would not marry. He would leave the propagation of his title to his younger brother. His mother had cured him of any desire to wed. His beautiful mother, who had never found time for him or his brother, who had spent her nights gambling and whoring, and her days sleeping and shopping and gossiping. Upon his father's death, he had finally been able to send her off to the Continent with an allowance and her latest lover.

He could make Jillian his mistress. No, that idea was preposterous. She was an innocent. He had done enough to her reputation by dancing the waltz with her and ruining her dress.

Unless she was not as pure as she appeared. He knew nothing about her except that she was Rystoke's ward. The relationship of guardian and ward could be a sham. She could be Rystoke's mistress. Rystoke was a conniver and sometimes a cheat. The man was as cold-hearted as a snake. Perhaps he already knew of the letter and urged Jillian to pretend ignorance. But that couldn't be true, because her response to his kiss spoke of her naiveté.

Pain in the palm of his hand made him glance down. He had clenched his fist so tightly his nails bit into his flesh. With a conscious effort, he unclenched his fingers. He remembered a rumor that Rystoke beat his women. Despite his misgivings about Jillian, she did not deserve to be abused.

He glanced out the window and made up his mind. He would let Diana have the coach to return to the city tomorrow. Tonight, he would return to London to get some answers concerning Miss St. Clare. He would risk being attacked by outlaws. His stallion, Madman Jack, could outrun almost anything.

CHAPTER 6

Jillian stood at a window of the drawing room and looked down at the street that ran by the townhouse of the Earl of Rystoke. Two days had passed since that horrible incident at Lord Bertram's country estate. Two days of living in disgrace. Two days of being confined to the house like a prisoner. Flowers bloomed and birds sang, but all she felt was gloom.

She watched a coach and four stop before the steps leading up to the front door. Several long minutes passed before a sparse gray head poked out, and then a shrunken little man tottered onto the street. He hunched over his cane and squinted up at the front door. His black, old fashioned coat was dusted with mildew, and his stockings, shirt and moth-eaten cravat were yellow with age. He leaned on his footman's arm as he shuffled to the stairs.

With a groan, Jillian turned away from the window. For two days, she had watched the comings and goings of prospective suitors for her hand in marriage. None of them had compared to the Duke of Dunbary. A couple of them had been young, a few middle-aged, and then this old man. She knew nothing about any of them, of course, but she tried to picture herself wed to each one as they stepped from their coaches. That only depressed her. She did not wish to marry any of them. The latest suitor made her stomach churn. He was obviously wealthy, for his black coach and matched set of four horses were elegant and well-maintained, but his person left much to be desired as a bridegroom. Jillian shivered as she contemplated being wed to such an elderly man and forced to endure his gropings in their marriage bed. She was sure he did not kiss like Dunbary, nor would he have the same strong arms to hold her.

As she tried to get that kiss out of her head, she paced the length of the drawing room, then returned to the window. The man had not even reached the top of the stairs yet. He finally shuffled below the window, out of sight. She heard the knocker fall on the front door. The visitor would be closeted with her guardian for quite some time. Jillian had become familiar with the routine by now. If the preliminary negotiations between the suitor and her guardian were agreeable, then she would be called down to meet the man, so that he might look her over like livestock. If the negotiations did not go as her guardian wished, she would be left alone.

Jillian clasped her hands together to keep them from shaking. She wanted to throw something. She felt trapped and helpless. When the earl summoned her, he expected her to smile and curtsy, be charming and demure. If she did not perform as he wished, he had threatened her with a beating. Not only was she anxious about the suitors appearing at the door, she was afraid of Rystoke's temper.

She wondered if Kip would make an offer for her hand. He was kind, and she enjoyed his company. They got along well together. He was handsome and strong. They might even grow to love each other eventually. But he did not make the air grow thin when he was near, nor did her stomach jig. Not like Dunbary, with his wicked eyes and devilish mouth. That mouth, those lips that had put her in this compromising position. She swung away from the window again and clenched her teeth. Her gaze fell on a delicate figurine, and she swiped it up, intending to smash it. But even as her fingers closed around it, she sighed. Creating a disturbance wouldn't help. She placed the figurine back on the table.

Kip was not coming. Her hope that he would suddenly appear was a foolish dream. It was not his responsibility to rescue her from her own stupid mistake. She had to accept the consequences of her actions.

She heard another coach pull up, and curiosity drew her back to the window. It had stopped behind the first. This coach was newer and painted an elegant deep burgundy. The horses were livelier than the others. The footman in his jaunty black and yellow uniform smartly opened the coach door and pulled down the step.

Jillian waited to see who this newcomer was. When the man finally emerged, she gasped. Dunbary!

Her hand flew to her mouth. Why had he come? To demand she hand over the letter? Or for some other, nefarious reason? She watched as he straightened the cuff of his dark blue coat and pulled his pale yellow waistcoat down to the proper line of the waistband of his trousers. Even in the grayness of this cloudy spring day, the silver head on his walking stick shone brightly. As he stood on the street and waited for his footman to lift the doorknocker, he glanced up to the window where Jillian watched. Quickly, she stepped away, but not before she caught a glimpse of those gleaming topaz eyes beneath the brim of his tall beaverskin hat.

She heard the doorknocker fall. An idea popped into her head. It was a preposterous idea, a wild, crazy idea. If she stopped to think about it, she would change her mind.

She had to reach Dunbary before he spoke to her guardian. As she hurried down the hall to the staircase leading to the floor below, she heard Williams greeting him. Warily, she descended to the first floor.

She was too late. Just as she reached the last step, she saw the duke enter the earl's study and close the door behind him. She heard her guardian exclaim angrily, "What is the meaning of this, sir?"

The possible repercussions of this meeting between the two men made her freeze. Dunbary would tell her guardian about the letter. He would request that Rystoke retrieve it. The earl would demand that she give it to him, intimidate her into handing it over to him. And then he would beat her for keeping it a secret. She would lose the one thing that gave her some power over her helpless situation.

But all was not yet lost. None of that had occurred. She still might have a chance to put her idea into action. She stepped into the dining room and left the door ajar so that she could waylay Dunbary before he left.

She did not have to wait long. When he emerged from the earl's study, his face was a stony mask as he closed the door behind him. No sound came from the room he had just left.

"Psst," Jillian hissed.

He looked up in surprise, and his mouth curved into a cynical smile. "Miss St. Clare," he greeted.

Jillian beckoned him into the dining room. She was relieved when he obliged her without question, and closed the door behind him.

Before he said anything or she lost her nerve, she said, "I have a proposition to make to you."

A dark brow curved up. "Really? How intriguing. I don't think I have ever been propositioned by a young, unwed lady before."

"It's not indecent," Jillian said sternly, trying to ignore the jig her stomach was doing.

"How disappointing," he murmured.

She sent him a quelling glance. "I have an idea that could benefit both of us."

"I'm fascinated." Dunbary tipped his head. "Will it require that we meet again? I think I might enjoy that. Although, you did give the impression the last time we met that you wanted nothing further to do with me."

Jillian blushed. "What happened between us was a mistake."

"I did not think it a mistake, at all. I rather enjoyed myself. It seemed to me that you enjoyed yourself, too, before you ripped your dress." His smile widened. With one finger, he lightly touched the brooch pinned to the shoulder of her dove-gray gown.

Jillian's blush deepened, but for some reason, she could not step back out of his reach. "I did not ask you in here to speak about *that*. I—"

"No?" The duke interrupted and dropped his hand to his side. A line appeared between his brows. "Then, pray tell, what did you wish to speak about, Miss St. Clare? The weather? The cut of my coat?" He paused. "Stolen property perhaps?"

She twisted her fingers together and ignored his reference to the letter. "Please, this is very difficult for me."

"Not as difficult as it is for me." Dunbary sighed. "Please, do go on."

Jillian took a deep breath. "I wish to make a bargain with you. I will return your property to you, if you –" She stopped, hesitating about laying out her bargain. If he were truly involved in treachery, then returning the letter to him would only help him in his villainy. But, if she did not make the bargain, she would continue to be under Rystoke's control. He could give her to the highest bidder, no matter the man's character. She ducked her head and gnawed on her bottom lip.

Dunbary sighed impatiently. "Yes?" he prompted. "What would you like me to do, Miss St. Clare?"

Jillian gulped. She could not delay any longer. "I will return your property if you will ask for my hand," she said in a rush, avoiding his gaze. "Just as a deception, mind you. I will break off the engagement after a month or two and you will be free to go your way."

Silence came from the man before her. Jillian did not dare raise her eyes. Abruptly, he threw his head back and laughed. Shocked at his reaction, her gaze flew to his face. She could only surmise he found the idea of even a sham engagement preposterous. Who was she, after all, but an insignificant young miss thrown into her first season in London? While he was society's most sought after catch.

Miserably, she said, "I'm sorry. I should not have been so forward."

Before he could answer, the door was flung open and her guardian strode into the room. He grabbed Jillian by the arm and pulled her away from Dunbary.

"What are you doing, you little jade?" her guardian demanded. "Are you determined to ruin everything by throwing yourself at this blackguard?"

Intimidated, Jillian shook her head in denial.

Dunbary stepped up and laid his walking stick across the forearm of the earl. "You will release the young lady, Rystoke." He tapped the earl's hand where he held Jillian. "You will also refrain from making slurs upon the young lady's character." His eyes glinted with menace.

The earl growled, "I will call her what I wish. She is still my ward."

"Quite," the Duke agreed. "But you will unhand her and keep a civil tongue, for she is *my* fiancée." He tapped Rystoke's arm again.

Jillian stared stupidly at Dunbary as Rystoke reluctantly released his iron grip on her. So the duke had agreed to her ruse?

Dunbary's smile was cool. "Thank you very much. It would have been rather awkward to fight a duel with the guardian of my betrothed, don't you think?" He turned to Jillian. "Your guardian and I have already come to an agreement concerning your betrothal to me. I would like the honor of calling upon you, if it pleases you.

I have business all day tomorrow which requires my attention, but perhaps the day after would be convenient?"

Stunned that her guardian had already agreed to have her wed the Duke of Dunbary, all Jillian could do was nod.

"Splendid," the duke exclaimed. "We can ride out into the country. Perhaps then we can discuss your interesting idea. Will two o'clock be satisfactory?"

Again, Jillian nodded in numb silence.

Dunbary bowed to her. "I shall count the minutes until our next meeting." He turned to her guardian and warned, "Touch one hair on her head, Rystoke, and you will have to answer to me."

He sauntered out of the dining room. His carefree whistle floated back as he descended to the ground floor.

Before he reached the front door, the doorknocker fell again. She heard Wilson open the door and the murmurings of another man as he entered.

"Ah, Bertie, old boy!" Dunbary's greeting to Lord Bertram echoed back up the stairs. "Come to sue for the young lady's hand, have you? Sorry, old boy, but you're a bit late. I've just contracted with Rystoke for that honor. Good day!" His whistle faded as he left.

Panic seized Jillian. Now that her suggestion was fact, terror clutched at her middle. She could not possibly become Dunbary's wife. With a cry of dismay, she turned and fled to her room.

Safely behind her bedroom door, she paced and wrung her hands. She had been stupid to offer that bargain to Dunbary. The line of potential husbands coming to the front door had panicked her, but the real prospect of being wed to Dunbary made her palms sweat and her head swim.

He had to want that note very badly to offer for her hand. With their marriage, her property became his, even the note. She did not know what would happen if she refused to give it to him, but she did not want to find out. What had been a fanciful idea to solve her problem about her reputation and get away from Rystoke had become a very real fact.

What would Dunbary be like as a husband? She knew so little about him, other than he was arrogant, wealthy, and too handsome for his own good. And kissed like the Devil, but that was beside the point. He was far too old for her. Why, he must be at least twen-ty-nine or thirty. That was nine or ten years older than she was. He made her feel strange sensations when he was near her, sensations that confused her. She wanted his arms around her at the same time she wanted to be as far away from him as possible. And what of his connection to the note? Was he involved in some treachery? How could she find out before it was too late?

How could she get out of this predicament?

The door to her room swung open and her guardian stalked in. A scowl darkened his face.

"Do not think you can run away from this marriage, girl," he snarled. "Marriages are arranged between families, not on the whim of some insignificant chit. Dunbary offered me far more than I had ever hoped to get for you. You will marry him."

Jillian said nothing, but her chin went up in rebellion.

Rystoke's eyes became like shards of ice. "I'm sure you saw the Earl of Flottendam. He was the doddering old coot who arrived just before Dunbary. Flottendam would be overjoyed to get his hands on such young, juicy flesh like yours. I hear he is quite depraved."

Jillian's stomach turned over. She felt the blood drain from her face.

His lips curled into a sadistic smile. "I see the idea of sharing the marriage bed with Flottendam does not appeal to you. So you will behave and wed Dunbary."

Jillian nodded in defeat.

"I knew you would agree," he said and wandered to the chair by the hearth.

Jillian had left her doll on the chair after sewing the secret note inside. She held her breath when he picked up the doll and stared at it. Then his lips twisted in distaste as he dropped it to the floor and sat. Relief flooded her.

Rystoke smiled and crossed his legs. "I think we can both profit from this marriage. Your mother wished for you to marry well, and Dunbary is quite the catch." His smile turned smug, as if he had instigated the betrothal.

Jillian waited in suspicious silence. Rystoke never conferred something without demanding some payment. In this case, he had *allowed* her to become betrothed to the duke.

When she did not express her gratitude, he shrugged. "I'd like you to do something for me, a small thing, really. Your future husband and I have been on opposite sides in Parliament since he first took his seat. I would be very interested in where he goes, who visits him, that sort of thing."

Appalled, Jillian searched for words. Finally, she blurted, "You want me to spy on him?"

"I would not put it in such harsh terms." He waved a negligent hand.

Her fist clenched in revolt. "I refuse."

Rystoke's gaze snapped and his mouth tightened. "You are still under my roof and my ward. Must I remind you about behaving?"

His threat of a beating still hung over her. She raised her chin.

"If you touch me, Dunbary will be very displeased and call you out," she said.

His eyes narrowed and he glanced away. When he turned back to her, he had banked his anger. Smoothly persuasive, he said, "Don't you wish to learn more about your future husband?"

She did. She barely knew him, and the manner in which they had become acquainted was unusual, to say the least. Her gaze slipped to the doll with its hidden secret lying in a heap on the floor. What if Dunbary's treachery ran deeper than passing stolen correspondence? But she did not trust Rystoke either, with his threats and smooth innuendoes and his desire to have her spy on her future husband.

"What would you do with that information?" she demanded. "Surely, knowing that he visited his club or met with friends would not help you."

Rystoke gave her a patronizing smile. "That is exactly the sort of knowledge that would help me. You are too young and innocent to understand politics and the dealings of men, but a man reveals his true affiliations by those with whom he associates. I have been watching Dunbary for some time, and I have my suspicions about his loyalty."

Jillian had her own suspicions, but she would not reveal that to Rystoke, nor would she align with him.

"With your help, I could prove his disloyalty," he went on. "I would report his activities to the authorities," he said. "He would be arrested. He might even be executed for treason. You could end up a widow with a prestigious title."

Jillian gasped. What he suggested was too terrible for her to contemplate. Besides becoming a widow, she would be treated like a pariah in society as a result of her husband's treason. She was suspicious of the duke, but what if her suspicions were wrong? What if he was actually working for England, not against? What if Rystoke destroyed an innocent man? And if Dunbary were executed…? The idea made her ill. Now that she had met Dunbary, she could not imagine the city without him. "No," she said, shaking her head.

Rystoke's brow lowered. "You *will* do this. Because, if you do not, I will — " With a shrug, he let his threat hang. A malicious smile curved his lips.

The silence hung menacingly. What would he do? She did not think his threat involved a beating, for he had backed down when she reminded him of Dunbary's warning. This time, his threat seemed more sinister, and although she could not imagine what he had in mind, she knew he was not bluffing. Whatever it was, it would be despicable. She had no choice. She jerked a nod. But she would be very careful about what she revealed to him.

The earl stood with a complacent smile. "That is a very good decision." He walked to the door. "Enjoy the rest of your day, Jillian."

His parting words sounded more menacing than mere good wishes. As the door closed behind him, Jillian's frustration rose through her like a pot about to boil over. She was caught in a double bind. The idea of escaping to the property she had inherited from her mother crossed her mind, but she dismissed it. Rystoke would know where to find her and drag her back. He would no doubt impose some horrible punishment, despite Dunbary's protection.

Jillian placed her hand over her mother's brooch. *Oh, mama,* she silently cried, *is this what you wanted for me?*

Rystoke returned to his study, a pleased smile on his face. The offer he had received from Dunbary was more than he had ever dreamed he would get for Jillian. In return, he would have to make a few concessions, but those were in the future, and he could find a way to circumvent them. His only regret was that the arrangement would benefit Jillian, and through her, his lifelong enemy, her father. He drummed his fingers on the polished surface of his desk. Perhaps, even those benefits could become damaging if he planned correctly.

He heard the doorknocker echo up the stairwell. Soon after, Williams appeared.

His butler bowed. "Mr. Stone is here, my lord."

Rystoke's eyes narrowed thoughtfully. "Show him up."

As Cooper Stone entered, his large frame dwarfed the butler, who silently closed the door behind the American. He had met the man through one of the other club members of White's. Although he did not particularly like Stone, the man had interesting connections and some persuasive ideas. Rystoke waved his visitor to a chair.

"What do you want, Stone?" Rystoke asked testily.

Stone's eyebrows shot up in surprise. "Are you always this ill-tempered?"

"My apologies," he said smoothly. "Just a minor problem with my ward."

The American studied his fingernails and smiled. "I heard some nasty rumors concerning the girl. Something about her lack of moral character and a torn dress. I believe Dunbary was involved."

"They are engaged," the earl snapped. "Dunbary just left here."

Stone crossed his legs as his smile broadened. "If Dunbary was engaged to my ward, I might be disagreeable, too. Perhaps I can brighten your day. I have received some interesting news."

"Oh?" Rystoke relaxed. The American's news was always useful. He had, on more than one occasion since his arrival in London, informed him of juicy rumors and tidbits that Rystoke could use to his advantage.

"You understand, of course, that my friends from Kentucky will want something in return," Stone warned.

"I have always repaid with useful information, Stone," Rystoke growled. "What have you learned?"

Stone cleared his throat. "A senator from Massachusetts wrote a letter to a colleague in Tennessee and urged patience to his friend from the south concerning certain grievances against England."

"So?" the earl snapped. "The northerners make money from trade with England. Of course they are going to urge patience. They don't want to upset the apple cart. That is no secret."

Stone shook his head. "Not everyone from the north is content to let England dictate how America should engage in trade. There are some who lose money with the forced stop in an English port before going on to trade in other countries. And the Americans are furious at the English impressment of their sailors. Parliament has made enemies with its Orders in Council."

Rystoke waved his hand in dismissal. "You Americans forget that if it were not for England, you would not have a country. You are all still Englishmen."

Stone's brow darkened. "We are free Americans. We fought a revolution for that honor. Don't forget that, Rystoke. I'm not a traitor. I'm just protecting my interests."

Rystoke hid his annoyance at the man's affront. The Americans never should have won their independence. They were Englishmen. If England had not been distracted by conflicts with France, Spain, and the Dutch, those Americans would never have won. But he was not about to anger Stone. The American's size was a bit alarming, and he could most likely break a log in two with his bare hands, not to mention the delicate chair on which he sat.

"I apologize," he said. "Please, do go on."

Mollified, Stone's brow cleared. "The letter I mentioned was intercepted on its way from Massachusetts to Tennessee. A copy was made and brought to England. Somehow, the copy was misplaced. It was supposed to go to someone in the Foreign Office, but it never arrived where it was supposed to go."

"What happened to it?" Rystoke demanded. Although curious, he knew he should not ask how the man came by his information.

Stone smiled. "We learned it was to be transferred at that ball you attended about a week ago. Someone found it, someone who happened to be standing nearby when the letter was passed."

"Well, who is that?" Rystoke was barely able to contain his impatience. Stone always acted as if he were his equal. He hated that he needed him.

Stone shrugged. "We don't know. That's your problem. Find the letter and you can convince Parliament that they have nothing to worry about with their Orders in Council. They can dictate America's trade as much as they want because they have friends in Congress."

Rystoke's mind raced. All he had to do was remember who was present at the ball. He might even request Jillian's help. Then he could give the list to his friends and they could make discreet inquiries.

Stone grinned at his silence. "You are a sneaky fellow, Rystoke. I'm sure you can discover who has the letter." He stood. "When I learn anything, you will hear from me." With another of his easy smiles, he left.

Rystoke drummed his fingers on the desk. He wondered what the American gained by helping him, but that thought slipped away as he pondered the information he had just been given. If he could find the note, he could use it to sway those members of Parliament to his side. The Orders in Council would remain in place, and England could focus on defeating Napoleon. Anticipation of keeping those brazen Americans in line made his lips curl.

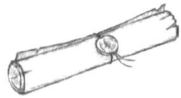

CHAPTER 7

The day after he had become betrothed to Jillian, Adrian dismounted from Madman Jack and handed the reins to Nat, his stableboy. He had just come from an early morning meeting with Lord Castlereagh, Secretary of Foreign Affairs, concerning England's Peninsular Campaign in Spain and Portugal. Distracted with his thoughts, Adrian at first did not notice Nat's averted face, but his usual bright grin was missing and his greeting was subdued. The boy's surreptitious wipe at his nose made Adrian look more closely. A dark purple bruise colored Nat's cheek.

"Did you get in the way of one of my stallions, lad?" Adrian asked.

"No, ah, I mean, yes, m'lord," Nat answered and swiped at his eyes. He led Madman Jack away.

With a confounded frown at the boy's behavior, Adrian entered his house. Boggs, his majordomo, took Adrian's hat and gloves as usual, but he seemed distracted, and his cravat was slightly askew. Adrian added Nat's bruise to Boggs's crooked cravat and suspected something had disrupted the household. Then he noticed the pile of trunks and valises in a corner of the hall.

Boggs cleared his throat. "You have…visitors, your grace," he said.

Boggs's hesitation did not prepare him for the voice that hailed him from the doorway of the salon.

"Adrian! Darling!"

Adrian stood very still, fighting to control all the emotions that voice engendered and hiding a grimace with great effort. He turned to greet his mother.

"Adrian!" His mother stood with her arms wide, as if she expected him to rush into her embrace.

"Madam." Adrian bowed politely. He observed that her figure had become a bit fuller, but her dark, chestnut hair was still rich and her face still beautiful. Only pale smudges beneath hard brown eyes showed evidence of her wild lifestyle.

His mother gave an insulted sniff. "I should have thought you would be more pleased to see me."

She turned and reentered the salon. Adrian followed and closed the door with careful precision. What he wanted was to tear it from its hinges.

"Here I have just returned from the Continent, and all I get is a polite bow," the lady complained. "I have not seen you in three years, Adrian." She sat on a chair by the fire, placed her feet on the footstool, and fussed with her skirt.

"Why did you not write to tell me of your arrival?" Adrian fought to keep his voice level.

"I wanted to surprise you. Aren't you surprised?" His mother peeked up at him coyly.

"More than you know," he acknowledged.

"There, you see? My arrival was a success." His mother clapped in delight.

"Why did you come back?" Adrian asked bluntly. "I thought you were having a wonderful time in Germany."

"I was, but I got bored, and I missed England." His mother pouted. "And I missed you, Adrian." She turned misty eyes on him.

Adrian was immune to her charm. Her theatrics annoyed him. "You have never missed me, mother. You were quite happy to leave England and your two sons."

"Only because you made it very clear that you wished me to leave." She glanced around as if searching for something. "Where is your brother? Why has he not come to greet me?"

Adrian's fist clenched at his side. "He's at his studies at Cambridge. You will let him be."

A discreet cough from the corner of the room drew his attention. Adrian swung about and saw a man, not much older than himself, step forward.

"Perhaps, it is vise I should leafe, yes?" the man said with a heavy German accent. "You must hafe much to speak of."

Adrian's mother smiled brightly. "Adrian, this is Gustav, Baron von Heisburg."

Von Heisburg bowed with military precision. The German was about Adrian's height, but broader through the shoulders. His blond hair was a bit long and shaggy for London fashion, and he wore a large mustache, intricately curled and waxed. His blue eyes were shrewd. Adrian disliked him on sight. He wondered if the bruise on Nat's cheek was a result of this man's temper.

"Welcome to my country, sir," Adrian greeted blandly.

"A fine country." The foreigner smiled. "But damp, fery damp."

Adrian turned back to his mother. One question needed to be answered, despite the rudeness of asking it before the German. "Where will you be staying?" He had thrown his mother out once. He had no compunctions about doing it again.

Anger glimmered in her gaze. Then she focused on a fold of her skirt. When she turned back to him, her smile was coy. "I thought we might stay here."

Adrian clenched his teeth so he would not say anything unseemly before the German. When he had his tongue under control, he turned to the other man. "If you will excuse us, sir, I would like to speak with my mother privately. I will have my majordomo show you where you might freshen up." He held out his hand to his mother. "Mother, if you please?"

Petulantly, Beatrice Bennett, Dowager Duchess of Dunbary, mother to the Duke of Dunbary, placed her hand in Adrian's and allowed herself to be led from the room. On the way out, she blew a kiss to her traveling companion.

After they had entered Adrian's office and he had closed the door, she complained, "That was quite rude of you Adrian, treating my...treating von Heisburg in that manner. After all, he is a baron."

Free from the German's presence, Adrian said bluntly, "Are you sure he is a baron? Or is he using the title to attach himself to a woman who enjoys throwing money about and taking younger men to her bed?"

Beatrice's hand landed with a crack on Adrian's cheek. "How dare you speak to your mother like that?"

He clenched his jaw for a moment to rein in his anger. "Don't flatter yourself, madam. You stopped being my mother a long time ago." Dispassionately, he watched his words bring tears to Beatrice's eyes.

"Oh, Adrian," she cried. "You are so much like your father. He never understood me and neither do you."

He turned away and walked to the window. "My father understood you too well. His understanding killed him."

With a sniff, Beatrice quickly regained her composure. Her voice turned hard. "Your father was a sentimental fool. He expected me to retire to the country with him and give up my entire life and all my admirers."

Adrian swung about to face his mother. "Don't you mean all your *lovers*? I don't believe my father was asking too much for his wife to remain faithful to him."

"Of course I was faithful," Beatrice declared. "But your father just didn't understand that I detested living in the country. Why, I would have withered and died on that isolated estate. I needed to see my friends, to live in the city."

Adrian realized that revisiting the old argument was useless. He sighed and sank into the leather chair behind his desk.

"How long are you staying in England, mother?" he asked.

"Why, I have no idea," his mother answered brightly. "Von Heisburg says he will stay as long as I like."

Adrian frowned. "You cannot stay here, not with that German."

"But Adrian, we have only just arrived. Our trip here was quite unexpected, so we did not have time to arrange for a suitable place to stay."

He remained resolutely silent and wondered why such a trip was *unexpected*.

His mother pouted, then casually examined her nails. "Fine. We will visit Lawrence at Cambridge. I'm sure he will be glad to see me."

"You will not," he nearly shouted. The last thing his brother needed was his mother hovering about and making a nuisance of herself. He could envision her seducing one of Lawrence's friends and causing a scandal that might get Lawrence expelled. The only thing to do was to allow her to stay here where he could keep watch on her. Adrian sighed. "You may stay here only until you find lodgings,"

Adrian said firmly. "I think a fortnight should be plenty of time. No longer."

Triumph briefly lit her eyes before she ducked her head. "Of course, dear. That is most generous."

"You may tell Boggs." Adrian nodded, satisfied that his mother understood he did not want her living indefinitely with her lover under his roof.

With a smile, she stood and started for the door. Halfway there, she hesitated and turned to him. "Adrian?"

He knew that tone of voice. She wanted something.

His mother caught her bottom lip between her teeth and gave him a calculating look. "Living in Germany has been so expensive," she said, "and finding decent lodgings will take a great deal out of my allowance."

He sighed and wondered why the German did not help with her expenses. "I will make arrangements. You will have enough to get settled."

"Oh, Adrian, you are a dear." His mother laughed and skipped out the door.

When she had gone, Adrian clenched his fists on the desk before him. His life had been peaceful since her departure to the Continent. Her letters came only when she needed money. He passed the requests to his solicitor who sent her enough to keep her happy and pay off some of her debt.

He wondered if he could tolerate her and the German for even a fortnight. Because of her, Adrian's father had drunk himself to death. The former duke could not bear the hurt and dishonor of a wife who slept with any man who struck her fancy, from nobleman to merchant to sailor. Two years after his father's death, Adrian had told her to take her lack of morals someplace else. Now, she was back.

With an effort, he unclenched his fists. The palms of his hands showed the imprints where his nails had dug into the flesh. His whoring, profligate mother was back just in time for his wedding. To Jillian. Who danced the waltz with him without permission, and met him unchaperoned in an empty room, and kissed with all the fervor of a woman aroused to passion. And dabbled in dangerous games she knew nothing about. Jillian, whose reputation had been ruined by an unfortunate accident, whom he had saved from social oblivion by asking her to be his wife. Was she another Beatrice?

He leaned back in his chair and let his gaze wander about the library. This room had been his sanctuary when his mother had still lived in the house. He would select one of the leather bound volumes and forget his problems in Cervantes, Scott, Defoe, Swift or Malory. Or, he would pace the thick Turkish carpet until his anger subsided. Now that his mother had returned, he could see himself spending more time in the room again. After he wed, would Jillian force him to seek sanctuary here, as well?

He closed his eyes and rubbed the bridge of his nose as a headache throbbed. He knew nothing about Jillian. Not where she came from, who her parents were, if she had brothers or sisters. Nothing. Except that she was the ward of the man whom he disliked intensely, who stood fiercely opposed to Adrian's political philosophy, the man who had scathingly rebuked Adrian when he had made his maiden speech in Parliament. Since then, the two men had derided the other's speeches and proposals made within those hallowed halls. Adrian shook his head. Offering for Jillian's hand in marriage made no sense at all, especially when he had already decided not to wed. He needed to learn more about her. He was a bloody spy, dash it all, trained to ferret out secrets. He should be able to discover more about the mysterious Miss St. Clare.

A knock on the door interrupted his musings. Boggs appeared at Adrian's call to enter and offered a sealed note on a silver tray.

Adrian recognized the seal and silently groaned. His grandmother. He had been expecting this summons since yesterday. The gossip connecting him with Miss St. Clare had evidently reached her ears. The old lady would be furious. He freely admitted she intimidated him. As the senior dowager duchess, she had connections and influence in places way beyond his scope. As the matriarch of the family, she kept watch over the morals and behavior of its members. As his grandmother, he loved her dearly. She had been his rock and comfort growing up. He hated to disappoint her.

"Have the messenger wait, Boggs," he said. "I will reply immediately." As Boggs nodded and turned to leave, Adrian added, "And send Nat to me." He meant to find out how the boy had gained the bruise on his cheek.

As Adrian penned a polite acceptance to his grandmother's invitation to tea that afternoon, he wondered if the dowager had heard of Beatrice's return. Perhaps his grandmother's ire could be diverted from her grandson to her daughter-in-law. But one problem at a time. Before he had to present himself to his grandmother, he had to arrive at the door of Miss Jillian St. Clare to begin his formal courting. That was a task he both eagerly anticipated and dreaded. How could two – no, three – females cause him such emotional turmoil?

Jillian sighed as she looked in the mirror and fussed with the neckline of her spencer jacket. "I don't want to go for a ride in the country. I don't want the Duke of Dunbary as my fiancé. I don't want *any* fiancé."

Anxiously, she readjusted the ribbon ties of the silly hat with the long front brim that sat on her head. When she had embarked on her season, she had never envisioned herself betrothed quite so quickly, and never to a man like the formidable Duke of Dunbary. She had thought at some time in the misty future she would be engaged to a nice, sweet, young man who endearingly stumbled over his complimentary words and fumbled with his cup at tea. Instead, she had the suave, debonair, worldly, enigmatic, handsome Duke of Dunbary as her fiancé, who scared her to death and at the same time drew her like a mouse to cheese. She tried not to think about the delicious sensations he created in her with his kiss.

Despite that, she could not believe she had actually made that outrageous proposal to him – the secret letter in exchange for his offer for her hand. And then he had the audacity to outwit her and make an offer to Rystoke. But at least, if – when – she married him, she would be away from Rystoke's cruelty. Dunbary had thrown a cloak of protection over her. Even if Rystoke still had some hold over her, the duke would protect her from her guardian's violence. That sense of security created a warm glow in her.

Not at all reassured by her musings, she sighed again, and retied the hat ribbons one more time.

Pennington echoed her sigh. "Unfortunately, your guardian has made the arrangements. You must go through with this betrothal, although I do wish he had consulted me first. I would have argued against it. He is much too handsome for his own good. He has a wild reputation. One might call him a rake. But he is a duke, and his income is beyond reproach. You could have done much worse." Having argued herself out of her disapproval of the match, her nod of acceptance held a bit of self-satisfied pride, as if she'd had a part in making it.

The sound of the doorknocker echoed up through the house. Jillian's eyes widened in alarm. "He's here," she whispered. She swung about to Pennington. "I can't go. Please, tell him I'm ill, tell him I have the megrim, tell him I have consumption, tell him I have the plague."

Pennington *tsked*. "I did not spend all this time teaching you how to behave in society to have you offend this man who was kind enough to offer for your hand. You will go downstairs, greet him civilly, and behave like a proper young lady."

"But shouldn't you be coming with us?" Jillian asked.

Pennington's gaze slid away. "I...have other things to attend to."

Jillian thought that excuse very odd. Suspiciously, she asked, "Has my guardian forbidden you to come along?"

Pennington smiled indulgently and straightened Jillian's bonnet. "You are formally betrothed to the duke. The announcement will appear in this afternoon's newspapers. If all goes well, you will soon be his wife. You have to learn to deal with him alone. He is a handsome, charming gentleman."

Jillian was about to argue that she thought Dunbary was not a gentleman at all, when the maid knocked on her bedroom door and announced that the Duke of Dunbary was waiting below. Swallowing hard to still the jig of her stomach, she went to meet her fiancé.

The Duke of Dunbary was waiting for her in the small room that served as a parlor on the ground floor. She noted that he had not been shown to the larger, grander drawing room on the floor above, evidently on orders from her guardian. Despite the small social slight, her fiancé seemed quite at ease.

He lounged in a chair by the fire. With his legs crossed at the knees, his highly polished Hessian boots reflected the flames. His buckskin breeches were molded to his thighs. A dark blue coat covered his broad shoulders, and beneath, he wore a pale yellow satin waistcoat and white linen shirt. A huge topaz gleamed in the folds of his cravat.

He unfolded himself gracefully from the chair, smiled and took her hand. "Miss St. Clare," he murmured as he bowed over her fingers. "You are a vision of loveliness."

At the warm touch of his lips on the back of her hand, Jillian's knees began to vibrate. Fighting for breath, she managed to reply, "You are too kind, your grace."

When he turned her hand over and kissed her palm, she nearly collapsed into a puddle at his feet. Annoyed at her body's response, she jerked out of his grasp and pulled on her gloves. "Shall we go?" Her words came out in a squeak. Pretending she was not at all flustered, without waiting for his answer, she turned and started for the door.

After they were settled on the high seat of his curricle, he turned to face her.

"So, Miss St. Clare, where is my secret correspondence?" he asked mildly.

Jillian blinked at his demand. Besides being aggravatingly smooth and suave, he also did not waste time getting to the point. "We are not wed yet, your grace," she told him primly.

His eyes narrowed. "A minor technicality."

"Not so minor when you consider that if this engagement is broken, my reputation will be destroyed. I have a great deal at stake, your grace. I intend to keep the letter and my reputation intact." She gazed at him steadily, leaving no doubt about her words.

A frown creased his brow and his mouth thinned. "You were not so concerned about your reputation when you danced the waltz with me."

She blushed. Turning away, she sniffed to hide it. "That was a minor transgression. Not at all the same as being left at the altar."

She braced herself against his ire. She was not going to give in no matter how angry he became. The letter was important, but she had to figure out who should get it.

With a disarming smile, he murmured, "I would never leave you at the altar, Miss St. Clare. You may keep the letter until we are wed." Jillian looked at him askance. She had the feeling she had just been out-maneuvered. Those topaz eyes were warm with some emotion she could not recognize. When he reached behind her, she jerked away, expecting him to wrap his strong arm about her and kiss her indecently there in the middle of the street. Instead, he pulled out a nosegay.

"Shy violets for the not-so-shy lady," he said with a grin.

Even though she was suspicious of his gallantry, she was charmed. "They are beautiful," she said. "Thank you." She smelled their fragrance.

"Just because we have not been on friendly terms in the past doesn't mean that we can't start over. Shall we call a temporary truce and shake hands?" he asked and extended his hand.

Still wary, Jillian stared at his hand, the same hand he had held out to her before they danced the waltz, the hand that had so invitingly lured her into this muddle she found herself in. But she was this man's fiancée now. What more harm could this hand do to her? She finally nodded and placed her fingers in his.

"All right," she agreed. "A truce."

His clasp was gentle. His hand was warm, even through her glove. Her hand fit perfectly in his. Her gaze locked with those tawny eyes. The world around her seemed to disappear. His mouth curved in an inviting smile, and the exciting memory of the touch of those lips swept through her. She very much wanted to experience that again.

The horses stamped and shifted, impatient to get started, jerking the curricle. The world came rushing back. Jillian blinked, took a deep breath, and disengaged her fingers. With a smile full of promise and a warning to hold on, Dunbary snapped the reins and they started off. Jillian sniffed the violets again. Perhaps this outing would be pleasant after all. She smiled a little secret smile. She was going on a ride in the country with the most sought-after bachelor in London. He had brought her flowers. She was betrothed to him. What more could any girl ask for on a spring day? She would deal with her suspicions and those strange, unsettling feelings he evoked with his kisses another time.

They left London behind with its noise and crowds. The road rolled through open fields divided by hedgerows. Dunbary pointed out manor houses and estates, and related stories about their inhabitants. Despite his charming manner, she was as nervous as a thoroughbred at Ascot on race day.

At a break in the hedgerows, he turned off the road. They bounced across a field to a copse of trees, where he stopped the curricle and jumped down.

"Here we are," he announced.

Jillian looked around. The spot was lovely. Beneath the trees that were beginning to bud, the ground was covered in soft grass. She could hear the splash of a stream. The sun appeared from behind the clouds, and its warmth spread through the glade.

Dunbary placed his hands on Jillian's waist to swing her down from the high seat of the curricle. As he lowered her to the ground, her body slid against his. With her hands on his shoulders for support, she was reminded of that day in Lord Bertram's trophy room. They had stood exactly like this when they had kissed. Boldly, she gazed up at him and wondered if he would kiss her again. She thought she might like that. With a smile, he leaned towards her. Giddy with anticipation, she closed her eyes. Instead of placing his lips against hers, he reached behind her.

"I brought a picnic," he said.

Jillian's eyes snapped open, and she saw him holding up a basket. An embarrassed blush heated her cheeks. What had she been thinking?

Dunbary took her hand and led her through the trees. She meekly followed, feeling very foolish. Yet, she thought she had felt a soft brush of his lips across her cheek. Or perhaps she had imagined it.

On the other side of the trees was a grassy space, and beyond, a stream flowed serenely past. Dunbary spread out a cloth on the grass and steadied Jillian as she sat. Then he opened the basket and pulled out its treasure—Cheshire cheese and fresh bread, scones and clotted cream, oranges, strawberries, and champagne. He served her on wafer-thin china plates with sterling utensils. They drank the champagne from crystal flutes. Jillian was overwhelmed by the elegance of the picnic. She was impressed by the sweet, exotic oranges, because they were rare and quite dear, but most of all, she was awed by the strawberries so early in the season.

"I have a greenhouse on my property in Cornwall," he explained. "My gardener forces the fruit to ripen early, then sends it to me in London."

"He must be a genius," she said as she picked up another huge strawberry and bit into it. The juice squirted out and ran down her chin. The duke chuckled, and wiped the dribble with his napkin.

"Please, your grace, you don't have to do that," she protested.

"I think it's about time you stopped using that form of address for me. You know my name. I would like you to use it," he said sternly.

His request sounded more like a command. Irritated, she agreed tightly, "Yes. Of course. Your grace. Dunbary."

"Adrian," he corrected.

"Whatever you wish." Her teeth clamped together. She was forced to be meek while living with Rystoke, but she was determined she would not be ordered about by her future husband.

Adrian sighed. "This situation is difficult for me, too. I had planned never to marry."

She fleetingly wondered why a duke would not wish to wed and produce an heir, but the unintended insult straightened her spine. "I certainly don't wish to ruin your plans. Your grace," she snapped. "I would never wish you to sacrifice your freedom to someone who dances the waltz without permission and has her dress ripped by a man who wants only one thing." Jillian did not understand why she was so angry, but his words twisted painfully.

A muscle jumped in his jaw. "The ripped dress was an accident."

"Was the kiss an accident, too? No, of course it wasn't. You had planned to do that all along to get what you wanted." Jillian took a large swallow of champagne. She hardly ever touched spirits, but this man made her furious enough to want to drink the whole bottle. Her blood pounded through her veins and buzzed in her head.

"I still don't have what I want," he shot back. "But you seem to have exactly what you want, since you had Mr. Giles interrupt at just the right moment to coerce me into offering for your hand."

Jillian gasped at the false accusation. "I never!" Outraged, she flung her champagne at him. It splashed across his face and into his hair. Bright droplets spattered his immaculate cravat, shirt, and waistcoat.

Appalled at what she had done, she stared at him with wide eyes and gasped. Now, he would break off the engagement. She would be forced to marry Flottendam. She was ruined.

He stared back, shock and anger chasing across his face. Then his mouth twitched. He threw his head back and laughed. His merriment was infectious. Hesitantly, she smiled, and then she was laughing, too. She pulled a lacy handkerchief from her reticule and dabbed at the droplets on his face and clothes.

As she wiped down his coat lapel, he became very quiet. His gaze became intense, his topaz eyes glinting with some odd, inner heat. She was transfixed by those eyes. As she stared, he reached across the space separating them, and pulled her over the plates with their crumbs and strawberry stems, the dishes with the remains of the bread, cheese, scones, and clotted cream. His glass of champagne spilled, seeping through her dress. The clotted cream smeared on her skirt.

"My dress," she protested weakly as she landed against his chest.

"I'll buy you a new one," he said carelessly. "You are the only woman who has ever doused me with champagne." He grinned as he fell back onto the grass, taking her with him.

She was sprawled across him in a most unladylike position, but she did not care. He planted a resounding kiss on her mouth. Jillian reared back in surprise and stared down at him. The impact of what she had just done struck her and her cheeks heated.

"I'm sorry," she whispered. "I don't know why I threw the champagne at you. I've never done anything like that before, but you make me so angry."

"Do I?" he asked, as he brushed a strand of hair away from her face. "You make me angry, too. But you also make me laugh." His fingers traced across her cheek to a corner of her mouth. "Who are you, Jillian St. Clare?" He untied the ribbons of her hat, pulled it off, and tossed it away. His fingers trailed up the nape of her neck and tangled in her hair. "Why do I find you such a mystery?"

Jillian was mesmerized by his touch. The angry words were gone, evaporated in the heat of his gaze. All that mattered was the feel of his fingers twined in her hair and the soft, warm glint in those tawny eyes. Despite her immodest position and that flip-flop in the pit of her stomach, she was quite strangely comfortable. She licked her lips.

Gently, their mouths touched. His fingers in her hair guided her like his arm about her waist had guided her in the waltz. Her eyes slipped closed and she followed his lead, allowing herself to be drawn into another kind of dance. She felt secure, safe, protected, as he embraced her.

His tongue traced her bottom lip, back and forth, softly seducing. In response, her lips parted, inviting him in. Heat spiraled through her. She was lost in the warm sensations he created.

He cupped her bottom and pressed her down into his hardness. A delicious shiver ran through her. Like acrobatic dancers, they rolled over. His weight pressed her down into the soft grass. She wanted to give him the same feelings he was giving her. She wanted to experiment, to explore his mouth. With a tiny thrust of her tongue, she met his and caressed it. She felt a tremor run through him, and her body echoed it.

He pulled back a little and lightly kissed the corner of her mouth, then trailed tiny kisses down the column of her throat. Somehow, her spencer had opened, and beneath that, the tiny buttons which closed the front of her bodice came undone. He kissed his way down the path between her unfastened clothes. Each touch of his lips felt delicious.

Cool air tickled her breasts as her chemise slipped away. The chill was replaced by his warm hand. Her nipple puckered beneath his touch. The heat of his skin radiated through her. She had no thought that he should not do this, no sense of indecency. The mistrust between them had disappeared. What he was doing seemed the most natural thing in the world, and she wanted it to continue.

His lips finally closed about the tight bud of her breast. She gasped as a spark of pleasure shot through her. Her hand slipped to the back of his head. Her fingers tangled in his hair, and she held him where he was. Each time he sucked, tingles swept through her to the very tips of her toes. His tongue tickled, his lips caressed. She had never felt anything so wonderful in her life. A tiny moan escaped her throat.

She wanted to kiss him again. She needed to feel his mouth against hers. With a tug on his hair, she recaptured his lips. Like a woman starved, she tasted and nibbled and licked. One of her legs was free, and she hooked it up around his thigh and ground her hips into his. His hardness against the apex of her thighs felt splendid. His fingers wandered beneath her skirt, up her calf, to her knee, to her thigh. His touch felt divine. She wanted this man. She was not quite sure for what, but she wanted him. And then his fingers tickled her most private place.

Jillian froze as awareness slammed into her brain. What was she doing? They were betrothed, not married. Her reputation was already hanging by a thread. Not to mention, Dunbary could very well be involved in some form of treachery. Goodness, she had to get hold of herself.

Dunbary pulled back. They stared at each other. With a blink, he rolled off her and sat up, then pulled her up next to him. Gently, he tugged her dress and spencer back onto her shoulders. Then he began to fasten the tiny buttons on her bodice.

Mortified at what she had just done with this man, she brushed his hands away. "I-I can d-do that," she stuttered and turned her back to him. Shame washed over her. This betrothal was a sham. They both knew it. And she had nearly allowed this man the liberties of the marriage bed. Would she become like her mother, a man's plaything, a mistress?

Adrian watched her a moment as he fought to get his arousal under control. Then he began to pack away the remains of their picnic. He had never been so swept away by a kiss. Surprised by her wild response, he had nearly deflowered her on the spot. That would have been disastrous. One more sword Rystoke could have held over his head.

He heard her draw a ragged breath. Apprehensive, he cast a quick glance over his shoulder. He hoped she was not going to fly into hysterics. He had never dealt well with hysterical women.

Her eyes were downcast as she tied the ribbons of her bonnet. As he had kissed her, those gray eyes were as turbulent and dark as a brewing storm. She glanced up at him, and with a mental sigh of relief, he saw her poise had returned. He wondered what thoughts were flying about behind those fathomless eyes. But her passion-bruised lips, the high color in her cheeks, the disarray of her honey hair, the slight wildness of her eyes contradicted her calm. She was still aroused, and he decided he liked the way Miss Jillian St. Clare looked after making love.

As he stood and held out his hand to help her up, he debated whether he should apologize, and thought better of it. She had manipulated him into becoming her fiancé. She would have to deal with the consequences, like his kisses and caresses, because he planned on kissing and caressing her often. Besides, there was still the matter of the letter she possessed.

Yet, to salve his conscience he asked, "Are you all right?"

Jillian pulled her hand out of his grasp as soon as she was on her feet. "Isn't it a little late to ask that now?" she muttered. "I understand why Lady Pennington was so against this betrothal."

Humor twitched his lips. "Why does Lady Pennington dislike me so?"

"It's obvious. You are no gentleman." She bent and retrieved her hat, plunked it on her head and tied off the ribbons. "She said you are much too handsome and a rake." Jillian's eyes widened, appalled at what she had just blurted. "Oh, my…I didn't mean… You're not…" With a strangled sound, she turned away. Trying to pretend she hadn't spoken, she tugged on her gloves, hoping to end the conversation.

She heard him make a strange noise, something that sounded suspiciously like a snigger.

Her cheeks heated. Her whole face felt hot. She wished she could disappear in a puff of smoke, for the earth to open up and swallow her. Perhaps if she moved to another spot, the ground would oblige her by splitting apart. She wandered closer to the stream. Hurried footsteps came up behind her, and Dunbary caught her arm.

"The ground here is marshy, and the bank of the stream can be slippery," he warned.

She shook him off. "I am quite capable of walking on my own."

He held up his hands. "I'm only trying to help."

Jillian sniffed and stepped back. Her foot sank almost to her ankle in mud. She yelped and hopped onto the other foot. It slipped from beneath her. With a plop, she landed on her bottom in the muck and slid down the bank towards the stream.

"Help!" she yelled and reached for the only thing that was near — Adrian's leg.

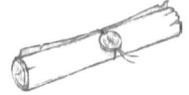

CHAPTER 8

Adrian was pulled off-balance, not expecting her to grab his leg. His heel slipped on the mud. His arms flailed. His other foot shot out from under him. With a complete lack of grace, like a buffoon, he plopped on his bottom. Damp seeped through his breeches.

But Jillian was slipping towards the water. She shrieked and reached for him. Adrian grabbed her arm, but not quite soon enough to prevent her feet and part of her skirt from slipping into the stream.

She squealed and tried to scramble back up the slimy bank. Adrian finally heaved her out of the water. She plonked beside him with a squish. They sat side by side, in the mud, in silence, as they caught their breath. He glanced at her. Her hat was askew and a streak of mud covered one pale cheek. Her shoes and dress dripped water, and muck smeared down her front. She looked like an adorable, wet kitten.

"Thank you," she said and dragged in a shaky breath.

Primly, she straightened her hat and scrambled to her feet. The back of her dress clung to her in a soggy mess. With a little cry of dismay, she pulled the skirt away from her backside.

"My dress is ruined," she mourned.

Now that she was safe on solid ground, Adrian's relief erupted into merriment. "I'll buy you *two* new dresses," he said, strangling on his laughter.

Her brow furrowed and she plucked at her dress. "How can I return to the earl's house like this?" she wailed.

"We can wait until dark and slip in like two thieves in the night," he suggested with a mischievous twinkle.

She groaned in despair and stepped away. A loud squish came from her shoes. She swung back to him. "I can't stay out here with you until dark. There will be gossip."

Adrian looked up at her with a grin and a raised eyebrow.

"More gossip than there is now," she muttered, and shivered in the cool air.

He stood and placed his coat about her shoulders. "Don't worry about the gossip."

"It's quite easy for you to dismiss the gossip," she sniffed. "You don't have Lady Pennington or the Earl of Rystoke watching over your every move." She pulled his coat tighter and sniffed again. Her eyes took on an impish light. "Besides, everyone already knows you are a rogue."

Her teasing startled him into releasing a chuckle. But her words reminded him of Rystoke's reaction at finding them together the day he had arranged for their betrothal. Concerned for her safety, he tugged the collar of his coat higher around her neck.

"If your guardian says one word to you about this, you must tell me immediately," he urged. "I will not have him cower you with his bullying. Will you promise to tell me if he torments you?"

Surprised at the solace she felt at his gallantry, Jillian blinked at him. Wide-eyed, she nodded. This was not the first time he'd protected her from her guardian. Perhaps her betrothed was not such a bad person after all. And she *had* been a priggish miss. Besides, his coat smelled delicious—like limes and *him*.

Dunbary flashed her a quick smile before he turned away to collect the remains of the picnic. When he bent over, Jillian saw a large, muddy, wet spot staining his backside. She covered her mouth to stifle a giggle. Even the fastidious Duke of Dunbary had not escaped unscathed.

She glanced down at her ruined dress and soggy shoes. The ridiculousness of the situation finally struck her. She looked like something that had washed up on the banks of the Thames. That giggle escaped. Dunbary swung around. As her eyes met his, her giggles erupted into laughter and she pointed at his breeches. He grinned and put a hand to his backside. It came away wet and muddy.

"We look appalling," she said with a twinkle.

"Ghastly," he agreed.

"My chaperone will be quite vexed," she said, repeating what she had told him while they had waltzed.

"Undoubtedly," he said solemnly. "Do you care?"

"No." Her lips twitched.

They simultaneously broke out into laughter.

Gasping with laughter, she said, "You know, I hate this dress."

"It is very…frilly," he observed.

Jillian nodded agreement. "And I hate this hat." She pulled it off her head. "Pennington will be furious. She'll be so concerned about the gossip…" Her laughter trailed off as she remembered the implications of what would happen if they were seen returning to the city in their present state. He had nothing to fear from the gossip. His reputation was already as black as pitch.

Sobering, she demanded again, "How are we to get into the city without being seen?"

Dunbary glanced at her with a mischievous glint. "I'll make sure no one sees us returning."

His offhand confidence made her suspicious that he had some outrageous plan in mind that would cause more gossip. But the gossip about her was already outrageous. Besides, she had no choice. He was her only way back to the city. And he looked nearly as disreputable as she did. With a nod, she squished her way back to the curricle.

Dunbary appeared with the picnic basket and helped her up to her seat. The sun had begun to go down and the air had become chilly. Her dress was wet. Her shoes were wet. She shivered despite his coat about her shoulders. The prospect of having Pennington or — God forbid — Rystoke see her in such condition sobered her. And Dunbary… What must he think of her for acting like a hoyden? Her cheeks flamed. It was enough to make a girl retreat into a convent.

She felt his searching gaze as he climbed up beside her.

"You're still cold," he observed. Without waiting for her answer, he unfolded the picnic blanket and placed it about her shoulders.

"Thank you," she murmured.

"If you don't wish to be seen, you can pull it over your head," he said.

She shot him a glance. Was he teasing or serious?

His lips curved, but his gaze was direct.

She realized it was a very good suggestion. The vision that popped into her head of the debonair, suave Duke of Dunbary driving in shirtsleeves through the streets of London in his fashionable curricle with a blanket-covered lump of humanity beside him made her laugh. He grinned, snapped the reins, and they set off.

Dunbary drove the curricle through back streets and avoided the fashionable areas of the city. Wide-eyed, Jillian gazed around her, viewing a part of the city she had never seen before, And Dunbary dropped tidbits of information about the sights they passed. He told her about the monolith called the London Stone, that legend said was supposed to have been placed in the city by Brutus, the son of the Greek hero, Aeneas. It was the point from which all the spokes of the Roman roads emanated. As they drove beneath Temple Bar, the last standing gateway into London, he related that in past centuries, the spokes around the main arch were used to display the heads of traitors. Jillian marveled and gasped and laughed while he expertly maneuvered through the streets and back alleys of the city. By the time they reached Rystoke's townhouse, she felt much more at ease about the afternoon.

Dunbary helped her down from her seat. He had driven the curricle around to the back of the house where the mews were located.

"Thank you for a delightful afternoon, Jillian," he said as he bent over her hand.

Suddenly shy, she slipped her hand from his fingers and ducked her head. She pulled the blanket from her shoulders along with his coat and held them out. "Thank you for the use of these." She shivered in the sudden chill, mourning the loss of the hug of his coat.

"You're quite welcome." He took the items and grinned. "I have reserved a box at the theater two nights from now. I would like you to accompany me."

Jillian's eyes went wide. The theater! What horrible catastrophe would befall her there? Vehemently, she shook her head. "I couldn't possibly."

"Of course you can," he contradicted smoothly. "You're my betrothed. We will be expected to appear together in public. Besides, there is the matter of your interesting bargain that we need to discuss further. I will send round the particulars tomorrow." With another grin and an insouciant bow, he strode to his curricle and drove off.

Apprehensive, Jillian quickly let herself into the house. His mention of the bargain scared her... Now that they were officially betrothed, he would expect her to fulfill her side. But that problem would have to wait while she avoided Pennington or Rystoke and changed her clothes. Before anyone could see her, she scurried up to her room.

Late that afternoon, Adrian waited in his grandmother's sitting room as she bade goodbye to the ladies who had been visiting her. After leaving Jillian, he had raced home, changed his clothes and hurried to arrive at his grandmother's on time. No one ever kept his grandmother waiting if they did not wish to invoke a sharp-tongued scolding.

As he waited, his thoughts traveled back to that afternoon. He had invited Jillian on the outing as the proper thing to do as her betrothed. He had never expected to kiss her, and he certainly never expected to be so aroused that he nearly lost his head. She was delectable. And impulsive. And a bit unconventional. When she had slipped into the water, she had laughed. With him. His lips curved in a smile. The afternoon had been delightful, unexpectedly so. He heard the swish of his grandmother's skirts approaching and stood to greet her.

"Grandmother." He bowed as Matilda, Dowager Duchess of Dunbary, entered the room. He moved forward to take her outstretched hand. "You are looking well."

"I do not," the old lady snapped. "My joints ache and my stomach is sour. Ring for tea."

Despite her tiny stature, she could be as commanding and temperamental as a queen. Adrian helped her to a chair, then did as he was told. With her cane, she tapped the seat across from her.

"Come, sit here. Let me look at you." She gazed at him with bright blue eyes and nodded with approval. "So. Why do I have to summon you here in order to get you to visit? What is this gossip I hear about you?"

Adrian smiled his most charming smile. "Grandmother, you know how busy I am with the Foreign Office."

She rapped her cane on the floor. "Pshaw. I know what I hear. You have been busy with the women, young man. Don't try to charm me. Now, tell me all." She tipped her head, studying him. "You're looking quite pleased with yourself."

He sighed in defeat and forced away all thoughts of the time spent with Jillian. He needed to tread carefully. Even though he was head of the family as Duke of Dunbary, his grandmother was the matriarch and made sure that everyone in the family behaved. Woe to anyone who did not perform to her expectations. Having betrothed himself to Jillian, an unknown and a ward of his enemy, he had stepped outside his grandmother's boundaries.

He was able to delay his answer for a few moments while his grandmother's majordomo arrived with the tea tray and poured for her. When the man left, Adrian reached for his cup, but his grandmother stopped him with a single word, as effective as placing her cane on his arm.

"Adrian."

He carefully placed his cup back on its saucer.

"Well?" she prompted. "I'm an old woman. I don't have time in my life to wait."

Adrian leaned back in his chair and met his grandmother's gaze. With more bravery than he felt, he announced, "I am betrothed, grandmother."

His grandmother's eyes narrowed. "So, it is true then. Tell me about her."

Adrian swallowed. This was the part he had dreaded. "Her name is Jillian St. Clare. She is the ward of the Earl of Rystoke."

His grandmother was silent for two heartbeats. "The Earl of Rystoke," she said, her flat tone indicating her displeasure. "Are you daft, boy? Have you taken leave of all your senses? That man almost ruined you."

Adrian turned away and set his jaw. The deed was done. His honor demanded he go through with the marriage, and his need to retrieve that letter compelled him to do so.

"All right." She backed down. "That is your affair. But who is this girl? Where does she come from?" his grandmother prodded.

Helplessly, Adrian shrugged. "I don't know."

At that, Matilda banged her cane on the floor twice. "I'll not have the family bloodlines watered down, Adrian. Rystoke could be using her for some devious scheme. For all you know she could be an imposter, an adventuress."

"She could," Adrian agreed, "but I don't think she is. I'm looking into the matter." He had set his solicitor to the task, but told him to take his time. Jillian St. Clare intrigued him too much to discover she was not exactly who she said she was. But he was not about to admit any of that to his grandmother — at least, not yet.

His grandmother studied him a moment, then asked, "What is this I hear about you ravaging the girl? Something about a torn dress?"

Adrian could not stop his chuckle. The old lady did not miss anything. "Grandmother, I did no such thing. The ripped dress was an accident."

Adrian watched her weigh the truth of his words.

With an abrupt nod, she said brusquely, "Drink your tea."

Relieved he was not about to get a dressing down, he picked up the delicate china cup and sipped. To change the subject, he said, "I have some other news you might be interested in." He reached for a custard tart. "Beatrice is back in London." As he bit into the sweet, he watched his grandmother's reaction.

A sour expression crossed her face. "Your mother always has a habit of appearing at the most awkward of times. With your betrothal, she'll want to be included in the celebrations. Quite unfortunate." She lifted her own cup and sipped.

"She didn't come alone," he added. "She has a traveling companion. A German. Some baron or other."

Her cup stopped halfway to her saucer. "Whyever would she bring home a German?"

Adrian shrugged. "Who knows what she thinks?"

"This German could be trouble," she said with concern. "Napoleon has taken quite a few German states and placed them under French control. This baron might be a spy in your own house. Be careful, Adrian."

He patted her hand. "Don't worry about me, grandmother. I have everything under control." *I hope,* he added silently, although with his betrothal to the unconventional Miss St. Clare and the arrival of his mother, he was not so sure. He placed his cup on the tiny tea table between them and stood. "If you will excuse me, grandmother, I have an engagement soon. Thank you for the tea." He kissed the parchment-like skin covering her cheek. "Thank you for caring."

Matilda smiled and patted his arm. "You know you are my favorite."

Adrian grinned. "You say that to all your grandchildren." Then he turned to leave.

"Adrian." Her voice stopped him at the door. "I want to meet this fiancée of yours."

He bowed in acquiescence. "Of course, grandmother."

Her eyes snapped. "Don't humor me. I wish to meet her soon, before all those busybodies arrive here asking questions I can't answer. You should have brought her with you."

Adrian suppressed a wince. He had enough trouble with Jillian St. Clare without her discovering how vulnerable he was with his grandmother. He needed that letter, and he had to guard against revealing too much to her. He still did not know where her loyalties lay, despite his attraction to her. And he was not sure Jillian had recovered after nearly falling into a stream. His lips twitched as he envisioned arriving here with Jillian, both of them dripping and covered in mud. The dowager duchess would have acted as if they had sinned against the state and should be clapped in irons.

"Tomorrow." His grandmother nodded. "I will expect to meet her tomorrow."

Fortunately, he had a meeting with the Foreign Secretary the next day. "I'm sorry, grandmother, tomorrow is impossible."

"Fine, then the day after." She narrowed her eyes. "If you don't bring her here, I will send for her myself, so don't try to wheedle your way out of this, young man." She waved him on his way.

Adrian was glad to escape with nothing more than a verbal rap on the wrist.

After watching her grandson bow stiffly to her and leave, Matilda turned a thoughtful gaze back to the tea tray and mulled over the bit of information he had given her about this girl he was engaged to. Jillian St. Clare. The name St. Clare nagged at her memory, something from long ago. Concentrating, she tried to retrieve the information. No, it was no use. She could not remember. Getting old was such a nuisance. Shaking her head at herself, she reached for her tea. But there had been something about that name…

Twilight had fallen by the time Kip drove the wagon onto the country estate of Lord Winslow. Relief swept through him as he guided the old horse around to the rear of the sprawling mansion. Although quite able to defend himself, he had been concerned on the trip out from the city about gangs of outlaws who might have seen the wagon with its lone occupant and decided it was an easy target for their thievery. Even more dangerous would have been meeting up with a troop of soldiers who occasionally patrolled the road. He would have found it very difficult to explain the kegs of contraband brandy in the back of the wagon, hidden under the mound of hay.

Disguised as a delivery man, he knocked at the service entrance to the mansion. After a maid answered, he was forced to wait until Winslow's haughty butler appeared. Kip pretended indifference at the delay, but unease made him vigilant. He wanted to turn over the smuggled brandy and disappear before he was caught. The butler finally allowed him into the house, and showed him to a small sitting room where he had to wait again, for Winslow was entertaining guests.

When Winslow finally appeared, he complained, "It's about time you got here, boy. How much brandy have you brought me?"

Kip hid his irritation at Winslow's arrogance. He slowly turned from his contemplation of the flames which crackled merrily on the hearth, sauntered over to a delicate, silk moiré chair and settled himself comfortably. He suppressed a grin at the faint hiss of distaste that came from the lord of the manor as his pristine chair was soiled by the dirt from Kip's disguise.

Gazing placidly at the older man, he said, "I think we have some other business to take care of first, Winslow."

"I told you the last time that my ship has been impounded by the American embargo. I have not received the load of cotton that was due, so I have not been able to sell it. I can't pay you. You will have to accept my credit."

"No, I will not." Kip casually crossed his knees.

Winslow blustered, "I have important guests. I must serve them French brandy."

Kip raised a cynical brow. "Then you will have to get it from another source."

Winslow's expression turned crafty. "Then what will you do with your contraband?"

Kip shrugged. "I can sell it to someone else. Lord Rystoke, for instance."

"Bah," Winslow snorted. "He won't buy it. He has everything invested in that pretty baggage who is his ward."

"I heard she was something other than that," he said, fishing for information.

Winslow's eyes narrowed craftily. "Are you interested, boy?"

Kip casually studied the dirt on his hand. "I may be."

With a snort of derision, Winslow said, "Then you won't get far. Rystoke will only settle for a marriage contract with a large bonus for himself. He'll never allow a smuggling Scot to get near her." He laughed and shook his head. "He's quite daft concerning the chit's suitors. Something about revenge on her father, I think."

"Interesting," Kip murmured.

Winslow turned to the bellpull. "I will have the brandy unloaded."

Kip sprang from his chair and grabbed the man. "You will not unload that wagon, Winslow." He released the man's coat, smiled and brushed out non-existent wrinkles. "You are too impatient. We have not yet solved the little problem of payment."

Winslow scowled and straightened his cuffs. "Impossible. You will have to accept my credit. I will pay you when I can."

Kip shook his head. "You must be going deaf. I told you I do not give credit, *my lord*. Mine is a risky business. Who knows if I will be around to collect on my debts when you finally decide you are able to pay me?" He sighed with regret. "I'm afraid that if you do not pay me now, I will be forced to take my goods elsewhere."

"The brandy is mine," Winslow declared.

Kip's patience was wearing thin. This man was incredibly thick-headed. "Perhaps I did not make myself clear. I am sure your wife has some jewelry lying about that would serve."

A look of panic crossed Winslow's face.

"Come, now, Winslow, stop delaying or I will announce myself to your guests. Did I happen to see Spencer Perceval's coach outside? I am sure the Prime Minister would be delighted to learn that his host is serving him contraband brandy."

Winslow's complexion turned ashen.

Kip smiled coldly but said nothing.

"Swine!" Winslow hissed and stalked out the door.

Kip sank back into the chair as he wondered why the Prime Minister was dining with Lord Winslow. He would like to corner Spencer Perceval and explain the reasons why he was forced to smuggle. He would like to tell the man of the hardships endured by the people of Ayton, all the dyers and weavers, because of his government's arrogant Orders in Council. He wanted to explain how he smuggled their woolen goods to America, traded them for rum and cotton which he then took to France, and exchanged those goods for brandy which he brought to England as contraband. The payments he received for the brandy went back to Ayton to keep his people from starving. He drummed his fingers on the arm of the chair and controlled his impulse to confront the Prime Minister. Getting arrested would not help his people at all.

Nor would it help Jillian. Winslow's comment about her intrigued him. If Rystoke's strange requirements for Jillian's suitors had something to do with her father, then it was possible… He let his thought trail off. He did not want to raise his hopes too much. But if he connected Winslow's information to the brooch that Jillian wore, he might be getting closer to the truth about her.

After many minutes, Kip became suspicious of Winslow's absence. He hurried to the service entrance, and was not surprised to see two of Winslow's footmen lugging kegs of brandy into the kitchen. He pulled two pistols from beneath his shapeless coat.

"I don't believe those have been paid for, lads," he said mildly.

The two men stopped short and glanced up at him in surprise.

"Why don't we go have a little talk with Lord Winslow." Kip punctuated his suggestion with a motion of his pistol.

The men obediently trudged back out the door. Standing beside the wagon, Winslow was giving orders to his butler.

"I don't like being swindled, Winslow," Kip said, making sure his pistols were visible in the gloom. "Pay me or I take the brandy to another buyer."

Winslow swung around in surprise. His brow lowered when he saw Kip. "The brandy is mine."

"Only after a fair trade of payment for goods," Kip said. He held one of the pistols against the throat of the man nearest him. "Would you care to lose one of your servants over a stolen keg of brandy?" he asked.

With a growl of anger, Winslow tossed him a pearl and ruby collar. Kip caught it with the barrel of his pistol. It would pay off Winslow's debt several times over. And provide several families of Ayton with sustenance for many months.

"You are very generous, my lord." Kip mocked him with a bow and dropped the piece into his pocket.

"This is robbery!" Winslow complained.

Kip laughed as he backed away into the shadows. "I hope to do business with you again very soon, my lord!" He spun about and disappeared into the night. Running into the woods, he caught the low branch of a tree and climbed up.

Winslow yelled a command to fetch the pistols and search for the smuggler. As Kip stretched out on a thick branch high up in the massive oak, he listened to Winslow's servants thrash about beneath him. With a quiet chuckle, he pulled out the bauble and held it up. It glinted richly in the moonlight. Well satisfied at the profit he had made, he tucked the piece away and made himself comfortable. He would have a bit of a wait before Winslow's men grew tired of searching. Then he could safely climb down, retrieve the horse he had hobbled just outside Winslow's property, and return to London.

The mystery of Jillian's identity awaited him there.

Adrian climbed the stairs to Diana's front door and waited for her butler to answer his knock. As he followed the man to Diana's drawing room, apprehension nagged at him. He had not spoken to her since that weekend at Bertie's.

He relaxed back into the downy cushions of the sofa. This room was very familiar to him. He had been here often over the past two years, both for pleasure and for business. It was decorated in pink, green and ivory. A fainting couch sat before a double window that looked out over a formal garden behind the house. That couch had been the scene of several intimate interludes. Two wing chairs sat sentinel on either side of the hearth, where they had planned clandestine missions. The deep pile of a pale, Chinese rug had softened footsteps as they paced and consulted. The walls shimmering in ivory silk had heard many secrets.

As he stared into the flames on the hearth, he smiled at some of the memories. He had sent round the usual single rose to her with his request to visit her this evening, but her reply had been coolly formal. His smile faded. Their affair was over.

A pang of regret shot through him, only to fade as the image of luminous gray eyes rose up before him. Jillian. A deep frown appeared between his brows. She invaded his thoughts at the most inopportune times. He focused on a figurine of a shepardess on the table next to him to distract himself, but the memory of eager lips and a warm, yielding body caused a throbbing in his groin. He shifted to get comfortable. Not even Diana had inspired such a strong and swift reaction at the mere thought of her. He was confounded at the reason.

The soft swish of silk and light footfalls announced Diana's appearance. As he stood to greet her, Adrian was stunned once again by her beauty. Never a slave to fashion, she renounced the pale colors that were all the rage and instead wore bright colors, like the turquoise dress that now clung to her curves. It made her eyes a vivid blue and her creamy skin translucent. But she did not stir him like she once did.

"Diana." He smiled and kissed her hand.

Her fingers lingered a moment in his before she pulled away and sat on the sofa. "So, you have asked the girl to marry you," she began without preamble.

Adrian sat beside her. "Yes."

"You realize, of course, that you should not have come here this evening." Her reprimand was delivered mildly.

"Why not?" Adrian's brow wrinkled in confusion.

"Because you are betrothed and I was your mistress," she said with exasperation.

"Oh, that." He got up and wandered over to the hearth. "I still need you to work for me, Diana."

Diana sighed. "I don't see how. You will be married soon. I'm sure your new wife won't appreciate that you are still seeing your mistress." Before he spoke, she warned, "Don't try to charm me, Adrian. It won't work."

He grinned. "All right. Then suppose I bribe you? Work with me just a while longer and I will see to it that you can pay off all your debtors and reopen Avingdon Hall."

Her eyes widened at the large sum he suggested. Then she asked suspiciously, "What do you want me to do?"

He was relieved that she had agreed. He would have missed working with her. "A German, the Baron von Heisburg, has arrived in London. I would like you to find out why he is here."

"The man who came home with your mother," she clarified.

Adrian winced. "Yes. I did not think the news had traveled that quickly."

Diana shook her head. "It hasn't. I was riding past your house this afternoon and saw them coming out the door. Your mother looked quite happy."

"My mother always looks happy when she has money and a man fawning over her." His tone was grim.

"I'm sorry, Adrian," she said, her voice gentle. "Is there anything else you want me to do?"

With an effort, Adrian turned his thoughts back to why he was there. "Yes. I've heard whispers about the missing secret correspondence. Someone from the other side has discovered its existence and has passed this information to Rystoke's friends. I want to know who this person is and how he learned about the letter."

Diana was silent a moment, then she ventured, "Your fiancée, perhaps?"

"She was the first person I thought of, but I don't think she told her guardian. Rystoke would have taunted me with the knowledge when I went to offer for the girl's hand." He shook his head. "There's someone else, possibly someone in the government."

Diana huffed with frustration. "That does not help much. It could be almost anyone."

Adrian strolled back to the settee, sat beside her, and brushed his lips across her cheek. "I have tremendous faith in your abilities, Diana."

"You flatter me, your grace," she teased.

He grinned. "Outrageously." Then becoming serious, he asked, "So you will discover what you can?"

She nodded. "I will do my best. But you know how men hate discussing politics with the ladies."

He raised her hand to his lips. "Diana, you could get the animals in the barn to talk to you."

"Charmer," she taunted.

Satisfied that he would soon have some information, he bid Diana goodbye and set off for an evening at Brook's Club.

As soon as Adrian left, Diana climbed the stairs to the next floor and stopped before the door of her sitting room. With her hand on the knob, she worried at her bottom lip. Adrian would be furious if he found out who else she was entertaining this evening. Even she had some misgivings about her visitor. With a shake of her head, she pushed the thoughts away and opened the door. She had to think of her own happiness occasionally.

"Mr. Stone," she gushed. "I am so glad you could visit this evening."

The tall American unfolded his muscular frame from the chair and turned to face her. "Call me Cooper, ma'am. It's much more friendly."

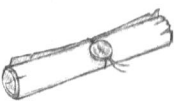

CHAPTER 9

Two days after the picnic, Jillian and Lady Pennington wandered through Picadilly on their way to Hatchard's book shop. They had visited earlier with Lady Matilda, Dunbary's grandmother. Jillian felt like she had endured a three-year siege. She was not sure she had passed the lady's inspection, for the dowager duchess's farewell had been as cool, polite, and distant as her greeting. Dunbary had been no help, sitting silent, watching the exchange with half-closed eyes, as if he had no interest. Jillian knew better. She sensed his attention as keenly as if he had been the one interrogating her. It sent her nerves skittering and her stomach jigging. Lady Pennington had been no help, for she had been as silent as the furniture.

Duchess Matilda had probed her background. Jillian had been hard pressed for answers. She had not fabricated, but her mother's past still remained a mystery to her. Her mother had told her that Rystoke was not her father — for which she was grateful — and that her father had died very soon after she was born. Rystoke had offered to take them in. Jillian did not reveal that her mother had also been Rystoke's mistress, an embarrassing fact which puzzled and saddened her, as she came to realize what kind of man Rystoke was. She had wondered why her mother had stayed with Rystoke. Why hadn't her mother sought refuge with her own family?

Rystoke's name had evoked Lady Matilda's curiosity, but what had truly grabbed her attention was the St. Clare name. When Jillian revealed that she had inherited a manor house from Lilith St. Clare, Lady Matilda's eyes snapped with interest. Even Adrian looked mildly engaged. Jillian wondered why, for a small manor hardly compared to the Dunbary wealth. She suspected their interest lay more in the fact that she was not completely penniless, nor a member of the anonymous masses.

When she and Lady Pennington and Dunbary had departed, her fiancé had left them with a murmured apology and the excuse that he had to see to some business. As Jillian watched him stride away, she wondered if that business had anything to do with the secret letter. She was thinking over the events of the afternoon when someone called her name and brought her out of her reverie. She glanced around and saw her friend, Phoebe Southwood. When Phoebe and her chaperone caught up with them, the two older women began discussing the latest gossip. Phoebe pulled Jillian aside.

"You're engaged to Dunbary!" Phoebe exclaimed in an awed whisper. "How did you manage it? Everyone is all agog over the news."

Jillian waved a nonchalant hand, pretending the circumstances around her betrothal were absolutely normal. "It just happened."

Pheobe's gaze darkened in concern. "I heard what happened at Lord Bertram's. It's all over the city. Did he hurt you?"

"Of course not." Jillian was surprised at Phoebe question. "It was just an accident."

"An accident?" Phoebe's eyes went wide. "I heard he tore your gown off you." She shivered in delighted contemplation.

"He did no such thing," Jillian denied, even as heat climbed her cheeks. All she could think of was that kiss, and more damning, what she and Dunbary had done on their picnic.

"Ooh, just the thought gives me goose bumps." Phoebe rubbed her arms. "You must have swooned."

"Absolutely not," Jillian denied with as much dignity as she could muster, for she *had* nearly swooned when he had kissed her in Bertram's trophy room. And then on the picnic…she couldn't even think about that.

Phoebe pulled Jillian close. "I heard something just this morning that you should know," she whispered. She hesitated and bit her bottom lip. "I don't want you to hear it from Jane Bicklesford. You know how catty she can be."

Jillian wondered what sly Jane Bicklesford could say about her that had not already been said. Jane had already attempted to destroy one young lady's chances with a good match when Jane saw her chatting on a veranda in the dark with a young man who was not her intended. Jane had tattled on them and exaggerated, saying she had seen them *in flagrante delicto* — kissing and nearly naked. Fortunately, the truth came out and the young lady's reputation was saved by her intended. Jillian did not want to contemplate what vile story Jane might make up about her.

Phoebe glanced around to see if anyone was near. Then she pulled Jillian closer. "My cousin Mary said her brother saw Dunbary going into Lady Avingdon's house last evening."

Jillian was stunned into speechlessness. Anger and hurt rose through her like a plume of smoke. He had the audacity to visit his mistress after becoming engaged to her. After what they had shared on the picnic. He had kissed her, touched her in places no one had touched before. He had made her feel things she had never felt.

Dunbary was without any decency. He was a cad, a bounder. He was… She could not think of enough despicable words for him. She stared at Phoebe as she searched for something to say.

"Good afternoon, Jillian," a deep male voice said beside her.

Startled, she thought for a moment that devil Dunbary had appeared. Instead, she saw Kip smiling at her. Still in shock after Phoebe's announcement, she forced a smile to her lips. "Kip! What a pleasant surprise."

As she gave him her hand, she glanced at Phoebe whose eyebrows were raised in eager interest. After introducing her friend to Kip, she watched as Phoebe flirted with the handsome Scot. Jillian wondered where he had been since that weekend at Lord Bertram's. Only a little more than a week had passed, but the time felt more like a lifetime, so much had changed in her life. She thought he might have sent her a note to inquire how she had fared after he'd rescued her from the duke at the country house party. He might have saved her from becoming Dunbary's fiancée.

The thought brought a fresh surge of anger at her betrothed. Dunbary obviously had no regard for her feelings, nor for gossip. Now that they were engaged, she thought he would refrain from seeing his mistress. She thought he might even come to care for her. But Dunbary was a rogue. She had known that and been foolish to fall under his spell at the picnic and allow him such liberties.

"May I call on you?" Kip's question snagged her attention.

She hesitated. She should not be receiving single men now that she was betrothed. But her fiancé did not stand on propriety. Why should she? Relishing the bit of revenge she could level on her Dunbary, she smiled. "Of course. I'd be delighted by a visit." That should keep her arrogant duke in his place. If he found out about Kip's visit, she could question him about his call on his mistress.

Phoebe's eyes widened and she shook her head in warning. Jillian ignored her.

Phoebe gave a little huff and announced, "Jillian is engaged to the Duke of Dunbary."

Kip's brow lowered. "Then perhaps I should not call on you until after you are wed."

Jillian smiled through gritted teeth as she fought the urge to strangle her friend. Feigning indifference, she said, "I am sure the duke will not mind if I continue to see my friends. After all, he still socializes with his." She sent a quelling glance at Phoebe.

Phoebe's mouth dropped open. Jillian ignored her shock and Kip's confusion. She glanced at her locket watch. "Goodness! Look at the time. We really must be going." She extricated Lady Pennington from her conversation with Phoebe's chaperone, bid goodbye to Phoebe and Kip, and hurried Pennington away.

Silently fuming, she paid no attention as they walked right past the book shop. She wanted to bang her fists on Dunbary's wide, hard chest. How dare he visit his mistress!

After they returned to the townhouse, Jillian had pleaded a headache to Pennington, who ordered tea for her and a cold compress. Jillian sipped the tea, but wanted to hurl the compress at Dunbary's face. When Pennington finally left her alone, Jillian stalked from one side of her bedroom to the other. She banged her fists on the bed. She pulled the pins from her hair and brushed it until it gleamed. Did Dunbary think he could do what he wished while she must conform to society's rules? Did he think she would not find out? That she would not care? Did he think that spending one afternoon in the country with her gave him the right to spend a night in the arms of the beautiful Lady Avingdon?

She had allowed him to kiss her, to touch her intimately. She thought the flowers, the picnic, and his soft words were the beginnings of his tender feelings for her. Obviously, she had been mistaken. They had laughed together, but the connection she had felt was apparently one-sided. It had all been a sham, a ruse to charm her into giving him the letter. Besides feeling stupid at being so naïve, she was hurt. She was his betrothed. He should care, at least a little.

Her hurt and anger subsided to a simmer, more from exhaustion than anything else. She sat by her window and absently gazed out at the bustling street below. A delivery cart turned into the servant's lane. Several minutes later, a maid knocked.

With a curtsy, the girl said, "This was just delivered, miss, from the Duke of Dunbary."

Jillian thanked the girl and watched with a muddle of emotions as the maid placed the large package on the bed. After the girl left, she stared at it suspiciously. Was Dunbary trying to salve a guilty conscience after a night spent with his mistress? She should send the unopened package back to him. But her curiosity was piqued. What had he sent her? How guilty did he feel?

Curiosity got the better of her. She pulled on the ribbon and pushed the wrapping apart. Underneath was another layer of wrapping, protecting the soft contents. It felt like clothing. Then she remembered he had said he would buy her a new dress, because she'd ruined hers with the strawberries and clotted cream. And the mud. Her cheeks heated at the memory of what she had done with him that afternoon. But if he had not been so charming she would not have let down her guard. She would not have begun to like him, despite her suspicion that he could be a traitor. Carefully, she pulled apart the last protective wrapping and gasped.

Before her lay an afternoon dress of pale yellow, watered silk. The sleeves were long and puffed at the shoulders. It had a tiny, stand-up collar that opened in the front into a small vee. A wide sash embroidered in green and gold circled the high waistline. The dress was beautiful.

When she pulled it out of the package, she saw there was another underneath. She placed the first dress across the bed, and shook out the second. It took her breath away.

It was a ball gown of white gauze with an underskirt of the palest blue silk. The scalloped hem was appliquéd in a double row of white silk petals and the same petals were scattered up the skirt. The sleeves were tiny puffs and the neckline was cut scandalously low. It was a gorgeous dress.

She stood before the cheval mirror and held the gown up in front of her. It would fit perfectly. When he had promised two new dresses, she had not truly believed him, but he had been true to his word. And extremely generous. As she admired the dress, a note fell from its folds. She picked it up and read:

I would be honored if you would wear this gown when we go to the theater.

Your servant, Adrian.

Jillian crumpled the note. His signature was a mockery. He had visited his mistress just the night before. He was no more her servant than the Prince Regent.

He must feel very guilty. Why else would he send her such beautiful and costly gowns? He was trying to impress her, most likely to gain access to the note. After all, wasn't that his true motive for marrying her? He did not truly care for her. He had proven that by visiting his mistress only the night before. The gowns were only a salve to his conscience.

Anger boiled through her. She held up the dress again and looked at herself in the glass. The dress was stunning. A plan tantalized, too alluring to discard. She would wear the gown to the theater, but she would make him suffer by flirting with as many gentlemen as she could. After all, Dunbary deserved to be punished after what he had done.

Dunbary arrived exactly on time to collect her that evening. They would be going to the King's Theater to see the prima donna Catalani perform in one of Mozart's operas, and then they would be taking a late supper. When the maid knocked on her door to tell her the duke was waiting, Jillian still fussed before the mirror. Pennington sat watching her with a frown.

"That dress is not suitable for the theater," her chaperone said for at least the tenth time.

Jillian bit back her sigh. "Don't you think the duke would care to see me wear his gift?"

Pennington *tsked*. "The man is a rogue. He is used to outfitting his mistresses, not his fiancée."

Jillian faced her chaperone with determination. "I am wearing the dress."

"Hmph." Pennington scowled. "Just remember that Rystoke will be in his box. He will be watching for any unseemly behavior."

Memories of the last time she was alone with Dunbary at the picnic made Jillian's cheeks heat. Her behavior then had been more than *unseemly*.

Pennington rubbed her temples and uttered a little moan. "I would be going with you if I did not have this headache. I really should lie down."

Jillian hid a smile. Pennington hated the opera, and would do anything to get out of going. Her chaperone's conscience had been soothed by the knowledge that Rystoke would be present at the opera. But Jillian would be on her own for the most part and able to execute her plan. She was out the door before the woman could say anything else.

As she descended the stairs to the drawing room, her hurt and anger sat like a hot stone in her chest. She would make the proud duke suffer for thinking he could still visit his mistress. He would learn that she was not to be easily dismissed.

Dunbary stood as she entered the drawing room. Despite her ire, she could not help but catch her breath by his overwhelming male allure. Even as she silently called him every vile name she could think of, she was drawn forward by his magnetism. Handsome in his black coat, creamy waistcoat and gray trousers, he smiled wolfishly as she approached. His topaz eyes gleamed with a predatory heat.

"Miss St. Clare," he murmured as he bowed over her hand. "I see that you received my gift."

The warmth from his touch seemed to spread up her arm, and she quickly pulled her fingers away. Breathlessly, she replied, "Yes, it arrived this afternoon, quite late." Angry at her reaction to him, she decided to begin her revenge a little early. She sighed as if imposed upon. "I had already dressed for the evening, but Pennington insisted I wear your gift instead." She flounced out the skirt with one hand. "It is quite satisfactory. Thank you."

She glanced up at him from beneath her lashes to see if her oblique jibe had any effect. It seemed to have none at all. His gaze had settled on the barely decent neckline of her dress.

"I am glad to see that it arrived in time for this evening," he said as he tore his eyes away from her cleavage.

I'm sure you are, she said silently, as she smiled and handed him her cape. When he placed it about her shoulders, his fingers skimmed her bare shoulders and sent a shivery tremor through her. Before she could move away, she felt his lips brush the nape of her neck. Surprised pleasure washed over her. She turned to berate him, but was halted by his disarming smile.

"My apologies," he said with a shrug. "You are too delectable. I could not help myself." He held out his arm to her.

Helpless before his charm, Jillian accepted his arm and allowed him to escort her out to his waiting coach. She would let him have his small caress. That would be all he would get. Tonight, he would discover she was not to be made a fool.

As Dunbary settled beside her against the comfortable leather squabs of the coach, he sent her a complacent smile, looking like the wolf that had just cornered the rabbit. That smile made her just a bit nervous, but she reminded herself that she had worn the gown specifically to get that reaction from him. Later, when he realized that she could bestow her charms on any man she wished, he would understand she was not some trifle to be picked up and discarded whenever he chose.

After they started off, he was charming and courteous as he spoke about *The Marriage of Figaro,* the opera they would be seeing, and

Catalani, the diva who would sing the lead. Jillian had heard of her and the incredible amounts she was paid for her performances. She could not wait to see her perform.

After they were seated in Dunbary's box, she gazed at the beautiful theater and the glittering throng. He pointed out the boxes of the Duchess of Richmond, the Duchess of Argyll, Lady Melbourne, and Lady Jersey. He bowed and smiled at those who greeted him from their boxes. Below them in the pit, the dandies strolled about like feisty cocks showing off their feathers. The young men talked and laughed and snapped their snuff boxes open and shut and made a great commotion. All that noise died away when the Regent's brother, the Duke of York, made his appearance in his box. Jillian was surprised when he bowed and smiled warmly in their direction.

"You seem to have caught York's eye," Dunbary murmured. "Be careful he does not make you his next mistress."

"And if he did, your grace, would you be devastated and call him out?" Jillian taunted, remembering to keep a smile on her face. "Or would you be glad of the freedom that afforded you?"

He raised a cool brow. "As you say, my darling Jillian," he said with an edge to his voice, "I would be devastated. I merely warn you of the danger."

"Danger?" Jillian flipped open her fan in agitation at her betrothed's obvious lie about his feelings for her. "I have heard York is a charming man." She allowed her gaze to slide back in York's direction.

Dunbary smiled coolly and lifted her fingers to his lips. "He is a worse rogue than I am, and he knows a beautiful woman when he sees one."

Despite her ire, Jillian felt herself blushing at his compliment. His warm lips sent shivers running up her arm. To hide her confusion, she asked, "Who is the young man in that box there?" She indicated a striking man who had entered a box almost directly across from them.

"That is Byron, author of the poem *Childe Harold's Pilgrimage.* Surely you have heard of him," he said.

"Of course. Who has not?" Jillian was awestruck at seeing the famous author. Even from this distance, she was struck by the penetrating gaze of his dark eyes. "He is quite handsome."

Dunbary's mouth flattened. "He is rather short-statured," he said, then turned his attention to the stage as the orchestra began the overture.

Jillian nearly giggled aloud at her fiancé's obvious jealous rancor. Perhaps her plan to provoke him this evening would be easier than she thought. Pleased, she focused on the opera.

The first part of the performance was magnificent, and Jillian sat enthralled through it all, despite the dandies in the pit who did not leave off their chattering. The soprano, Catalani, was spellbinding. Before Jillian realized it, intermission arrived.

Intermission was a time for the gentlemen and ladies to visit the boxes of their friends and acquaintances, stroll along the mezzanine, and refresh themselves with punch or champagne. As she and Dunbary wandered through the crowd, they were met by Lord Byron. Jillian had read *Childe Harold* despite Lady Pennington's admonitions that it was not suitable for a young lady. Like many others, she believed that the hero was Byron himself. As Dunbary introduced them, Byron's dark eyes bored into her.

Lord Byron bowed over her hand. "You have always been able to find the prettiest ones, Dunbary," he drawled, retaining his hold on Jillian's hand. "You realize, of course, that I shall have to do my utmost to steal this gorgeous creature away from you."

"You will find that next to impossible, I'm afraid," Dunbary said. "Miss St. Clare and I are inseparable. Aren't we, my dear?" Those cat-like topaz eyes speared her, daring her to contradict him.

A devil took possession of her and she paid little attention to her inner voice of caution. Laughing lightly, she flipped open her fan. "I am surrounded by gallants." She turned to Byron with a conspiratorial air. "Now I know for certain that the passionate hero of your poem is none other than yourself, my lord."

Byron bowed his agreement. "You have found me out, Miss St. Clare. Only a lovely, virtuous woman such as yourself can save me from my ruin. Leave this doddering old goat to whom you are betrothed and run away with me to be my salvation."

Jillian cast a sidelong glance at Dunbary. He appeared amused, but his jaw twitched with irritation. Pleased at the result of her flirting, she turned to Byron.

With a smile, she said, "Nothing would please me more, my lord, than to be the savior of such a man as yourself, but I believe the next act of the opera is about to begin and I do so enjoy the voice of Catalani."

"Ah, well, then I must bid adieu, to wander the world in my doom, and perhaps watch the next act of the opera myself." Bending over her hand once more, he smiled and then was caught up in the crowd.

Alone once again with Dunbary, Jillian fanned herself furiously. "He is so charming. Those eyes can pierce your soul."

"That is exactly how he seduces all the women." His tone was dry with disapproval.

Jillian glanced at him in surprise. "Why, your grace, are you jealous?"

He gave a short bark of laughter. "Jealous? Why should I be jealous? You are, after all, betrothed to me, are you not?" He scanned the crowd over her head. "I see the boy with the champagne tray. I will get us some."

Bemused at his reaction, Jillian watched him push through the crowd.

Adrian bore down on the servant with the tray of champagne. Just before he reached the man, another servant offered him a note. It was an invitation from the Duke of York to visit his box. Adrian crumpled the paper in his fist. The only reason for the invitation was because York had seen Jillian. The regent's brother would not be above trying to seduce her into becoming his mistress. Adrian would risk expulsion from court before he allowed that to happen. She was *his* fiancée, after all.

When he had collected her this evening and she had appeared at the top of the stairs, she looked like an Ice Queen. But the feel of her warm skin beneath his fingers and the tremor that ran through her at the touch of his lips convinced him she was anything but icy. Although she might be an innocent and unaware of her own passion, he had no doubt that it simmered hotly just beneath the surface of her cool exterior. He had evidence of that when he'd kissed her.

He placed his hand over his chest where an inside pocket hid a document. The soft crackle of stiff parchment made him smile wolfishly. Before the evening was over, she would belong to him — body and soul.

Byron and York could go to blazes.

Jillian waited nervously for Dunbary to return. She knew no one in the crowd. She smiled and nodded at couples as they strolled past and tried to look unconcerned at being left alone.

A deep voice with an odd accent spoke near her. "Did your escort desert you, miss?"

She swung about and saw a very tall man smiling at her. Uncomfortable at the stranger's forward approach, she flipped open her fan and backed away a step.

"He merely went to get us some champagne," she said coolly.

"Of course." His smile deepened. "Allow me to introduce myself. I am Cooper Stone, a friend of your guardian's."

Jillian immediately became wary. She smiled politely, but said nothing.

"I am new to your country, so I do not know many people here," Mr. Stone said.

"Where are you from?" Jillian asked, curious despite her caution.

A humorous glint lit his eyes. "From the state of Kentucky in America."

Jillian was intrigued. She wondered how he had become acquainted with Rystoke. And she wondered if he knew anything about the information in that secret note. But she dared not ask him about his views on war with England. And she wondered why he had sought her out.

When she remained silent, Cooper Stone went on, "I understand your fiancé is the Duke of Dunbary."

"Yes." The whole city knew that. Jillian wondered where this conversation was going.

"You must find it awkward to be engaged to the adversary of your guardian," he observed.

"It is not difficult at all, sir," she said, affronted at his obvious prying.

He raised his brows in surprise. "No? Dunbary has not plied you with questions about Rystoke?"

"Whyever would he do that?" She fluttered her fan in annoyance. "I am not a spy for my fiancé."

"Of course not," the American soothed. "And neither are you a spy for Rystoke."

Jillian remained mute. What did this man know?

"I must admit to a certain amount of curiosity," he went on.

Jillian sent him a sharp glance. "Curiosity about what? You are being very impertinent, sir. Are all Americans like you?"

He grinned. "I'm afraid so, miss. Curiosity has always made us want to see what is beyond the next hill."

"How quaint," Jillian murmured and searched the crowd for Dunbary. Why was he taking so long to get that champagne?

"Maybe," he conceded. "But my curiosity has led me to discover that pretty young ladies like yourself aren't always what they appear to be."

She did not like the man's implication. "What do you mean, sir?"

His brows lowered. "I mean that you are hiding something, Miss St. Clare, and I intend to find out what it is."

Panic swept through her. He knew about the letter. Forcing herself to remain calm, she laughed. "Oh, Mr. Stone, you are amusing."

At that moment, Dunbary appeared at her elbow with the servant who carried the tray of champagne. "What is so amusing?" he asked.

"Why, Mr. Stone was just telling me all about America," Jillian gushed, desperately trying to cover her fear.

She introduced the two men who were barely civil to each other. Immediately, Cooper Stone found an excuse to leave.

"What were you really talking about?" Dunbary demanded. His eyes flashed angrily.

Jillian shrugged. "Just what I told you." She did not lie exactly, but she did not tell the whole truth. How could she tell him that Cooper Stone was after the letter? If she mentioned it, he would demand again that she hand it over. After hearing that he still visited his mistress, she was not about to concede anything to him. She mistrusted him as much now as when she first danced with him.

125

Dunbary's eyes narrowed. With one hand, he waved away the servant with the tray of champagne, and with the other hand clamped down on her wrist. "Come with me," he ordered, and pulled her through the crowd.

Jillian was so surprised that she followed without a word. She caught a glimpse of Rystoke with his current mistress, but Dunbary whisked her through the crush too quickly for her guardian to stop them. When they reached the lobby of the theater and he placed her cape about her shoulders, she was able to catch her breath.

"Where are we going?" she asked.

"To get married," he growled.

"I beg your pardon?" She did not think she had heard correctly.

"Don't make a scene, Jillian," he warned. "You heard perfectly well."

Panic shot through her. "We can't get married. Not yet. It's not proper. We only just got engaged. The banns haven't been announced. I refuse to go with you."

"You will." He glowered. "Or I will take you back to my box and make love to you in front of the whole theater. Then you will have to marry me."

The idea that he might do such a thing made the blood drain from her face. "You wouldn't."

"Don't make me prove my words." His tone was grim as he took her arm, guided her out into the night and into his coach.

Jillian huddled back against the leather squabs of his coach as they sped away from the theater and through the London night. She clutched her cloak about her as if it would protect her from Dunbary's taciturn profile. Apprehension tightened her muscles. He actually meant to go through with this wild notion. Despite the fact that plans were underway for their eventual wedding, she'd wanted to delay that day that as long as possible. And she definitely was not ready to become his wife on this very night.

"We can't marry tonight," she declared into the silent darkness of the coach. Her words finally made him turn in her direction.

"Why not?" he asked coolly.

She searched for an answer. Because she was frightened of him? Because she would have to turn over the secret letter sooner than she thought? She couldn't blurt out either of those. She spoke the only one she could. "Because plans and arrangements have already begun." Inwardly, she cringed at her anxious tone.

"Plans can be changed." He waved a dismissive hand.

"My wedding gown has been ordered." She tried to sound practical instead of panicked.

His gaze ran over her. "The gown you are wearing will serve very well."

She came up with another excuse. "Rystoke will be furious."

He huffed a sardonic laugh. "Rystoke will be thrilled."

"I don't want to marry you," she declared desperately.

Silence fell within the coach. It stretched out as the horses drew them nearer to their destination. Her heart pounded noisily in her chest. She damned her loose tongue and waited tensely for her fiancé's reaction.

What did she know of this man? She had danced with him twice, had kissed him twice. She disregarded the enjoyable time she'd had on the picnic and his consideration afterward. He had a terrible reputation. He flouted the rules of accepted behavior, went after whatever he wanted. Perhaps he was even involved in some sort of treachery. But what sort of man was he? Was he kind or cruel? Was he even-tempered or moody? Was he generous or stingy? She knew that last answer. He was generous. He had proven that by gifting her with two beautiful gowns. He was also charming and witty and terribly handsome. When he touched her, he made her feel things she had never felt before, lovely, warm, tingly things. His kisses made her melt. Then she discovered he had visited his mistress. And her heart had collapsed in her chest. How could she trust him?

She jumped when she felt his hand brush her shoulder. His fingers swept lightly up the back of her neck. Even though his touch was warm, shivers rolled down her spine.

"Why don't you want to marry me?" His low voice vibrated in the darkness.

Jillian swallowed as his free hand undid the clasp of her cape. "Because I hardly know you…" His fingers left a hot trail on her bare skin, down her throat to the edge of her neckline.

"You know me better than a lot of women know their husbands." His silky tone caressed her as well as his hands.

"You asked me to wed you only to save my reputation." Jillian forced herself to concentrate on the discussion as his thumb dipped into her cleavage.

"That is not the only reason." His tone of voice did not change, but she understood the threat in his words.

"People should marry for love," she gasped as his hand covered her breast. She felt the nipple harden and strain against the thin material of her gown.

"Don't be naïve. People marry for all sorts of reasons. Love is rarely the main one." He pushed the tiny, puffed sleeve of her gown off her shoulder. "You offered me a wonderful reason to wed you – a bargain."

His touch was making it difficult for her to breathe. She was desperate to have him stop so that she would not lose control as she had before when he had kissed her. His words made her uneasy. She could not give him the letter. Anxiously, she blurted the only thing that she could think of. "I don't like you."

He took her chin and turned her to face him. Although the coach was dark and she could not see his features clearly, still, the feral glitter of his eyes was visible. He was silent for a moment. Frightened, she waited for him to react to her bald statement.

A low chuckle reached her ears. "So, the incorrigible Miss St. Clare does not like me. You lie, Jillian."

She drew in a breath. She wanted to deny that she lied, but she could not repeat that she did not like him. She remained silent.

"Do you want to know why you lie?" he asked. His thumb moved across her jaw to her lips where it stopped to rest.

Jillian only blinked as she tried to concentrate on his words.

"You lie because you like it when I kiss you. You want me to kiss you now." His thumb grazed her mouth – back and forth, back and forth. "You lie because you want me to do more than just kiss you."

"No." Her single word came out in a hoarse whisper. She sensed his answering smile in the dark.

"We will wed tonight," he went on conversationally. "Everyone at the theater saw us leave abruptly. I have no intention of returning you home tonight. Do you think people will believe that we spent the time together—all night—conversing about politics?"

Jillian stared at him in the dark. He was right. If she did not marry him tonight, the gossip would ruin her completely. Worse than the fiasco at Lord Bertram's. But why had he dragged her away with him tonight? Why not wait until the date that had already been set for their nuptials? Why was he in such a hurry to marry her when he had stated so bluntly that he had never planned on marrying? Why was he blackmailing her into marrying him? Why? Why? Why?

"Why?" Unconsciously, she spoke her thought.

"Why, indeed?" he asked sardonically and gave another soft chuckle. Releasing her, he leaned back into his own corner of the seat.

Like a flash of lightening, the answer came to her. The letter. His desire to wed sooner rather than later must have something to do with the letter. He wanted the secret letter and would stop at nothing to get it, including eloping instead of waiting for the set date. He had agreed to wait for the letter until after they were wed. That would occur in the next few hours. What was she to do?

She was doomed. She had no hope for a happy marriage. He'd proven to be a cad by visiting his mistress, and now he threatened to compromise her. She had no choice but to elope with him, or risk complete ruin. All for that letter. She wished she'd never taken off her shoes at that blasted ball. She wished she'd never hidden the note in her shoe. She wished she'd never danced the scandalous waltz with the most handsome, charming, and seductive man she'd ever met. She had made a bargain with the Devil and now must live with it. She tugged her cloak back around her shoulders and clutched it tightly for security. And tried not to think about the future.

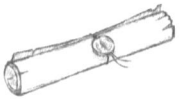

CHAPTER 10

Hours later, Adrian sat before the fire and sipped at his brandy. Upstairs, his new wife waited for him. He frowned into the flames and wondered what had possessed him to whisk Jillian out of the King's Theater and off to a tiny hamlet to wed. He had roused a sleepy vicar and demanded that the man marry them immediately. The coat of arms on the door of his coach along with an exchange of currency had helped convince the protesting vicar. The man had barely glanced at the special license Adrian handed him.

A log fell and sent a burst of sparks up the flue. Adrian took another sip of brandy. He had been angry, angrier than he had ever been before. He had watched Jillian flirt with Byron, had seen the hot glances of the Duke of York. But as soon as he saw her talking with the American, his temper flew out of control. All he had wanted was to take Jillian away from the charming smiles and ogling eyes of other men. He wanted her all to himself. His fingers curled into a fist.

He had planned to charm and seduce her into agreeing to marry him tonight, foregoing all the folderol of a formal wedding. That was why he had obtained the special marriage license. He had wanted to thrill her with the theater, then overwhelm her with a lavish dinner for two. But his temper had destroyed his clever plan. Instead, he had dragged her away from the theater like some ill-mannered boor.

He told himself the need to retrieve the secret letter had made him do it. Seeing her flirting with the American had angered him beyond all reason. What if she passed the letter back to the Americans, those who wanted war with England? What if the Americans had already contacted her and her flirtation had all been a ruse in order to gain information? After all, that's how Diana worked to extract information for him. Or what if Jillian were like his mother, seeking attention and admiration from any man she met, falling into bed with one after another? Was Jillian a spy like Diana, or a trollop like Beatrice? He didn't want either to be true, so he had whisked her away from Stone before his suspicions took root.

By marrying Jillian, all she possessed was now his, including the letter. She had even made that bargain with him—his hand in marriage for the letter. He had kept his side of the bargain. Now, she must keep hers. She would have to hand the letter over to him. He would make her. But how? He had forced her to marry him tonight by threatening to ruin her, but how could he get her to give him the letter? By more threats? By soft persuasion? By trust?

He smiled grimly. Jillian didn't even like him. She had said so, rather bluntly. And he had given her no reason to trust him, for he had been rather single-minded and a bit underhanded in trying to wrest that letter from her. He doubted she trusted him enough to give an accurate report of the weather. But neither did he trust her. She was the ward of his enemy in Parliament. Who knew what hold Rystoke had on her, what secrets she had divulged to the man? She held a letter that could mean the difference between war and peace for England. And now she was his wife.

He did not truly believe that she didn't like him. She had seemed to enjoy his company on the picnic. Her blunt statement tonight had been merely a frightened, desperate attempt to persuade him not to elope with her. He was quite confident he could charm his way back into her good graces. But for some reason, her lack of trust bothered him more than her dislike. He wanted her to trust him so she would give him the letter. That was the only reason. That's what he told himself.

Adrian sighed and leaned his head back against the chair. She waited for him upstairs in his huge bed. She waited for him to possess her. She waited for nothing.

He had decided on the ride back into London that he would not consummate this marriage. There would be no children as a product of their union, no children who could be hurt by a mother who did not care. He could not bear watching a child of his be ignored, like he and his brother had been by Beatrice. That would destroy him. Having no children was safer. His brother could carry on the title.

Miss St. Clare had received his name and all its benefits, but she would receive nothing else from him. He would guard against giving her his soul.

The darkness of the room, lit only by the fire on the hearth, seemed a bit lighter. Glancing out one of the windows, he realized that dawn was not far off. Jillian had looked like the dawn tonight. She had sparkled with a freshness that had invigorated him. Those mysterious gray eyes had glittered with excitement at attending the opera. And he had been pleased to show it to her.

He smiled. She had floated like an angel in the gown he had given her. It had hinted at the womanly curves beneath. The low neckline had made it difficult for his eyes to focus on anything else. His blood had raced through his veins. In his coach on their way to be wed, the silkiness of her skin and her soft gasps as his fingers stroked made the muscles in his groin tighten.

He closed his eyes and tried to banish those thoughts. He would not make love to her. He would not bury his fingers in that golden cloud of hair, or trace his fingers along that soft shoulder. He would not lose himself in those mysterious eyes. Yet, she was his now. She waited for him upstairs. He had whisked her out of the theater tonight just for that reason—to possess her.

He tossed back the last of his brandy and set the glass down on the table beside him. Just this one night. It was his right after all. She was his wife now. He would make her his. Just this once, he would feel her beneath him, would hear her gasps of pleasure and her soft sighs. He would not leave her with a child, but he would indulge himself. And then, he would never touch her again.

The bedroom was nearly dark when he entered. The fire was smoldering cinders on the hearth. Only a single candle sputtered on the bedside table, and that had just about burned out. He undressed quietly and approached the bed. Jillian lay asleep on her back, her face turned toward him. Her golden hair lay spread across the pillow in a tangled curtain. She had been waiting for him to come.

In sleep, her expression was serene, her youth evident. Those deep eyes were hidden by blue-tinged lids and a sweep of thick lashes. This was a far different Jillian than the anxious young woman who had trembled by his side in the dark little church with shaking hands, pale face, and eyes wide with trepidation.

A twinge of guilt made him wince. He did not want her to be afraid of him. He wanted her to be trusting, soft, loving. He shook off his musings. What he wanted and what he had were miles apart. This was the woman who had burst into his world, and played a dangerous game by keeping that note. Was she a spy or merely foolish? Neither option mattered. He needed that letter. And he wanted her tonight no matter what she was.

Kneeling on the bed, he braced his hand on the bar of the canopy above his head. The dip of the mattress brought Jillian awake. With a gasp, her eyes flew open and she stared up at him. For a moment, apprehension showed in those gray depths, then embarrassment made her lower her gaze, a hot blush staining her cheeks.

He softly brushed a golden strand away from her face. "I won't hurt you, Jillian."

She nodded, but refused to look at him.

"Jillian," he coaxed.

She squeezed her eyes shut.

Bewildered by her response, he frowned. Was she that afraid of him? Had this spirited woman suddenly lost all her courage? Then a thought occurred to him and he smiled. "Jillian, have you never seen a naked man before?"

Her eyes flew open. "I—ah—" She shook her head. Her cheeks turned an even darker shade and she looked away.

With a chuckle, Adrian climbed under the covers. "Men don't look like monsters. We don't have horns or tails, not even cloven hooves. You'll get used to the way I look. Just as I'll get used to the way you look." He punctuated his statement by dipping his hand beneath the covers and running it lightly down her body. He smiled as he encountered the silky material of her chemise still modestly covering her.

She gasped and squirmed away.

He caught the shimmer of tears in her eyes. Guilt flooded through him. He shouldn't have teased her. He did not want her to cry. "I know you are frightened," he said gently. "There's nothing to be afraid of."

Jillian sniffed and shifted her teary gaze back to him. She clutched the covers to her chin. His heavy signet ring hung loosely, on her delicate finger and looked incongruous. He had neglected to obtain a proper wedding band before the nuptials, so he'd used his, bearing his family crest when they had exchanged vows. A serious omission in his planning. He touched it with a finger.

"I'm sorry I did not get you a wedding band before we wed." He smiled. "We will have to get you one a bit more suitable. One that will not slip off your finger."

She looked down at the ring. "This one is fine, your grace," she said softly. "But I will give it back to you if you would like."

She started to take the ring off, but he stopped her by folding his hand about her fingers. "Everything I have is yours, now, Jillian. Including my name. I would like you to use it."

Her eyes were unfathomable deep pools as she stared up at him. He was drawn into their depths, into the mysteries that were hidden there, into the untapped passion that smoldered there. He brushed his lips against hers. At the touch, he felt her tremble, and a swift thrill ran through him, throbbing in his groin.

"Adrian," she whispered.

Jillian did not realize she had spoken aloud until she saw his lips curve in a smile. He overwhelmed her. She was not afraid of him, but of how she reacted to him. He made her forget everything but him. When he had touched her in the coach, she would have succumbed to him if he had not stopped.

Now, she was wed to him, this man of topaz eyes and cat-like grace, of subtle touch and honeyed words, of mysterious secrets. What lay in those golden depths? Truth or treachery? She pushed her thoughts aside. Now was not the time to speculate on the future. Now, this man was lying naked with her in this grand and elegant bed, and she knew without any doubt that she wanted him to possess her.

That knowledge confused her. She didn't trust him. She did not like the way he seemed to know her thoughts and intentions.

Yet, all that faded away as he held her in the embrace of those tawny eyes.

Her gaze flicked down to his mouth. He could do strange, wonderful things to her with that mouth. She watched as his smile turned seductive.

"Do you want to kiss me, Jillian?" he asked in a husky whisper.

Surprise drew her glance to his eyes, but she was too embarrassed to utter the truth. She shook her head.

"Yes, you do," he contradicted. "Come here." He wrapped his arm about her waist and pulled her against him.

"No," she protested mildly as she pushed against his chest.

Laughing, he let her wriggle away. "All right. Then I will kiss you." He flung the covers off her. "Let's see, where shall I begin?"

Like a mouse mesmerized into immobility by the hypnotic gaze of a cobra, Jillian could not move as she waited to see what he would do. She nervously clutched her chemise.

He traced his fingers down her throat. "Shall I begin here? No, not there."

She swallowed convulsively.

His fingers trailed down to her breast where he softly massaged the tip. "Here?"

She sucked in a breath.

"No, not there, either." His fingers danced across her belly and slipped beneath her thin linen garment, up her thighs, to the curly patch between. "Here."

She clamped her legs together.

With an exaggerated sigh of disappointment, he said, "Ah, well, not there...yet." He glanced at her with a puzzled frown. "Where shall I kiss you, Jillian?" His gaze wandered over her body, and his hand smoothed down her leg. His fingers curled about her toes. "Here!" he exclaimed triumphantly. He sat at her feet. With a mischievous grin, he cupped her heel in his hand, lifted her foot and kissed each one of her toes.

Surprised and relieved that he wanted only to kiss her toes, Jillian relaxed and allowed herself to enjoy the feel of his lips. The journey of his fingers down her body had alternately made her nervous and excited at the same time. Now, as he sucked and licked each individual toe, she giggled at his tickling and gasped from the thrills that ran up her leg. She had never thought her feet could be the source of such delicious sensations.

When he ran his tongue around the arch of her foot, she laughed and tried to wriggle away, but his grip was firm. His tongue slowly moved up to her ankle and stroked the sensitive area just behind the bone. Jillian watched, enjoying what he was doing to her, waiting to see what he would do next. This was not at all how she had pictured her wedding night. Although she had no clear idea of what would happen, she knew it had not been this.

He moved up her leg, tickling the back of her knee with his tongue and licking across the pulse that throbbed there. Jillian closed her eyes at the sweet sensation. She felt as if he had cast some spell over her. His fingers traced up the inside of her thigh. A sigh escaped her.

The bed dipped as he moved closer. She opened her eyes and found him above her. His smile suggested wicked things that she wanted to know. She had the overwhelming desire to kiss him. Without a thought, she pulled him down. Their mouths came together, gently at first. But she wanted more. She parted her lips, inviting him to explore. Their tongues met, entwining, caressing. Jillian felt like a woman starved. She could not get enough of him. When he pulled away, she gave a tiny whimper of disappointment.

But he did not go far. Before she had time to think, he had pulled off her chemise. She lay before him naked, exposed to his eyes. Oddly, she felt no embarrassment. She felt deliciously free and wonderfully wanton beneath his warm gaze. His lips kissed down her throat, down, down, to cover the tight bud of her breast. Ripples of desire coursed through her. Each time he sucked, her toes curled. She had never felt such pleasure. But she knew there was something more, even though she was not quite sure what it was.

His fingers traced across her ribs and down to the triangle of curls between her thighs. Before she realized what was happening, his fingers were there, playing, teasing, caressing. She wanted him never to stop. She writhed against his hand. Delicious. She had never experienced anything like it before. A great tension built within her. And then it burst, pulsing, spreading through her like wildfire. She cried out with surprised pleasure and clung to him as if only he could keep her from floating away.

Slowly, her breathing returned to normal and she opened her eyes. He was above her, braced on his elbows, and grinning down at her. She grinned back. Whatever he had done to her was the most marvelous thing she had ever felt.

"That was wonderful," she murmured.

"Was it?" His smile turned smug. "That was just the beginning."

"The beginning?" Puzzled, she frowned.

"Umhm. Are you ready, Jillian?" he whispered.

"For what?" What more could there be?

"For this." He kissed her nose. "And this." He brushed his lips across her mouth. "And this." He bent his head and touched his tongue to her throat. "And this." He nudged her thighs apart with his knee. She felt something push where his fingers had just played. And then he slid inside her.

Jillian stared up at him in surprise. He filled her. The sensation was strange at the same time it felt wonderful. Perfect. But she had felt no pain, and she knew she should have.

"Take a deep breath, Jillian," he said gently.

Not knowing why, she obeyed. He plunged deeper inside her. A sharp pain cut through her, making her gasp.

"I promise, it won't hurt ever again," he whispered as he kissed away the tears that formed at the corners of her eyes.

His gentleness soothed. When he captured her mouth, she forgot all about the pain. His kisses drugged her, blanking out everything except his mouth, those sensuous lips, that talented tongue. Then he began to move inside her. That other thing he had done with his fingers was wonderful, but this was magical. She was swept away on wave after wave of pleasure. Up, up the wave, higher and higher, until it crested. She screamed in release. And then like a leaf caught in the tide, she cascaded down, down the wave until she landed gently on the beach, languidly drifting on the shore.

With a shout, Adrian pulled out and collapsed on top of her. Something warm trickled across her belly. She wrapped her arms about him and held him to her, loving the weight of him, the feel of his body against hers. The salty tang of his skin. His breathing slowed and after a few moments he propped himself up on an elbow and grinned down at her.

"You are mine, now," he said. "Everything is mine."

Jillian did not like the sound of that. "What do you mean?" She frowned at his smug smile.

Without answering, he rolled off her, yanked the covers over them, and pulled her up against his body. "Go to sleep, Jillian," he whispered as his arm curled about her, erasing any idea of escape she might have.

Jillian lay quietly in his embrace, and listened as his breathing became deeper and regular, indicating that he'd fallen asleep. She tried to analyze his words, figure out what he'd meant, but her body was tired from their love-making and her eyes grew heavy, no matter how hard she tried to stay awake. He had claimed her and given her pleasure unlike anything she had felt before. His hard body at her back and his arm curled around her spoke of his possession. She was his. But his words held a subtle threat. Everything was his, and that *everything* included the secret note. As she slipped into sleep, worry, like a demon, invaded her dreams.

When Jillian awoke, rain was pelting against the window. The grayness of the day gave no indication of the time. She felt lazy and quite cozy beneath the covers. As she rolled onto her side, her gaze wandered about the pleasant room. It was decorated in dark blues and reds, a masculine room with heavy mahogany furniture and two soft leather chairs guarding the hearth. The large four poster bed where she lay with its swagged canopy of heavy, dark blue damask dominated the room.

The coolness of the sheets where her husband had slept indicated that he had risen long ago. Her husband. The words made her mind stop short. Her life had abruptly taken a new route.

Dunbary was her husband now. She was married. A flutter of nerves erupted in her stomach. Heat crept into her cheeks at the memory of the night before. Nothing her mother had ever told her about men or marriage had prepared her for the wildly exciting sensations her new husband had made her feel. He had been kind, gentle, teasing, had swept her away on a tide of pleasure. But before she had fallen asleep, he had let her know the real reason he had wed her. Those words came back to her. *You are mine now… Everything is mine.* He possessed everything she owned, including her. Including the secret letter.

He would not get it. The bargain be damned. No matter how much he wanted it, no matter how sweet or caring he was, no matter how many times he made love to her, she would not give it to him. It was treachery in its darkest form. Somehow, she would have to evade her husband's demands for the letter. It had to go to the authorities, but who? She was too naïve to know the answer to that. And she certainly was not going to give it to Rystoke.

Jillian winced. Rystoke had to be told she was wed. He would be furious, for he had spent a huge sum on preparations for the wedding. But she couldn't change that now. It was done. He would have to be happy that she was finally wed to his enemy and could play the spy for him. That thought depressed her even more. She didn't want to spy on her husband. She didn't want to spy on anyone. She rued the day she'd ever found that note. If only…

She wished she could trust Dunbary — Adrian — her husband. She could hand the note over to him with a clear conscience. Then they could begin to build a life together. But that was a pipe dream. The reality of their relationship was much messier.

Footsteps approached the bedroom door and distracted her from those dark thoughts. She heard a knock and a maid poked her head in. Jillian remembered her from the night before.

"Ah, your grace, you're awake," she said and entered.

Jillian started to correct the girl's form of address, then realized she was now the Duchess of Dunbary.

The maid was several years older than Jillian, plump and rosy, with her brown hair pulled into a tight bun. She had an air of authority and confidence about her. "His grace said to let you sleep and not bother you, but, well, it's a bit difficult to pack him up with yourself sleepin' in his room."

Jillian sat up, then realized she was stark naked. She quickly pulled the covers up to her chin.

"Why are you packing up his grace?" she asked. "Where is he going?"

"Why, to Dunbary, of course." As if she performed the task every day, the maid picked up Jillian's chemise from the floor and handed it to her.

Jillian slipped the garment over her head. Deep disappointment settled on her at hearing that her new husband was deserting her so soon after their wedding.

"When is he leaving?" she asked, trying to sound merely curious.

"Well, now, that's hard to say, your grace, seein' as how you just awoke and all, and he has to wait for your clothes." The maid went to the large wardrobe and pulled out a man's blood-red silk dressing gown. "Here, this'll keep you a mite warmer than what you're wearing. His grace won't mind you wearing it."

Jillian climbed out of bed and wrapped the dressing gown about her. The sleeves hung way past her fingertips and the hem dragged on the floor, but the woolen lining warmed her. The maid added fuel to the fire and stirred up the embers, so Jillian moved closer to the hearth to absorb its warmth.

"What's your name?" she asked.

"Dory, your grace." She straightened and bobbed a curtsy. "Me gram served his grace's gram, and me mum served his mum, until…"

Something defensive lurked in Dory's gaze and her unfinished sentence told Jillian this girl knew a great deal about "his grace" and his family. She decided she would question her later.

"Then you must know all about the house," she said. "You will have to guide me as its new mistress. I want to make his grace a good wife."

Dory nodded. "As you wish, your grace." With crisp movements, she shook out Jillian's gown that was lying across a chair and hung it in the wardrobe. "Your clothes should arrive soon. His grace sent round for them this morning. I'll tell Cook you're awake and to send you up something to eat." She moved toward the door.

"Dory." Jillian stopped her. "I should like to see his grace before he leaves for Dunbary."

Surprise crossed the girl's face. "I thought you were going with him. It's your wedding trip."

Embarrassment at her misunderstanding made Jillian's cheeks burn. "Of course. I forgot."

"Yes, ma'am," Dory mumbled with a smile as she left.

Jillian sank onto one of the leather chairs by the fire. Giddiness swept through her. Dunbary was not leaving her alone in London. She laughed a little, then immediately sobered.

Why did she want him to take her with him? She did not even like him, despite his tender love-making. He had blackmailed her into marrying him last night. He just wanted that letter. That was why he had married her, and that was his only reason.

If he thought that taking her out of London to some secluded place would turn her meek and compliant, he was very mistaken. She was even more determined he should not get the letter. She would not be swept away by his soft words of seduction, or cowered by his bluster. But deep inside, a spark of excitement bubbled at the possibility of sharing more nights in his bed.

While she was eating a hearty breakfast of eggs, ham, kippers, muffins, and coffee, a knock came at the door and it swung open before she could answer. Her new husband sauntered in, looking quite pleased with himself.

"Good afternoon, Jillian," he said. "Did you sleep well? Of course you did. It is nearly one o'clock. You have slept away quite a bit of the first day of our married life together."

Jillian felt at a distinct disadvantage because she was still wearing his dressing gown and had not even brushed her hair. Covering her discomfort, she said coolly, "I would prefer that you wait until I bid you enter my bedchamber rather than barge in."

Adrian lifted an amused brow and glanced about the room. "All this time I thought this was *my* bedchamber." He dropped down into the chair opposite her. "My dressing gown looks quite fetching on you."

Blushing, Jillian ducked her head and laid down her fork. Her appetite had suddenly fled.

"Do go on with your meal, Jillian." He motioned at her plate. "We won't be stopping to break our journey until quite late this evening."

"You could have told me we were going to Dunbary," she accused, glad to turn the direction of the conversation away from her dishabille.

He grinned. "I know. Dory mentioned your misunderstanding, rather emphatically, I might add." He cocked his head and studied her a moment. "Do you know, I find red quite becoming on you. A shame it is worn only by Cyprians."

Embarrassment at her wanton behavior the night before made Jillian's temper flash. "What are you insinuating, your grace?"

He chuckled. "I am not insulting you, sweet Jillian. Although for a new bride you were very ardent last night."

Jillian turned crimson and gasped.

Adrian laughed. "Don't ruffle your feathers, dearest. I expected nothing less from the unconventional Miss Jillian St. Clare. Last night was quite pleasurable, almost as pleasurable as… well, never mind." He continued to grin at her like an addled idiot.

Jillian was incensed that he appeared to be comparing her to some other woman. He was insufferable. She wanted to rake her nails down his cheek. And in a small corner of her heart, she felt a tiny pang.

"I am sorry I do not measure up to your high standards, your grace," she said with a huff. "Perhaps it would be best if we did not share the same bedroom." Even as she said the words, she regretted the loss of those delicious sensations of the night before.

His grin faded into a cynical smile. "Perhaps you are right," he agreed and stood. "There is no reason to force ourselves on each other."

"Perhaps you would prefer to travel to Dunbary on your own," she suggested.

His reaction was swift and frightening. He leaned over her. "So that you may forestall keeping your side of our bargain?" his voice lashed out. "No. You will accompany me to Dunbary, as is proper for the new Duchess of Dunbary. You will act the blushing bride and the devoted wife as long as there is breath in my body. There will be no outrageous acts or deviations from society's norms. And you will give me the letter. Do I make myself clear?"

Jillian gazed up into those topaz eyes, as hard and cold as the stones, and saw a deep anger in them. This was a man who had demons chasing him, who kept those demons firmly leashed and only occasionally allowed them loose, like now. Jillian was not sure she wished to know what those demons were.

Realizing this was a time to retreat gracefully, she nodded. "I will travel to Dunbary with you, your grace, if that is what you wish."

He straightened. "That is exactly what I wish. Finish your meal and make haste. Your clothes have arrived. I wish to leave within the hour." He strode to the door and stopped with his hand on the knob. "By the way, your guardian sends his felicitations upon our marriage. As a matter of fact, he was quite delighted. You must have been a great trial to him. Do try to behave now that you are my wife."

Her temper flared at his parting words. *He* was the one who had asked her to dance the waltz without permission. *He* was the one who began this train of events that led to her becoming his wife. She would behave, but only when it suited her. And that included keeping her side of the bargain.

She leaned back and blew out a breath. Relief washed through her. He had mentioned the letter but had not demanded that she give it to him. But she did not have it with her. It was still hidden in her ragdoll which was at her guardian's house. Somehow, she would have to evade Dunbary's demands until she could figure out what to do with it.

In the meantime, Rystoke expected her to spy on her new husband. Now that she had faced Dunbary's wrath, she was not sure she was brave enough to do that. What if her husband learned of her deceit? But if she did not spy on him, then Rystoke would devise some evil punishment, guaranteed to make her life a living hell and most likely cause a scandal that would make her a complete outcast.

She picked up her fork and absently played with her food. She was caught between her husband's wrath and her guardian's evil punishment. She sighed and dropped her fork to her plate again. All she could do was take one step at a time and hope that she was going in the right direction. A knock came at her door and Dory entered to help her dress. For now, she had to hurry so she would be ready when her new husband wished to leave for Dunbary.

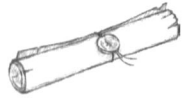

CHAPTER 11

A week later, Jillian sat before the fire in the salon and worked on a piece of embroidery. Across from her, Dunbary sipped an after-dinner glass of brandy. Their trip to his ancestral home had been uneventful. On the way, they had fallen into a routine, with Dunbary riding his massive stallion and Jillian stuck inside the coach. She itched to ride as well, but decided not to press the issue, behaving as he had suggested. But she had also decided she would not always be the demure, withdrawn wife.

Since arriving at Dunbary, her new husband had shown her about the house with pride, telling her of its history, how the original part of the house was built by his great-great-grandfather, and how each succeeding generation had added a new section or remodeled an old one. They had dined together each evening in the family dining room, which was smaller than the enormous formal dining room, but still quite large with its table that seated twenty. He had been polite, but cool and reserved. Each evening he had retreated to his library and left her on her own. And he had not once visited her bedroom, connected to his by an elegant sitting room.

But tonight, he had decided to sit with her. She felt his gaze and purposely did not look up. But his focus on her made her next two stitches crooked. Annoyed with herself, she tugged at the threads. She wished he would say something. The air in the room felt pulled tight. A log fell on the hearth, popped and sparked. She jumped. When he rose to poke the logs, every inch of her was aware of him. He carefully placed the poker back in its holder and faced her.

"I think we should end this charade, Jillian," he said.

Jillian pricked herself with the needle. "What do you mean?" she asked casually, but her insides trembled. He was going to tell her that he was leaving her, that he was going back to London, to his mistress. He was going to tell her that he never wanted to see her again. Despite her ambivalence to this marriage, she did not wish to be left alone at Dunbary.

"You know what I mean." He stood directly before her. She had to crane her neck to look up at him. "You need to keep your side of the bargain. I want the letter."

Jillian's mind raced, at once relieved he was not leaving her, but panicked that he was demanding that secret bit of treacherous parchment. "Oh, that." She sucked at the tiny wound on her finger and peered up at him. "Why is it so important to you?"

His eyes narrowed, then he shrugged and turned back to the fire. "It's a task left unfinished. The letter must go to people who will use it wisely."

His answer was vague and ambiguous. *Use it how? Which people?* she wanted to ask. He would tell her nothing. But she was not about to hand the letter over to him. She needed to discover more about it.

"I don't have it," she said with as much nonchalance as she could muster.

Dunbary was silent for a moment. Then he rumbled, "What do you mean you don't have it? Where is it?"

She hesitated only a moment before she came up with a suitable excuse. "I burned it," she lied with a shrug.

"You burned it?" he repeated incredulously. Swiftly, he leaned over her, supporting himself on the arms of her chair. "Are you lying to me, Jillian?"

She gazed up into those tawny eyes. They seemed to search her soul. A chill ran through her, despite the heat that radiated from his body. His lips were a tight line. His eyes were hard. She did not want to know what might happen if his fury were unleashed. But even if she wanted to give him the letter, the doll where she had hidden it had not been packed up with her clothes. It could still be at Rystoke's or her guardian might have cruelly thrown it in the trash.

"I am not lying," she said quietly.

Dunbary studied her a moment. "Did you read it before you destroyed it?"

Her honor compelled her to tell the truth. She had made a bargain with him and he had upheld his part. She gave a jerky nod.

He perched on the arm of her chair. His presence overwhelmed her, made her feel very small. She was acutely aware of his arm across the back of her chair, his hard muscular thigh against her arm, his broad chest looming over her. He traced his fingers down her cheek. A chill skittered down her back.

"Since I have kept my side of the bargain, you must tell me what was in the letter." His hand curved gently about her neck. "A husband and wife should trust each other," he murmured.

Jillian shivered at his touch, at once intimate and threatening.

"Do you trust me, Jillian?" His whispered question sounded like seduction.

She remained silent while her mind whirled.

"I see you don't." He laughed softly. "I don't trust you either."

She knew that, but hearing him speak the words caused a shaft of pain to pierce through her heart. She kept her gaze averted and stared at the fire, not wanting him to see her hurt.

His hand retreated from her neck. With a finger beneath her chin, he turned her to face him. "Trust is something that is earned."

Jillian could no longer stand his intense, powerful presence. His touch did strange things to her. It made her a little mad. She wanted him to make love to her, but her pride and apprehension kept her from reaching out and telling him. He did not want her for herself. He wanted only the letter. She pushed his hand away, jumped from the chair and swung to face him.

"Yes," she agreed hotly, "trust is something to be earned. But you have not earned *my* trust, your grace. You wed me only for your precious letter. I don't have it, and if I did, I doubt I would give it to you. The bargain be damned!" She bent to gather her embroidery, intending to flee and hide in her room.

He grabbed her arm, halting her. "I have to know what was in the letter. You must tell me."

"Go to blazes." She glared into those topaz eyes.

"What was in the letter?" He gave her arm a little shake.

Furious at his concern for the letter and his disregard for her feelings, she was determined more than ever not to tell him. "I've forgotten," she shot back. "Will you divorce me now because I have not held to the bargain?"

His eyes widened. He dropped his hand from her arm, stepped back and shook his head. "No, I won't divorce you," he said flatly. "Go to bed, Jillian. It's late." He strode across the room and out the door.

Jillian stared at the closed door a moment before she gathered the rest of her embroidery threads. An ache closed around her heart. If only he would tell her why the letter meant so much. If only he had denied that he had wed her only for the letter. If only he had taken her up to bed and made love to her. If only...

As she passed the library, she saw light coming from beneath the closed door. A shadow crossed back and forth. Soft footfalls marked his progression across the carpet and back again. What demons was her husband battling in his solitude?

Lying in bed in the darkness, she stared up at the yellow silk canopy above her head. She was finding little trust at Dunbary. The servants, although impeccably polite and correct, watched her every move. Her husband trusted her so little he would not even visit her bed.

Tears of loneliness crept from the corners of her eyes. Marriage was not supposed to be this charade of bargains and mistrust. With a furious swipe, she dashed the tears from her cheeks. She couldn't live this way. She would not give in. Determination overcame her anger and hurt. She resolved that somehow, she would begin to gain the trust of someone at Dunbary.

A week later, Adrian walked out to the stables for his usual morning ride on Madman Jack. One of the stableboys, Danny, met him just as he entered the building.

"Yer lordship!" the boy exclaimed. "Are yer 'ere to ride?"

Adrian frowned at the odd question. "Of course. Don't I ride every morning?"

"O' course, yer grace, but—well... I'll saddle a 'orse fer yer straight away, yer grace." The boy trotted off.

Adrian turned and stared out the door while he waited. His gaze took in the rolling lawn, the tiny duck pond, and the woods beyond. He loved Dunbary in the spring. The clouds obscured the sun and mist clung to the land. The air was damp, but there was a hint of warmth to it. Spring was slowly awakening the countryside.

He wondered if Jillian would come to love it as he did, then immediately pushed the thought aside. Why should he care whether she liked it or not? She cared little for him. She had proven that with her cool suggestion that they share separate bedrooms. And then she had asked if he would divorce her if she did not hold to her side of the bargain. Her question had caused an odd, painful tightening in his chest. It had turned him into a coward, avoiding his wife at every turn for the past week. He shook his head at himself. Marriage was quite different from what he had thought it would be.

He heard the clip-clop of a horse behind him and swung about, expecting to see the fiery eyes of Madman Jack. Instead, another stallion stood saddled and waiting for him.

"What is this?" he demanded.

"Yer 'orse, yer grace," Danny answered. He would not meet Adrian's eyes.

"Where is Madman Jack?" Concern swept through him. Was his favorite stallion ill or injured?

"Out, yer grace," the boy mumbled.

"Out? What do you mean?" His concern was replaced by the heat of anger.

Danny averted his eyes. "Um, 'Er grace -"

Adrian exploded, "Is the duchess riding Madman Jack?"

The boy bobbed his head. "Aye, yer grace."

Fear clutched at Adrian. He swept the boy aside and swung up onto the horse. "Which way did she go?"

"Toward th' beach, yer grace." The boy pointed, as if Adrian needed direction.

Adrian barely let the boy finish before he dug in his heels and urged the horse into a full gallop. As he raced across the lawn, all he could think of was how fragile Jillian had looked beside the brute that was his favorite stallion. He remembered how Jack reacted every time Jillian had gotten close, rolling his eyes, snorting, sometimes even trying to bite. A vision of her lying somewhere, crumpled and broken, sat in his mind like a carrion specter, waiting to swoop down, laughing cruelly at his neglect.

He reached the beach and saw the deep hoofprints in the stony sand. Jack was at a gallop. He followed the prints a short way and saw they veered off to head back across his land toward the road to the village. He knew a shortcut. He could head her off.

Adrian first caught sight of Jillian as she and Jack jumped a low hedge. They had not yet made it to the road to the village. Two became one as Jillian leaned over the neck of his stallion and they flew across the open field. A fence, four rails high, was in their path. Surely Jack would balk at that. Jillian would be thrown. She would break her neck. Adrian leaned over the neck of his own horse and prodded him with his heels. He had to catch up with her and stop her.

Jillian grinned as the wind whipped her hair out behind her. She was having a marvelous time. Madman Jack was the finest horse she had ever ridden. When she was growing up, living on Rystoke's estate, the stable master had taught her to ride, and he let her help him exercise the horses. Her guardian had no idea she galloped wildly across his fields, splashed through streams, jumped fences, and returned to the stables looking like a hoyden. The fence coming up was quite high, but she knew this horse could clear it with no trouble. She laughed out loud.

The sound of other hoofbeats approached very fast. She glanced over her shoulder and saw her husband bearing down on her. His expression reminded her of an angry god, bent on vengeance. She dismissed him as she focused on the fence. She was not going to allow him to spoil her fun, no matter how furious he was.

He came abreast of her just before they reached the barrier. Side by side, they sailed over the top rail. As soon as the horses had landed, Dunbary grabbed Madman Jack's bridle and brought them both to a halt.

"What the hell do you think you are doing?" he erupted.

"Riding," Jillian said coolly as she nudged Jack into a walk.

Dunbary still held Jack's bridle and stopped him. "Are you mad? You could have been killed!"

"And then you would never learn the contents of your precious letter," she snapped. She was angry at his outburst. Angry that he'd ignored her for days, then chased her down and abruptly stopped her from the only enjoyment she'd had in a long time. And most of all, she was angry that he had not even attempted to make love to her.

Dunbary swung off his horse and pulled Jillian from Madman Jack before she had time to protest. "Is that what you think?" He pressed her against Jack's heaving side.

Jillian stared up into those wild, tawny eyes. "Why should I think any differently?" she asked coolly.

His fingers clutched her arms. Something desperate and hurt flashed through his eyes, and was gone. "Then you know very little about me, madam."

Calm enveloped her, blanketing the anger she had carried about with her for days. Finally, she saw an opening into the secret side of the man she had wed. "You're right," she said. "I know very little about you, your grace. I know only that you are furious that I have not kept to my side of the bargain."

His eyes darkened. "Then perhaps it is time I taught you something about me."

Jillian was unprepared for his mouth swooping down. Her lips were parted, and he took full advantage of his surprise attack. His tongue tangled with hers, tasting, teasing. Pleasure coursed through her. Caught between the horse and the wide chest of her husband, she could not escape his exquisite onslaught.

His hands moved between them. He opened the jacket of her riding habit, then loosened the tie of her chemise. The cool air made her gasp. His warm touch on her breasts made her sigh. A tiny thought nagged that she was supposed to be angry with him, that she was hurt by his neglect and coldness towards her. She should not allow him to do this. Her body rebelled against that fleeting thought. As he brushed his thumbs back and forth against both tight little buds, a whimper escaped her throat. This was what she wanted from him, this need, this intimacy. She clutched the sides of his coat in her fingers and held on for dear life. The blood pulsed through her veins from the wild ride and the recklessness of his kiss and touch. Lightheaded, weak-kneed, she leaned into him.

He broke away abruptly as a voice hailed them. He cleared his throat and said gruffly, "Compose yourself, Jillian. My groom has arrived with help and a more suitable horse for you to ride."

Flustered, embarrassed, and angry at herself that she had once again succumbed to him, Jillian turned her back and buttoned herself up. She smoothed her hair as best she could. She felt dazed from his touch, and her lips throbbed from his kiss. When she had put herself back together, she watched Dunbary casually approach the men. She suspected he knew they had been going to arrive soon. Damn him for being such a treacherous bastard.

He led a prancing little filly to her. "This is Vixen Lady. She is yours when you wish to ride. *Not* Madman Jack." His cool tone emphasized his controlled anger.

Jillian turned from the banked ire in her husband's gaze to admire the horse. The filly was delicate and graceful, with an underlying strength to her sleek form. A smile of pleasure lit Jillian's face as she ran her hand over Vixen Lady's silky neck, and she turned to thank Dunbary. "She's a beauty, your grace. Thank you."

He blinked and seemed at a loss for words at her thanks. He cleared his throat and motioned for her to mount. As he boosted her into the saddle, he murmured, "Do not think our conversation is over, madam. We will finish it at the house."

He swung up onto the stallion he had ridden out and trotted off. Jillian raised her chin and urged Vixen Lady to follow. She was not about to let her husband's men see that Dunbary's murmured words made her heart pound and her knees quake. She peeked at him from beneath her lashes to gauge his mood. His set profile was daunting. She took a deep breath. He would not intimidate her. They rode back to the stables in silence.

After they dismounted, she whispered a few words of praise to Vixen Lady, and promised she would steal a carrot from the kitchen for her later. When she turned to bid a cool farewell to Dunbary, she noticed his raised brow and a suspiciously humorous glint in his eyes. She huffed, and swung away, hurrying back to her room. Dunbary, no doubt, was cheerfully concocting other ways he could seduce and embarrass her in front of his staff.

As soon as she had shut the door to her bedroom, she began to unfasten the jacket to her riding habit. She saw that in her haste to cover herself before Dunbary's servants, she had buttoned it wrong. She felt her face heat. That man could so distract her that she couldn't even dress herself. He had known the men were on their way, and he had seduced her anyway. With a frustrated cry, she ripped her jacket open and stripped it off, flinging it across the room. A guilty blush warmed her cheeks at her own childish behavior. With a growl, she grabbed up the jacket and laid it over a chair.

She was still angry. Spitting mad in fact. With her hands on her hips, she paced the room. He was an ogre. How dare he seduce her out in the open. He was a rogue. A devil. A fiend.

The door opened behind her as she continued to pace. "I wish a bath, Dory," she said. "I do not wish to be disturbed. I feel a headache coming on."

"Does that headache have my name on it?" Dunbary asked.

She swung about in surprise. Apprehension made her stomach flutter. He had removed his coat and wore only his waistcoat over his soft shirt. His doeskin breeches clung to his muscular thighs.

"Yes," she said bluntly. "It does."

He advanced into the room. "I know several cures for a headache, but right now, I wish to discuss your conduct this morning."

"I did nothing unseemly," she said with a defiant lift to her chin.

"You were out riding alone." He prowled closer.

She shrugged. "I have ridden alone many times."

His eyes narrowed. "You were riding my horse, Madman Jack."

"He is a magnificent beast, your grace." She thought she might disarm him with a compliment.

"He is unruly, barely tame," he snapped.

"He was very docile when I rode him." She dismissed his statement with a wave of her hand.

He glowered. "He could have balked at the fence."

"But he didn't." She blinked innocently.

"You could have been thrown." He stalked closer. "He might have broken a leg and had to be destroyed, a valuable piece of horseflesh gone to waste."

Jillian sucked in a breath through her teeth. "If I had been injured, would you have felt the need to destroy me, too?"

"Don't be ridiculous." A muscle twitched in his jaw.

Jillian forced a sarcastic, little laugh. "How silly of me. Of course you wouldn't have me destroyed. I still haven't told you what was in the letter."

An odd look flickered in his eyes. Surprise? Hurt? It was gone before she could tell what it was. Then he was back to the confident, sardonic duke.

"Something else which belongs to me," he growled, "and which you have brazenly taken over as your own." He sauntered a few steps nearer. "I would say that some payment is due, wouldn't you, Jillian?"

Jillian stepped back at his intense presence. She felt very exposed, since all she had covering her from the waist up was her thin chemise. She had not forgotten his comment out in the field about finishing their conversation at a later time.

She shook her head. "There is no payment due for something that is found."

"Truly?" A dark brow lifted. "Not even when the owner comes forward to claim the lost article?" His hand snaked out and caught the neckline of her chemise.

Jillian swallowed against the tightness in her throat. One of his fingers plunged into the crevice between her breasts. "Finders, keepers," she whispered.

"Not so, Jillian. Not in this case." He was interrupted by a knock and the entrance of Dory. "Yes? What is it?" he asked impatiently.

"Begging your pardon, yer grace." Dory bounced a curtsy. "Her grace's bath is ready."

Dunbary turned back to Jillian with a wicked grin. "A bath? How delightful," he murmured. Then he tossed over his shoulder to the girl, "The duchess will be there presently." After Dory had bobbed another curtsy and hurried out of the room, he told Jillian, "Payment begins now, my pixie." He loosened his hold on her chemise, traced his fingers up her throat and into her hair. "I want to see what wet gold looks like."

Aghast at what he proposed to do, Jillian stepped away from him. "You are going to watch me bathe?"

"Why not? We are husband and wife. There should be no secrets between us." His smile was wicked and his eyes held heat. With a flourish, he motioned her on to her dressing room where her bath waited. "After you, your grace."

Stiffly, Jillian walked past him and into her dressing room. He followed like an overpowering phantom. She tried to think of some way to get rid of him. The last thing she wanted was to have him watch her bathe. But she could find no excuse to send him away as Dory helped her undress.

He settled in the small chair in the corner of the room. She could feel his eyes devouring her. When the last piece of clothing dropped from her, she proudly stepped into the tub. She was not going to scuttle about like a timid mouse.

She quickly washed then ducked her head so Dory could wash her hair. She enjoyed having her scalp massaged. Gradually, she became aware that the strokes of Dory's fingers were softer and slower than usual. The girl's thumbs ran down the nape of her neck and back up again.

Jillian was not in the mood for a relaxing bath, not with her husband watching. "Dory, please hurry. The soap is running into my eyes."

"Dory is gone," Dunbary answered. "I dismissed her."

Jillian's head jerked up and she frantically wiped soap from her eyes. "I did not want her dismissed," she said.

Dunbary chuckled and pushed her head forward again. "You had little to say in the matter."

"But I need her to help me dress," Jillian complained.

"No, you don't." He continued to stroke her neck and soap her hair.

"But—"

"Hush. Not another word. Consider this punishment for riding Madman Jack without permission." His fingers threaded through her hair and gently massaged.

Jillian ground her teeth together. If he had not been such a knave, she would not have felt the need to ride his damned horse in the first place. Although Madman Jack was a magnificent animal, he was a devil, just like his master.

His thumbs caressed her neck. His hands kneaded the tight muscles in her shoulders. Slowly, under his expert ministrations, despite her self-consciousness and anger, she relaxed.

His touch worked magic. Even when he stopped to rinse out the soap, the feel of the warm water running through her hair and down her back reinforced what his fingers had been doing.

As if in a dream, she heard him say, "Stand up, Jillian."

She wiped the water from her eyes, rose and faced him. He had removed his waistcoat, opened the neck of his shirt, rolled up his sleeves. Dark curls peeked through the vee of his open shirt. His eyes glinted warmly. His mouth curved up with amused arrogance. He reminded her of a pirate about to claim his prize.

With one finger, he traced a line from her throat to the valley between her breasts, then across one plump mound to where an impudent glob of bubbles clung to the tip. He pushed the bubbles around and around. She gasped at the delightful sensation.

"You are beautiful, Jillian," he said reverently.

She shook her head, denying, scattering droplets, but his compliment created a warm spot in her chest.

He smiled, a secret, satisfied smile. "Yes, you are. And you're mine." He placed a towel around her and lifted her out of the tub, He had her sit on a small stool near the fire, rubbed warmth back into her limbs, and dried her hair.

His touch was gentle, caressing. Jillian was confused. Was he still angry with her for riding his horse? Or had he forgiven her? Was he planning some cruel torture after being so kind? Even though one part of her enjoyed his ministrations, another part of her watched warily for any sign of a sudden attack.

He knelt behind her and with great care, combed the tangles out of her hair. Even after the tangles were gone, he continued to comb her hair in long, even strokes. Jillian's wariness ebbed away with the mesmerizing effect of his touch.

Her eyes closed in rapture. She murmured a protest when he stopped combing her hair. But then he gently massaged up her neck, down her back. His hands slipped over her shoulders beneath the towel and cupped her breasts. His lips touched the sensitive spot below her ear.

"Wildflowers," he murmured.

CHAPTER 12

"You smell like wildflowers."

Jillian sighed her answer. His fingers traced down across her belly and nudged her thighs apart. Her head fell back against his shoulder. He created those wonderful sensations again, the same ones he had created the night they had wed. She wanted more of them. She remembered how they had swept her along in a great rush. Without any sense of shame or embarrassment, she opened herself to him.

Tendrils of pleasure curled deep within her. Tiny moans caught in her throat. She reached behind her and clung to his shoulders, arched into his touch, sucked in gulps of air. Slowly, his fingers withdrew. She uttered a wordless cry of protest. He hushed her with a caress on her cheek and a kiss on her jaw.

She heard him moving behind her. When he pulled her up from the stool and turned her to face him, she saw he had undressed. His naked body was beautiful. Broad shoulders narrowed down to waist and hips. Dark hair sprinkled across his chest and a stygian line pointed to his manhood, proud and erect. She had never seen a naked man before. On their wedding night, he had come to her in the dark. She should have been appalled at his nakedness, or at least embarrassed. Instead, she wanted to feast her eyes, touch him, explore every plane and hollow. When he drew her to him, she went willingly, pliantly. Their mouths came together in a crush.

Jillian had learned a bit about her needs and those of the man she had wed on that one night when he had introduced her to love-making. Now, instinct and that fledgling knowledge took over as she clung to him. She pressed against him, and allowed him to feel all of her, made him aware of her curves, the hills and valleys of her body. In response, she felt the hardness of him throb against the hollow of her hip.

With a firm grasp on her hair, he forced her to look into his eyes. "Vixen," he growled, and dragged her down to the floor.

He lay back across the velvety carpet and she sprawled across him. With his hands framing her face, he held her still as he teased and nipped and licked her lips. When she could stand it no longer and pressed her mouth against his, when her concentration was centered on his kiss, she felt him enter her. She drew back and gazed at him in surprise.

He traced his fingers down her cheek. "Do what you want, Jillian," he whispered.

Despite the wild excitement that coursed through her, some tiny bit of reticence held her back. He was giving her control, but she did not know what to do with it. She would have to expose her deep desire for him, and she was not ready to do that. She would not only be naked on the outside, but on the inside as well.

She shook her head and murmured, "I can't."

With a little smile, he clasped her firmly and rolled them both over. He was above her now. She closed her eyes, memorizing every touch, every sensation. This was what she craved, to feel his weight on her, pressing down, pressing into her. When he moved inside her, she purred.

Pleasure built within her, higher, higher. She spiraled up, up, into the dark vortex he created. She clung to him as her only grasp on reality and followed him on this soul-stirring journey. As she reached the top of the whirling coil, she exploded out of it in a dazzle of exquisite release and a cry of unbridled passion.

His own release was marked by an animal growl deep in his throat. He collapsed on top of her and buried his head in the hollow of her shoulder. She wrapped her arms about him and listened to his deep, regular breaths come and go. Sated, her body relaxed into a state of contentment.

The sweet moment did not last. With a jerk, he rolled off her and abruptly rose to his full height. As if nothing had happened between them, he began pulling on his clothes.

Startled, suddenly cold, bereft of the warmth of him, Jillian sat up and hugged her knees. "Where are you going?" She could not hide the plaintive note in her voice.

"I have an appointment with my estate manager," he said as he pulled on a polished boot. "I have already kept him waiting too long."

"You have spent every single day with him since we arrived," Jillian said. "Perhaps you should have married him." She knew she sounded childish but she didn't care. That he could make love to her and then discard her so easily cut deeply, more than she expected.

Her husband stopped buttoning his vest and stared at her. "I am master of this estate and several others. I have a duty to see that they are properly maintained. I believe my duty to you has been fulfilled, madam."

Jillian turned away so he would not see the tears that sprang to her eyes at his cold words. Yes, he had performed his duty to her. He had deflowered her, and this time, he had not retreated at the end, so the job was done properly. Legally, he was not at fault. But emotionally… She did not wish to probe that wound too deeply. She had begun to believe he might have some affection for her, now she feared he never would. She blinked back her tears and turned to him once more. He was dressed and nearly at the door.

"I wish to return to London," she announced.

He stopped with his hand on the door handle. "Absolutely not. We will return to London at the end of the fortnight, together, as any newly married couple should. I will send your maid to you."

After he had gone, Jillian jumped up and stepped into the tub again. The water had chilled, but she did not care. Angrily, she scrubbed all vestiges of their love-making from her body. By the time Dory entered, she was sitting before the fire and brushing her hair. The hurt was buried deep within her.

As Adrian closed the door to the dressing room behind him and walked down the long hall, guilt stabbed through him. He had been very harsh with Jillian, harsher than he had intended. His fear at her riding Madman Jack had annoyed him. But that was not the only irritation. She had looked magnificent atop the beast as they galloped across the meadow. Not only that, Jack had looked like he was enjoying himself as well. The horse had never allowed anyone but Adrian to ride him. Until Jillian.

He thought to punish her with that kiss in the field. A grave mistake. His need had risen like some hungry serpent, frustrating him even more. When he followed her to her bath, he had expected to exchange angry words with her, not sweet endearments and passionate embraces. He had intended to chastise her for riding Madman Jack. Instead, the sight of her soap-slicked body had made him forget his anger and think of only one thing. He wanted to caress all those secret places where the bubbles tickled her. He wanted to feel the pliant muscles beneath his hands that had ridden Jack. He wanted to assure himself she was not harmed from that wild ride.

He had not planned that such feelings should enter into his marriage. Wedding Jillian had been only a means of retaining his honor and her reputation. And the way to gain the letter she said she had destroyed. Yet, the soft feelings he had for her after their love-making chipped away at his resolve to not become emotionally entangled with her. He had learned a hard lesson on the cruelty of women from his mother. His resolve not to father a child had been destroyed, for their coupling had been completed. He'd not had the presence of mind to pull out before his release. When he touched his new wife, everything else dissolved into a hazy muddle.

He entered his own bedroom and called for Symmes. His valet scurried out of the dressing room with a coat of dark blue wool over his arm.

"Help me change quickly, Symmes," he said as he stripped off his shirt, irritated that he had forgotten his waistcoat in Jillian's room. "Duggan is waiting for me to go over the estate records."

As Symmes brought a fresh change of clothes, Adrian's thoughts once more returned to Jillian. He had not missed the hurt expression that crossed her face at his hard words. He felt like an absolute cad. He could not understand why that should be. He had never had any compunction about telling a woman exactly how their relationship stood. But he hadn't been married either. And the women with whom he had relations had never been young and innocent. Jillian was certainly young, but was she so innocent? After all, she could still play him for a fool with that bloody letter.

He had vowed he would never be duped as his father had been by a woman like Beatrice, his *loving* mother. He would never allow himself to feel anything beyond a slight fondness for any woman. Yet, the recent interlude with Jillian had shaken all those resolves. She had opened herself to him completely, had been warm and giving. And he'd repaid that gift with callousness. He'd never been so swept away with any other woman. The feelings were new to him. Both thrilling and threatening to his peace of mind. But his demons had gotten the better of him. And he had treated his wife abominably.

His wife. Those two words jolted him. Jillian was *not* a passing affair. They would be married for life. He did enjoy her company, at least when she was not battling with him. But even that he found energizing. Perhaps he should spend more time with her. She must be quite lonely here at Dunbary. She was a charming, beautiful young woman. He had called her a pixie. Wondering where that term had come from, he realized it was perfect. From winsomely giggling over a mud-splattered gown, to whimpering with pleasure as he caressed her, to riding his stallion as though she'd been born to it. She fascinated him. But he would just have to keep those weak feelings locked tightly away. It would not do to let her know how he felt and give her such an advantage over him.

With a satisfied nod at Symmes for helping him look presentable, he headed out the door to his meeting. His step had a bounce to it. He looked forward to dinner with Jillian, when he would invite her to go riding with him tomorrow.

The following morning, Adrian stood outside the stables and slapped his gloves against his thigh in annoyance. The sun had broken through the clouds and warmed the spring air, but the fine weather did not lighten his spirits. He waited impatiently for Jillian to appear so they could ride together. He had been disappointed at her cool acceptance of his invitation at the dinner table the evening before. He had expected her to be pleased at the suggestion to ride together.

Instead, he had received a mild, "As you wish, your grace." And now she was purposely vexing him by making him wait

He heard a horse approach from the stable behind him, and he swung about expecting to see his groom leading out Madman Jack. Instead, he saw Jillian already mounted on Vixen Lady. As she came abreast of him, a mischievous smile curled her lips. He suddenly had an unreasonable urge to kiss those lips.

"Are you coming for a ride, your grace?" she asked. "This is the hour you suggested, is it not?"

He squashed the desire to pull her from her horse and kiss her silly. Coolly, he lifted an eyebrow. "I only awaited your sparkling presence, madam." Then he turned into the dark interior of the stables to mount his own horse.

Jillian watched him go and bit her lip to keep from giggling aloud. He had been waiting for her with impatience, while she had been hiding in the tack room. She wanted to teach him that an invitation to ride together did not compensate for hurtful words or actions.

The night before, she had lain awake probing the pain she felt after his cold words. She did not understand why she should feel such hurt. After all, their marriage had only occurred because they each needed something.

If he wished to treat her merely as a possession, something which he was duty-bound to have, then she would guard her feelings zealously. She would be charming and gay with him, but he would not have access to her bed ever again. For when they came together in passion, she was lost. She became vulnerable and defenseless. Last night, she had vowed she would never allow that to happen again. Her mother had schooled her well.

Her husband emerged from the stables on Madman Jack. She had to admit they made a devilishly handsome pair. Before Dunbary came abreast of her, she nudged Vixen Lady into a trot.

She called back to him over her shoulder, "Hurry up, your grace! I am anxious for you to take me riding." Laughing, she allowed her horse to break into a canter. Before her husband could catch up, she gave Vixen Lady her head. At a gallop, she dashed across the lawn.

An expletive exploded from her husband. Enjoying the slight advantage she had, she headed toward the beach. Madman Jack was more powerful than Vixen Lady, and Dunbary would soon catch up, but she wished to keep ahead of him as long as possible.

She was surprised that she reached the narrow path down to the beach first. Dunbary was only a few yards behind her, but she was able to claim her designated finish line to the race before he did. As she slowed Vixen Lady to a walk, he reined in his horse beside her.

"Good God, Jillian, are you trying to break your neck?" he burst out. "That path down here is treacherous."

With a sly grin, she asked sweetly, "Are you concerned for my welfare, your grace?" Before he had a chance to answer, she said, "You know I ride very well. I proved that yesterday on Madman Jack."

"Only too well," he grumbled.

Laughing, she cajoled, "Come, your grace, don't be a poor loser. Show me the secrets of Dunbary, where ancient invaders landed and smugglers hid their booty."

Adrian was entranced. Her eyes sparkled like the sea beneath the sun, and her cheeks were flushed from the excitement of the ride. Her lips were soft and rosy with her smile. He wanted to reach out and brush his fingers down that warm cheek and crush those lips beneath his mouth. The blood began pounding through his veins. Remembering her sweet surrender to him the day before, his fingers tightened on the reins. Madman Jack gave an annoyed toss of his head, and Adrian's thoughts halted their journey down that road of foolishness. Memory of his wild attraction to her made him realize the folly of following through with his desire. He would not be a reincarnation of his father. He would not allow himself to be duped by another Beatrice.

He turned away from her bewitching loveliness. "You have guessed the history of Dunbary. Norsemen and Picts landed here in the time of the Druids, and smugglers have always used it as a place to hide their contraband."

"Do smugglers still land here?" She glanced around as if hoping to see some pop out between the rocks.

He nodded. "On occasion. I have men patrol the cliffs, but it's impossible for them to cover every place at once. There are too many caves and dens for the bandits to hide in."

"Can you show me one?" she asked eagerly.

He smiled at her excitement. Despite wanting to remain aloof, he could not help but be charmed by her. "Of course. I'll show you where my ancestor hid his booty. I don't think even the modern day smugglers have found this hidey-hole."

She drew in a surprised breath. "Your ancestor was a smuggler?"

He chuckled. "You did not know you had married into a family with such a disreputable past, did you?"

"I think every family has its disreputable members." Her tone was subdued.

He glanced at her sharply, wondering if she was revealing something about her own family, but she was intent on guiding her horse across the slippery shale. "You are probably right," he agreed. "Come this way."

He turned Madman Jack toward another track that wound back up the cliff from the beach. Making sure that Jillian followed, he led her across the top of the cliff and through a grove of trees, which ended abruptly at the edge. Another path, very much overgrown, zig-zagged down to a minuscule patch of rock-strewn sand.

"It's low tide," he said. "We'll be able to get into the cave, but we'll have to leave the horses here."

He dismounted, then helped Jillian slide from Vixen Lady. His hands nearly spanned her waist. He wanted to press her back against her horse and kiss her until she was dazed. Instead, he stepped away and turned to find the way to the beach, which led him to wonder why he was revealing this part of himself to her. He had never revealed this to any woman. Why did he want to tell her, the woman who had forced him into marriage?

As soon as Jillian's feet were on solid ground, she moved away from him to tie the reins to a low branch. She was not about to expose herself to another onslaught of her husband's touch. She did not want to feel the blood pounding through her nor the wild sensations he caused by just being near him. She did not want to lose control of her emotions again. Not after her husband had seduced her, then acted as if they had merely conversed about the weather. She would not be hurt again.

Dunbary took her hand and led her down the steep path. She tried to ignore the feel of his fingers gently cradling hers. Instead, she concentrated on her surroundings. The rough sand on the beach scrunched wetly beneath her riding boots. The wall of the cliff showed signs of high tide several feet above her head. Large boulders, covered with seaweed, lay strewn about the beach and were scattered among the swell of the waves. He led her around a group of huge rocks that towered over her. He seemed to be leading her into the sea, but instead, a small sandy path curved back to an opening into the cliff. Before her, the cave gaped blackly.

He dropped her hand and searched for something on the slimy rock wall. "Ah, there it is," he said, and began to climb. He reached for something above his head, then backed down a few steps before he jumped to the ground. He held an old torch and piece of flint.

"I used to play here when I was a boy," he explained. "There are footholds carved into the wall. I discovered the torch holder left from the days of my ancestor. I hid a torch and flint there so I could see my way to the back of the cave." As he struck the flint to light the torch, he mused, "I was not sure they would still be there. It's been a long time since I used them."

Jillian was touched by this glimpse into his boyhood. She could envision him playing pirate, being brave and daring against imaginary foes. What had made him change, become so cynical? She had no time to ponder. He took her hand and, holding the torch high, led her into the inky dark.

The floor of the cavern was wet sand, punctuated here and there by a rock. Water dripped down the sides. Occasionally, they had to skirt around large puddles left by the ebbing tide. After several minutes, they reached what appeared to be the back of the cave. The wall slanted up and away from them.

"Do you feel like climbing?" he asked.

Curious about what lay ahead, she said, "Lead on, pirate captain." Warning that the rocks were slippery, he helped her climb up the face of the wall. When they reached the top, she saw a flat sandy surface that opened into a large chamber. Here, the sand and walls were dry.

"At high tide, the cave we walked through is flooded almost to the ceiling," Dunbary explained. "This chamber remains above water level and so it stays dry. It's a perfect spot for hiding contraband."

Jillian saw a few old barrel staves partially buried in the sand. There was no evidence of recent use. "You said that smugglers use your property for landing their cargo. Haven't they used this cave?"

He shook his head. "Unless you know the cave is here, you can't see it from the sea. The mouth is cloaked by some large rocks that look like a dragon's head." He dropped her hand and wandered over to one of the barrels. "I slayed a lot of dragons in here," he reflected as he ran his fingers through the coating of sand on the staves.

In the flickering light from the torch, Jillian thought she saw a look of pain cross his face. Had his childhood been so very terrible? When he turned to face her, he was smiling self-consciously.

"I guess I sound a bit silly," he said as he walked back to her.

This vulnerable side of him was a revelation. She wanted to reassure him. "You don't sound silly at all. I always played the damsel in distress, captured by the evil wizard's dragon." She smiled. "But I never had a knight in shining armor to rescue me. I always escaped on my own."

He laughed and chucked her under the chin. "I should have guessed. The unconventional Miss St. Clare would not need a knight to help her." He took her hand. "We'd better head back before the tide turns and traps us in here."

Jillian was thoughtful as they slipped their way back down the wall of rocks, then followed the sandy floor out into the open. The tide had begun to close in on the mouth of the cave, and they had to dodge the waves in order to reach the beach. Gaining the clifftop, they found their horses side by side contentedly cropping the grass.

Slowly, allowing Madman Jack and Vixen Lady to find their own way, they headed back toward the house. Jillian wondered at the glimpse of vulnerability her husband had revealed. She had never thought they would share their childhood fantasies to each other, especially not after the difficult week they'd had. The contrast between what she had first perceived the Duke to be and what she now knew of him confused her. Perhaps she was wrong about his aloof distance. Perhaps something prevented him from being the warm, loving husband she wanted him to be.

As she listened to him describe the boundaries of Dunbary and relate the history of his family's ownership of the land and title, she fell under his charm. By the time they reached the stables, she was astonished that she had enjoyed being with him.

As he helped her down from her horse, he said, "Perhaps you would enjoy a stroll through the gardens with me this afternoon?"

Their morning had been delightful and he had been the perfect gentleman. Why not take advantage of his good humor? "I would enjoy that very much, your grace," she replied in a soft voice.

She smiled all the way back to the house.

Jillian checked her appearance in the cheval mirror for the third time in ten minutes. She felt as though thousands of butterflies were dancing around in her stomach. *It's just a stroll through the gardens.* According to the standards of society, she was supposed to be bored by the prospect. And yet, Dunbary had asked her, and that made all the difference.

She accepted a shawl from Dory, then sedately made her way to the stairs, even though she wanted to dash down to the main floor where her husband waited. Instead, she took a breath, and gracefully descended the steps.

She saw him standing at the bottom, waiting for her. Her heart quickened at the sight of him. He was handsome in his dark blue coat and pale gray trousers. His topaz eyes gleamed in appreciation as they raked over her. She placed her fingers in his outstretched hand, and a familiar thrill ran up her arm. Even a simple touch, a connection of their fingers left her breathless.

"You will be my lovely wildflower among the cultivated blooms," he said as he brought her hand to his lips.

Touched by his compliment, she giggled. "Wildflowers are usually considered weeds, your grace. They are plucked out by the gardener and tossed away on the dung heap."

"Then the gardener has no sense." He tucked her hand in the crook of his arm. "Let me show you my garden, Lady Wildflower, and you will see the truth in my words."

His broad smile and gleaming eyes punctuated his words, and she felt the answering heat in her cheeks as they strolled out into the sunshine. Her husband explained that his grandmother had laid out the plans for the gardens. Duchess Matilda loved flowers and, until a few years ago when she could no longer manage it, had spent many an hour on her hands and knees in the dirt tending the blooms.

"I can imagine what the society matrons had to say about that." Jillian's lips quirked in a smile.

He chuckled. "Years ago, my grandmother caused quite the scandal. The matrons told Lady Matilda she was acting like a common peasant woman. To retaliate, she gave a grand ball and decorated the whole house in garlands of flowers from her own gardens. The society matrons were entranced by the decorations and never said another word to her about working in the dirt."

"Does your mother enjoy gardening, too?" she asked.

A cold mask dropped over his face. "No," he answered abruptly. "She has nothing to do with the gardens. I keep them up for my grandmother."

Jillian was surprised at his sudden change in mood. She searched for something to say. They were just passing a bed of white roses, not quite in bloom.

"What beautiful roses. Your grandmother must have loved them," she said.

"My father had that bed planted. For my mother." He quickly averted his gaze to the opposite side of the path.

She wondered at his clipped tone and the mystery behind his words. She lapsed into silence, trying to find a subject that would break through his sudden chilliness. With relief, she heard footsteps on the path behind them.

They stopped and turned. The butler held out a silver salver with a note on it.

"I was asked to present this to you immediately, your grace," he said.

Dunbary took the note and read it. "Have the messenger wait for my reply, Boggs," he said. "I will be in presently." He turned to Jillian. "I have been called back to London. We will leave early tomorrow morning."

"So soon?" Jillian could not hide the disappointment in her voice.

"I thought you would be pleased. Isn't that what you asked of me yesterday?" His tone was cool, sardonic.

Where had her attentive husband gone? Her heart constricted in her chest. She had thought they had turned a corner in their marriage. That perhaps they were finding a way to be happy together. Glancing at his stony expression, her mouth flattened as she realized she had once again been foolishly beguiled by his charm. "Of course," she said stiffly. "If you will excuse me, your grace, I must direct the packing."

As she walked back to the house, she thought she heard him whisper her name. But it could have been the breeze.

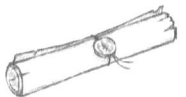

CHAPTER 13

Several days later, Jillian stood in the middle of all the confusion. Around her were trunks, boxes, and piles of clothes. She and Dunbary had arrived back in London late the night before. Dory and another young serving girl were attempting to create order out of the chaos. Besides the luggage from Dunbary, the belongings she had left behind at Rystoke's had arrived.

She was looking for the ragdoll with the secret letter hidden inside. She had to figure out what to do with it. Her husband was still an enigma. She still had not decided where his loyalties lay. Just as she thought he might be letting her see into his heart, he had slammed the door shut with his cool demeanor since leaving his estate. Sighing, she opened the last trunk. If the doll was not there, then her guardian had played one of his cruel little tricks on her.

As she felt about in the clothes, she heard a knock on the door. Absently, she called out to enter.

"So, this is the young lady who has brought my son to the altar," a woman said.

Startled, Jillian jumped up. Before her stood an older woman, still very attractive. Her hair was rich and vibrant and her dark eyes sparkled, but her heavy makeup was unable to completely cover the dark circles beneath her eyes and the lines on her face. An artistic application of rouge brought an artificial, youthful blush to her cheeks.

From the family resemblance, the woman had to be Dunbary's mother. Jillian dropped into a curtsy and murmured, "Your grace."

"Well, at least he married someone with good manners and a pleasant face," the woman said in a haughty tone as she advanced into the room. "What is your name, girl?"

"Jillian St. Clare," she said, forgetfully giving her maiden name. A flash of surprise crossed the woman's face, but she smiled. "What a delightful name." She held out a delicate hand. "I am Beatrice, but I am sure my son has told you all about me."

Jillian took her hand, limp and cool. "No, your grace, he has said very little. We have not known each other very long."

"Didn't you just spend time at Dunbary?" Beatrice asked. "Did my son bury himself in the estate books as he usually does and leave you alone?"

Jillian felt a compulsion to jump to Dunbary's defense, but she simply shook her head.

"Well, that is just like him," Beatrice went on, ignoring Jillian's denial. "He has absolutely no understanding of women. He never understood me." The woman's annoyance switched to sadness. "Just like his father before him." She had left the door open and footsteps approached in the hallway. Her expression brightened. "Gustav, come meet my son's new bride," she called.

A man much younger than Beatrice appeared. As Dunbary's mother introduced them, he clicked his heels together and bowed with precision. He was suave and handsome, but Jillian disliked him on sight. His cool blue eyes appraised her up and down, as if she wore no clothes. Uncomfortable under his blatant scrutiny, she wondered what attracted Dunbary's mother to him. She remembered her husband's tone when he spoke of his mother on their walk through the gardens. Now she had a glimmer of understanding.

"Ah, *vunderbar*," the German gushed. "The English rose is so fery fair. An honor to meet you, madam. Ve must meet again and chat. Now, I hafe appointment vith man who sells me horse."

He bowed again to Jillian and raised Beatrice's hand to his lips. Even though he murmured soft words to Beatrice, his last glance before he left rested on Jillian. Dunbary's mother watched in silence as her lover closed the door behind him. Then she turned to Jillian.

"Watch yourself, miss," she warned coldly. "The baron is mine. Stay away from him." With an angry swish of skirts, she stormed out, slamming the door behind her.

Astounded, Jillian stared at the closed door. She was wed to Lady Beatrice's son. What sort of woman would give such a warning to her own daughter-in-law? Besides, the German made her very uncomfortable. His last glance had sent a trickle of apprehension down her spine. It had held something far more sinister than a lecherous gaze. If possible, she would avoid crossing paths with Gustav, Baron von Heisburg.

Dismissing him from her mind, she sank to her knees before another trunk of clothes. As she searched for the ragdoll, her thoughts returned to the relationship between Dunbary and his mother. When Jillian had walked with him in the garden at his estate, he had become distant at the mere mention of Beatrice, as if he could not bear to speak of her. Was his mother's unsavory lover the cause? Surely, Dunbary would not wish for that association. Or had his mother done something else that hurt him?

Even as the question rose in her mind, it was blocked by another concern. The ragdoll was not in the trunk. Worried, Jillian sat back on her heels. She was convinced Rystoke had kept the doll to taunt her. If he examined it closely, he would see that some of the stitching up the doll's back was new. Jillian had no doubt he would open the doll and discover the letter. His rage at being tricked might lead him to carry out his malicious threat to destroy her.

Sighing, she stood and surveyed the disarray in the room. The mess reflected her life. But no one must know. Society demanded that she send out her calling cards to announce that she was in residence in London. She had to act the part of the serene, newly-wed Duchess of Dunbary.

Before she could direct Boggs to send out a footman on her errand, a message arrived from Rystoke, who wished her to call on him. A moment of panic gripped her. Had he discovered the letter? Then reason overcame her fear. He wanted information about Dunbary. The demand made her seethe. Although she and her husband were not on the best of terms, he was her husband. She owed him loyalty, more than to her sly, cruel guardian who used her for his own gain.

She rang for Dory to help her change into something she could don like armor.

Too soon, she was standing before Rystoke in his study, as he sat at his impressive desk. She had to wait until he finished writing something. He finally looked up and leaned back in his chair with a venomous smile.

"Back so soon from Dunbary?" he asked snidely. "Did you and your new husband not get along?"

Now that she was no longer under his control, she would not let him intimidate her. Without being invited to do so, she sat in one of the leather chairs before the desk.

"He was called back to London on business," she answered coolly as she pulled off her gloves.

"How unfortunate." Rystoke's tone mocked.

"What did you wish to see me about?" she asked bluntly.

His brows went up in false surprise. "My dear girl, you are so suspicious. Shouldn't a guardian be concerned for the welfare of his newly-wed ward?"

Jillian stared straight into those bland, pale eyes. "You have never been concerned about my welfare except when it profited you. But since you seem so interested, I am doing quite well, thank you."

"Excellent. We should celebrate. We never had the chance since your new husband whisked you off so quickly. After all, it is not every day that a girl in your circumstances makes such a successful catch." He chuckled. "The poor boy could not even wait until the prearranged date to marry you."

"I do not wish to celebrate," Jillian said flatly. "I did what you wanted and what society obliged me to do. I married Dunbary. I see no cause for celebrating something he and I were both forced into."

His mouth twitched with humor. "Do I detect a bit of discord between the two newlyweds?"

Jillian bit down on her anger. She would not rise to his bait. "Please, just tell me what you want," she said with an exasperated sigh.

The mask of congeniality and mocking humor dropped from Rystoke's face. "Tell me what you did at Dunbary and what he did. I want to know every detail. I want to know why you came back to London earlier than you had planned."

Relieved that she had nothing of consequence to relate, Jillian gave him a brief account.

"What did you talk about?" he demanded.

Jillian shrugged. "Nothing of consequence. The estate, his family history, his horses." A blush heated her cheeks. The memory of the morning she had ridden Madman Jack, when Dunbary had watched her bathe, was still fresh.

"What about his horses?" He pounced.

"We merely went riding," she said.

"Where did he take you?" Interest showed in his pale eyes.

"Around his estate." She wondered at his intent.

"Where?" His single word was more than merely curious.

She shrugged carelessly and tried to give him insignificant information. "He showed me some caves. He said smugglers sometimes use his property, and he has to have men patrol the area."

Rystoke was silent for a long moment. "How unfortunate," he finally murmured. "I'm sure that is quite an annoyance."

Jillian stared at him. Somehow, she had given him information that he could use, although she had no idea how. The thought made her heart sink. Before she could repair her mistake, he smiled at her in dismissal.

"We are off to a good start," he announced. "Do you see how easy it is to keep me informed? If you keep your side of the bargain, I will keep mine and not tell your husband your true origins."

In frustrated anger, Jillian stood. "I am betraying my husband and that is despicable. Good day to you, my lord." She turned and left.

As she closed the door to the study behind her, she let out a sigh of despair. She hated what she had just done. Everything she had told Rystoke was very innocent, but something had made his devious mind begin to churn. She did not want to see Dunbary hurt by his enemy, but somehow, Rystoke would find a way to use what she had just told him against her husband.

Just before she reached the front door, someone hissed at her. She looked around at the empty entrance hall. An eye peeked out and a finger crooked at her from behind the door to the small drawing room. Curious, she walked closer. The door opened wider and Lady Pennington pulled her into the room.

"Did anyone see you come in here?" she whispered breathlessly.

Jillian shook her head. "Lady Pennington, why are you hiding?"

"Hush, girl, I'm not supposed to be talking with you." The woman glanced around, took Jillian by the arm, and directed her away from the door. Her turban was slightly askew and two bright spots colored her cheeks. "Rystoke thinks I am superfluous and a bad influence on you now."

"But why?" Jillian was confused.

Lady Pennington waved away the question. "It doesn't matter. I'm leaving tomorrow. I'm going to live with my sister in Derby. But I wanted to make sure you got this before I left." She shoved a wrapped package into Jillian's hands.

Puzzled, Jillian stared at the bundle. "A gift? That is most generous of you."

Pennington shook her head. "No, not a present. Your doll. The one your mother made for you. He was going to burn it."

Relief washed through her that the secret note was safe. And tears filled Jillian's eyes at Pennington's thoughtfulness. "Thank you." She hugged the package to her. "This doll means a great deal to me."

Pennington nodded once, decisively. "I know. I know *exactly* how much it means to you. Do the right thing with it."

Surprise at Pennington's oblique reference to what the doll contained made Jillian stare at her.

Pennington reached out and cupped Jillian's chin in her hand. "Goodbye, Jillian. Be happy." With a little shove towards the door, she said urgently, "Now go on, get out of here. I'll write to you when I get settled."

Jillian opened the door, but before she walked through, she turned and kissed her chaperone on the cheek. "Thank you, Elenora." Then she slipped out of the room and hurried to the front door. All the way home, she clutched the package to her heart.

The day after arriving back in London, Adrian sat in the back corner of the common room of the Cat's Paw, one of the more disreputable taverns near the docks. He hunched over his pint of ale as if someone might come along and steal it from him. From his position, he had a perfect view of the entrance. In his threadbare coat and breeches, soiled shirt and cravat, he appeared to be just one more poor soul who was down on his luck. The dark stubble on his chin added more credence to his charade.

The door opened and a large man swaggered in. His striped neckcloth, grimy white pantaloons, and blue jacket, salt stained and missing a few buttons, identified him as a sailor. As he surveyed the room, Adrian pulled his wide-brimmed hat down lower over his eyes and took a sip of ale. He forced himself not to grimace at the abominable brew.

The sailor caught one of the serving wenches about the waist and ordered rum. As she went to fetch it, the sailor slapped her behind and guffawed. At this time of day, there were few empty seats. The man approached Adrian's table.

"Mind sharin' a table, mate?" he asked.

Adrian gave a noncommittal shrug and returned to staring into the depths of his pint. The man sat, leaned back in his chair, and gazed about the noisy room.

"Not much 'appenin' 'ere," he observed. "Me mates tol' me, 'Go t'the Cat's Paw,' they said. 'You'll 'ave a good time there.' Not bloody likely."

Adrian remained silent. The serving wench brought the sailor's rum and graced him with an inviting smile.

"Ah, sweet'eart, you are th' ripest thing I've laid me eyes on in months," the sailor crooned as he wrapped his arm about her waist. "Care for a tumble wit' ole Willy Breen?"

The well-endowed girl wriggled out of his embrace and returned tartly, "I'm too good fer th' likes o'you."

"Maybe, sweet'eart, but what about me gold?" Willy threw a guinea on the table.

The girl's eyes widened and she whispered, "Meet me around back at 'alf after th' hour." With a disdainful sniff in Adrian's direction, she sashayed away with a haughty tilt to her head and a swing to her generous hips.

The sailor guffawed again and took a swig of rum.

"You're going to catch something vile rolling with her," Adrian muttered to his agent.

Willy slapped his tankard down on the table and wiped his lips with the back of his hand. Under cover of the action he said, "Don't worry, I've no intention of touching her." He took another drink, then mumbled, "News from the North."

Adrian gave a barely perceptible nod to indicate he was listening.

"The Luddites are threatening to shed blood and blow up Parliament if nothing is done to help them," Willy murmured. "Opening up trade with America would help."

Adrian took a sip of ale and grimaced. The Luddites were laborers who knitted stockings on frames. New types of knitting frames had replaced the traditional ones and put many knitters out of work. War with France and trade restrictions with America had reduced the demand for stockings, so the laborers' wages had fallen. Frustrated at conditions they could not control, the Luddites had rioted, smashing and burning the new frames and sometimes even murdering their owners.

"I'll pass that along," Adrian said into his cup. "Any other news?"

"About that missing letter," Willy whispered. "I heard it was a woman who told the other side of its existence."

Adrian's chest constricted at his agent's words. Had Jillian lied to him when she had told him that the letter was destroyed? What if, instead of burning it, she had already passed it along to Rystoke? With difficulty, he brought his attention back to Willy.

"They don't know what's in it. They're just guessing it will help them," Willy muttered into his tankard.

Relief passed through Adrian that his wife had not given the letter away.

Willy banged his mug on the table. "'Ere, girl!" he called to the serving wench and waved his tankard in the air. "Fill me up again!" Hunching over the table, he said under his breath. "If the Orders in Council remain in place, the weavers won't get the raw cotton from America. I've heard that some members of Parliament from the North have formed a conspiracy to keep the Luddites out of work and prices for cotton goods high."

Adrian pretended to doze off over his ale as he said, "See if you can find out who's involved. And try to discover the name of the woman who's passing along secrets." He jerked his head up as if suddenly awakening. Rubbing his hand across his face, he mumbled, "Contact me in the usual manner when you have news." He stood, tossed a few coins on the table and stumbled out the door.

Outside, he shambled along, keeping his disguise. What he wanted to do was stride angrily through the streets and confront his wife. But he could not do that. He had to remain anonymous in case anyone was watching. And he could not reveal anything to Jillian. She might run to Rystoke with the information. Somehow, he had to get her to disclose what was in that damned letter. With each passing day, he sank deeper and deeper into a morass of questions, suspicions, and mistrust. Naïvely, he had believed the enchanting Miss St. Clare held no danger. Now, he realized that she was as threatening to his sanity and his well-being as any enemy agent—more so since she had become his wife.

Late that afternoon, Jillian paced impatiently as she waited for her husband. They were expected at Lady Matilda's for tea, and he had gone out. They had to leave soon. The coach had already been brought around to the front of the house.

She paced to the window and stared down into the street. A ragged stranger shuffled past. He passed the front of the house, then ducked around to the back. Suspicious about the stranger's intent, she rang for a footman, but before the servant arrived, she heard Dunbary's footsteps pass by her door. She hurried through the sitting room and with a light tap on the door, entered her husband's bedroom.

She had not been in the room since their wedding night. Memories of her wanton response to her husband's touch brought a deep flush to her cheeks. Her gaze landed on the large bed, then immediately slid away. This was not the time for her to be thinking about such things.

"We are due at Lady Matilda's within the hour," she said as she focused on Dunbary.

She stopped abruptly with a gasp. He looked like he had just come from the sewers of London. His clothes were filthy and torn. His face sported a stubble of beard and black smudges. His hair was wildly disheveled.

"Where have you been?" she asked in shock. At the same moment, she realized her husband had been the person she had seen shambling past the house.

Both Dunbary and his valet froze. Her husband was the first to recover, and he motioned for Symmes to continue pulling off his boot. He ducked his head but not before Jillian caught the angry flash of his eyes.

"Isn't a man allowed any privacy?" he complained mildly as he took off his ragged coat.

Jillian searched for any sign of injury. She was relieved to see he appeared unharmed. The memory of his ogling her while she undressed came to mind and she grinned, crossing her arms over her chest. "Fair is fair, your grace. You owe me this display."

"I would prefer to satisfy your curiosity some other time, madam," he said, as he handed his ragged shirt to Symmes.

Jillian feasted her eyes on his broad chest with its matting of dark hair, then forced herself to look away. "What happened to you?"

He waved his hand airily as he turned his back and began stripping off his breeches. "Nothing that a bath and a change of clothes can't remedy."

With her toe, Jillian poked at the pile of dirty clothes Symmes had dropped on the floor. They did not appear to be the quality of clothing that her husband usually wore, and they had hung on him as if they had been several sizes too big.

"These are not your clothes," she accused.

"If they are not mine, whose would they be?" he asked coolly as he turned to face her.

Jillian's gaze swept over the naked body of her husband, this time drinking him in. He was magnificently formed, with muscled arms and chest narrowing to a taut stomach and hips and sinewy thighs. His manhood was proudly displayed before her. The memory of what he could make her feel with that body caused her blood to heat. She remembered how he felt beneath her fingers, how hard those muscles were, how crisp that dark sprinkling of hair. A throbbing began between her thighs. She thrust the thoughts away. This was not the time.

Symmes stepped between them and held up a towel. He murmured in embarrassed agony, "Please, your grace."

Jillian turned away to give Symmes and herself some relief. Her gaze landed on the pile of dirty clothes. "Why were you wearing such rags?" she asked.

"I enjoy mingling with the poor folk to find out how they are getting along," he said, as if it were quite obvious.

Jillian did not believe him. She swung around. "You can't be serious."

He shrugged and moved past her to his dressing room where a bath waited. "Believe what you wish."

Fascinated by this side of her husband, Jillian followed. Her instincts told her he was not telling her the truth. Despite Symmes' scowl of disapproval, she watched Dunbary climb into his bath.

She decided to go along with his charade. "Mingling with the poor is very commendable."

He squinted up at her through the water that Symmes poured over his head. "An interesting tidbit that I'm sure you will tell Rystoke."

"How...?" she stuttered in surprise that he knew she had to report to her guardian. She sniffed in offense. "I'll do no such thing."

He grunted in disbelief.

Jillian motioned for Symmes to leave them. She quietly moved to the tub and began soaping her husband's hair.

"You don't believe me." She massaged his neck with her thumbs. She would use his seductive technique against him. Perhaps he would divulge some of *his* secrets.

Adrian's shrug was dispassionate. "You may tell him whatever you wish. He won't discover any secrets of mine."

"Then you hide things from me?" Her hands slid down from his neck to his shoulders and rubbed the muscles there. The feel of him beneath her fingers was intoxicating.

"Why should I trust you when you withhold secret correspondence that was meant for me?" he demanded.

"How do I know that you do not commit some treachery?" She rubbed her thumbs up and down the tight cords in the back of his neck.

His chuckle was sardonic. "Do you really believe I am involved in something treacherous and underhanded? What of Rystoke? Is he as pure as the lily?"

"I don't know." She let her hands slip down his chest where she created a thick lather in the matting of hair there.

"Always denying knowledge," he murmured as he caught her hands. "If you don't stop bathing me, you will end up in the tub with me, my little innocent."

"We have to be at Lady Matilda's soon," she reminded him without much conviction.

He ran his hands up and down her arms. The sensation was delicious.

"I think Lady Matilda can wait this once." He guided her around to the side of the tub.

"No, we really must go." Jillian shook her head. "I am all dressed, and all of Dory's hard work will be for naught." She tried to pull out of his grasp. The fear of a drenching was not all that made her want to be free of him. Something in his manner made her wary, as though he were keeping himself on a tight leash.

"I will give Dory a bonus," he said. "It is time you learned how risky it is to play with fire, my pixie."

With a jerk, he pulled her against the side of the tub. Jillian lost her balance. With a cry of surprise and a splash, she landed across his lap. As she tried to wriggle out of the bath, one of his hands wound up beneath her dress on her thigh. With the other hand, he cradled her head.

"My gown! I am soaked!" she protested, very aware of that warm hand inching upward along her skin.

"Shh. The servants will hear you," he warned. "You would not want them gossiping about your scandalous behavior."

She gasped in outrage. "*You* pulled me into the bath."

"But I am supposed to be where I am. You are not." His eyes held a dangerous gleam.

"Please." She tried to reason with him. "We will be so very late."

"Not if we are quick. And your wiggling about will make everything go quicker." He grinned wickedly.

Jillian reached behind her, grabbed the pitcher of water Symmes had left for rinsing, and dumped it over his head. He sputtered and coughed, but he did not release her.

"Vixen," he muttered as the hand beneath her dress found her most sensitive spot.

"We can't do this in a tub," she protested weakly as pleasure began streaking through her.

"Why not?" His mouth captured hers and shut off any further argument she might have made.

Jillian realized there was no use fighting. She loved what he did to her, how he made her feel. His touch, his kiss made her want whatever he did. Despite the odd undercurrent of anger she sensed in him, she craved him. She kicked off her shoes and gave herself up to the mastery of this man.

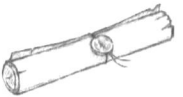

CHAPTER 14

That evening, Jillian wandered through the guests crowding Lady Jersey's elegant salon. She smiled at various acquaintances as she moved toward the window seat in the back of the room. All she wanted was to go home, but Adrian had insisted that they make an appearance at the fashionable gathering. This strange impulse of his to be in the midst of society puzzled her, for when she had first met him, she had sensed that he cared little for the glitter of the fashionable set. But that afternoon at tea, when Lady Matilda had asked how long they would remain at home in seclusion, he had answered that they were not. The lady had raised her eyebrows, for newly-wed couples did not appear in society so soon. Even his grandmother's censure did not dissuade him from insisting they appear at Lady Jersey's.

Jillian finally reached the window seat and sat down with a sigh. Not only was she tired from their arrival from Dunbary, but her husband's love-making was enough to wear out the most wanton of women. A blush crept into her cheeks at the memory of their bath together. Despite her sopping, clinging dress, Dunbary had quite thoroughly taken her senses to a fever pitch before he relented and gave her release. She had been clay beneath his touch, allowing him to do as he pleased, and delighting in every minute. In return, she could not get enough of him, needing him as much as she needed air to breathe.

She clasped her hands in her lap and ducked her head. She had behaved like a strumpet. How could she have been so wild with a man who cared so little for her? What must he think of her?

"May I bestow my best wishes on the lady at her propitious marriage?" a deep voice asked.

187

Startled from her thoughts, Jillian jerked up her head and saw Kip bowing before her.

"Kip! How wonderful to see you." She swept her skirt aside to make room on the window seat. "Please, sit down."

With a smile, he sat beside her. "It seems we are destined to sit together on window seats," he observed.

Jillian waved her hand vaguely at the gathering before her. "I am not up to this tonight, but my husband insisted we come."

"Did he abandon you?" he asked, as he swept the crowd with a glance.

Jillian shook her head. "No, not at all. I am tired and did not wish to impose on his enjoyment." For some reason, she felt the need to defend Dunbary.

"I was very surprised to hear of your wedding. I thought it was not for some weeks yet. I was out of the city and never had the chance to call on you before you left for Dunbary."

"Our plans changed suddenly." Jillian looked away to hide her embarrassment. She caught a glimpse of a woman with pale, blond hair. Lady Avingdon. Next to her was a familiar dark head. Was that why her husband wanted so much to come tonight? To meet his mistress? A strange, ugly feeling twisted within her. Hot rage followed swiftly. If he could come here and openly flaunt his mistress before her, especially after what they had shared that afternoon, then she could repay him in kind. Turning back to Kip, she said, "You must come and visit me now that I have returned from Dunbary. My husband is away from the house quite often and I am very lonely. I miss seeing my friends." She placed her hand on his. "Please. I need someone to talk to."

Kip gave an uncomfortable little cough. "Jillian, you are a married woman. I couldn't."

"Please," she said again.

"Only if you are sure the duke will not mind," he said with concern. "I refuse to stand against him on the field of honor."

"He will not mind," she said flatly.

Kip took her hand. "Jillian," he began, then stopped.

"Please, come and visit me." With a smile, she withdrew her hand. "I must mingle with the guests so I do not disgrace my husband. Excuse me." She stood and walked into the crowd.

As Jillian neared the spot where Adrian and Lady Avingdon stood together, she saw her husband raise that lady's hand to his lips. Even from where she stood, Jillian could see the warmth in his eyes as he gazed at the lady. Hot rage and sharp pain swept through her. Adrian was *her* husband. Despite the circumstances that forced them to wed, he had no right to seduce another woman. She bit down on her lower lip to control her emotions and approached Dunbary and his mistress.

"So, my dear, you have decided to join us," Dunbary said as he appraised her coolly. "Had enough of your Scottish friend?"

Jillian gritted her teeth and smiled. How dare he insinuate that she was at fault? He was the one who flaunted his mistress before her so that everyone might see. She wanted to rake her nails down his handsome face. Instead, she said sweetly, "I fear I have a wretched headache, your grace. Could you please take me home?"

"Oh, you poor dear," Lady Avingdon exclaimed. "You must be exhausted after arriving in London only yesterday." She turned to Dunbary. "You must see to this poor child's health, Adrian. Why, if you had brought me back from Dunbary only last evening, I should not have ventured out for days."

Jillian smiled tightly and wondered how many times the lady had visited her husband's estate. "Oh, the trip was nothing," Jillian said, then confided wickedly, "but my husband is very — ah — virile." She blushed. "He quite exhausts me. You understand." She glanced at the lady to see if her remark struck home.

Instead of being angered, Lady Avingdon chuckled. "Take your husband home, dear. I won't keep him any longer from your marriage bed."

Jillian could not stop a flush of embarrassment from coloring her cheeks at Dunbary's raised eyebrows. With a murmured word, she excused herself to bid good-bye to her hostess. She hoped her husband would follow.

She waited for him in a corner of the entrance hall and tried to appear inconspicuous as people milled about and passed from one room to another. Absorbed as she was with her anger and humiliation, she did not hear anyone come up behind her.

"We meet again, Miss St. Clare," an accented voice said.

Jillian swung about. Before her stood the American, Cooper Stone.

He bowed and smiled. "We seem to be always running into each other. But, you are no longer Miss St. Clare, are you? My apologies. You are now the Duchess of Dunbary."

"You seem very well informed, sir," Jillian retorted coolly.

"I have excellent sources, duchess." He smiled and clasped his hands behind him. "For instance, I have heard that a certain piece of correspondence has come into your possession."

"I am sorry, sir, I don't understand what you are talking about." She flicked open her fan and scanned the crowd for her husband. Fear clutched at her. What did this man know about the letter she held?

Stone grasped her arm and forced her to look at him. "You do know what I am talking about," he growled. "You have the letter which was to be passed in secret to your husband."

"I have no such letter, sir," Jillian lied. She needed to decide quickly what to do with it.

Cooper Stone's eyes narrowed angrily. "Keep denying that you have the letter and something very serious could happen to your husband."

Terror raced through her at his words. Despite that, Jillian shook off his hand. "You try my patience, sir. I have no knowledge of this letter, and even if I did, my husband is perfectly capable of protecting himself."

The American bent close and whispered, "But can he protect himself from scandalous rumors that his wife was spawned on the wrong side of the blankets? He would be shunned."

The blood drained from Jillian's face as she stared up at him. "You wouldn't dare spread such a lie."

Cooper Stone merely smiled, bowed and moved away.

Soon after, Dunbary arrived at her side. His look was dark as he placed her wrap about her shoulders. Without a word, he took her by the elbow and guided her out of the house and into their waiting coach. Jillian, still trying to recover from the American's threat, thought her husband was angry at her for dragging him away from his mistress. Between the American's nastiness and Dunbary's pique, her temper soared. She was not about to let her husband get away with his churlishness and deceit.

As soon as the coach was underway, she turned on him. "How dare you flaunt that woman in my face?"

Dunbary whipped around to face her. "Don't say another word, madam," he ordered coldly. "Your conquests were many this evening."

"My conquests?" she gasped.

"I saw you chatting intimately with that Scot, and I saw the American whispering in your ear." His voice vibrated with his anger. "Did you invite them to sample your charms?"

"You cad!" she spat. "The only reason you wished to attend Lady Jersey's salon was to meet your mistress. I saw how you warmly kissed her fingertips. What else would you have kissed had you been alone?"

His hand snaked out and caught the neckline of her dress. With a yank, he pulled her across the seat so that she was pressed up against him. "Lady Avingdon is not my mistress," he said between clenched teeth. "That relationship ended when I married you, madam. But perhaps I should renew it, since I find that you seek satisfaction for your needs in places other than in my bed."

"I do not!" Jillian denied hotly as she tried to pry his fingers from her gown.

"Liar," he said flatly.

"Let me go," she demanded. She wanted to pummel him, but at the same time, the feel of his fingers against her breast was doing strange things to her insides.

"I think not." His free hand pulled up the hem of her dress and slipped beneath to her naked thigh. "I think you should know how it feels to be a whore, for that is what you will be if you continue on your present path. You will have to meet with your lovers on the sly. Coupling with them will be urgent, done quickly, in hiding." He pushed her back across the seat and covered her with his body.

Jillian was aghast at his crude statements and his cruel intent. She pushed at his shoulders. "No, please." Despite her pleading denial, his touch was sending tendrils of pleasure through her.

"Why not? You should learn how to make love in a coach. It is the safest place for a whore to meet with her lover." His hand dipped into the neckline of her dress and cupped her breast. With his thumb and finger, he squeezed its hard nub. His other hand slipped to the apex of her thighs where she was wet and warm.

Jillian gasped as pleasure shot outward from his touch. "No, not like this," she cried.

"Yes," he whispered. "Like this."

His mouth came down hard on hers, devouring, claiming. Her ardor shriveled at the onslaught. This was not the husband who had so tenderly introduced her to making love. This was a man whose demons rode him hard. Somehow, she found the strength to push him away.

"Adrian!" She used his given name as a rebuke, not like the only other time she had used it, sighing in passion.

He froze and stared down at her, as if just now seeing her. His eyes squeezed shut. Without a word, he sat up and retreated to his corner of the seat.

"Cover yourself, Jillian. We are almost home." His voice was a monotone, devoid of expression or feeling. He stared out the coach window.

With an effort, Jillian pulled herself to a sitting position. She felt as if she had just been run over by the very coach in which she rode. Straightening her clothes and smoothing her hair as best she could, she glanced quickly at her husband's set profile, then turned to regard the passing scene out her own window.

What had just happened? Something had gone very wrong. She had thought to put her husband in his place concerning his mistress. Instead he had accused her of infidelity. The injustice made her want to scream. Her wanton reaction to his kiss made her want to disappear.

She peered out at the houses they passed. Their dark façades reminded her of her husband—stony on the outside with hidden depths within. She would not open herself to him again. She would keep her soul intact. Her hand covered her mother's brooch where it was pinned to the shoulder of her dress. No daughter of Lilith St. Clare would allow a man to own her.

The coach came to a stop before the lit entrance of Dunbary's house. Without a word, he climbed down from the coach, then turned to offer his hand to her. As if nothing had occurred between them, she accepted his aid. Together, they entered the house.

After handing their wraps to Boggs, Dunbary once again offered his hand in silence to Jillian. Curious about what he might want of her, she accepted it. He led her into his study and closed the door behind them. He moved to a side table where a decanter of brandy and several glasses stood. After pouring himself a portion, he tossed it down in one swallow. Jillian wondered at his inner turmoil.

He turned slowly to face her. "It seems that we have made a mistake," he said.

Jillian silently agreed. His mistake of seeing his mistress. Her mistake of attending the salon.

"We do not seem to complement each other," he went on.

Jillian's breath stopped.

He placed his glass on the table behind him, turned back to her, leaned against the table and crossed his arms at his chest. "Perhaps it would be best if we led separate lives."

A sharp pain arrowed through her heart. She hid it with an outrageously scandalous suggestion. "If you wish a divorce, your grace, you may have one." The only way to obtain a divorce was for one partner to accuse the other of adultery before all of Parliament, laying out their sins before the world. She wondered which of them would accuse the other.

Dunbary pushed away from the table and stalked toward her. His eyes glinted with angry menace. "There will be no divorce," he said. "Would you destroy the Dunbary title with the scandal?"

She lifted a shoulder. "I was only suggesting—"

"No divorce," he interrupted.

Jillian nodded once. "If that is what you wish."

"We shall lead separate lives," he dictated. "You may come and go as you wish. But if there is the least hint of scandal with that Scot or anyone else, I will send you to Dunbary for the rest of your days."

Jillian's temper rose with each word. His unfair assumption that she was having an affair with Kip angered her, but his dictatorial ultimatum turned her wrath icy. She would not be treated like a troublesome piece of chattel.

Her hands clenched into fists. Coldly, she said, "Have no fear, your grace, I will not cause you any scandal. And if there is a child from our coupling, I will not bother you with its upbringing. But what of you? Will you run back to your mistress? I'm sure tongues will wag when that becomes known." Before he could respond, she said, "I find I am quite exhausted. Please excuse me." She swept from the room.

She was numb. She had not known what to expect from marriage, but it had not been this. How could a man who had so gently, warmly, and thoughtfully introduced her to making love become so cold? As she sought the sanctuary of her room, as the tears fell, she decided tomorrow she would deal with this curve in her destiny.

Adrian silently watched her go. When she closed the door behind her, he felt as if a part of his life had been sliced away. He had done the right thing by giving Jillian her freedom. Then why did he feel so bloody awful?

He had been enraged when he saw her with that Scot and then with the American. A reincarnation of Beatrice rose up before him with her taunting, profligate ways, flaunting what she did before his father, making him miserable. He wanted to hurt and punish Jillian in some way. That was what he had started out to do in the coach, but when he had touched her, all reason had fled. His rage had become mixed up with his need for her. He had nearly violated his own wife. His eyes squeezed shut as guilt wrenched his heart. Then he poured out another glass of brandy and downed its contents.

He had made a mess of their marriage. Sighing deeply, he picked up the decanter and sagged into a chair before the fire. Suppose there was a child? Would she keep it from him? He had certainly made her angry enough. His plan not to impregnate her had gone to hell. Every time he touched her, his brain shut down. All he wanted was more of her. Her scent, her sighs, the feel of her beneath him. She was too delicious.

The thought of a child whom he might never see disheartened him. Guilt and pain sat like rabid demons on his shoulders. He splashed more brandy into his glass and gulped it down. The only way to erase what had occurred this night was to drown in drink. He could not face the knowledge that he had married another woman like his mother. That was why he had given Jillian her freedom. Only an emotional distance from her would give him the peace of mind he sought. He understood why his father had drunk himself to death. It was the only protection he had against the pain.

He suspected that with her visits to Rystoke, she was passing along information. And she still had not told him the contents of the letter. She might even have lied about destroying it. Whether she had burned it or not, he was certain he would never learn its contents. He refilled his glass. Tonight, England's security could go to hell.

Tomorrow, Jillian would become an intimate stranger. After he wiped away the pain.

Alone in her room, Jillian unpinned the brooch from her dress and laid it on the dressing table. The amethysts and diamonds winked at her in the light of the candle. Gently, she ran her fingers across the hard stones and the gold filigree. *Oh, mother, what have I done?*

The stones gave her no reply. She pulled off her shoes and walked to the huge wardrobe. The carpet was damp beneath her feet. Thoughtfully, she rubbed her toes back and forth across the spot. She had dropped her wet dress here after making love with her husband that afternoon in the tub. That would never happen again.

Tears clouded her eyes. His touch had been gentle as usual, had aroused her as always, but there had been unleashed anger in him. Something was tormenting him And it concerned her. Recalling his ragged clothes when he'd returned from his outing earlier in the day, she wondered what sort of secret mission he was on and what he'd learned.

She sighed deeply and swiped the tears from her cheeks. Perhaps the pain at her husband's cold words came from her wounded pride. She had thought entering society would be easy, an enjoyable lark. She had failed miserably at that, making many a *faux pas* and creating scandal at every turn. Now, it seemed, she had failed at the rest of her life, as well. Her husband did not love her. He could be charming and kind, and he could turn her into a quivering mass of desire at his touch, but that was not love.

She swiped her toes across the damp carpet again and thought back to that afternoon. She had succumbed to her husband's desire because she had wanted his touch, but more than that, she had wanted him to want her. She wanted to feel close to him, connected. And his rejection made her feel pain and despair.

Because she loved him.

The realization made her gasp and then brought a fresh spurt of tears. But he did not love her. How could he when he had made the outrageous suggestion that they lead separate lives? She dashed away her tears. Crying did not solve anything.

She rang for Dory to help her undress. Tomorrow, she would begin to build her life without her husband. Perhaps, along the way, she might discover the key to make their marriage work, although she held little hope of that.

For now, she would avoid her husband and his cold rage, and bury the deep, searing pain at his harsh words.

CHAPTER 15

Jillian stared morosely out the window to the small park across the road. Her needlepoint sat unheeded in her lap. A week had passed since that awful confrontation with Dunbary. He came and went as if nothing had changed. He left early, returned to change for the evening, then was gone until the small hours of the morning.

She, on the other hand, remained at home. She could not bring herself to go visiting, as she knew she should, and she had declined what few invitations she had received. The situation between her and Dunbary distressed and embarrassed her. And angered her. She had done nothing wrong, nothing to cause the duke to set down the present rules of their marriage.

What had occurred at Lady Jersey's salon had been so innocent. Except she still had the letter. She never should have kept it. If she had tossed it back out the window that night at the ball, she would not be in this marriage with a man who wanted nothing to do with her. She had to decide what to do with that letter. And soon.

A knock came at the door and Boggs appeared.

"You have a visitor, my lady," he announced. "Mr. Kenric Giles."

A surge of excitement ran through her. "Tell him I will be right down," she told the major-domo. "And please, bring tea and some port for Mr. Giles."

He bowed and left. Jillian checked her appearance in the glass. She bit her lips and pinched her cheeks to bring some color to them, then went to greet Kip.

He stood when she entered the salon, and she held out her hands to him in greeting. "Kip, what a delightful surprise." As he took her hands and bowed over them, she smiled for the first time in days.

"You brighten my day, as always, your grace," he murmured.

She laughed and guided Kip to the sofa. "Such formality."

Boggs entered with the tea tray and a decanter of port. As Jillian poured the beverages, she said, "I'm so glad you have come to visit. Tell me, what have you been up to? I see you once, then you disappear. Are you doing something illegal, Mr. Giles?" she teased and handed him a glass.

Kip regarded her over the top of his glass. His expression was bland, but something in his eyes told her she had come close to the truth. She realized she knew very little about this man, despite their easy friendship.

He swallowed the rich port and smiled. "Your husband keeps an excellent cellar," he said, changing the subject.

Jillian placed her cup and saucer down on the table with a clatter. "My husband keeps up the appearance of a perfect gentleman, while in truth he is the most barbarous of cads." She had not meant to say anything about Dunbary, but the wound of their separation was still too raw, too close to the surface. Embarrassment at what she had revealed heated her cheeks. To keep her tongue under control, she gritted her teeth and stared into the fire on the hearth.

Kip's hand closed about hers. "Tell me, Jillian," he prompted quietly. "I want to help."

The warmth from his touch was reassuring. Like taking hold of a lifeline, she grasped his fingers. She glanced down at his hand, tanned and dark against her fairness. It was a strong, well-formed hand, a hand that could protect. His presence soothed her. Words tumbled out.

"My husband and I have an agreement, made the night of Lady Jersey's salon. We will lead separate lives. Our marriage is in name only. He cannot stand the sight of me." Saying the words aloud released the pain which she had locked away. Tears teetered on her lashes. She had not wanted to reveal the awful truth to anyone. She had too much pride to admit defeat in a marriage that had barely begun. But confiding in Kip was easy. He was a friend. She was comfortable with him, and so she felt no embarrassment at her tears. The anguish she felt over her failed marriage cut at her heart like a thousand knives.

Kip put his arm around her. "I'm sorry, Jillian. Please let me be your friend."

His words comforted. Because of her guardian, she had schooled herself to hide her feelings. But for some reason, she trusted Kip. His strong, comforting arm about her broke through her dam of reserve.

She clung to his coat and let her tears flow. If only she had not picked up that secret letter... If only her mother's brooch had not caught in Dunbary's coat...

She should not be crying on Kip's shoulder. He should not be holding her so close. Their position was quite improper. She pulled back.

"I'm sorry," she said with a shaky smile. "I don't know what possessed me." She searched for her handkerchief.

Kip pulled out his and handed it to her. "Here, use this."

Gratefully, Jillian took it. "I must look a fright," she murmured, as she dabbed at her eyes.

"You look wonderful." He pushed a stray lock of hair away from her cheek.

"I have cried all over you." She brushed her hand across the damp shoulder of his coat. "I have ruined your coat."

Kip caught her hand in a gentle squeeze and smiled. "It's nothing."

"Oh, Kip," she sighed. "You are such a kind man."

She placed her hand against his cheek, clean-shaven, smooth and warm beneath her touch. Her husband's words echoed in her mind: *There will be no divorce, but neither will we live as husband and wife. We will lead separate lives.* Her husband would retreat to the arms of his mistress. She had no one.

"Why couldn't I have fallen in love with you?" she whispered.

Kip jerked away. "No, Jillian," he said.

Mortified at what she had done, she jumped to her feet. "I'm sorry," she said in a strangled whisper. "I don't know what came over me." She twisted his handkerchief in her fingers.

"Jillian." He reached out to her.

She stepped away, wishing she could disappear. "You must think me quite forward."

"No, Jillian." Kip rose and followed her to where she stood wringing her hands in the middle of the room. "That's not what I think of you."

She could not look at him. "I am so foolish."

"No, you are not." He took her hands. "I am very fond of you."

She dropped her gaze to their hands and pulled away. "I understand. You don't have to explain. I have been much too forward. I should not be crying about my failed marriage to you.""

"No." He ran a hand through his hair. "That's not it."

On the verge of tears again, she kept her face averted as she said, "It's all right, Kip. I told you, I understand."

"No, you don't understand at all." With gentle pressure, he turned her to face him. "Come, sit with me." He led her back to the sofa. "There's something I must tell you."

Puzzled, Jillian sat beside him. "What is it? Are you in some kind of trouble?"

He smiled. "No, I'm not in any trouble. At least, not yet." He touched the brooch pinned to the shoulder of her dress. "Do you know how your mother came to own such an expensive piece of jewelry?" he asked.

Confused at his change of subject, she shook her head.

"She received it as a gift from your father," he said.

Jillian's frown deepened. "How do you know that?"

"Because he told me." A corner of his mouth twitched.

"You knew my father?" she gasped. This news was more wonderful than anything she had expected.

"Quite well, actually." His head dipped.

"Oh, Kip!" she exclaimed. "You must tell me everything about him. What did he look like? Was he kind? Did he love my mother as much as she loved him?"

At her last question, surprise flitted across Kip's face. "I will tell you everything I can about him, but not right now." He took her two hands in his and held them tightly. "Jillian, your father is still alive."

Jillian stared at him a moment, not sure if she had heard him correctly. "Alive?" she whispered, not daring to say the word aloud.

Kip nodded.

She was speechless. Her father was alive. Not dead. Rystoke had implied the same thing. But then suspicion descended on her euphoria like a pall. She had dealt too long with her guardian and his torments to believe something this wonderful could actually be true. And Kip's own secrecy added to her suspicion. His sudden appearances and disappearances were odd. What did she really know about him?

"How do you know this?" she demanded. "How do you know he is my father and not some imposter hoping for a handout now that I have wed a wealthy man? If he is truly alive, why would my mother lie and let me believe him dead? Why are you telling me this? Why do you wish to hurt me with such a lie?" She pulled out of his grasp.

"I'm not lying, Jillian. Your father is very much alive." Kip's level gaze spoke the truth.

She was not convinced. "What proof does this man have that he is my father?"

"You have the proof, Jillian," he said.

Confusion creased her brow. "I?"

"The brooch you wear." Once again, he touched the gold filigree and sparkling stones.

Jillian protectively covered the piece of jewelry. "How is this proof?"

"It belonged to your mother, did it not?" he asked.

Jillian nodded.

"And your mother left it to you when she died?"

"Yes." Her answer was subdued at the painful memory.

"It was how I found you, Jillian," he said. "I was told to look for a woman who wore a distinctive brooch rendered like a stalk of heather."

"My father sent you to find me?" Jillian's eyes widened at the thought that perhaps Kip was telling the truth, that someone in the world cared for her.

Kip nodded. "He did."

"But why now, after all these years?" she demanded.

"Your mother sent him a letter just before she died telling him where you might be found." His statement landed like a cannon ball in the middle of the room.

In shock, Jillian stood and wandered aimlessly to the long windows overlooking the small, formal garden. She did not see the clipped greenery nor the perfect beds of flowers spread out before her. All she saw was her mother's pale face against the pillow as she lay dying. *Why, mother? Why did you hide this from me?*

She turned abruptly at another thought. "Why did my father send *you* to find me? What connection do you have to him?"

Kip hesitated before he shrugged and said, "I have known him since I was a wee babe. He thought it prudent that a younger man make the journey to London to find you."

"Journey from where?" she asked.

"From Ayton, in the Borders, near the east coast of Scotland," he said.

"Scotland," she murmured. She realized now why the pipes Kip had been playing when she first met him had seemed so familiar to her. "Tell me of him," she demanded.

"Your father is a kind man, concerned for the people in his charge," Kip began. "He is a laird, the Scottish equivalent of an English earl. I believe he loved your mother very much, and he grieved at their separation."

"What caused them to separate?" she asked.

Kip took a sip from his glass of port. "It is not my place to answer that."

"But you know, don't you?" Jillian probed.

"Yes." He nodded.

Jillian's thoughts raced. What had made Kip suddenly reveal this information to her? Why had her mother led her to believe that her father was dead? Why had her mother lied to her?

With a sigh of confusion, she turned back to the window. She wanted to believe Kip, but his announcement that her father still lived was contrary to what she had believed all her life. Kip's apparent concern for her, combined with his odd absences, were strange at the very least, suspect at the most. What secrets of his own was he hiding?

If Kip was lying, what did he hope to gain? Her eyes focused on the very large garden before her. Something clicked in her brain. She was wed to a wealthy, influential man, despite the fact that they were estranged.

Jillian spun away from the window. "What do you want?" she demanded coldly.

The look of dismay that crossed Kip's face confirmed her worst suspicions. He did want something. Only a man who had something to hide could look that guilty. Why was he doing this to her? She had thought he was her friend.

He carefully placed his glass on the table beside him, then stood and approached her. "I want nothing," he said quietly and reached for her hand. "I only want you to know the truth."

Jillian evaded him. "What proof do you have that my father is alive and that he is truly my father? *Who are you?*"

He backed away a step and motioned to the sofa. "You might wish to sit down for this."

"I will stand." Jillian was cool and determined.

"As you wish." Kip again ran a hand through his hair, took a deep breath, and said quietly, "Jillian, I am your brother."

She remained absolutely still. She did not blink, and she barely breathed. Of all the things Kip might have said, that was the last she expected. If it were true, that would explain the immediate sense of rapport she had felt with him. If it were true... She grabbed the back of a chair for support as her knees went weak. "My brother?"

"Aye. Y'r brother." He lapsed into his native burr.

"We share the same mother and father?" Her voice trembled with her shock.

"The same father, different mothers."

Jillian sank into the chair. "Tell me."

Kip stood before her. "As I told you before, there are some things your father — our father — must explain himself. I can tell you the events. He must explain the reasons. Some of the events may be painful to you."

Jillian looked into his gray eyes. His expression was open, unguarded. Somehow, she knew deep inside that this man did not lie. He waited for her permission to begin. "Tell me," she repeated.

He crouched before her and sandwiched her cold hand between his. This time, she did not reject his touch. His gaze remained on their connected hands.

"Our father wed my mother when she was just a girl, younger than you are now," he said quietly. "She was a sweet Scottish lass who bore her husband three sons. I was her last child. Something went wrong during my birth. She was never the same after that. Her mind was gone, and she retreated back into her childhood.

"I was three when my father brought home your mother. She was kind to all of us and became our mother. You arrived within a year of her coming. I remember you as a tiny little babe, all pink and white and gold." He looked up at her and smiled. "You are still lovely." He dropped his gaze to their hands again. "Your mother left suddenly and took you with her when you were about two years old. She disappeared, telling no one where she was going and taking only her maid with her. My father was frantic with grief and worry. Finally several months later, a letter came from your mother. I don't know what it said. I was only five or six, and I did not understand such things. After it arrived, my father seemed to shrivel up inside. Then just over a year ago, he received the letter your mother had written before she died. It invigorated him. He had found a reason for living again — you, his daughter." He met her eyes with a candid gaze.

Jillian stared at him as she pondered his story. Finally, she asked, "Why did my mother run away?"

Kip's gaze slid away. "I was never told the reason, but I have guessed." He paused. "My mother, our father's first wife, was still alive when your mother ran away."

Jillian sat in shock as Kip's last bit of information burrowed into her brain. Finally, in a monotone, she restated what he had just told her. "Your — our — father married my mother when he was still wed to another woman."

Kip nodded once. "Yes."

Jillian sat frozen. Kip rose and disengaged his hand. Hers sat limply on her knee. Here was another piece to the puzzle of her mother. The information Kip shared opened up many questions. And revealed one very numbing truth — she was illegitimate.

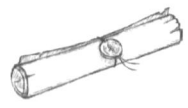

204

CHAPTER 16

Illegitimate. The word curled around her brain like a venomous snake. Was this what Rystoke had been hinting at with his threat? Would he use this to ruin her? The exchange of gossip at Dunbary's grandmother's about Viscount Chombly's broken engagement came back to her in a rush. She was no better than the scheming adventuress who had tricked the man into a betrothal. If Dunbary ever discovered… No, she could not think about that. The consequences were too awful to imagine.

"Jillian."

Kip's voice made her jump. He knelt before her again.

"What is it? What frightens you?" He placed his hand gently over hers.

Jillian looked at him, but instead of Kip, she saw Dunbary's cold, angry face as he threw her out of his house. "You should leave," she said, unable to speak above a hoarse whisper. "My husband… the duke…" She swallowed, fighting to make the words come. "He will be back soon. You should not be here."

Kip stood. "All right, I'll leave if you wish," he said. "But if you need me, I want you to send for me. Here is my card." He placed the calling card in her lifeless fingers. "Promise you will send for me if anything troubles you."

She stared at the engraved lettering on the white card in her hand, her brain stunned. Above Kip's name was his family's crest, and depicted in the upper right quadrant of the shield was a stalk of heather that had been copied into a brooch of gold, diamonds, and amethysts. The brooch she now wore pinned to her dress, proof of his declaration.

"Promise me, Jillian," he urged, his words demanding her attention.

She looked up at him and nodded.

He pulled her to her feet and wrapped his arms about her. Limply, she leaned against him.

"I am your brother, Jillian," he whispered. "I will protect you."

"I know," she said, her voice muffled by his coat. She pulled away and smiled bravely. "You must go now. Quickly, before he returns. I need to be alone. I will send a note round tomorrow to let you know when you may come again."

He kissed her cheek and left. Jillian sank back into the chair as soon as he was gone. She tried to absorb everything she had just learned. Her father was alive. She had a brother. She was illegitimate. That last made her thoughts stumble. Her perception of herself shifted. She was not the product of a legal marriage, but the child of a woman who had been duped. Her world had abruptly tilted, and she felt very much off-balance. She shook her head and heaved a sigh. She would never have been able to predict the events of this afternoon.

The clock in the hall struck the hour. Dunbary would be home soon. She did not want him to see her in such a distracted state. Despite their estrangement, they still treated each other with civility. He would question her about her odd mood. Quickly, she left the salon to go upstairs to her room to avoid him.

As she crossed the hall, she saw Baron von Heisburg before the door to her husband's study. She wondered if he had been about to sneak inside. His calculating, cruel eyes coupled with his smooth manner made her uneasy. The relationship he had with Dunbary's mother made her uncomfortable.

Suspicious of his intent, she asked, "May I help you with something, baron?"

He stepped away from the door and blocked her way. "Maybe, ve could haf little chat, ya?" he said with a suave smile.

Jillian forced a smile. "Perhaps some other time. You must forgive me. I have a headache, and I really must lie down," she lied.

"I vish fery much to speak vith you. Perhaps you vould vish to lie down later, ya?" He remained firmly in her way.

"Please, I really must go," Jillian said as she tried once more to get past him. "Later, at dinner perhaps, we will chat."

He caught her arm. "You vill not vish me to tell your husband of the young man who just left. The young man, he is fery handsome, ya?"

Jillian stared up into the cold blue eyes of the German. Apprehension slithered through her. What could this man want?

Von Heisburg shook his head. "It is fery sad vhen husband pays no attention to his vife, ya? You must be fery lonely."

"What do you want, baron?" she asked coolly.

"Only chat. I only vish to gife you chance to chat vith me." He smiled innocently.

The German's grip on her arm and his threat to tell Dunbary of Kip's visit contradicted his mild words. They convinced her to agree to his request. She nodded once. "All right. We will chat. And please let go of my arm."

The German's smile did not reach his eyes, and he did not release her. "Not here. In my room."

Jillian frowned at his selection for a place to talk, but something in his manner warned her not to protest. With a hand clutching her arm, he escorted her up the stairs. She was not able to shake off his hold until they reached the door leading to his room. Smiling blandly, he waved her inside. Jillian hesitated only a moment before entering. If he tried anything unseemly, she could scream. The servants would run to her aid.

She put space between them as he closed the door. Being alone with this man in his room was quite improper, and she did not like the way he had coerced her to be there. Nervously, she watched as he leaned back against the door and crossed his arms at his chest.

"So, baron, what do you wish to chat about?" she asked.

"Your husband." The German's answer was flat and direct.

"My husband?" she repeated in surprise. "Why?"

He pushed away from the door and stepped closer. "I vill not— how do you say?—beat about the bush. I vish some information."

"What kind of information?" Jillian's suspicions were instantly raised.

"Information such a man in his position might hafe," he said.

"I don't understand." Jillian was truly puzzled.

"Of course you do. I know you are not stupid voman. I know how you tricked your husband into marrying you." The German's gaze bored into her.

"That is absurd," Jillian said with an insulted sniff. "I did no such thing."

"Vhatever you say." The German's smile was loaded with scorn. "I think ve may be useful to each other."

"I can think of no way that you can help me, baron," she said coolly. "I would like to leave now."

"I am fery goot at keeping secrets." He winked suggestively.

"A useful talent," she murmured sarcastically and started towards the door.

The German did not move out of her way. "*Nein, nein,*ve hafe not finished." He shook his head. "Do not be in such hurry. I hafe bit more to say."

Jillian gestured for him to continue.

He smiled smoothly. "Your husband, he is spy, ya?"

With an effort, Jillian kept her face expressionless. "I don't know what you are talking about."

"Come, come, Jillian—I may call you that, ya?" he wheedled.

"No, you may not." She tilted her chin to a haughty level.

He ignored her protest. "Ve are both grown people. It is no secret that your husband vorks for the Foreign Office."

She congratulated herself on not reacting. How did she not know *that* about Dunbary?

"He is spy," the German concluded.

"I think you are quite mad, baron. My husband is no spy," she said firmly as she tried to reconcile all she knew about her husband with what she had just learned.

He showed his teeth in a predatory grin. "Perhaps. Perhaps not." He stepped closer.

Jillian stepped back. His threatening manner made her wary.

"You like this handsome young man who just left, ya?" he speculated. "You vould not like me to tell your husband about this handsome young man."

Jillian shook her head. "I am sorry, baron, but he won't care."

With lightning speed, he grabbed her arms. "Ya. He vill." With each word he gave her a little shake.

Frightened at his sudden ferocity, Jillian tried to break his grasp. "Please, you're hurting me."

The German released her and backed off a step. "Forgife me. You must understand I do not vish to harm you. But you must do as I ask."

Alarm streaked through her. This man was both desperate and dangerous. Hiding her fear, she asked, "What is it that you want me to do?"

"I vant information from your husband." He laid out his demand as if only asking for another cup of tea.

This man was a spy, just like Dunbary. But he was obviously not on the same side as her husband, whatever side that was. "Why do you wish this information?" she demanded.

"There are those who vill pay dearly for information known by man who vorks for the Foreign Office," he said.

Jillian nearly choked at his casual reference to Dunbary's position. She forced herself not to react.

"If you do this little thing for me," he went on, "I vill see that you vill get revard. *I must hafe this information.*"

She caught a flash of dangerous desperation in the man's eyes before they became cool and calculating. Despite her fear of him, she asked calmly, "What exactly do you wish to know?"

"Then you vill do this little thing for me?" His words were eager, hopeful.

"Perhaps," she hedged. "It depends on what you want."

"I vish to know if England vill go to var vith America," he stated baldly.

Jillian blinked her shock, although she wondered why she was surprised by his demand. Everyone seemed to be concerned with that question. A war between America and England would naturally affect most nations on the Continent.

She would never pass that information along to him even if she had it. Not wanting to provoke him, she said, "I don't know how I can get this information."

"You vill find vay, ya?" His words held an undertone of threat.

Jillian fussed with her sleeve, pretending indifference. "It may be some time before I can get any information that would be useful to you."

The German merely smiled. "I vill vait, but not too long." He stepped back, allowing her access to the door.

She did not like that smile.

As she slipped past him and murmured her excuses, he caught her arm. "Ve vill speak again soon, ya?"

She did not answer as she pulled out of his grasp and made her escape.

By the time she reached her room, her head throbbed. The German was a dangerous threat. She did not want him telling lies about her seeing another man, especially now that she had learned that Kip was her brother. She had to protect Kip as well as herself.

If her husband did work for the Foreign Office, then she had to protect him as well. She wanted to believe that Dunbary was working for the English, but was the German telling the truth? If her husband's loyalties lay elsewhere, why would von Heisburg want information from him? She would have to find a way to discover the truth.

In the meantime, she somehow had to avoid von Heisburg's demand, for she would never reveal anything to the German. Finding him at the door to Dunbary's study made her wonder where else he had been snooping. His presence in the house and his threat made her decide to send the ragdoll containing that vital, secret letter to Kip for safekeeping. In the meantime, she would learn where her husband's loyalties lay. She had not thought her life could get any more complicated. How wrong she had been.

She rang for Dory to help her deal with the very real headache that pounded in her temples, and decided for now, everyone could go to blazes.

When she entered the dining room that evening, Boggs greeted her solemnly as she headed toward her usual lonely seat at the foot of the large oval table. Her place had not been set there. Her stomach dropped. Had Dunbary decided to send her away? A discreet cough from the majordomo drew her attention to the head of the table. He stood behind a chair to the right of Dunbary's usual place, waiting to seat her. She saw a setting laid out for her there, as well as one at the head of the table.

As she sat, she asked, "Is his grace dining at home this evening, Boggs?"

"Yes, he is," a dry voice said from the doorway.

Jillian glanced up in surprise and watched her husband enter the room. She watched his graceful walk, like that of a predatory animal, and his noble profile, like some ancient warrior god. He was dressed impeccably, as usual, which emphasized his handsome maleness. The sight of him triggered memories of their love-making, of the feel of his hard muscles beneath her fingers, of his hungry mouth blazing across her skin. Jillian lowered her eyes. She could not torture herself with such thoughts. He had made it perfectly clear that he wanted nothing to do with her.

After he was seated, he took her hand and raised her fingers to his lips. "You are looking lovely this evening, Jillian."

In surprise at his compliment and his warm gesture, her mouth dropped open.

He chuckled. "Do I surprise you, my pixie?" He grinned wolfishly. "I truly enjoy surprising you. You appear so innocent when you are surprised."

Jillian snapped her mouth closed and pulled her fingers out of his grasp. She was not sure what his purpose was or what he meant by his remark, but she was determined not to be lulled into any false sense of complacency by his manner. Sensing some underlying reasons for his presence, she decided to let him direct the conversation. She signaled Boggs to begin serving.

"Since you have dined at home so little recently," she observed after Boggs had gone to fetch their meal, "I merely assumed that you would be dining out this evening as well."

"That is precisely why I decided to dine at home. With you." His topaz eyes seemed to gleam wickedly in the candlelight.

"I am pleased for your company, your grace," Jillian said demurely.

"Are you?" A dark brow arched upward.

"Of course." Jillian waited as Boggs poured wine and a footman served them. The interruption gave her a chance to gather her wits. When the majordomo had finished and retreated into a discreet corner, she went on, "My first duty is to your grace, to please you in all things. If it pleases you to dine at home, then I am pleased."

At that, Dunbary released a bark of laughter. "If only I believed that rubbish. You do not have the temperament of a lord's subservient mistress. You are more vixen than dove."

Jillian's eyes flashed. "And if I am, your grace, is all the fault mine, or should not some of the guilt lie with you?"

He gave a crooked grin and forked a piece of smoked salmon into his mouth. "Touché."

Jillian said nothing, turning her attention to her own meal. She wondered what reason he had for dining with her. They ate their salmon in silence. Boggs was clearing the plates before Dunbary spoke again.

"We have received an invitation," he began, "one we cannot decline."

"*We*, your grace?" she echoed.

"Yes, the invitation is for both of us." He grimaced. "Will you please stop calling me that?"

"Calling you what, your grace?" she asked guilelessly.

His eyes narrowed dangerously. "You know what."

"What would you have me call you?" Jillian blinked innocently. "I don't know what to call a husband who is a stranger to me," she baited.

Dunbary glared as if he wanted to strangle her. He was distracted by Boggs returning with the next course. After they had been served, Dunbary took a deep breath and let it out, appearing to get his anger under control.

"We have been invited to dinner at Carlton House," he said. "Prinny wishes to meet you."

"Prinny?" she asked.

"The Prince Regent, His Royal Highness. We must appear together. If we don't, Prinny will be disappointed, to say the least." He played with his wine glass and frowned darkly.

Jillian picked up her knife and fork and focused on cutting her slice of roast beef into small pieces. The action gave her something to concentrate on besides the pang in her heart. When her husband had first joined her at the table, she thought that he had changed his mind about the arrangement concerning their marriage. But he had not. That hurt nearly as much as when he revealed he did not want her as a wife.

When she had meticulously carved all the meat on her plate into tiny pieces, she discovered she was no longer hungry and put down her utensils. What had she expected? She should have realized there would be times when she would have to appear in public with Dunbary as his blushing bride. He had dined with her only to tell her what she must do.

"If it is necessary to attend this dinner at Carlton House, then I will do it," she said. "On one condition, your grace."

"And that is?" He leaned back in his chair and raised his wine glass to his lips.

She stiffened her spine. "That you refrain from seeing Lady Avingdon for a week."

Dunbary sputtered and nearly choked on his wine. When he had recovered, he exclaimed, "Damn me, woman!"

"I have already done *that*, your grace," she retorted.

A twist of guilt wormed through Adrian at Jillian's demand. He was annoyed he should feel such an emotion. After all, he and Diana had ended their affair, but she remained his informant. His suspicions whirled. Why did his wife wish him to refrain from seeing Diana? Was this some new secret game Jillian was playing?

Anger surged through him. Damn this woman, this vixen, this vision of his sleepless nights. This pixie. She haunted him with her silky skin and luscious lips, her hair of gold and stormy eyes. Glaring at her, at her defiant little chin and set expression, he realized that she was stubborn enough to refuse to accompany him if he did not agree to her request. If they did not appear together, the Prince Regent would be insulted. Prinny might get angry enough to banish him to his estate for an extended period. Then he would never be able to prevent the war brewing with America. He had to convince Jillian she was wrong.

"Diana—Lady Avingdon is not my mistress any longer," he ground out. "I told you that."

"Appearances say otherwise, your grace." Jillian gave a delicate sniff.

Adrian's brows snapped together. "She is a friend."

"Then surely she won't mind if you do not visit for a while." She blinked innocently.

His wife had him in a corner. What could he do?

Finally, he gave a curt nod. "All right. If that is what you wish."

"Thank you," she said simply.

He rewarded her with a dark scowl. His anger escalated. The calling card he had found on the floor seemed to burn a hole in the pocket of his coat. While his lovely wife demanded that he stop seeing Diana, she was receiving that annoying Scot. His appetite fled.

Standing, he pulled the card from his pocket. "You might be more careful where you leave your lover's card," he snarled as he tossed it across the table toward her. "If you'll remember, I demanded discretion in your life."

Her cheeks paled. "I have done nothing—"

"I don't give a damn what you have done," he growled. "Fair is fair. One demand begs another. If I am restrained from seeing Diana, then you are restrained from seeing your Scottish lover."

"But—"

He leaned over the table. "No arguments. I do not want you to see him from now until after the dinner at Carlton House. Not him, nor anyone."

"There is no one—"

"Enough!" His hand came down and slapped the table so hard that the dishes jumped. "Don't lie to me. I know you are seeing him. That proves it." He pointed to the card. "But do you know where I found it?" He went on without waiting for her answer. "In front of the German's door. Are you lifting your skirt for my mother's lover, too?"

Jillian's eyes widened and she shook her head. "No," she denied hoarsely. "No, never." She reached out to him, then paused.

Adrian took her hesitation as an admission of guilt. He straightened, slighting that beseeching hand. "Don't bother trying to convince me otherwise," he growled. "I don't share my women with other men." He turned on his heel and stalked away.

He entered his room, closed the door firmly behind him, and paced across the space. His anger seethed like a roiling, viscous liquid about to boil over. He wanted to break something. Instead, he stalked back and forth, from one side of the room to the other.

Damn her conniving, unfaithful soul. She had the audacity to make demands on his fidelity while she was as faithless as a rabbit. He had suspected that before and had married her anyway. To save her reputation. He had been so stupid. And desperate to retrieve the letter.

She was another Beatrice, another woman who cared nothing for others, only for herself and her own pleasures. He wondered what reward she would receive when she finally turned the information in the letter over to Rystoke. Would it be some monetary reward? Or perhaps something a bit more intangible, like an introduction to some foreign dignitary who piqued her interest. Someone who might reveal his secrets for Rystoke and titillate her desires at the same time.

No. He sank into a chair and covered his face with his hands. That image was more than he could handle. She was *his* wife. His. No one else's. He had married her because...

For once, he faced the truth squarely. He had married her because she intrigued him as no other woman had. She was beautiful and bright and charming and unpredictable. Her ruined reputation had been merely a convenient excuse. Her bargain of the letter in return for his hand was only a bonus. He wanted her. In his life. In his bed. During the time on his estate, he thought that they might be able to build a life together. But that had been a stupid dream. That would never happen now. He had denied himself that after Sally Jersey's salon to preserve his sanity and his self-esteem. He knew he could not let his wife worm her way into his affections and then watch her stomp on his feelings as his mother had done to his father.

But there was something he could do. He sat up straighter as an idea came to him. He could see just how well she kept to the agreement they had made at the dinner table. If he had her followed during the time between now and the dinner at Carlton House, he would be able to discover if she spent time with that annoying Scot. The servants would be able to report if she visited the German here in the house.

Satisfied with his decision, he blew out a breath. His wife had better behave herself, or she would find herself exiled to one of his more distant estates. A boring existence in the country was the perfect punishment for a disobedient, profligate wife.

Jillian sat at the table long after Adrian had left. She wondered how her marriage had reached such a low point, how she and Adrian could have become so estranged. Kip's calling card lay on the table where Dunbary had left it, silently accusing. But she had done nothing wrong, so why did she feel so guilty? With a sigh, she rose from the table and returned to her room.

What had she done to Adrian to make him despise her so? She tried to remember everything that had occurred between them since they had first met. Perhaps because he had felt forced to wed her. Perhaps because she had bargained with him—the letter for his hand—and had reneged on her side of the bargain. She hadn't known at the time whom to trust, and she worried about the consequences of giving Adrian the letter. But now…

She remembered von Heisburg's words to her, that Adrian worked for the Foreign Office. If her husband did work for the government, that would explain his receiving secret correspondence, his being called back to London from Dunbary, his long hours away from the house. That would also explain why Rystoke wanted her to spy on her husband. If what the German had told her was true, then she was the biggest fool on the face of the earth. Why had she not known? Why had no one told her? Why had she not asked?

Jillian sat before the hearth in her sitting room and stared at the flames dancing in front of her eyes. The vision of a shabby derelict shambling along the street appeared in her head. Adrian. He had told her that he mingled among the poor to see how they fared. She had found the idea commendable. But what if he mingled among them for a different purpose? What if it was a way to receive information?

She leaned back against the chair and squeezed her eyes shut. What if England and America went to war because she had not turned over an important piece of information? How could she discover the truth?

She could ask Adrian, but she doubted he would tell her anything. She doubted he would even speak to her. Rystoke would laugh at her and tell her only a perverted version of the truth. The German, von Heisburg, frightened her. She did not trust him. Whom could she ask? Lady Beatrice? No, she did not trust her and doubted the woman knew anything about what her son did. There was no one she could trust to tell her the truth. She would have to discover it on her own.

Perhaps, in the morning, she would be able to think of someone she could ask. But even if she could find someone, her husband had put serious restrictions on her until after the dinner at Carlton House. She sat up as an idea came to her. Why had she not thought of it before? The Prince Regent would certainly know if her husband worked for the Foreign Office. If she were very clever, she could discover the truth from him. In the meantime, she would have to keep the letter very safe. Tomorrow, first thing, she would send it to Kip.

Feeling a bit better, she went to the library to fetch a book to read.

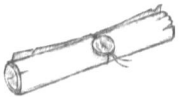

CHAPTER 17

"More wine, Duchess Dunbary?"

Jillian smiled nervously at Lord Castlereagh, who sat on her left at the Prince Regent's enormous dining table. "No, thank you, my lord. I'm afraid if I have more than one glass I will make a complete fool of myself."

"It's a wise person who knows how much she can handle," he observed with a kind smile. "Isn't that so, Constance?" he asked of the lady seated on his other side.

With a silent sigh of relief at having the Foreign Minister's attention turned away from her, Jillian poked at the food on her plate. She was seated about halfway down the long table in the formal dining room at Carlton House. At the head of the table, the Prince Regent was regaling those around him with a raucous, bawdy tale of the exploits of one of the more outwardly sedate members of Parliament. At the foot of the table, Mrs. Fitzhugh, the Regent's long-time mistress, was directing a discussion of the latest production by Edward Garrick, the famous actor. Conversation swirled about Jillian as the other diners at Carlton House consumed their meal.

So far, she felt that she had acquitted herself quite well for being in such august company for the first time. Dining at Carlton House was not anything like the dinners and balls she had attended before. She felt that she was under close scrutiny from everyone present, especially her husband. Casting a surreptitious glance to where he sat, across the table and several seats nearer the head, she saw that he was engaged in conversation with those about him. He turned in her direction. His manner was solemn, the expression in those topaz eyes unreadable, but he sent a nearly imperceptible nod her way before he turned back to his discussion.

Jillian did not know whether to be consoled by that small acknowledgment or disturbed by it. Since their disastrous dinner together only a week ago, they had not even spoken, although she was quite aware that her husband spent his nights in his own bed. For that, at least, she could be grateful. He had acquiesced to her request that he not visit his mistress. For her part, she had sent a message with her ragdoll containing that troublesome little letter to Kip the very next morning. She had explained that the doll had been made by her mother, that their father might like to see it, but she would not be able to communicate with him until the day after the dinner at Carlton House. The week had been very long.

She had buoyed her spirits with the anticipation of this dinner, where she might learn if her husband did work for the Foreign Office. Yet, so far, she had only discovered that he was well-liked by the Prince Regent, Mrs. Fitzhugh, and the others who crowded about the long dinner table. She had met Lord Castlereagh, the charming gentleman to her left, the Foreign Minister, but how was she to find out about her husband's loyalties to England? She could not very well blurt it out at the dinner table.

Besides, table conversation about the war with Napoleon or the tensions with America was not proper with the ladies present. That would happen after the ladies withdrew. Jillian wished she could remain to listen in.

Then from several seats away, a gentleman said, "I have stated many times, sir, that I will back rescinding the Orders in Council as soon as the French have revoked their decrees."

Jillian glanced down the table. The man who spoke was Prime Minister Spencer Perceval.

"And I say, sir, that unless you support the rescinding of the Council's orders, you will force us into war with America," another man answered whom Jillian did not know. He was a young man and very elegant.

Other conversation at that end of the table ceased. To her left, she sensed Lord Castlereagh's disapproval at the raised voices. Adrian leaned back in his chair and watched the two men with shrewd eyes.

At the other end of the table, the Prince Regent was still engaged in relating a story and was unaware of the tension at the foot of his dining table.

"I have stated my position more than once in Parliament, that we cannot rescind the Orders without jeopardizing our economic security," Mr. Perceval lectured. "Since Napoleon has seen fit to seize any neutral ship which has touched upon an English port in order to cut into our trade, we must retaliate by seizing any vessel which has *not* touched upon an English port."

"You are losing sight of the issue in legalities, Mr. Perceval. Our trade with America, a neutral, is being hurt, and therefore, our people are suffering from lack of American goods and raw materials," the handsome young man said.

"America can trade with England through licenses, Mr. Brougham," Perceval answered. "Repealing the Orders would allow the profits from those licenses to fall into the coffers of other nations besides England."

"How long do you suppose America will put up with having to pay for the right to trade with us, Mr. Perceval?" Brougham shot back. "How long before she becomes angry at the seizure of her ships on the high seas? How long before America loses her patience and declares war?"

At that point, when all conversation had completely stilled, Mrs. Fitzhugh stood to signal the end of dinner and saved the party from dissolving into unpleasantness. "Come, ladies," she trilled. "I do believe the gentlemen wish to be left to their brandy and conversation. We all must refresh ourselves before the dancing."

Jillian was thoughtful as the ladies moved out into the hall and up the stairs to a room where they could refresh themselves. The letter she had given to Kip inside her ragdoll would help convince the members of Parliament, perhaps even the Prime Minister himself, that war with America must be avoided, that it was closer than they realized. She would have to retrieve the letter as soon as she could. Deep in thought, she was surprised when someone gently pulled her aside. She saw the Duchess of Wyndham smiling at her.

"You are the Duchess of Dunbary, Adrian's new bride," the duchess said.

Jillian nodded, amazed that the lady should take notice of her. "I have just come out of my confinement after the birth of our second child, and I am afraid I have not had the chance to extend my best wishes to you on your marriage to Adrian," the duchess confided.

"I should be the one congratulating you, your grace," Jillian told her. "I understand you had another boy?"

The duchess chuckled, her lovely face glowing with motherly happiness. "Yes, it seems I will have to try again to get the little girl I wish for. Of course, Damien, my husband, is as pleased as a father of two boys could be. He loves them dearly, and spends time with them every day. After his time in foreign service, I never thought I would be able to keep him home."

Jillian was unable to respond, for they had reached the upstairs room, and the duchess was surrounded by a group of the ladies who congratulated her over the birth of her new son. The duchess was not many years older than herself. Her lovely face radiated a youthful beauty, and her gown slipped over the curves of her figure, still svelte after bearing two children. A tiny lump formed in Jillian's throat at the obvious happiness and contentment of the duchess. Jillian stepped to a mirror and smoothed her hair as she blinked away the sting in her eyes. She doubted her marriage with Adrian would ever be as wonderful.

The duchess was finally able to break away from the other women, and she came back to Jillian's side. "We must have a long talk," she said. "Wyndham and Dunbary have been friends since they were boys. I am sure we will be seeing quite a bit of each other." She hooked her arm through Jillian's and began to walk with her back to the ballroom where the dancing would take place. "Now, tell me, how did you happen to meet Adrian? He has been quite the best catch in London for several seasons. I am sure you have all the other girls crying on their mother's bosoms at the loss of such a prospect for marriage."

Jillian had to smile at the mischievous twinkle in the sapphire blue eyes of the duchess. Here, she felt, was someone who might understand the problems she was having, someone to whom eventually she might confide her secrets.

With a shrug, she answered, "We met at a ball, your grace."

"Ah, a ball." The duchess nodded. "And I understand at a weekend in the country?"

Jillian blushed. Of course the news of the ripped dress and ensuing scandal had been in all the papers. The duchess grinned and patted her hand.

"Someday, I will tell you how I met Wyndham," she said with a little laugh. "Have you ever heard stories of the dashing spy, Le Chat, and the notorious French spy, Madame du Barré?"

Puzzled, Jillian nodded, wondering what connection this composed, genteel lady had with spies.

"I have known them both," the duchess confided. "Beneath this socially acceptable exterior lies the heart of an adventuress." At Jillian's look of astonishment, she laughed again. "You see? I have shocked you with my confession, so nothing you have done will shock me."

"But, your grace, you have such standing in society…I mean, the Prince Regent is holding this dinner in your honor," Jillian protested.

The duchess showed her dimples. "Yes, I have to admit, I have become quite staid since my marriage. Well, Wyndham advises the Foreign Minister, you know, so I am not allowed to be naughty anymore."

Jillian became aware that she had found her chance to discover the truth about her husband. Tentatively, she said, "I did not realize Wyndham was involved with the Foreign Office. Does he work with Dunbary?"

"Why yes, they have worked together many times, although Damien is no longer as involved as he used to be. Estate business and our boys keep him occupied." The duchess shook her head ruefully. "But sometimes, I think he wishes he could trade places with your husband. I think he misses the excitement."

As they walked the last few steps to the ballroom, chagrin churned through Jillian. She had discovered what she most wanted to know about Dunbary. He was no traitor to England, only a man who was trying to help his country avert war. She had been so wrong about him.

Just before they entered the ballroom, the duchess said warmly, "I have the feeling we have much in common and will end up being great friends. Please, call me Jessica."

As soon as they walked through the door the Duke of Wyndham stepped forward, took Jessica's hand and raised it to his lips. He was handsome, with bright golden hair and extraordinary green eyes. The contrast between Jessica's dark head and his bright one, her startling blue eyes and his green ones, made them an extremely attractive couple.

"I missed you, my love," Wyndham murmured to his wife.

Jessica smiled and blushed as her fingers lingered in his. "You demonstrate an unfashionable amount of affection in public, my husband."

He grinned back at her and shrugged with casual unconcern. "Let the gossipmongers have their say. What is wrong with a man loving his wife?"

"Indeed," Jessica agreed. "Except that your manners need improving." She turned to Jillian beside her. "May I present the new Duchess of Dunbary? And this is my incorrigible husband, Damien, the Duke of Wyndham."

Jillian received the full force of that intense green gaze before the duke took Jillian's outstretched hand and bowed over it. She wondered how anyone could withstand the potency of the combined scrutiny of both dukes. At the thought of her husband, she glanced over Wyndham's shoulder to where Dunbary stood. He watched her a moment, then turned his back to engage another man in conversation. The gesture shouted of his feelings toward her and thrust a cold wedge of pain through her.

"Adrian mentioned that he took a bride," the duke commented, regaining her attention. "I must commend him on his lovely choice."

Jillian forced herself to answer lightly, "You are much too kind, your grace. Your own wife far outshines me on points of grace and beauty."

At that moment, they were interrupted by the entry of the Prince Regent and Mrs. Fitzhugh into the ballroom.

"Please excuse us, Lady Dunbary," the duke said. "Prinny has opted to open the dancing with my wife for a partner. I'm afraid I must present her to him."

Jillian watched them walk away. She was saved from the embarrassment of standing by herself throughout the dance when Lord

Castlereagh came to claim her for a partner. Dunbary partnered Lord Castlereagh's wife.

As the Foreign Minister led her onto the dance floor, he said, "I have looked forward to our meeting, Lady Dunbary. I'm glad I finally have the chance. Your husband spoke of you with great feeling when he first met you. I, in turn, wished to meet the lady who could raise such emotion in him."

Believing that the only emotion she could rouse in Dunbary could be anger or dislike, she said, "I apologize if I have disappointed you, Lord Castlereagh. Or if my husband gave you the impression I was somewhat of a hoyden."

The older gentleman laughed. "My dear young lady, your husband does not speak of you in those terms at all. Rather, he believes you to be quite charming and a bit mysterious."

Bemused by this revelation, she murmured, "I had no idea."

"Dunbary is not one to expose his thoughts," Castlereagh said. "He is also too much of a gentleman to force someone to do something against his or her wishes."

Jillian glanced at him sharply. She immediately understood his subtle point. "If there is something you wish to say, my lord, please do not fear that I will faint away if you speak plainly."

He smiled. "Adrian also mentioned how forthright you are."

"He probably called me stubborn," she muttered.

Castlereagh merely smiled.

"What is it you wish to tell me, sir?" she prompted.

The Foreign Minister immediately sobered and said, "Dunbary works for the Foreign Office, Lady Dunbary. He receives very sensitive and sometimes quite secret correspondence from those who are involved in other foreign offices. What he does is vital to how England forms her own policy. Do you understand?"

Jillian nodded as guilt tore through her at this gentle rebuke from the Foreign Minister. She had initially suspected Dunbary of treachery, when all along he had been working for the English government. She had denied him an important piece of information.

"Yes, I understand," she managed to say in a choked whisper. "The letter…" Her voice failed her.

"Exactly," the Foreign Minister said. "If you could be so kind to turn the information over to your husband or myself, England would be very grateful."

"As soon as I am able," she agreed. She would have to send for Kip immediately. Raising guilty eyes, she said, "I am so very sorry, my lord. I had no idea…"

"Do not fret, your grace," Castlereagh soothed. "You did not know what you had. It was an honest mistake."

Jillian nodded, but silently she disagreed with him. It was not an honest mistake at all. It had been stupid. She could not erase the terrible guilt that she hadn't trusted Dunbary. Perhaps, she had also been mistaken about his mistress. He had not visited her for the entire week. But neither had he denied spending time with the lovely Lady Avingdon. That was another problem, she decided, as the dance came to an end. For now, she would have to see that the letter was returned to the rightful owners.

Lord Castlereagh escorted her to the side of the dance floor. When the next dance began, she was partnered by another gentleman. During the course of the evening she found that she had actually enjoyed herself, much to her surprise. Although she was not able to ask her new friend, Jessica, more questions about her husband, and despite the fact that she only saw Dunbary from time to time across the room or dancing with another of the ladies present, she discovered that the Prince Regent held engaging social events. She forced her guilt over the letter and the pain of her strained relationship with her husband to the back of her mind. Tomorrow, she decided, would be soon enough to dwell on unhappy thoughts and right the wrong she had committed against her husband.

When the evening was nearing its end, the small orchestra began playing the opening strains of a waltz. Jillian had retired to a quiet corner of the ballroom in order to rest for a few moments. She watched as the Duke and Duchess of Wyndham swirled past, their love for each other obvious. They were two halves of a perfect whole. That knot of envy which had squeezed at her insides earlier in the evening tightened once again. Perhaps, the problems she was having with Adrian were mostly her fault.

A presence beside her made her glance up. She saw Adrian bowing to her.

"May I have the pleasure of this dance, my duchess?" he asked.

Adrian had observed Jillian all evening. He had seen her dance with Castlereagh and watched her chat with Damien and Jessica. All three had told him what a charming and bright young lady his wife was. As the evening progressed, he had agreed with them. When sadness crossed his wife's lovely face, guilt had stabbed through him.

Perhaps he had been at fault for causing the strain between them. Perhaps he should have trusted her more and told her exactly why the letter was so important. Perhaps he should have confessed that Diana was his informant, not his mistress. But he had not.

Jillian had kept her promise to him and not seen the Scot as he had demanded. According to Boggs, she had avoided the German still living under his roof. If she were another Beatrice, why would she have honored her side of the bargain? The question gnawed at him.

When the opening measures of the waltz played, an invisible string pulled him in the direction of Jillian. Now, gazing into those fathomless gray eyes, wary at his request yet at the same time shimmering with hope, he knew he had not made a mistake in asking her to dance.

He smiled. "I believe the next dance is mine," he said, repeating the words that had first brought them together.

Jillian's expression relaxed into a small smile and she placed her hand in his.

"I hope you won't think me too forward for agreeing to dance with you," she said, echoing her part of the conversation at that first fateful meeting.

He chuckled as he led her onto the dance floor. "Do you remember how to dance the waltz?" he asked as his arm slipped about her waist.

"I could never forget," she answered a bit breathlessly. "I had a wonderful teacher."

"Do you think London society ever recovered from the scandal we caused by dancing the waltz without permission?" he wondered.

She laughed. "Probably not. I'm sure mothers now have to keep their daughters on a much tighter leash in order not to have them whirling across the dance floor. After all, they saw how I was able to marry the bold devil who asked me to waltz."

"A bold devil, am I?" Adrian's lips twitched. "What of you, my pixie? I should say you were a bit headstrong."

"Perhaps. Or perhaps just heartstrong," she murmured, then sent him a wary glance from beneath her lashes.

Adrian heard the wistful tone in her words. Perhaps she was as confused and heartsore about their marriage as he was. "Do you always allow your heart to rule your head?" he asked.

"Always," she answered playfully, lightening the mood. "Doing that, you see, gets me into mischief, and extricating myself keeps me from being bored."

"Is that why –" He stopped in mid-thought. He did not want to turn this conversation to unpleasant subjects, such as the letter and her lover. "Are you bored, Jillian?" he asked instead.

His question made her eyes widen in surprise. Then her lashes swept down as she answered. "No, I'm not bored, only lonely."

A fresh wave of guilt assaulted him at her candid response. Was her loneliness his fault? The answer came swift and hard. He had been a cad to leave his wife adrift in her new life. So she had turned to that Scot to comfort her. Whom she had not seen since their dinner together. Did she pine for him?

Her next words nearly undid him. "I am lonely for you, Adrian."

His steps slowed at her confession. Her gaze was open and without guile. It cut him to the quick, and he could not meet it. He glanced away to focus somewhere across the top of her head. They moved to the music in silence.

The waltz had almost come to an end when he found some bit of courage. "Perhaps we should call a truce to our little war."

Jillian's mouth dropped open and she stared at him.

Pleased at her response, he smiled as he murmured, "You'd better not look at me like that, Miss St. Clare. People will begin to spread the rumor that we are lovers."

Her laugh bubbled up at the words he repeated as they had danced at Almack's.

Adrian gazed down into his wife's soft, laughing gray eyes and realized he would very much like to make that rumor true. Leaning toward her, he asked, "A truce, your grace?"

Jillian nodded. "A truce, your grace," she agreed.

"Will you be my lover, at least for tonight?" he whispered in her ear.

Blushing hotly, she replied playfully, "I am yours to do with as you please, your grace."

At that, Adrian chuckled. "Vixen," he teased, just as the music ended.

As he led her from the dance floor, anticipation surged through him. He could not wait to get his wife home. He was relieved when the Prince Regent retired immediately after the dance was over, and the guests were now free to leave. Adrian wasted little time gathering Jillian's wrap and ushering her out the door.

They were silent on the ride back to the house, but his hand stole across the seat of the coach and held Jillian's in a firm embrace. Her fingers twined with his, but he sensed her apprehension.

Just before the coach came to a stop before their door, he lifted her fingers to his lips. "Your hand trembles, Jillian," he murmured. "Are you afraid?"

She shook her head in denial.

"If you would prefer not to do this tonight..." He allowed her the freedom to back away from their truce, at the same time hoping she would not.

She caught her breath at his concession, more evidence of what a bounder he had been. "No," she answered. "I want to be with you. I just need a bit of time..." She glanced down at their hands, then met his eyes. "I will come to you."

He nodded his agreement just as the coach rolled to a gentle stop before their front door. As he escorted her into the house, he noticed that her hand trembled. At the top of the stairs, before they parted to their separate rooms, he raised her fingers to his lips once more with a silent promise of what was to come. Then turned into his room.

Hope that she would come to him warred with apprehension that she would not. But he would not force her. If she stayed away, he vowed he would woo her every way he could think of. The time had come to create a real marriage with his wife.

Jillian turned slowly toward her own room. She was nervous. She wanted this night to be perfect. So perfect, in fact, that her husband would not ever feel the need to return to the arms of his mistress.

She woke Dory, who was napping on a cot in her dressing room, and sat before her mirror. Examining her reflection, she decided she did not look any different than she had several weeks ago before she had met Adrian, but she felt very different. Older, somehow. Less innocent. More aware of the world about her. More concerned with the feelings of others, Adrian in particular.

Excitement swept through her as Dory pulled the pins from her hair and let it cascade about her shoulders. Her husband wanted her, at least for tonight. A thrill ran through her. Impatiently, she waited while Dory finished brushing her hair, then made the girl hurry as she helped her undress. The girl had laid out a plain nightrail, but Jillian directed her to take another out of her wardrobe. It was part of her trousseau, a frothy, white, nearly sheer linen slip of material that skimmed her curves and dipped very low over her bosom. A matching robe of white velvet edged with miles of Spanish lace disguised the provocative gown beneath with its demure appearance. After tying the ribbons and fluffing the lace, Dory stepped back and nodded her approval.

Jillian blushed and bid her good-night. She waited until she heard Dory's footsteps fade, then she took a deep breath and walked to the door which led to the adjoining sitting room. After knocking softly, she turned the knob and entered.

Adrian rose from his seat before the fire. He wore the blood-red dressing robe she had borrowed on the morning after their wedding. The color accentuated his thick black hair and dark good looks. His masculinity hung about him like an invisible vapor. Her blood surged through her veins.

"I was beginning to think you would not come," he said. His low voice vibrated through the room.

Jillian swallowed and smiled nervously. "I'm sorry I took so long. I wanted to look… different." She carelessly swept out the skirt of her robe then let it fall.

Adrian's gaze slipped down to her toes and back up. His eyes darkened and he stepped closer. "You look beautiful," he murmured.

Jillian gave a little laugh and shook her head in modest denial.

Standing before her, he wrapped his fingers around her arms. "Yes, you do."

The warmth of his hands seeped through the material of her robe to her cool skin and made her shiver. She wanted more of his warmth. His chest was bare beneath his robe. She wanted to feel that muscled expanse beneath her fingers. Tentatively, she placed her hand between the gaping lapels. The short curls of black hair across his chest tickled her palm. She could feel the thud of his heart echo under her hand, could feel it accelerate beneath her touch. Amazed that she should have that effect on him, she raised her gaze.

He smiled. "The sight of you always makes my heart race."

Jillian ducked her head to hide her blush.

With a finger beneath her chin, he raised her face. "Don't be embarrassed. It's natural for a man and woman to want to be intimate. I thought you knew that by now."

"I did, but…" She shrugged, too shy to say that she wanted more than anything to be intimate with him. Hearing that he wished the same, made her want to sing to the heavens for joy. Perhaps he cared for her just a little.

He took her hand and drew her to the fire. "Come sit with me and have a bit of brandy," he invited.

She held back. "No," she said.

Disappointment flashed though his eyes.

"I don't want to sit by the fire." She held his hand and stepped close. "I don't want a bit of brandy." Her voice dropped to a whisper. "I want you, Adrian. Only you."

His gaze heated and his fingers traced her cheek. "You are quite a woman, Jillian, Duchess of Dunbary."

He cupped the back of her neck and pulled her against him. His lips lightly touched her mouth. And then, as if he could not get enough, he crushed them, taking her breath. She gave herself up to him. Her arms slipped about his waist as she leaned into him. She loved his muscular maleness, his hardness against her softness. She loved being next to him, having his arms about her, engulfing her. She loved feeling as if she were seeping into him, becoming part of him. She loved *him*, every part of him.

His tongue caressed her lips, tasting, prodding, seducing. With a tiny whimper of desire, she allowed him entry beyond, inviting him to explore and take possession of her mouth. She wanted to taste him as well. Mimicking him, she stroked and touched with her tongue. Only when they had no more breath did they break apart, panting.

His eyes gleamed hotly in the light of the fire. Their heat seared her. She wanted this man. More than anything.

"Make love to me, Adrian," she whispered.

Without another word, he swept her up into his arms and carried her from the sitting room into the room beyond where his huge, four-poster bed waited.

He placed her on her feet beside the bed. With agonizing slowness, he untied the ribbons holding her robe together. When it fell open, he ran his hands beneath it, skimming his palms across her ribs, her breasts, her shoulders, and pushed the robe down her arms. His fingers closed about her wrists.

The suggestion of capture by this man made her blood pound in her veins. She licked her lips as if she could already taste him. His topaz eyes burned with molten heat, and her body was consumed in their fire. Ducking his head, he nibbled her neck and ran his tongue around her ear.

"Wildflowers," he whispered.

Jillian threw back her head, offering herself to him, arching into him. With only her thin nightrail and his robe between them, his need throbbed against her. She wanted to hug him to her, but his hands held her captive. Instead, she leaned into him, conforming her soft curves to his hard planes.

"Vixen," he growled, as he let go of her wrists and pulled her tight against him.

His mouth captured her lips, and all coherent thought fled. Heat throbbed between her thighs. He bunched up her nightrail, and his hands cupped her bare bottom. His erection pressed against her belly.

She needed to feel bare skin against bare skin. Unclasping his robe, she slipped her arms inside, wrapping them about his waist. But he was already pulling her nightrail over her head. She pushed the robe from his shoulders. Coming together again, they fell back onto the bed.

His mouth left hers only to fasten gently upon one breast. At her moan of pleasure, he kissed slowly down her body — her shoulder, her collarbone, the crevice between her breasts, her belly, her navel where he swirled his tongue, the hollow of her hip, her thigh, her knee where he nipped, her ankle, her toes where he sucked. Streaks of hot sensations swept through her. Everywhere his mouth touched made her tingle. His hands traced in divine counterpoint. She throbbed with need. And then he moved up her body until he reached the curls between her thighs. A single finger swept between her folds. She shuddered in response.

"Wildflowers," he murmured.

And then his finger was inside her, and then two, curling and touching, and she flew apart with a cry.

As her world came back into focus, she saw his small, gratified smile. With a feline growl, she made him roll onto his back. It was her turn to make him mindless.

She used her mouth and her hands on him as he had used his. Kissing, licking, caressing, she moved down his body, making his muscles twitch, making him groan in pleasure. She wrapped her hand around his manhood and licked, delighting in the steel enclosed in silk. But he did not let her play for very long. With a tight rumble, he pulled her up by the arms and impaled her on it. She gasped in sweet delight and smiled like a sated cat at this ability to arouse him.

"Pixie," he whispered. "Pixie of the wildflowers. Do your magic. Weave your spells."

She did not need any more urging. Instinct took over where she was unpracticed. Moving slowly at first, then faster, matching her rhythm to his, she took them away to fly on the winds of desire. Their wild cries of pure pleasure echoed up to the clouds and stars, and softly, together, they floated back to earth.

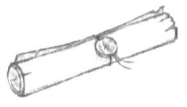

CHAPTER 18

Daylight was streaming through the window when Jillian awoke. The bed was empty beside her, but warmth from Adrian's body still lingered. She ran her hand over the sheets as the memory of their love-making washed through her. The feeling of contentment after being well-loved made her sigh happily. Smiling widely, she stretched.

Today, she decided, would be the beginning of her new life as her husband's lover. Today, they would put all the pain behind them. But first, she had some things to do. Ringing for Dory, she sat up in bed. She needed her writing materials. She had to send for Kip immediately and ask him to bring the doll back to her. She would introduce Kip to Adrian, let him know Kip was her brother, and give her husband the letter. He would see that she had not betrayed him with either the letter or Kip. The rift between them would be healed. She smiled. This day was going to be wonderful.

As the day progressed, Jillian's euphoria began to evaporate. Boggs had informed her that Adrian would be gone until late in the day. The nasty little thought that he had gone to see his mistress insinuated itself into her brain, but resolutely, she pushed it away. After all, she had made the demand that he not visit the lovely Lady Avingdon. Besides, she and Adrian had spent a wonderful night together.

Wonderful. She kept that word before her as she waited for Kip to appear that afternoon. The word was like a beacon, guiding her away from the shoals and rocks of her misgivings. When Kip was finally announced as she sat doing needlework in the drawing room, relief washed through her. She smiled brightly as he advanced into the room.

He took both her hands and placed a chaste kiss on her cheek. "You are beaming like a ray of sunshine, Jillian," he said with a smile. "You must have resolved some things with your husband."

She led him to the sofa and sat down with him. "I soon will resolve some things," she said happily. "I want to tell him you are my brother."

His brows went up in surprise. "You haven't told him yet?"

"No. I haven't had the opportunity," she said blithely, ignoring the tiny nag that she had left it too long. "I would also like you to return my doll."

He shifted in his seat. "The doll isn't here in London, but I can get it for you in a few days."

"Oh." Disappointment crashed through her. "What have you done with it?" She tried to keep her voice steady as horror welled up inside her. She had to have the doll today to prove to Adrian that she was to be trusted. She clutched his hand. "I must have that doll, Kip." She realized she sounded too desperate. She could not reveal what was hidden inside the doll. Calmly, she took back her hand and let her gaze slide away. "The doll is very precious to me."

Kip's eyes narrowed. "I think you are keeping secrets."

Jillian's gaze snapped around to him. "As are you."

He laughed. "Secrets? What secrets?"

The questions tumbled from her. "Where do you disappear to when you are not in London? Why does no one know where you go? Why do you have few friends, yet you are invited to the best social events?"

He smiled and shrugged wordlessly.

Suspicious at his evasion, she asked, "Where is my doll, Kip?"

"It's more than just a precious keepsake, isn't it?" he demanded. "The doll has some other meaning."

Jillian drew a breath at his insight. Was he trying to learn her secret? She barely knew him. Even though he was her brother, could she trust him? She stood and paced a few steps as her mind whirled. As she turned back to him, she decided she did not need to tell him everything. "I need the doll to rectify a stupid mistake."

"If your husband is upset that you gave me the doll…" he began.

"No. He does not even know you have it." She sat down and faced him. "I thought I could trust you. You told me you were my brother. You convinced me that I could rely on your help if I needed it."

"You can trust me, Jillian." He leaned forward. "I suspected the doll was very precious to you, so I hid it. I'll bring it back, but I have to retrieve it."

She said nothing. Her silence asked more questions than she could ever speak aloud.

A muscle jumped in his jaw. Then with a sigh, he ran his hand through his hair. "I'm going to tell you something that could ruin my life. Once I tell you, the knowledge is yours to use as you wish." He paused. "The doll is on a ship I own. I am an outlaw, a smuggler. That is why I disappear from London."

Jillian stared at him as comprehension seeped into her brain. She had not expected him to tell her anything quite so damning. He had laid his life in her hands. He trusted her. She could denounce him to the authorities or she could keep his secret. The choice was hers.

"Why?" she asked.

He stood, stepped away, turned to face her, then stuck his hands in his pockets and hunched his shoulders defensively. "Because there are people in Ayton who are out of work and starving. I bring them work and extra coins to help them buy food. These damned Orders in Council have played havoc with the economics of the country. The people can't get enough cotton from America to fill their looms, so they have no product to sell to support themselves."

"So you smuggle in cotton," she finished. "Where does the cloth go?"

"To France."

"And from France?"

"I bring back brandy."

"Which you sell to members of society."

He nodded.

Jillian thought that over. Kip might be breaking the law, but he was helping the people of the country. More than she had done by holding on to that letter.

PATRICIA BARLETTA

"I think you should be commended for helping your people,"
she said. "I won't reveal your secret." Then she smiled. "Even my
husband's ancestors smuggled."

He chuckled and sat down. "The doll is on my ship on its way
to Ayton. I won't be able to retrieve it for a few days."

Jillian hid her disappointment. "But you will bring it to me as
soon as your ship returns?"

As Kip nodded his assurances, Boggs entered with the tea tray.
Just as Jillian reached for the teapot to pour, von Heisburg's voice
rang out, "My dear Jillian, vhat good luck to find you here."

Her head snapped up in surprise as she watched the German
enter. Her stomach flipped. He would see her with Kip and be convinced she and her brother were lovers.

Boggs straightened from setting out the refreshments and sent
her an apologetic look. "My apologies, your grace," he murmured.
"I had no idea he had returned to the house." He sniffed disdainfully
as he passed the German on his way out.

Kip stood at von Heisburg's entrance, and Jillian made the intro-
ductions. With a toothy smile, Baron von Heisburg sauntered farther
into the room as if he planned to stay for some time.

"So you are the young gentleman who has captured the affections of our lovely Jillian, ya?" von Heisburg said, as he leaned his
elbow casually on the mantle.

"I think you are mistaken, baron," Kip corrected. "The duchess
and I are merely friends."

Jillian sent her brother a small smile of thanks, and turned coolly
to the German. "Is there something that you wished to speak to me
about, baron?"

His chilly blue gaze warmed as he looked at her. "Any time you
speak vith me is special, *Liebchen*."

Jillian's lips compressed at the German's too familiar endear-
ment. She felt Kip's confused glance and sent him a tiny shake of
her head.

Kip turned a stern gaze on the German. "I don't think the lady
likes such familiarity, sir," he said.

Von Heisburg's eyes went cold. "Perhaps, it is only because you
are here, ya?" he said.

Kip leaned back on the sofa, casually draped his arm across its back, and crossed his legs as if he were prepared to stay for quite some time. "Perhaps, it is because you are here, and she does not like the way you speak to her, ya?" Kip answered, mimicking the German.

Jillian saw that the situation could degenerate into something nasty. She stood, forcing Kip to do the same. "You will let me know the minute we can conclude our business," she said briskly as she led him to the door. "I will be quite anxious until it is finished."

Kip smiled reassuringly. As he opened the door to the room, he said, "I will send word as soon as I can. Don't worry, Jillian. It will all work out." He raised her hand to his lips and gave her fingers an affectionate squeeze.

A movement in the hall beyond caught her attention. Jillian gasped. Adrian stood, stiff and silent, as his gaze traveled from her to Kip and back again. Her heart stilled in her chest. Adrian's jaw tightened. He took a step toward her, then stopped. Frozen, she stood with her hand still in Kip's. Adrian's eyes impaled her like white-hot lances.

"Jade," he ground out, and flung a huge bouquet of wildflowers at her feet. Without another word, he spun around and stormed out.

"No," she protested, but her voice barely carried beyond her lips. It certainly made no impression on her husband, who was already gone. Devastation settled upon her like a pall. Her plans for the day, her hopes for her marriage were snuffed out by a stupid misunderstanding.

She quickly withdrew her hand from Kip's grasp. "Please, leave," she pleaded, barely above a whisper.

She felt Kip hesitate, then he nodded and stepped away. When she turned back into the drawing room, everything seemed painfully exaggerated, too bright and too sharp. The sensation made her close her eyes for a moment. When she opened them again, her glance fell on von Heisburg, still leaning negligently against the mantle. She realized Adrian had not only witnessed Kip's farewell, but had also seen the German.

Wanting more than anything to be alone in her misery, she took a stiff step forward. "I don't think we have anything to discuss, baron," she said, forming the words from instinct rather than conscious thought. "As you see, my husband does not speak to me."

The German straightened, threatening with his presence. "I think you vill speak to him," he contradicted. "Perhaps I tell him vhat vas happening vith you and the young man vhen I arrive, ya?"

Jillian stared up into his cold eyes. She felt brittle, as if she would break into a thousand pieces if she did not move carefully. Yet, his threat hardly made an impression. Her heart felt like a lump of river mud in her chest. The truce with Adrian, her hopes for a wonderful day, had crumpled to dust with her husband's one word to her. He had made it very clear how he viewed her. The German's ultimatum could not hurt her any more than she was already.

"I don't care what you tell him, baron," she answered. "If you want information from him, you can get it yourself."

His expression turned dangerously seductive. "*Nein, Liebchen,*" he said, as he reached out and stroked her cheek. "You are confused, ya? You vill get this information." His hand moved to her neck, his fingers circling her throat. "I think you vill do this thing for me."

Jillian had hardly been aware of his fingers on her cheek. The man's gaze was mesmerizing in some dark, sinister manner. Her mind seemed to be on another plane of existence. Yet, his hand closing about her throat, although barely touching her, was menacing. Its threat brought her immediately back to her surroundings.

Stepping back, she pushed his hand away. "I think not, baron. I want nothing to do with your intrigues. I don't care what you do to me."

He smiled cruelly and bowed to her. "As you vish, dear Jillian, but I think, perhaps you vill be sorry, ya?" Stepping past her, he left her alone.

At that moment, Beatrice swept into the house. She stopped in mid-step as she saw her lover emerging from a room where Jillian stood alone. Her eyes moved from the baron to Jillian and back again. Color rushed to her cheeks. Her mouth tightened. Her gaze landed again on Jillian with animosity.

Stepping forward, the German said smoothly, "Ah, *Liebling,* you hafe finally come home, ya? Vas your shopping a success, then?"

Distracted, Beatrice's manner instantly switched. She turned a bright smile on her lover. "Oh, Gustav," she gushed. "You must see the delicious bonnet I have purchased."

As she spoke, one of the footmen entered, burdened with numerous packages and boxes. Jillian noted that Beatrice had purchased quite a bit more than just a bonnet.

Beatrice sent another murderous glance at Jillian. "I'm glad we are moving to our own lodgings in a few days," she observed. "Some in this household step beyond their bounds." With a furious swish of her skirts, she headed up the stairs and commanded, "Come, Gustav."

Jillian watched her in silence. The woman suspected that she had invited the German's advances. How could she convince Beatrice otherwise? As the baron placed his foot on the bottom step, he turned to Jillian and gave her a meaningful little smile, then he followed his lover to the floor above.

Suddenly cold, Jillian hugged her arms about her and stood before the fire. Disappointment, anger, regret, and fear, were a tangle in her chest. The implied danger of von Heisburg hung like a dark presence in a corner of her mind. But her sharpest emotion came from her shattered relationship with her husband. She had planned wonderful things for the day. A tiny sob erupted from the strafed, painful area around her heart. She clapped her hand over her mouth, halting what could become a torrent of self-pity. Sucking in a deep breath, she straightened her shoulders. She had to find a way to bridge the gap between her and Adrian. Last night, she had seen a glimmer of what their marriage could be. She had to find the means to reach out to him, to be able to tell him the truth about Kip, to be able to hand him that letter.

A quiet knock on the door interrupted her thoughts. "Your grace," Boggs said. "Shall I have the coach brought around? It is almost time for you to leave for your visit to Duchess Matilda."

Jillian stifled a groan. She had asked to visit Adrian's grandmother several days ago. In the turmoil of the morning, she had forgotten. That lady was the last person she wished to see at this moment. Lady Matilda seemed to notice everything, and knew everything about the family. Jillian's thoughts stopped short. Of

241

course! Adrian's grandmother was the perfect person to give her the key to begin opening doors in her marriage.

"Yes," she told Boggs, as hope began to glimmer inside her. "Please bring the coach around. I will be ready to leave in a few moments."

"And the flowers, my lady?" Boggs asked, as he held up the huge bouquet he had rescued from the floor. "What would you like me to do with them?"

Jillian caught her bottom lip between her teeth to keep back the tears which abruptly blurred her vision. "Have them put in my room, Boggs, where I can see them when I go to sleep."

As Boggs bowed his acquiescence and left, Jillian turned back to the fire. At least, if she could not have Adrian beside her at night, she could have the flowers he had brought her in that single, fleeting moment of their shared harmony.

When the Dowager Duchess Matilda entered the old-fashioned drawing room, Jillian rose from her seat, murmured a greeting, and dropped into a curtsy. With a curt gesture, Adrian's grandmother motioned for Jillian to sit. After the lady settled herself stiffly in her own chair, she gazed at Jillian with piercing eyes.

"So," she said. "Why hasn't my grandson seen fit to visit me along with his new wife?"

Jillian flushed hotly at the lady's sharp question. "I don't know, your grace," she said meekly. "Perhaps he has been too busy."

"Rubbish!" Duchess Matilda rapped her cane on the floor. "Too busy, is he? I wager he won't be too busy to come when I'm on my deathbed and the inheritance I promised him is at stake."

Jillian gasped at the woman's outrageous statement.

The old lady's eyes narrowed thoughtfully. Giving a tiny nod, she said, "Perhaps you're right, girl. Adrian is not like that. Something else keeps him away. What is it?"

Jillian had a moment of panic as she floundered for an answer. She had so many problems to choose from—marriage problems, spying, illegal activities. Finally, she answered weakly, "I don't know, your grace."

The lady's majordomo entered at that moment with a tea tray, allowing Jillian some respite. Duchess Matilda directed her to pour, which gave her something to do besides clasping her hands tightly in her lap to hide her nerves. But as she handed the tea to her, the cup rattled in the saucer.

With a quick, searching glance at Jillian, the lady took her tea and sipped delicately. As she placed her cup and saucer back on the tiny table between them, she observed, "You do not appear to be the blushing bride I would expect after so short a time married to my grandson."

Jillian was unprepared for the direct remark. Heat rose in her cheeks, and she kept her eyes lowered on her teacup as she tried to think of an appropriate answer.

"Well, out with it, girl," Duchess Matilda prompted impatiently. "I don't have forever to sit here and wait. I'm not a young woman in the first bloom of youth."

Jillian gulped down her apprehension and looked into the snapping dark eyes of the lady. Despite the duchess's abrupt manner, she sensed a kindness behind those eyes. Taking a fortifying breath, she replied quietly, "Marriage to your grandson has been difficult, your grace."

Duchess Matilda nodded once. "I thought so. It seems to me that you did not wed for the right reasons."

"What do you mean?" Jillian was so surprised at the lady's answer that she did not consider her impertinent words.

A sharp glance from the duchess reminded Jillian of her place, but the old woman answered evenly, "He wed you out of a sense of honor because he felt he had ruined your reputation. You wed him to be free of your guardian. It was not an arrangement of respect, but of fear — running away from something to avoid something else. Now, you must face the consequences."

Jillian stared at the old lady in astonishment. She had not expected such a frank declaration. She had thought the lady might help, but Adrian's grandmother was right. Despair washed through her. Tears welled in her eyes.

The duchess rapped her cane on the floor in annoyance. "Don't snivel, young lady," she ordered. "Spilling tears never solved anything. Do you want this marriage to work or not?"

Sniffing, Jillian answered, "I want it to work very much."

The old lady pursed her lips. "Yes, I think you do. Does my grandson trust you?"

Jillian shook her head dolefully. "No, he doesn't."

"Why not?" She barked with the precision of an officer drilling his troops.

Jillian kept her eyes on the cup resting in her lap as she answered, "I did something that was very foolish."

"Did it have to do with another man?" the lady asked bluntly.

Shocked at the direct question, Jillian did not know how to answer, but knew she had to say something. "Well, sort of. It did and it didn't."

Duchess Matilda rapped her cane on the floor again. "Well, did it or not? I can't help if you don't tell me."

With a sigh, Jillian gave up trying to hide things from this woman. Quickly, she explained the situation about the letter, her foolishness, and Kip's part in the affair. The only thing she left out was the fact that Kip was her brother and a smuggler.

When she finished, the old lady nodded sagely. "You were very foolish, young lady. The letter might have been something else entirely. You could have put yourself in a great deal of danger."

Chastened, Jillian said, "I know that now."

"Are you going to turn this information over to my grandson?" Duchess Matilda asked.

Jillian nodded. "Oh, yes. As soon as I have it again."

"Well, that should help, but about this other young man— Kip." Duchess Matilda shook her head. "That is very serious. You will have to stop seeing him."

"But there is nothing—"

The old lady put up her hand to stop her. "There are some things about my grandson I think you should know." She paused and took a sip of tea. "I am sure," she began slowly, "that you are aware that my grandson and his mother do not get along. The reason for that goes back many years, to when Adrian was growing into a young man.

"Beatrice always ran with a wild crowd, but my son, Adrian's father, did nothing to stop her. She spent little time with Adrian, who adored his mother and did everything he could to make her notice him. When Adrian was about twelve, Beatrice announced she was with child."

Jillian's mouth dropped open.

"Yes." Duchess Matilda nodded. "Adrian has a brother. *But he is not my grandson.*" Pausing, the old lady picked up her cup again. Her hand shook as she sipped.

Jillian sat in stunned silence. She was beginning to understand. Adrian thought he was wed to a woman like his mother.

Duchess Matilda cleared her throat and took up her tale once more. "My son, Adrian's father, loved his wife. But he could not stop her from sleeping with every man she could entice into her bed. We have no idea who fathered Adrian's brother. It could have been any number of men, from a member of the House of Lords to some soldier who happened to strike her fancy. The boy has been brought up as if he were Adrian's full brother, but we know he is not. Of that we are certain, for my son had not shared a bed with his wife for several years. His love became whiskey and rum. Adrian blames his mother for driving his father to the bottle and drinking himself to death."

The old lady bowed her head. The parchment-like skin stretched over her cheekbones was pale, and her hands shook as they rested on her cane. Concerned that the lady was ill, Jillian poured some hot tea into her cup and handed it to her.

Duchess Matilda waved away the teacup and pointed to a delicate cabinet decorated with intricate marquetry. "Fetch me some gin from that cupboard."

Jillian found the decanter of gin and a tiny crystal glass next to it. She filled the delicate glass almost to the rim, then watched in astonishment as Duchess Matilda drank it down in one gulp. The gin brought some color back to the lady's face.

With a mischievous twinkle, Duchess Matilda explained, "I keep that for medicinal reasons, you understand. My physician tells me I should drink nothing stronger than tea, but I find that tea does not warm the blood like gin. But please don't tell my grandson. He would be scandalized."

Jillian murmured her promise, bemused and charmed at this side of Adrian's quite proper grandmother.

The dowager duchess took up her story once more. "Between Beatrice's recklessness and his father's drinking, Adrian had no one to raise him. I did that. He, in turn, has raised his brother."

"Where is Adrian's brother?" Jillian asked.

"At Cambridge, getting educated. Adrian wanted his brother to have every advantage when he reached manhood." The old lady gazed at Jillian, then she asked abruptly, "Do you love Adrian?"

Jillian blushed and ducked her head. Now, more than ever, she knew the answer to that question.

"Yes," she said slowly, "I do."

The old lady gave a short nod. "I think he loves you, too."

That surprised Jillian even more. "He does?"

"Yes." Duchess Matilda nodded again.

Sadly, Jillian shook her head. "No, your grace, he does not."

Duchess Matilda drew herself up. "Don't be impertinent," she snapped. "Of course he does. Except he does not realize it. Go home, girl. Fight for him."

Stunned, Jillian did not move.

The old lady rapped her cane on the floor. "Well, what are you waiting for? I want to see some great-grandchildren before I die, and I won't get them with you sitting in my drawing room."

With a grin, Jillian jumped up, dropped a perfunctory curtsy and hurried to the door. Adrian loved her! Just before she left, she turned and said shyly, "Thank you, your grace."

"You may call me Grandmother," the old lady allowed regally.

"Thank you, Grandmother Matilda," Jillian said shyly and closed the door behind her.

A bubble of happiness danced in her chest. Somehow, she would gain Adrian's trust and make him see she loved him.

The old lady stared at the closed door. Something about the girl's smile, the curve of her cheek, the way she moved, triggered a memory. Full-blown, it popped into her head. Now she knew who the girl was. And she had just learned the day before that the Laird of Ayton had taken up residence in his London townhouse. At the time, she wondered what had brought the Scot to the city when he rarely visited. Now she knew.

Laughing to herself, she picked up the glass of gin and frowned because it was empty. She remembered the scandal — all of it. The girl, Jillian, looked like her mother, Lilith St. Clare, the Baroness St. Clare. Jillian was a baroness in her own right. Without realizing it, her grandson had chosen himself a wife of exceptional bloodlines. This was cause for celebration. With another happy chuckle, she rang for her majordomo. When the man appeared, she said, "Ackers, bring round the carriage. I think I will take a drive through Hyde Park this afternoon."

The duchess chuckled at Ackers' bemused expression as he bowed and left to do her bidding. Normally, she detested the crowds in the park, but today she would make an appearance. It would get the gossips wondering, and re-direct the whispers about her grandson's abrupt marriage. After all, in a few months, if all went well, she could announce the impending birth of a great-grandchild.

After seeing his wife entertaining two of her lovers so soon after their hesitant reconciliation, Adrian had stumbled blindly out of his house and back into his coach. He ordered his driver to take him to Boodle's club where he was determined to get roaring drunk and forget his wife. Except he discovered the deed was impossible to accomplish. No matter how hard he tried, the vision of Jillian, the memory of her soft skin beneath his hands, her golden hair tumbled about her shoulders, her gray eyes dark and wild with passion, haunted him. But then he remembered seeing her with the Scot and the German — both of her lovers — after she had enticed *him* with her charms only the night before.

The evening before, when he had seen Jillian standing sadly at Prinny's ball, he thought he might have been mistaken about her. He had been swayed by Wyndham's and Jessica's glowing comments about her, and blinded by her innocent beauty. When he had asked her to dance and seen the warm glimmer in her eyes, he had been lost. All he had wanted was to take her home and make passionate love to her. She had rewarded him by flaunting her heartlessness.

All women, he decided, were deceivers and cruel creatures bent on the destruction of men. They were all like his mother. The only woman he trusted was his grandmother. He understood more than ever why his father had turned to strong spirits, and saw no reason why he should not do the same, for he had to deaden the pain that was twisting inside him.

He had considered visiting Diana, but for some reason, her beauty and charms did not entice him. Damn all women. The race was composed of fickle, treacherous creatures, none of which, with few exceptions, could be trusted.

Rousing from his morose thoughts, he decided to visit another club to see if he could find more consolation there. He went from club to club throughout the evening and eventually ended up at White's, that bastion of conservative Toryism. But he was barely more drunk than when he had first set out.

In the small hours of the morning, Adrian was doggedly emptying a decanter of brandy in a secluded corner when he heard the murmur of voices and his name mentioned. Through the liquor-induced fog in his brain, he recognized the voice of the Earl of Rystoke. Even in his blurred mind, the presence of his nemesis made alarms ring. He cursed himself for consuming so much brandy, and he cursed his wife for driving him to it. His job with the Foreign Office required that he be quick-witted at all times. Now he felt as stupid as a sheep.

Forcing his brain into action, he blinked away his grogginess, straightened his cravat, stood and faced the two men. Surprise at seeing Rystoke's companion quickly dissipated the fog in his brain.

The earl stopped in mid-stride and mid-sentence, and a cruel smile crossed Rystoke's face.

"See, Mr. Stone," the earl crowed to the man beside him, "we have interrupted what appears to be a journey down the road to forgetfulness."

"I never forget those whom I dislike, Rystoke," Adrian said coldly.

"Tut, tut, sir, such poor manners, and before a guest to our country," the earl admonished. "But where are my manners? May I present Mr. Cooper Stone, lately arrived from America?"

Adrian's gaze flicked over the tall American. "Mr. Stone and I are already acquainted. I believe he was annoying my wife at the theater one evening."

"Your wife, sir, is never annoyed by the attentions of gentlemen admirers." Stone's mild comment was accompanied by a slow, significant smile.

Adrian's fingers dug into the back of the chair, but he managed to keep his expression blank.

Rystoke chuckled as his glance moved from one man to the other. "My ward has always had a rather wild streak. I'm not surprised that she encourages the advances of many gentlemen. Perhaps that is why you sit here alone with your bottle, Dunbary, rather than dancing attendance upon your new bride. Is she entertaining a close acquaintance?"

"You go too far, Rystoke," Adrian growled.

"But you dare not call me out," the earl said smugly. "Rather awkward to do that, wouldn't you say? After all, I was the girl's guardian."

Stone added solemnly, "The scandal of a duel would certainly not help your position in the Foreign Office. Especially with the rumors going the rounds about your smuggling."

Adrian waved away the man's remark. "Old rumors. They have been replaced by juicier gossip."

"I beg to disagree, Dunbary," Rystoke said, as he studiously studied the cuff of his coat. "Why, only this evening I overheard our Prime Minister and Lord Castlereagh in a discussion about these rumors. How scandalous that a man of your position in the Foreign Office should flaunt the laws of the very government he serves."

Adrian felt that he was somehow missing something. How had these rumors come into existence? Who had started them? He fervently wished again that he had not consumed so much brandy.

"You are mad, Rystoke," he said flatly. "You know there are no such rumors."

The earl laughed. "But there are, sir. And now, there will be the further rumor of your fondness for the bottle." He shook his head. "A sad state of affairs."

Frustrated and befuddled by drink, Adrian muttered a curse and commented on the morals of the earl's ancestors.

"I could call *you* out for that," the earl said, "but then I might be accused of trying to do away with my ward's husband in order to take advantage of her wealth. That would not do." He shook his head. "No, I believe I will let matters run their course. Who knows? My ward may be a widow very soon without my having to stand on the field of honor. A gentleman in disgrace knows where his duty lies." He turned to the American. "Come, Stone, we will leave Dunbary to his bottle. Perhaps he will find a solution in its depths." With a nasty laugh, the two men moved off.

Adrian sank back into his chair and covered his face with his hands. How had his life become such a mess? What had he done to make the fates so cruel? He had a faithless wife, and false rumors about his smuggling threatened his position in the Foreign Office. Rystoke's suggestion that he take his own life as a means of saving his honor was a cruel taunt. Even in his low state, he was not about to fall into any trap the man set.

With a deep sigh, he dropped his hands from his face. It was all too much for his befuddled brain. He poured himself another glass of brandy. He would drink himself into oblivion tonight and straighten everything out in the morning. Perhaps, with the help of the elixir in the crystal decanter, he could have a decent night's sleep without dreams of a witch with golden hair and fathomless gray eyes.

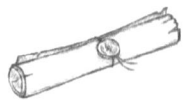

CHAPTER 19

Beatrice opened the door to her room and peered out. A few lamps were lit in the hall to force away night's gloom, but the house was quiet. The evening was well advanced, and the servants had all retired except for a footman, who napped in the small butler's room while he waited for the return of the master and mistress of the house.

She had watched Adrian and his wife leave in separate carriages. Beatrice smiled to herself. Her son, who had reviled her for enjoying herself, was now wed to a woman who took her pleasure seriously and left her tedious husband to his own devices. She had been quite aware of the cold antipathy which characterized her son's marriage to the young beauty.

Beatrice frowned. Gustav had become enchanted with Jillian. Too enchanted. Dear, charming Gustav. Sly, treacherous Gustav.

Beatrice moved out into the hall and quietly closed the door behind her. Gliding down the hall, she came to a stop before another door, not far from her own. She glanced about to be sure she was alone, turned the handle and slipped inside.

The room smelled of her lover, of his pipe and the heavy scent he wore. A lamp had been lit in a corner for his return, but other than that, the room was in deep shadow. She knew he would not be back for several hours, for he had gone to a gaming hell. She had begged off, pleading a headache.

She stood in the middle of the room and looked around. Where to begin? The wardrobe seemed the most logical place. Determined to discover if he were truly dallying with her son's wife — the little hussy — she opened the wardrobe doors and proceeded to search.

Almost an hour later, Beatrice sat back on her heels and heaved a sigh. She had found nothing — nothing in the wardrobe, nothing in any of the drawers, nothing in his pockets. Perhaps her fears were unfounded. Yet, something in her lover's manner caused her unease. He was just as attentive, just as exciting between the sheets as he had always been, yet something... His suave dismissal of her questions concerning his meeting with Jillian made suspicions nag at her.

Glancing about the room once more, her gaze happened to land on the small, bedside table. Perhaps it was a trick of light, perhaps it was her odd position on the floor, but there seemed to be something attached to the underside of the table, mostly hidden by the carved, wooden apron.

She crawled over to the piece of furniture and peeked underneath. There, stuck to the underside, was a packet of papers. Carefully, she pulled them free of the wax which held them to the wood. Untying the cord that bound them together, she laid them out on the floor before her.

There were two letters, one unfinished, obviously begun by Gustav, and another addressed to him. They were both in German, but she had lived in that country long enough to decipher most of the words. The one written by Gustav described his meetings with various members of Parliament, and conversations he'd had with them concerning the war with Napoleon. The second complimented him on his timely escape from Germany and the hope that England would prove more hospitable and a fertile source of "that knowledge which will be most helpful to our Emperor in his glorious quest for the supremacy of France." As she read quickly through them, devastation enveloped her. Both letters incriminated her lover as a spy for Napoleon. Both made her painfully aware of how she had been duped.

Gathering the pages together, she slowly rose to her feet. She felt old, ancient, and saw herself as pitiful, pathetic, despicable. She was a fool for believing a virile young man like the Baron von Heisburg would want her as a lover. All he wanted was the protection she could afford him from those men who despised what he did and what he stood for, men like her son. Rage swept through her. She would not allow this man, this *spy*, to use her any longer. No more would he wander freely about London as he gathered information to send back to England's enemies. No more would he charm her with his suave lies. Tomorrow, despite the difficult relationship she had with Adrian, she would tell her son of von Heisburg's deceit and confess her stupidity. Perhaps, just this once, she could be the type of mother Adrian wanted her to be.

Clutching the letters in her hand, she slipped out of the German's room and down the hall. As she neared the top of the stairs, she heard the front door open and close and the murmur of male voices. The footman welcomed Gustav home. The German dismissed the servant and insisted that he retire for the night. At the man's protest, von Heisburg assured him that he would remain up to answer the door when his master and mistress arrived home, an oddity, to be sure.

Beatrice heard the footman retire and made a mental note to speak to Adrian about dismissing him. The servant should not have been so eager for his bed. However, she wondered at the German's reason for retiring him.

His footsteps echoed across the entry, and she watched as he came into view. He glanced up as he placed his foot on the bottom step. Frozen by her raging emotions, she remained unmoving as he hesitated and smiled at her. Somehow, that smile seemed so cold, so calculating, so evil, now that she knew what he truly was.

"My dear Beatrice," he greeted her. "You are feeling fery much better, ya?"

"Yes, thank you, Gustav," she replied as she hid the papers behind her. "My headache seems to have left me."

"That is goot." He gained the top of the stairs and stopped before her. "Did you miss me, *Liebling*?" He reached out to stroke her cheek.

She stepped around him and kept the letters in her hand hidden. "No, not at all. Actually, I was quite busy."

"Ah, *Meine Liebe*, you crush me. I thought you vould be vaiting for my return. But, perhaps, there vas someone else here to entertain you, ya?" His blue eyes glittered coldly in the soft light of the hallway.

Beatrice laughed, a brittle sound. "You are a strange one to accuse me of infidelity, Gustav, when I see you dallying with my son's wife."

He shrugged off her accusation. "She is a beautiful voman. I pay her respect that is due her."

"More than respect, I think." Even now, when she knew the truth about this man before her, jealousy gnawed at her.

"Ah, *Liebchen*, ve must not argue. It is only vasted time, ya?" He stepped closer to her and ran his hand seductively down her arm. "Vhat is this you are hiding?" he asked mildly when he noticed her hand behind her back.

Rage and betrayal surged through her at his attempt to beguile. But she forced herself to keep her voice light. "Something I found that told me what type of man you truly are."

He smiled, a bit uncertainly. "Vhat did you find?"

Waving her free hand airily as if it did not matter, she turned and walked away a few steps. "Oh, papers."

"Vhat papers?" His smile turned to a displeased frown.

"Papers that were cluttering up your room," she told him with a nonchalance she did not feel.

"Beatrice, *Liebling*, you must gife me back those papers, ya?" His voice was quiet, pleading.

She turned to face him. Resolve hardened her tone. "No, I don't think so. I think I will give them to my son. He will know what to do with Napoleon's spy."

A change came over his face. His mouth turned down and his eyes went cold. He was no longer the suave, urbane gentleman, but became the cruel, devious villain he truly was. "So, you hafe discovered my secret. I am glad. Now, I do not hafe to pretend to make lofe to a vithered, old hag."

Instead of crumbling beneath his vicious words, she became more determined to see this deceiver brought to justice. Raising her chin, she said, "Your insults don't touch me, Gustav. But I am curious. Why did you choose me as your pawn?"

He smiled, a nasty, cold smile. "You vere easy prey, *Liebchen*. I needed to escape Germany because the gofernment suddenly did not like Napoleon. You gafe me the perfect reason to leafe one country and come to another vhere I could gather information. Vhen I discofer that you are the mother of a man who vorks for the English Foreign Office, I think maybe I hafe come to Heafen, ya?"

"You are a weasel, Gustav."

His smile widened. "Ya. Now, gife me the papers." He took a step towards her.

She whipped them behind her back and retreated. "No. I told you, these are going to my son."

"You are wrong, *Liebling*. They are not." He lunged forward, reached around her, and grabbed the letters.

Beatrice clutched her end with both hands as she struggled to wrench them free. "You won't get them," she panted, as she tried to pull them away. "I am going let my son know he has a spy living in his house."

The German abruptly stopped struggling with her, but retained his hold on the letters. Calm replaced the anger on his face, as if he had seen his error. "Perhaps, you are right, *Liebchen*." Stepping forward, he forced her to back up.

Confused, Beatrice stared up at him. Only when she felt the edge of the top step dig into the bottom of her foot did she understand. Panic swept over her. She tried to inch forward to more solid footing. The German was an unyielding wall. She knew what was about to come. Her only thought was to hold onto the letters in her grasp.

Stepping forward, von Heisburg forced Beatrice off balance. Only their mutual hold on the letters kept her from toppling backwards. An evil light came into his eyes. He abruptly released the letters. She teetered on the top step. Her arms waved wildly. Clawing at her lover's coat, she tried not to fall backward. The German caught her wrist and pried her fingers from his coat. He held her above the yawning stairs. She was suspended on the brink between danger and safety. She met his gaze—cold, cruel, dispassionate. And knew what was coming. She felt no fear, only a sense of calm and triumph. She was finally doing something for her son.

"I hate you, Gustav," Beatrice spat out.

Distaste twisted his lips. With an annoyed shove, he released her wrist. She flailed, her arms wind-milling as she teetered on the step. Losing her balance, she fell back into space. A tiny cry escaped her as she tumbled down the staircase. She heard the thudding of her body as it pinwheeled from step to step. She felt the hard impact of each stair. A sharp pain in her neck. Then she felt nothing. Her last thought was victorious. She had held onto the letters.

Von Heisburg watched her unpleasant descent. It ended when she landed in an unnatural heap on the floor at the bottom. He stood at the top of the stairs a moment and listened. He heard no cries of alarm from any of the servants. The old hag had not even screamed as she toppled down the stairs, and so had wakened no one in the house.

Straightening his cravat and waistcoat, he sauntered down the steps. He stood over the formless pile of humanity for a moment and surveyed his handiwork. Her head lay at an odd angle and indicated a broken neck. She did not move. Crouching over her, he felt for a heartbeat. There was none. She had died instantly.

With a grunt of satisfaction, he reached beneath her for the letters she still held. She clutched the top half of them in her death grip. He tried prying her fingers open, but with little success.

As he knelt over his victim, he heard the approaching sounds of a carriage. Realizing it could be Dunbary or his wife returning home, he desperately yanked at the papers again, but with little success. All he could do was tear off the parts that were free of Beatrice's hold. With a vicious, snarling oath at the woman who had turned against him, he stood and bolted up the stairs to begin his flight.

Two nights after his drunken wallow in self-pity, Adrian stepped wearily down from his carriage onto the front drive of his house. He was returning from a dinner with his friend, Wyndham, and several other friends. Out of courtesy, he had been forced to be sociable, laughing and chatting as if his world were perfect, when in truth, he felt as if he were living in Hell.

He looked up at the house. Something made him uncomfortable. Except for a few dim glimmers of lamps lit for his return, the house was in darkness. He did not expect all the lights lit, but Boggs usually left more lamps burning. Wondering if his wife were at home, he slowly climbed the stairs and reached for the doorknob.

His thoughts churned. Wyndham had taken him aside at the end of the evening and told him he had heard von Heisburg was asking probing questions around the city concerning the government's policies and activities. The German living beneath his roof was very likely a spy. Adrian sighed. While he wanted very much to catch the German with incriminating evidence, he was relieved that his mother and her lover would be moving out of his house in two days.

He paused with his hand on the door handle. That sense of wrongness descended on him again. Boggs usually had a footman waiting up, who would open the door at his approach. But the hour was quite late. The footman had most likely dozed off. Shrugging off his unease, he opened the door and walked in.

No servant greeted him. That thought had barely registered when his glance fell on a jumbled pile of clothing at the bottom of the stairs. Annoyed at the mess, he stepped closer to investigate. His breath halted. The pile was a body. His mother.

With a low cry, he dropped to his knees beside her. Her head was bent at an awkward angle. Her eyes were open, staring blankly into space. "Mother?" he asked tentatively, not really expecting an answer. He listened for her breath and felt for her heartbeat. There was none. She was dead.

Stunned, emotions poured through him. Horror. Anger. Regret. Grief. His mother's eyes were fixed on a point at the top of the stairs. She must have tumbled down the steps and broken her neck. Taking a deep, shuddering breath, he reached out a shaky hand and shuttered that unseeing gaze.

Her skin was cool. She looked as if she only slept. In death, peace had finally found her. A great, wrenching sob tore itself from Adrian's throat.

"Oh, mother," he whispered, as emotions tumbled through him.

Gently, he smoothed her hair back from her face. Deep regret stabbed him at their terrible, strained relationship. Anger at her lack of maternal instincts quickly followed. Sorrow that now they could never resolve their differences swamped everything else.

Lost in grief, he remained on his knees beside the mother who had never been a mother to him.

Jillian, returning from an evening recital at the house of an acquaintance, alighted from the coach and glanced up at the house. Annoyance crossed her face at the lack of lights. Since Boggs had the evening off, the first footman had been left in charge of the household. She made a mental note to discover why he had been so negligent. She hoped there had been no emergency.

Sighing, she climbed the stairs to the front door. This petty annoyance did not improve her depressed mood. Her relationship with her husband was still terribly strained. Even though their paths did not cross in the evenings, she was quite aware of his chilly anger and his nighttime excursions. So far, the dowager duchess had been wrong about Dunbary's feelings. She opened the door and stepped into the house.

Her gaze immediately fell on her husband kneeling over someone laying at the bottom of the stairs. Something about the droop of his shoulders alarmed her.

"Adrian?" she asked as she stepped forward.

At her voice, his head snapped up, but he did not turn to look at her.

She walked closer. "Adrian, what is it?" Her breath caught in her throat when she saw Beatrice. "Oh, dear God! What happened? Is she—?"

"Dead," he finished flatly.

Jillian crouched beside him. "Oh, Adrian, I'm so sorry." Tentatively, she placed her hand on his shoulder, fully expecting him to shrug it off. She was surprised when he let it remain. "How did it happen?"

He shook his head. "I found her when I arrived home. Her eyes—" His voice broke. He swallowed and went on. "Her eyes were still open, staring up the stairs."

Jillian watched him smooth the hair back from his mother's face. She did not know what else to say to comfort him. The terrible, strained relationship between Adrian and his mother made ordinary, sympathetic words seem meaningless. She looked down at Beatrice, at the unnatural angle of her neck, at the crumpled heap that had once been a vibrant, living being.

The heavy quiet of the house made her glance around. The servants should have been rushing about in response to such a tragedy. Silence greeted her. Something was very wrong.

"Why is there no footman about?" she asked. "Where is everyone?" Adrian's answer was a disconsolate shake of his head.

Her husband was too overcome with grief to understand the problem. She looked at the body. Beatrice's fist was clenched tightly around something white.

"What is she holding?" she asked.

Adrian seemed to shake off his lethargy as he glanced at his mother's hand. He pried open her fingers and pulled torn sheets of parchment from her hand. His features hardened as he read them.

"It's the German," he said, his voice cold and hard. "Wyndham was right. Von Heisburg is a spy for Napoleon. My mother must have found these letters." He glanced up the stairs. "They must have struggled, and that German cur pushed her down the steps. That's why she was staring at them."

"Then we should have the footmen detain him." Jillian began to rise, but Adrian's voice stopped her.

"No doubt he's fled by now. I'll send word to the authorities to watch for him." He gazed at Beatrice and crushed the papers in his hand. "Oh, mother," he sighed, those two words filled with regret.

Jillian wanted to comfort Adrian in his anguish, but their strained relationship made her hesitate. She wondered if she should tell her husband about the German's desire to get her to pass along information. Would Adrian see it as a device to gain his trust at a time when he was vulnerable? She opened her mouth to tell him, then shut it again. The moment was lost when her husband spoke.

"She was always a willing victim of someone who would pay her pretty compliments and make her feel young," he said, his voice low and brooding. "She never wanted responsibility for anything, including me. She despised my father for getting her with child because it made her ugly. She always needed to be reassured about her youth and beauty." His tone turned sorrowful. "All I wanted was for her to notice me."

He shuddered. Jillian put a hesitant, comforting hand on his shoulder. Silent tears welled in his eyes. His pain made her ache. Wanting to console him, she wrapped her arms about him. He clung to her, his face tucked against her shoulder.

Her heart clenched at his anguish. But he had turned to her in his grief. He had exposed his rawest emotions to her. Perhaps he felt something for her after all.

Adrian's loss of control lasted only a few moments. He straightened and turned from her.

"My apologies," he said stiffly. "I did not mean to subject you to such an indecent display." He stood as he surreptitiously wiped his eyes.

His abrupt withdrawal shafted through her. She could not allow him to walk away after he had allowed her to see his grief. As she rose to her feet, she said, "I think we should talk, Adrian."

He glanced at her, then turned away. "I fear there is nothing to talk about. Besides, there will be little time over the next few days." He motioned to his mother at his feet.

She was not going to let this opportunity slip away. "There is something you should know about von Heisburg."

He raised a curious eyebrow in her direction. "Yes? What is it?"

She shook her head. "Not now. Tomorrow. After arrangements have been made for—for your mother."

His gaze was cool. Then he turned to the bellpull to summon the servants. "Very well. Tomorrow afternoon. Shall we say five o'clock, in my study?"

"Five o'clock will be fine," she said. Then added, "Your grace."

At her formal address for him, he hesitated as he reached for the bellpull, but only for the tiniest moment. Straightening her shoulders, Jillian closed away her own hurt in order to contend with that of her husband's. The ordeal of the next several hours would be difficult enough without the added burden of her own broken heart.

At precisely five o'clock the following afternoon, Jillian stood before the door to Adrian's study. After patting her hair into place and smoothing her skirt, she knocked. His low, muffled voice bade her enter. Taking a deep breath, she opened the door and walked in.

The room was dim. Out of respect for the death in the household, the drapes had been drawn across the front windows. Only a small lamp burned on Adrian's desk. Her husband stood when she entered. Gingerly, she sat on the edge of a chair before the desk.

His face was drawn. Dark shadows beneath his eyes and stubble on his jaw testified to his grief and distraction. The day had not been an easy one for either of them, but particularly for Adrian. Lack of sleep had only aggravated the terrible situation and placed an extra burden on strained nerves. Jillian knew this conversation would be difficult. She only hoped that by its end, she would have begun to bridge the gap with her husband.

Giving a tiny smile of sympathy, she said, "Please, sit down, Adrian. You look exhausted."

Her words brought a frown to his face as he sat. "What do you wish to speak to me about?" His tone was abrupt. His gaze was cold.

Jillian folded her hands in her lap and studied her fingers a moment as she collected her thoughts. Raising her head, she said, "I knew von Heisburg was a spy."

"Your confession is a little late." Chilly anger flared in those tawny eyes. "My mother is dead — murdered — and the cur has fled."

Jillian flinched. He was right. She should have told him when the German had first approached her. Except at the time, she thought her husband was committing treason as well.

Despite his contempt, she forged on. "He wanted me to watch you, listen to your conversations, read your correspondence."

A dark brow quirked sardonically upward. "Did you?"

"No! I told him I would never spy on you."

"That is terribly kind of you, since you are doing that already for Rystoke." His sarcastic words were as barbed as a fishhook.

Jillian sucked in a breath. How did he know about her guardian's demand? "I have never told Rystoke anything that could hurt you."

"Why do I find that difficult to believe?" Adrian leaned back in his chair. "Have you ever told me the truth, Jillian?"

Yes, she had been truthful about the most important thing — that she wanted only him. But he did not — would not — believe her. She remained silent.

He pursued relentlessly. "What about the letter? What about the bargain you laid before me — my hand in marriage for the letter? You told me you burned it, but I don't believe you. I don't think you would destroy something as important as that. I think you lied. *Where is the letter, Jillian?"*

Wretchedly, she stood and wandered away a few steps. She knew it was time for the truth. "You're right. I didn't burn it. But..." She swallowed, then confessed, "I don't have it." She wished she had never given it to Kip. She wished she could just hand it over to her husband.

"You don't have it," he repeated grimly. "I have been hearing excuses ever since you made that bargain with me. I don't think you ever meant to keep your side in the first place. I think I was the dupe in a very clever scheme you and your guardian put together. I kept my side of the bargain. You have my hand and my name, Duchess Dunbary. Unfortunately, I don't have the energy to pursue a divorce, nor the willingness to withstand the resulting gossip."

Shock made her blurt, "I don't want a divorce."

Adrian's smile was cold and cynical. "Of course not. Why should you want to give up the prestige of your title?"

"No." She shook her head. "You don't understand."

"Of course I do. A divorce will cause you quite a bit of discomfort, but that is only a bit of repayment for what you have caused me."

Jillian closed her eyes at the pain of his words. Opening them again, she looked directly into that topaz gaze. "I don't want a divorce because I love you," she said quietly.

He stared at her a moment, then he barked a laugh. "Love?" he mocked. "You don't know what love is. All you want is to be surrounded by admirers, men who will say anything to gain your favors."

"That's not true." Tears, desperate and painful, balanced on the edge of her lashes.

"Please, don't insult my intelligence." He paused, then sighed as if too exhausted to continue. "Don't worry, I won't divorce you. Just try to behave while the house is in mourning."

Holding onto her pride, hiding her pain, she stood. "You do not need to lecture me. I know perfectly well how I should act." She turned toward the door. "Thank you for your time, your grace. This has been a most enlightening conversation." She stopped with her hand on the knob and turned back to him. "I would like you to know that I have never bestowed my favors on any other man besides my husband — you, your grace — and especially not on von Heisburg. He was your mother's lover, not mine."

Adrian watched her leave. Leaning his elbows on the desk, he dropped his head into his hands. Her words rang in his ears... *your mother's lover, not mine.* If only it were true. If only he could trust her. If only she would show him something that proved her faithful. All he had was evidence to the contrary — that meeting with the American at the theater and again at Sally Jersey's, the meeting with that Scot behind his back, entertaining both the Scot and the German the morning after they had shared a glorious night of love.

Memories of soft murmurings, silky-hot skin, and wild, panting breaths slipped through his mind. He shook his head to chase away the images. He could not dwell on that marvelous night. She was a deceiver, a wanton, who would do anything to get what she wanted. Somehow, he would have to deal with that fact. Somehow, he would have to separate himself from the fact that she haunted him with those fathomless gray eyes, that hesitant smile which came so rarely to her lips.

She said she loved him. If only that were true. If only he could believe those quietly spoken words. She must be very frightened to voice such drastic lies. Perhaps he had scared her by his talk of divorce. Or, perhaps, the death of his mother and the flight of the German worried her. Perhaps she was afraid the German would return for her. Perhaps by admitting to knowing the German was a spy, she was trying to turn suspicion away from herself. Perhaps, she, too, was a spy for Napoleon. He sighed heavily. All these possibilities with no definite answer.

He raised his head. He would decide what to do with her later, after he had buried his mother. He had been stupid. How could he have fallen into the same trap as his father and married a woman who cared only for herself? But knowing what he had done did not ease the horrible ache in his heart.

He sighed again, stood and eased the cramps in his neck and shoulders. His brother would be arriving from Cambridge tomorrow. Perhaps, while the young pup was home, he could begin to teach him about the vices and vagaries of women. Maybe one male member of the family could escape the unhappiness women could cause.

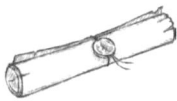

CHAPTER 20

"You must be Duchess Dunbary."

The young man's voice startled Jillian from her contemplation of the black bombazine and crepe mourning gown she would wear at Beatrice's funeral. He stood, looking a bit uncertain, in the open doorway of her sitting room.

She knew immediately this was Adrian's younger brother. He had inherited the same square jaw as her husband, the same chiseled mouth. He was a handsome youth. She smiled warmly.

"You must be Lawrence," she said. "Please, come in."

He bowed and said, "I apologize for my intrusion, your grace, but I wished to introduce myself."

"Please, call me Jillian." She sat in a chair near the hearth and motioned to another across from her. "I heard you arrive last evening, but I didn't wish to intrude on you and your brother. Please, join me in a cup of tea. I just had it brought up." As Lawrence seated himself, Jillian poured the tea. "I would like to extend my sympathy on the death of your mother," she said. "It must have been a great shock to you."

Their gazes met as she handed him his cup. She caught a flash of pain in his eyes before he lowered them. "Thank you."

Jillian studied him as she took a sip of tea. He had inherited his mother's rich, dark hair and bright, dark eyes. At the age of about sixteen or seventeen, he had not yet reached his full growth, but already he showed signs of the attractive man he would become. He was keeping tight control at the moment over some very disturbing emotions, for his shoulders were stiff and his jaw was tight.

"I did not know your mother very well, but her death was a tragedy," she said.

"Her death was a blessing." His words were defiant, as if he expected her to argue.

Jillian caught her lip between her teeth. Here was another son whom Beatrice had hurt badly. "I think I understand how you feel, but you must not speak ill of the dead."

He leaned forward intently. "I don't think you have the right to lecture me on what I should not do."

Surprised by his antagonism, Jillian carefully placed her cup on the table between them and leaned back in her chair. "I did not mean to insult you," she said. "But I believe your mother died trying to rectify a wrong."

He laughed bitterly. "That attempt came a bit too late, didn't it? Adrian said you are just like her."

Hurt and anger swept through her at his accusation. A knot formed in her chest. Her declaration of love to Adrian had not changed his mind about her. She suspected it had convinced him of her duplicity. But his brother had no right to condemn without knowing her.

"We have only just met," she said, keeping her tone level. "How do you know I am just like her?"

"Adrian told me how you got him to marry you. He does not even know who your family is. He suspects you may be some nameless adventuress."

Jillian wanted to slap him for his superior attitude. He was illegitimate, just as she was. "Do you know who your father is, Lawrence?" she asked quietly. "Duchess Matilda related some intimate family secrets to me."

A vivid blush crawled up his neck to the tips of his ears, and he ducked his head.

Taking pity on him, she said, "Your secret is safe. No matter what Adrian's opinion of me is, I am still a member of this family. Its secrets affect me, as much as they do you."

When Lawrence raised his head, his mouth was tight. "Adrian said you reneged on a bargain you made with him."

Guilt made her shift in her seat. "Yes, I did, because I did not understand something which was very important. I am trying to rectify my mistake."

"How?" he lashed out. "By having all manner of men visiting you under this very roof?"

Jillian stared at him as she tried to control her temper. "Before you make accusations, I think you should be sure of your facts. Only one man has visited me here in this house. He is—"

She halted before she blurted the truth about Kip. She had not yet been able to tell Adrian. If she told Lawrence and he told Adrian, would her husband think she was keeping secrets again?

She glanced at the young man seated across from her. Suspicion was etched on his face. He deserved the truth, and he needed to learn that not all women were like his mother. Even if—when—he told Adrian, nothing could worsen her husband's opinion of her.

She took a breath and said, "The man who visited me is my brother."

His eyes widened. "But...Adrian said..." His brows crashed together. "I don't believe you."

She had expected his skepticism. "Believe what you wish. It is the truth."

Lawrence sat in confused silence.

"I have not had the opportunity to tell Adrian," she confided. "I only discovered he was my brother a short time ago."

Doubt clouded Lawrence's eyes.

Sighing, she leaned forward and poured more tea. "I am telling the truth, Lawrence. You see, your accusation about my background was not far off the mark. I am illegitimate, too." She didn't know why she was confiding to him. Some instinct told her that perhaps, in time, they might become friends.

At his silence, she went on, "It's a long story, and I don't know all of it yet. I'm not sure your brother would believe me because of other deceptions." She turned away as tears blurred her vision.

Lawrence was quiet for a moment. Then he asked, "Why did you tell *me*?"

"I thought you should know. I'm not the monster your brother thinks I am." She shrugged fatalistically. "It seems that our lives have been twisted by secrets and deceptions. If I could start over... Well, it's too late for that, isn't it?" She smiled bravely to cover the terrible pain in her heart.

"I'm sorry," he murmured, then fell silent for a moment. "I know why Adrian fell in love with you," he blurted.

Jillian blinked. "I beg your pardon?"

Lawrence grinned. "He's in love with you, you know."

She reached for her cup to cover her confusion. "I'm sure you must be mistaken. Adrian and I have a very strained relationship."

"I know. He told me all about it." His mouth curled in a suppressed grin.

"Then how can you say that he is in love with me?" she asked.

"Because when he talks about you, he has a look in his eyes..." He shrugged, unable to explain it any clearer.

Hope fluttered in the vicinity of her heart. If what Lawrence said was true, then perhaps her relationship with Adrian held some promise. She shook her head. No, their marriage was beyond redemption. "I'm sure you believe that, but I don't think what you see in his eyes is love. All the same, I thank you for trying to help."

At that moment, Adrian stopped in the doorway. "Lawrence, I need to discuss some important matters with you," he snapped out. "Please come to my study. Now." He bowed in Jillian's direction as his cold gaze raked over her. "Madam. My apologies." Then he turned on his heel and left.

With a brave smile to hide her pain, Jillian turned to Lawrence. "Thank you for sharing tea with me. I will see you at dinner."

Lawrence stood and bowed over Jillian's proffered hand. "He does love you, you know," he whispered. Then he went to attend his brother.

Jillian sighed and turned to her cold and lonely tea.

The next day, Jillian glanced out of the coach as it pulled up before the house. Rain streaked the windows and smudged everything into shades of gray. The funeral had been depressing. The ride back home had been worse, made in sad silence. Wet, black crepe draped about the door and front windows, shaded from inside. A black wreath hung on the door. She hated black. It reminded her of her mother's sad funeral, attended only by her and a few loyal servants. With

Beatrice's death, now she would have to wear the awful color for the next year and a half.

Adrian stepped down from the coach and helped Duchess Matilda alight. As he walked his grandmother up the front stairs, he bent down to hear something the old lady said. The knot which tangled in Jillian's chest pulled a bit tighter. To her, Adrian had been as cold and remote as the weather.

Lawrence stepped down onto the drive, then turned to hand her out. As she stepped onto the drive, she smiled up at him. The young man had been stoically brave during the whole ordeal of the day, and had been kindly concerned for her well-being. She felt a sisterly fondness for him.

Upon entering the house, Jillian was relieved to throw off her mourning veil and remove her dull, black hat. Adrian and the dowager duchess had already disappeared into the drawing room. Extra black gloves, those that had not been needed for the mourners, still sat in a pile on a small side table, along with a large tray of calling cards left by those who had come to express their sympathy. The muted clatter of dishes being cleared after the funeral feast came from the dining room. She was relieved that all the fuss surrounding the funeral was over. As the wife of the Duke of Dunbary, society would never have permitted her any deviation from what was expected.

Boggs announced that there was tea and refreshment in the drawing room, and with a grateful smile at the majordomo, she joined her husband and his grandmother along with Lawrence.

When she entered, Adrian halted his conversation with Duchess Matilda. Jillian felt the old lady's gaze as she sat and poured herself tea in silence. It dragged on as Jillian sipped from her cup. Lawrence wandered over to a window that faced the back gardens and stood gazing out.

Duchess Matilda patted Jillian's knee. "Your preparations for today were commendable, dear. I dare anyone to find fault with your arrangements or your conduct."

Adrian started to say something, but Boggs knocked on the door. "Excuse the interruption, your grace, but there are some...er...gentlemen here to see you."

Surprised silence fell into the room, for these visitors breached the code of acceptable behavior by intruding upon their grief.

Adrian frowned. "Didn't you tell them we're not receiving?"

Boggs nervously cleared his throat. "I did, your grace. They were quite adamant. I believe they will not leave until you speak with them."

"I will see them in my study, Boggs," Adrian finally said.

As her husband placed his cup and saucer on the table, Jillian heard several men passing by the door. She caught a glimpse of a red soldier's uniform. Uneasiness made her frown as Adrian walked out the door. His footsteps echoed in the entry hall. She glanced at Lawrence and saw her apprehension mirrored in his eyes.

"I would like another cup of tea, young lady," Duchess Matilda announced. "Or shall I have to pour it myself?"

Jillian mumbled an apology and poured. Handing the cup to her, she said, "I can't imagine who would be so discourteous and call at such a time."

"No doubt someone who has no idea of proprieties," the old lady sniffed.

"One of the men was an officer in the Tenth Regiment, the Regent's Own," Lawrence observed.

Jillian had a sick feeling in the pit of her stomach. She could think of no reason why soldiers should call on her husband so soon after burying his mother. Was the visit connected to the note hidden in her doll? Or was it connected to something more sinister? She could think of only one person who might orchestrate something so audacious and cruel — the Earl of Rystoke.

She watched Lawrence pace to the doorway, listen a moment, then pace back. To distract him, as well as herself, she asked, "More tea, Lawrence?"

"I could use a glass of port," Lawrence announced.

"You'll have no such thing," his grandmother scolded. "Spirits at this time are inappropriate." She emphasized her words by sharply rapping her cane once on the floor.

Looking thoroughly chastised, Lawrence started pacing again.

After his fourth trip to the door to listen, he announced, "They're coming out."

Footsteps sounded in the hall and Adrian entered the drawing room. His face was grim, but his eyes blazed with fury.

"I'm afraid I must leave," he said. "I am being arrested for smuggling." His gaze landed with piercing directness on Jillian.

She felt the blood drain from her face. Like the first time she and Adrian had met, the rest of the room dissolved into vagueness, leaving just the two of them. Only this time, no delicious thrill and no enveloping warmth washed through her. This time, only a cold chill and antagonized tautness stretched between them. Adrian thought she had instigated the arrest. She had tried to prevent it.

"No," she whispered and gave her head a little shake.

Adrian turned from her in contempt. The connection between them broke, leaving emptiness in her heart.

"Smuggling!" Lawrence exclaimed.

"This is an outrage!" Duchess Matilda declared.

Adrian smiled grimly. "I'm sure this is all a misunderstanding. I'll go with these gentlemen and clear this up."

"How could they possibly arrest you for smuggling?" the old lady demanded.

"Some contraband brandy has been discovered at Dunbary." Adrian sent an accusing glance at Jillian. "Someone found the caves to be a convenient hiding place."

The room tilted when Jillian heard his words. Swallowing hard and taking a deep breath, she forced herself not to faint. Had she told Kip about the caves at Dunbary? She couldn't remember. If the contraband belonged to him, how could she possibly clear her husband without incriminating her brother? Closing her eyes, she tried to shut out the horrible dilemma and the accusation in Adrian's gaze.

When she opened them again, he had beckoned Lawrence to his side. "I don't want this to keep you from returning to your studies at Cambridge," he said. "Even if I have not returned by tomorrow, I want you to take the coach as you had planned."

"But—" Lawrence began.

"I won't hear any argument," Adrian told him firmly. "If something happens, you can best help by finishing your education. Promise me that you will."

Reluctantly, Lawrence nodded his agreement.

Bowing, Adrian took his leave. "Ladies, forgive me." Then, turning on his heel, he allowed himself to be arrested like a criminal.

Heavy silence descended in the drawing room. Jillian glanced at Lawrence. His brow was furrowed and a muscle jumped in his jaw. He looked as if he wanted to hit something. Jillian felt the dowager duchess's gaze, but could not meet it. Somehow, she felt responsible for her husband's arrest. Anger at Rystoke's plotting tangled with guilt at her association with him.

"There is something foul afoot here," Duchess Matilda remarked. "Smuggling, indeed."

"Didn't our ancestors smuggle, Grandmother?" Lawrence asked.

Duchess Matilda sent him a sharp glance. "That was a very long time ago, young man. It is ancient history. There is no reason in the world why Adrian should resort to such a thing."

Jillian cleared her throat. "I'm sure it must be some mistake." She tried very hard to sound normal.

Duchess Matilda's eyes glittered in her direction. "Hmm," was all she said. She studied Jillian a moment, then turned away. "Have the coach brought round," she ordered tersely. "I am going home to rest and think on this. I still have a small amount of influence. Perhaps I can discover something about this nasty business."

Jillian rang for Boggs and resolved that she would also discover something about "this nasty business." She would pay a visit to the Earl of Rystoke and confront him, but she would have to go alone. She would never involve Lawrence in her guardian's web. Somehow, she had to sneak out of the house, for social convention required that she remain at home, secluded, for some weeks in order to pay the proper respect to Beatrice. Even if Lawrence did not argue social proprieties with her, she suspected that he would insist on accompanying her.

She resigned herself to wait until she could slip out undiscovered, and kept watch with Lawrence for Adrian's return in the drawing room. The endless afternoon stretched into evening. Adrian still had not returned. She and Lawrence shared a light supper, but their conversation was desultory. Jillian had little appetite. Each time a vehicle passed by the house, she thought it might be Adrian returning, released from custody. Each time, she was disappointed.

After supper, she and Lawrence played chess, but she couldn't concentrate. She picked at a handkerchief until its edges were frayed and ragged. After Lawrence had placed her king in check for the fourth time, he took her hand. "Adrian will be all right," he said. "He's innocent."

Jillian forced a smile. "I know he is, Lawrence. It's just the waiting." She did not say that she was anxiously waiting for her chance to sneak out of the house to visit Rystoke.

Two hours later, Jillian hurried through the dark streets. She had successfully slipped out without anyone seeing her. Her plan was to confront Rystoke and return home before anyone knew she was missing. Her thoughts whirled in her head. Somehow, she would force the earl to get the charges against Adrian dropped, even if Rystoke carried out his threat and revealed she was illegitimate.

She loved Adrian. Now, she must prove it.

When she knocked on Rystoke's door, Williams was astonished to see her. The butler hurried away to announce her to his master. She waited in the drawing room, the same room where she had watched Adrian arrive to offer for her hand in marriage. The room had not changed, but she had. She was wiser now, and very much in love with her husband. If only she had known that then.

She heard Rystoke's footsteps approach, and then he appeared, smiling broadly, looking quite pleased with himself. She hated the sight of him.

"My dear Jillian," he said smoothly. "This is a surprise. Is your husband aware that you are venturing out so soon after the death of his mother? That was a tragedy, to be sure. Please accept my condolences." He did not look saddened in the least.

Jillian scowled. "You always have the right words to say, my lord. A pity your true feelings don't match them."

"Jillian, you do me an injustice. I have great sympathy for your husband's loss." He managed to compose his features into a semblance of sorrow.

"Which loss is that, my lord?" she tossed out. "The loss of his mother, or the loss of his freedom?"

"What are you are saying? Dunbary's freedom?" Victory glinted in his eyes before he hid it with false concern.

"He was arrested soon after we arrived home from the funeral. For smuggling." Jillian spat out the last word.

"Smuggling, you say?" He appeared suitably appalled. "My dear girl, I had no idea. What a misfortune coming so soon upon the death of his mother. Goodness, the scandal that will cause. *Tsk, tsk.*" He shook his head sadly.

"You may stop pretending, my lord. I know you wish to shout with joy. Isn't this what you wanted? To have Dunbary discredited?" Jillian demanded.

A slow, cold smile crossed Rystoke's face. "You are right, of course. I could not have planned it any better. The powerful Duke of Dunbary arrested for smuggling." He chuckled with satisfaction.

"So you *are* the one behind his arrest," she accused. "You put the contraband brandy in the caves at Dunbary."

He gave a negligent shrug "I have friends who are willing to take on unsavory tasks for a price." He looked quite pleased with himself.

"Why do you wish to ruin him?" she demanded.

"Because he has stood in my way for too long. He blocks every move I make in Parliament. And because he is married to *you.*"

"What has that to do with anything?" she asked. "I thought you were pleased with the connection."

"Oh, I was very pleased with the connection. After all, not every man can claim his ward is wed to the Duke of Dunbary." He gave her a condescending smile. "And now that Dunbary is ruined, I have ruined you, and gained a small bit of revenge on your father."

Bewildered and shocked by his words, Jillian sank into a chair. "I don't understand."

"You don't need to understand." Contempt twisted his lips. "You are only the pawn in this game of chess."

Insult and pride straightened her spine. "Some games are won by a pawn," she declared. "If you do not have these charges against my husband dropped, I will tell the authorities that you were the one who hid the brandy on his land."

The Earl of Rystoke threw his head back and laughed. "Who would believe you?"

"I have powerful friends. They will believe me." Jillian knew she sounded more positive than she actually felt. The only powerful friends she knew were the Duke and Duchess of Wyndham, and she was not sure they would believe her.

"Tell your powerful friends," Rystoke dared her. "Tell them, and I will let it be known that the Duchess of Dunbary comes from the wrong side of the blanket. Do you think they will believe you then? Do you think they will remain your friends when they discover what you are? Do you think your loving husband will appreciate what you do when he learns the truth about you?"

Jillian knew what she risked, but she could see no other way of proving her love for Adrian than to let him know the truth. "I don't care. Either clear his name or I will go to the authorities with what I know."

Rystoke's eyes narrowed. "I believe you would throw away everything to get him released." He chuckled. "Well, well, the lovely Jillian is in love with the biggest rakehell in London. How touching. It almost brings a tear to my eye." He wiped away an imaginary drop.

Jillian surged to her feet. "You are a snake, my lord. I'm leaving."

"No, I don't think you are." The earl stood resolutely between her and the door.

"Get out of my way. I am going to the authorities." She took a step around Rystoke.

The earl caught her arm. "No, my dear, you are not. You will remain as my guest until your husband is well and truly dishonored."

"You are mad." She tried to pull away.

"I am in complete control of all my faculties, my dear." He smiled smugly. "But you, on the other hand, are terribly distraught over the death of your mother-in-law and the arrest of your husband. You have come to me, your guardian, for comfort. It is my duty to keep you here until you have recovered."

"You are going to keep me a prisoner," she gasped.

"Oh, my goodness, no. You are merely a guest with restrictions." His smile was crafty.

She tried to wrest her arm from his grip. "I will scream and bring the servants," she threatened.

"I would advise against it," he said as his fingers dug painfully into her flesh. "They would come, but they are paid to keep a silent tongue in their heads. They would be distressed if they saw something which they should not see." He pulled her across the room toward the door. "Now, come quietly, my dear, or I shall have to use force."

Knowing his cruel streak and his temper, Jillian stumbled along with him. Fear nagged at her, but she pushed it away. She tried not to dwell on what might happen if he lost his temper. Somehow, she would think of something that would allow her to use that temper to her advantage. Something that would allow her to escape and return to Adrian.

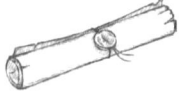

CHAPTER 21

"Where are you taking me?" Jillian demanded of her guardian as he propelled her through the house.

"To greet some friends who dined with me this evening," Rystoke said. "Good manners dictate that I include you in our gathering."

Jillian looked at him askance, but he would not meet her eyes. His smug expression widened into a smile when they entered the dining room. "Gentlemen," he announced, "we have an unexpected visitor."

Several men rose from the table. She recognized Lord Winslow and Lord Bertram, but she did not know the other two men. And at the foot of the table was Cooper Stone, the American.

"Duchess," Cooper Stone greeted. "This is a surprise."

"I should have known I would find you here, Mr. Stone," she said coldly. "Vipers tend to congregate in a comfortable nest."

"Manners, Jillian," Rystoke admonished. He pushed her to a chair at the table and forced her to sit, then took his seat at the head of the table. He glanced in triumph at his guests as they resumed their seats. "I told you we would hear about Dunbary's arrest. My dear Jillian has just confirmed that."

"You will clear his name, or I will go to the authorities," she threatened again. Turning to the other men at the table, she asked, "Has he twisted all of you? My husband is innocent. You know he would never bring dishonor on his name."

Cooper Stone shrugged. "This is war, your grace."

Appalled, she demanded, "How can you be so casual about something so horrible?" She looked at the men around the table. "You would destroy an innocent man and force two countries into war for your own ends."

Lord Bertram's glance slid away

"See here, Rystoke," Lord Winslow complained. "I do not enjoy being tongue-lashed by a young woman who should be at home plying her needle."

"My ward knows quite a bit more than she should," Rystoke said with a dark glare in Jillian's direction. "If I do not keep her here, she'll go to the authorities and ruin everything."

Lord Bertram stood. "I will have none of this, sir, if it involves the safety of an innocent young woman."

"Nor will I," one of the other men said. "Come, Bertie, let us take our leave and wash our hands of this whole affair."

Another man also stood. "I'm afraid I must join these others, Rystoke. I will not be a party to this."

"By all means, gentlemen," Rystoke said generously. "Just remember that your silence on this is crucial. If you implicate us, you incriminate yourselves."

"You needn't threaten, Rystoke. We are well aware of our guilt," the man sniffed.

Before Lord Bertram left, he bowed before her. "My humble apologies, duchess. I had no idea how low Rystoke would sink to gain his victory in Parliament." With great dignity, he followed the other two men out.

Winslow puffed on his pipe and leaned back in his chair as if this were an innocent gathering, as if these men were not plotting war. Jillian remembered the dinner at Lord Bertram's where this man spoke of smuggling goods into England as if he spoke of nothing more vexing than the weather. Not content with breaking the laws of his country, he conspired with her guardian to bring that country to war.

"You hid the contraband found at Dunbary," she accused Winslow. "I told Lord Rystoke about the caves, and he had you put the French brandy there."

"An intelligent young woman," Stone observed. "But would the authorities believe her over a distinguished member of Parliament?"

Rystoke gave a dismissive shrug. "Most likely not. But I think we should be cautious. We cannot have her casting doubts on Dunbary's guilt." He gazed at her thoughtfully. "I believe a stay in your room upstairs is just the thing."

"You can't keep me here," Jillian said as apprehension gripped her. "I will be missed. Someone will come looking for me."

Rystoke laughed. "Who? Your husband? I think not."

"She has a point," Cooper Stone observed. "You can't keep her here, Rystoke. It's too risky."

"Then Winslow can take her to his house in the country," her guardian suggested.

Jillian's apprehension turned to fear. If they took her to Lord Winslow's country house, she would never be able to help Adrian. She had to escape. She jumped up and ran for the door. She had nearly reached it, but Cooper Stone grabbed the back of her dress. She heard tearing cloth and felt cool air across her shoulder.

She struggled to free herself. "Let me go."

His arms clamped about her waist and lifted her clear of the floor. "I don't think so, Duchess."

She kicked and squirmed, landing several good blows against his shins, but he held her fast. He plopped her down in her chair and held her in place with heavy hands on her shoulders.

"Sit still," he ordered. His fingers closed painfully around the back of her neck. "I know all about taming wild animals."

She cried out in pain as his fingers dug into the soft areas below her jaw.

"I will keep her on my ship," he said to Rystoke and Winslow. "No one will think of looking for her there."

Rystoke gazed at her thoughtfully. "What will we do with her when this is all over?" he mused. "She knows enough to incriminate us all."

"That's simple," Stone said "I'll take her with me when I sail back to America."

Jillian's stomach clenched into a knot. She was in far more danger than she could have imagined. No one knew where she was. She would disappear without a trace. Somehow, she had to convince them to release her. Then she remembered the letter.

"I have something you want," she said. "If you let me go, I'll give it to you."

The three men stared at her.

She swallowed, gathering her courage. "It's secret correspondence. I think you might be interested in it."

The American's grip loosened.

"The letter," Rystoke said.

"Yes." She nodded. "I'll give it to you in exchange for my freedom and getting the charges against Dunbary dropped."

Rystoke exchanged a triumphant look with his two conspirators. When he turned back to her, his eyes glittered coldly.

"You are just like your mother," he said. "She always had something to bargain with. She was a scheming doxy. I hated her."

"Why?" Jillian demanded angrily. "Because she was smarter than you?"

Rystoke flushed. His hand whipped out and he slapped her across the mouth. "Bitch."

Pain exploded in her lips and cheek. She tasted blood. When her eyes focused, she glared at her guardian. "I hate you."

Winslow's mouth twisted in distaste. "See here, Rystoke, you may torment the young lady all you wish after we have the letter."

Her guardian's cruel lips curled into a thin smile. "Yes," he agreed. "After we have the letter." Cunning gleamed from his dark eyes as he turned to Jillian. "Now, my dear, where is it?"

She glanced from Rystoke to Winslow. They waited expectantly. She felt the fingers of Cooper Stone tighten about her neck. Praying that Kip had the letter by now, swallowing against her rising terror, she said, "I will have to send for it."

Dowager Duchess Matilda sat in her bed with an open book on her lap. She had not looked at the pages since she had opened the cover. Her mind whirled with thoughts and unanswered questions. Her grandson had been arrested for smuggling. The very idea was preposterous.

She thought over the events of that afternoon. When Adrian returned to the drawing room and made his announcement, they had all been shocked, but Jillian's eyes had betrayed anxiety as well. The old lady's mouth thinned into a line. The girl knew something about why Adrian had been arrested.

Matilda mused about that for a while, and then her thoughts turned to the girl's guardian, Rystoke, an unscrupulous man. A long-standing enmity had burned between Rystoke and Jillian's father. The girl's mother had stoked it with the scandal. Rystoke must have laughed with glee to have Jillian St. Clare fall into his clutches.

Matilda came to a decision and yanked on the bellpull. When her maid arrived, she ordered, "Send a man around to the residence of the Laird of Ayton to inform his lordship I will be calling on him presently. Then come back and help me dress." At the look of disapproval on her long-time maid's face, she snapped, "I'll have none of your lectures, White. This is a grievous matter which must be cleared up immediately. Now, off with you."

Soon, Duchess Matilda was riding in her coach toward the old house on the outskirts of London. Exhilaration coursed through her veins. Too many years had passed since she had maneuvered and plotted to gain prestige for her family. Since Jillian St. Clare was now a member of her family, she meant to see that no dark stain soiled the girl's reputation. At the same time, she would be enlisting the aid of a powerful ally in clearing her grandson of these ridiculous charges.

The coach pulled up before the old house, and she climbed down as the footman ran up to the front door and rapped the knocker. The door was opened immediately by the butler, who showed her into an old-fashioned but cozy parlor. The fire drew her with its warmth. No sooner had she stretched out her hands to the heat than a voice, rich with a burr, spoke behind her.

"Ye have brightened my evening with y'r delightful presence, Duchess Matilda."

She turned and studied the handsome, middle-aged man bowing before her. "Ayton," she acknowledged. "It seems our families are now connected by marriage. And it appears that unless we act swiftly, both of our families may be destroyed by a common enemy."

"So, the viper has struck, has he? Then come, m'lady, an' tell me what ye ken," the Laird of Ayton invited.

After Matilda had seated herself, she looked directly into gray eyes that had been duplicated so perfectly in another. "My grandson has been arrested for smuggling," she said. "And I believe your daughter suspects the reasons for it. Rystoke has woven his web

281

very tightly. If you wish to save her, then you must save my grandson as well."

A smile crossed the laird's face. "I knew th' viper would make his own end," he said. "Begin at th' beginning, y'r grace, an' we'll ken what must be done."

The dawn was barely pearling the edges of the night sky when Adrian wearily entered his house. It was silent, for the servants had not yet roused. He immediately made for his study where he usually found solace. Embers still glowed on the hearth. Someone had spent most of the night hours on watch. A pair of booted feet stuck out before one of the chairs. Lawrence.

Not wanting to wake the lad, he stepped over the outstretched legs and stood staring at the shimmering ashes. With an exhausted sigh, he leaned on the mantle. Deep-seated anger roiled inside him. He was furious at his wife's treachery, and at himself for being duped. He glanced at the decanter of brandy sitting on a side table, but decided this was not the time to indulge. He needed a clear mind to deal with Jillian's betrayal.

She had done it. She had put him in the middle of a scandal—again. Except this time, her name would not be mentioned. She could play the innocent, bewildered wife as she watched his disgrace. What had he done to her to make her hate him so? Or was she so under the influence of that bastard Rystoke that she could not think for herself? If he were not so tired, he would throw something.

"Adrian." Lawrence's voice was slurred with sleep. "Sorry I dropped off. I meant to be awake when you returned home."

Adrian's lips twisted bitterly. At least someone had the decency to worry for him.

"I appreciate your waiting up for me," he said, "but I'm back, all of a piece, so you needn't worry anymore."

"I should say I'll worry," Lawrence argued. "My brother, arrested for smuggling. How can I not worry? You might have been tried and sent off for transportation."

"I hardly think I would have been sent to Australia quite so soon. You would have at least had time to bid me safe voyage," Adrian said drily.

Fully awake now, Lawrence straightened. "This is not a time to jest, Adrian. Why, you could be ruined by this arrest."

Adrian sighed. "I know. Forgive me. It's been a very long day and night."

"Have the charges against you been dropped? Tell me what happened." Lawrence leaned forward.

"I was able to convince the authorities that I have never owned a ship and have thus been unable to carry on any sort of smuggling operation. There is still some doubt, however, about the contraband brandy found at Dunbary."

"But it's not yours!" Lawrence exclaimed. "How can they think that someone in your position would keep that sort of thing on his own land?"

"Precisely," Adrian agreed. "Which is why they decided to release me. That, and the word of Lord Castlereagh that I am an honorable man." His lips twisted. "A pity my own wife does not believe that."

"Of course she believes it," Lawrence contradicted.

Adrian sent his brother a bleak smile, and swayed on his feet.

Lawrence jumped up and steadied him. "Sit down. I'll ring for Boggs or Symmes."

"No." Adrian shook his head. "I need to work out how this all came about. I need to decide what I am going to do about Jillian."

Lawrence dropped his hand from his brother's arm and stepped back.

"What is it?" Adrian asked tiredly. "What has she done now?"

Stuffing his hands in his pockets, Lawrence stared down at his feet.

"Out with it, man," Adrian demanded.

With his head down, Lawrence mumbled, "She's not here."

Adrian heard the words, but he could not process them. "Not here? What do you mean?"

His brother glanced at him, then his gaze slid away. "She's gone. She left early last night."

Adrian felt as if he had been stabbed. "So, she's run off."

Intense, blinding rage surged through him. With a swipe of his arm, he smashed the ormolu clock from the mantle. It crashed to the floor in a cacophony of discordant chimes and shattered glass.

As he surveyed the destruction, he said, "Don't ever marry a woman who fires your blood. She'll only bring you heartache."

Lawrence stared at the broken clock, then gazed at him with wide eyes. "I'm sure she'll be back."

"I don't want her back," Adrian shot at him. "She can go to blazes."

Lawrence's mouth dropped open. "I don't think…that is, she's probably…" He shook his head and cleared his throat. "Um, why don't you get some sleep? You look about done in."

Adrian wondered what his brother was trying to say, but he was too tired to pursue it. Instead, Adrian placed his hand on his brother's shoulder. "I must look dreadful for you to say that. Perhaps you're right. I'll retire for a while."

Adrian trudged up to his room. His feet felt like lead and every muscle in his body ached. He felt as if he could sleep for years, but his mind kept circling around the painful fact that Jillian had left him. His anger congealed into a hard knot in his chest. She had betrayed him. He had wed her to protect her reputation, and now she had thrown his honor and his good intentions back in his face.

He paused before the door to her bed chamber. For some reason, he felt if he rapped on its panels, he would hear her lilting voice bidding him to enter. He wanted that very much. But she was gone. And he had no idea how to cope with that.

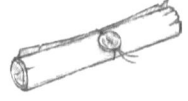

CHAPTER 22

Later that morning, in a spacious room, bare of furniture but for several racks of swords, rapiers, and daggers, Adrian fenced with Lawrence.

"Keep up your guard," Adrian warned, as he executed a series of deadly moves.

The pain and rage inside him felt like a caged animal clawing to get out. He knew Lawrence had suggested this fencing match to distract him. He had only slept for a couple of hours. When he had risen, all he had been able to do was pace, his thoughts chasing themselves. He had been arrested for smuggling. Jillian was gone. The two events were connected, but not in an obvious way. Something, some bit of information eluded him. He just didn't know what it was.

The ringing of steel on steel sounded like the cacophony that was ringing in his head. His frustration emerged in his aggressive attack. Lawrence tried to defend and backed away, but Adrian slipped beneath his defense. The covered tip of his rapier landed in the middle of Lawrence's chest protector.

Lawrence froze. "God's teeth! You're like a madman."

Adrian stepped back and dropped the point of his rapier. He had not realized how belligerent he had been. Lawrence's eyes were wide with alarm behind his face mask.

"Sorry," Adrian said. "But you dropped your guard on your left."

Boggs cleared his throat from the doorway. "Your pardon, your grace," he intoned. "There is a gentleman here who wishes to speak to you. He says it is most urgent."

Adrian frowned in annoyance. "I am not receiving anyone, Boggs," the Duke told his majordomo. "Send him away."

Boggs hesitated. "I believe it concerns the Duchess of Dunbary, your grace."

Adrian ripped off his face mask. "Then I especially do not wish to see him."

"Adrian, perhaps Jillian is in some difficulty," Lawrence suggested. "Perhaps the man knows something of her whereabouts." He turned to the majordomo. "What is the man's name, Boggs?"

"Mr. Kenric Giles, sir."

The name caught Adrian's attention. A cold smile crossed his face. "Mr. Giles? Show him down, Boggs. I will receive him here."

As the majordomo left, Lawrence demanded, "What are you planning, Adrian? I don't like that look in your eyes."

Adrian shrugged. "I merely wish to speak to this Mr. Giles and discover what he knows of Jillian's disappearance."

"I don't believe you."

Adrian sent a sharp, warning glance at his brother. "Believe what you wish, but remain out of this. I have some history with Mr. Giles that needs settling."

Boggs announced the Scotsman, then retreated.

Giles took one step into the room and halted.

"Mr. Giles," Adrian greeted sardonically. "This is an unexpected pleasure to find myself face to face with you in my own house."

"I apologize for the intrusion, Dunbary, but I have come about Jillian," Giles said.

Adrian sauntered a few steps closer to his visitor. "Has she left you, too? And so soon after running into your arms. *Tsk.* She is such a fickle woman."

"See here, Dunbary, I'll not have you speaking of her like that," Giles said.

"No? Then will you defend her honor? Or perhaps you would prefer to defend your own." Adrian pulled a rapier out of the rack near him and tossed it to his visitor. "I have wanted to cross steel with you ever since I first laid eyes on you." He pulled the protective button off the tip of his rapier.

"Adrian, what are you doing?" Lawrence demanded, horrified.

"Something I should have done long ago: rid myself of this pesky Scot." He tapped the tip of his rapier on the floor. "Since I am a gentleman, I will allow you to remove your coat. I would not wish it said that I was unfair to my opponent." He turned and stepped away.

"I refuse to fight with you, Dunbary," Kip announced.

Adrian swung about and raised his sword. "I don't think you have a choice," he snapped as he circled the point of his weapon in the air not far from his visitor's chest. "If you do not defend yourself, I will run you through."

"Very well," Giles agreed stiffly. "But this is wasting time. Jillian needs you."

Adrian's lips twisted bitterly. "I'm sure she does. She most likely needs to be rescued from a change of clothing or lack of coin."

The Scot did not bother to answer. He stripped off his coat and pulled the tip off his rapier.

Adrian ripped off his protective, padded vest.

"*En guard!*" Adrian ordered as he assumed the attack position.

He watched the Scot mirror him. Their swords touched briefly, and the fight began. His rage blotted out everything. All he wanted was this man's blood seeping across his floor. The Scot had taken what was his. The man had gained Jillian's affection in place of him, her husband.

The ringing of the rapiers, the grating of steel sliding against steel filled the room, music to Adrian's ears. His anger flowed through his arm and down his weapon. Murder was a black blot in his mind, blanking out everything else. For a long time, Giles seemed an equal match. Finally, Adrian's cold fury began to win. The Scot was tiring. Adrian sensed victory.

Their rapiers slipped together, only the hand guards keeping them apart. They stood chest to chest, panting with their exertions. Adrian glared into his opponent's eyes, where he saw determination and something else. Was that pity? His anger hardened. He refused to be pitied by this man who had stolen his wife.

Lawrence suddenly brought his weapon down between them, at the point where their swords crossed. "Enough!" he cried.

Startled, Adrian glowered at him. "Step away, or I won't be responsible if you get hurt."

"No!" Lawrence grabbed Adrian's arm. "I won't see you do murder in this house."

"Damn you, Lawrence! Get away!" Adrian tried to shake him off.

"Don't push me away as mother did," Lawrence grated.

"This is different, you fool," Adrian snarled.

"I'm trying to save your life." Lawrence shook Adrian's arm.

"And I'm trying to save Jillian's," the Scot added.

Adrian startled. "What's that you say?"

"Jillian's life is in danger." Giles words were quiet with truth.

Adrian disengaged and backed away from him. "Explain yourself."

Giles sucked in a breath. "I came to you because your wife is in danger." He turned to where he had tossed his coat and pulled a paper from its pocket. Shoving it at Adrian, he ordered, "Read this."

With a dubious glance at the Scot, Adrian took the offered paper and read. When he finished, his mouth twisted in a sarcastic smile. "How touching that she should have given you, her lover, this ragdoll for safe-keeping instead of me, her husband."

Giles ran a hand through his hair. "Damn it, man! I'm not her lover!"

Adrian raised a disbelieving brow.

With an impatient sigh, the Scotsman announced, "I am her brother. Didn't she tell you?"

Adrian gave a cynical laugh. "That is a convenient explanation."

Lawrence placed his hand on his brother's arm. "Adrian, it's true. Jillian told me she had a brother." He stared at the Scot. "Look at him. Isn't there a resemblance?"

Adrian gazed at the Scot. What he had never noticed before were the man's eyes, similar in color and shape to Jillian's. Had he been wrong about his wife?

"I suppose there is some resemblance," Adrian grudgingly admitted. He glanced down at the paper in his hand. "She says she is being held by Rystoke, and won't be released until you deliver her ragdoll." Incredulously, he asked, "Her ragdoll? Really, Mr. Giles. What would Rystoke want with a ragdoll?"

"I don't know, but I'm sure it must be important," Giles answered. "Jillian wanted me to give it back to her. That's why I was in your home the day—" He halted and swallowed. "—the day you saw me with Jillian," he finished. "She had asked me to bring the doll back to her."

Adrian stared at the man before him as he began to make connections. The day this man was in his home. The day after he waltzed with Jillian at the Prince Regent's. The day he thought they might mend their relationship. The day he had believed the worst of his wife.

He turned and wandered away a few steps. Why had Jillian wanted the doll returned the day after they had waltzed, the day after they had made love? What significance did the doll have? He glanced again at the pleading note in his hand. Why did Rystoke want a silly ragdoll? Unless it was not a doll that he wanted at all. He swung about abruptly.

"Do you have the doll with you?" he asked.

Giles nodded. "I left it with your butler."

The three of them hurried to the entrance hall where Boggs had placed the Scotsman's hat and gloves. And the ragdoll. Giles handed the doll to Adrian.

He quickly examined it, then said, "Come into my study."

When they had gathered about Adrian's desk, he placed the doll in the middle and stared at it. It was old and well-loved. The woolly yarn used for hair was thin, and one of the embroidered eyes was ragged with missing stitches. The dress had been patched. Adrian was touched by seeing something that had belonged to his wife when she was just a small child. Tenderly, he ran his fingers around the doll's face.

Forcing himself back to the present problem, he said, "There has to be a reason why Rystoke should demand something of so little value." He examined the doll more closely, turning it about and squeezing it with his hands. "There seems to be something inside." He pulled the doll's dress open in the back. "This seam has been freshly sewn," he observed. "See how new the stitches are in comparison to the others." He grabbed a letter opener and slit the stitching. When he pulled the seam apart, stuffing popped out and a tightly wound, tiny piece of parchment sat nestled snugly in its midst.

"The letter," he murmured.

He dropped into his chair as the ramifications of finding the letter in this way crowded into his head. The day after he had waltzed with Jillian at the Prince Regent's, Jillian had said she had something to tell him about the letter. She had sent for Kip to bring her the doll.

Inside the doll was the letter. Had she meant to turn the letter over to him? Had he horribly misjudged her?

He had. She was not having an affair with the Scot. She had not given the letter to Rystoke. In fact, if she did not give the letter to Rystoke, her life might be in danger.

Jillian's words to him the day after they had found Beatrice echoed in his head: *I love you… I have never bestowed my favors on any man besides my husband.* She was telling the truth. She did love him. And he had laughed at her declaration. How that must have hurt her. She might be in very grave danger. He closed his eyes to block out the terrible guilt that washed through him. He had been a fool. An utter and complete fool.

"Adrian, are you all right?" Lawrence asked anxiously.

He opened his eyes and sat forward. "Yes." Glancing at Giles, he said, "I apologize for my previous behavior. It seems I was wrong about you, as well as several other things."

The Scot waved away his apology. "There were too many secrets and deceptions. You could not be blamed for seeing things as you did without knowing the whole truth."

Adrian was grateful for his graciousness, yet aggravated at the same time by that very generosity of spirit. "Quite," he said shortly. He turned to Jillian's note. "Jillian says you are to bring the doll to Rystoke, and then he will release her. You can't give Rystoke the secret correspondence."

"But—" Giles and Lawrence said at once.

Adrian held up his hand for silence. "I'm sure Rystoke has no idea what the secret letter contains. So, what I propose is to make up our own secret letter, place it back inside the doll, and give the doll to Rystoke. He'll find *a* secret letter in the doll and release Jillian." His words held a conviction he did not feel. Rystoke could be a wily cur.

The three of them forged a letter and had one of the maids sew it into the doll.

As they were waiting, Boggs knocked on the door and announced, "The Laird of Ayton to see you, your grace."

"Who the bloody blazes is the Laird of Ayton?" Adrian demanded peevishly.

Giles said quietly, "He is my father. And Jillian's."

An hour later, Adrian stared out his coach window as the vehicle wended its way to the home of the Earl of Rystoke. Across from him sat Lawrence and Jillian's brother—Kip. Adrian ignored them as his thoughts whirled around in his head. He felt as if he had been thrown over a waterfall, tumbled about at its bottom, and then flung onto the shore. Meeting both Jillian's brother and her father in the same day had been unsettling. His wife was as complicated as a maze, and he wanted more than anything to unravel all her mysteries. But first, he had to save her.

He had sent the Laird of Ayton to Lord Castlereagh with the information that the secret correspondence had been recovered, in order to keep the laird from storming his enemy's house. Now, it was up to him to save Jillian. He had brought Lawrence and Kip in case something went wrong.

The coach pulled up before Rystoke's house. Adrian and Kip stepped down.

"Are you sure you don't want me to go in with you?" Lawrence asked, a bit plaintively.

"I need you out here, in case something should go wrong," Adrian said. "It's important that someone should go to Lord Castlereagh if Rystoke escapes."

Lawrence slumped back on the seat. With a smile at his brother's disappointment, Adrian turned to the front door. Rystoke's butler showed them into the drawing room. They did not have to wait long.

Rystoke entered, arrogant and sly. "I never thought I would see the Duke of Dunbary inside my house again." He turned to Kip. "I don't think I've had the pleasure, sir."

"Kenric Giles," Kip snapped out without bowing.

"Ah, of course! The brother. Well met, sir." He offered his hand, but Kip refused to shake it. Shrugging, he went on, "You have brought the letter?"

"Jillian wrote to bring this." Adrian held out the doll.

Rystoke stared at it. "She had it here all the time and I never guessed. That sly little bitch. Just like her mother."

"First, we must see Jillian," Adrian said coldly. "Where is she, Rystoke?"

"Not here." Rystoke's smile was crafty. "Give me the doll and I'll tell you where she is."

Grudgingly, Adrian handed over the doll. Rystoke examined it, then ripped it open. Digging into the stuffing, he pulled out the tiny, tightly wound piece of parchment. Triumphantly, he held the letter in his hand.

Rystoke laughed. "I knew I made the right move in allowing you to wed my ward. She has finally proved her worth."

"You have what you want, Rystoke. *Where is Jillian?*" Adrian contained his temper with difficulty.

The earl waved his hand airily. "Oh, you'll never find her, Dunbary. She is safely locked away and in due course will be shipped off to America. I daresay she'll come to some sort of unfortunate end there."

The thought of never seeing Jillian again wrenched his insides. How could he lose her now, when he realized he wanted her? That he loved her. He was determined to find her.

Kip surged forward to attack Rystoke. "You bastard!"

Adrian grabbed Kip to stop him. He needed information from Jillian's guardian. "How will you get her to America, Rystoke? Who would take a woman across the Atlantic against her will?"

"Mr. Stone, the American, has been quite helpful," the earl said, as an evil smile curled his lips.

Despair washed through Adrian. He had to find Stone's ship among hundreds of others at the London docks. If Jillian were lost forever… His anger erupted, fueled by his desperation. Balling his fist, he slugged Rystoke in the nose.

The earl dropped to the floor and clutched his face as blood spurted out between his fingers. "My nose!" he screamed. "You've broken it! You'll pay for this!"

Adrian stood over him. "I don't think so, Rystoke. Not after you have been brought up before the King's Bench on charges of treason." He stepped over the earl's legs. "Come along, Mr. Giles. Jillian needs us."

They hurried out of the house and into the coach. As they headed toward the docks, Kip told Lawrence what had occurred, describing Adrian's punch in great detail.

"I always miss the excitement," Lawrence grumbled.

Adrian barely heard him as his doubt and despair threatened to overwhelm him. He couldn't lose Jillian now. He had been so wrong about her. He wanted to apologize, to tell her he had been a blind idiot. He wanted to kiss away the sadness in her eyes. He wanted to tell her he loved her.

Dragging his thoughts out of that dark place, he turned to his brother and the Scot. "Jillian is being held on Stone's ship, but how are we going to discover which is his? He may have set sail already." Just saying the words made his heart squeeze in pain.

"Who is Mr. Stone?" Kip asked.

"An American, who evidently sides with Rystoke in wishing to keep the Orders in Council in place and forcing America and England into war." Adrian said.

"Can you describe him?" Kip asked.

"Very tall, broad through the shoulders, acts as if he owns the world," Adrian said.

Kip thought a moment. "I think I know his ship."

For the first time that day, Adrian felt a glimmer of hope at finding Jillian. When they reached the docks, he instructed his driver to stop the coach out of sight. The three of them alighted and Kip led them to one of the docks.

He pointed to a large, well-maintained ship. An American flag flew from the mast. "There. I think that might be his."

Longshoremen rolled barrels and heaved crates up its gangway. Sailors scurried about the deck.

"It looks like they're preparing to sail," Lawrence observed.

Kip nodded. "The tide will turn soon."

Anxiety gripped Adrian. He would not let Jillian sail away. A blond-headed man, tall and broad through the shoulders appeared on deck. Cold, calculating anger suffused Adrian.

"That's Stone," he said, then turned to Kip. "I don't know how you know so much about the docks, and I'm not sure I want to know, but if Jillian is on that ship, you have my undying gratitude for the rest of my days."

Kip grinned. "I have a stake in her well-being, too. She is my sister, after all."

"Then we are brothers-in-law!" Lawrence exclaimed.

"Before we have a family reunion, let's rescue Jillian, shall we?" Adrian suggested drily. "Here's what we do. Lawrence, take the coach and go to Lord Castlereagh. Tell him where we are and what we're doing. We'll probably need reinforcements. Mr. Giles — "

"Kip," the Scot corrected.

"Yes. Right. Kip and I will sneak on board, find Jillian and release her."

"You always get all the action," Lawrence complained.

"That's because I'm older and have more experience. Besides, if something happens to me, you will have to carry on the family name."

"There's always Cousin Reginald," Lawrence suggested helpfully.

Adrian gave him a playful cuff on the side of the head. "Off with you now, and hurry. I don't want to be caught and find myself sailing to America as Mr. Stone's guest."

He watched Lawrence scurry back to the waiting coach. Then he turned to his brother-in-law. "Here's my plan."

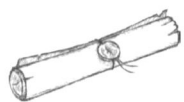

CHAPTER 23

Jillian sat in the only armchair on board Cooper Stone's ship. Her ankles were bound together. Her wrists were tied to the arms of the chair. A silk scarf covered her mouth and prevented her from uttering a word.

At Rystoke's, the American had pointed a nasty little pistol on her and forced her into her guardian's coach. When they had reached the docks, she had tried to escape, so he had tied her up. Now, she watched Lady Diana Avingdon pace across the spacious main cabin of the ship.

"Please understand," Diana said, "I have no ill feelings toward you. But a woman has to watch out for her own welfare. I have the greatest fondness for Dunbary. I had hoped at one time that he might consider offering for my hand, but that was not to be, so I broke off our relationship." She shrugged, turned toward Jillian and smiled. "Our friendship could not compete with his love for you."

Jillian raised her eyebrows dubiously.

"Oh, yes, he does love you," Diana said. "He may not even realize it himself, but I have seen that look in his eyes whenever he speaks of you or your name is mentioned." She sat across from Jillian. "That is why I agreed to all this deception and unpleasant business." She waved her hand gracefully in the direction of Jillian's bonds. "I know he will eventually come looking for you. I do not wish any harm to come to you. Cooper has assured me that you will be safe."

Jillian wanted to believe her, but Adrian did not care about her, and she had seen the cold ruthlessness in the American's eyes. She would be taken across the ocean and then she would disappear in the American wilderness.

Diana smoothed her skirt. "I know what you are thinking. How could I have plotted against Adrian when I have been his...when I have been so close to him? A woman in my position with little income must be realistic. I need to do what I must to maintain a certain lifestyle. Besides, I find Cooper Stone to be quite an exciting man." She smiled.

A knock on the door and the announcement that her tea had arrived interrupted her. After a sailor had placed the tray on the table between them and departed, Diana poured herself a cup. Jillian watched enviously while the lady added milk and a touch of sugar, then took a sip. As Diana reached for a scone, she glanced up.

"I do apologize for not offering you some refreshment, my dear," Diana told her. "But I cannot risk taking off that annoying scarf across your mouth and having you give an alarm. We wish to depart without any unpleasantness."

Jillian made some unintelligible noises and shook her head vigorously, trying to communicate that she wouldn't scream.

Diana looked doubtful. "Are you sure you will not raise a fuss if I take off the scarf?"

Jillian nodded.

"Do you absolutely promise?" Diana leaned confidentially across the table. "You see, I don't wish Cooper to be angry with me."

Jillian nodded again and mumbled to assure Diana that she would behave.

Diana pursed her lips. "Well, all right. But just until you have finished your tea."

When the lady had untied the scarf, Jillian gasped a deep, shuddering breath and licked her dry lips. "Please, could you also untie my right hand so that I might feed myself?" she asked meekly. If one hand was free, she might be able to untie herself and escape.

Diana's brows crinkled.

"I promise I won't try to escape," Jillian lied.

"Well, I suppose it would be quite awkward for me to feed you." Diana tipped her head thoughtfully. "All right." She untied one of Jillian's hands, then poured Jillian some tea. "Milk and sugar?"

"Please." After taking a fortifying sip, Jillian said, "I still don't understand how you came to be involved in this business of the secret letter."

Diana chuckled. "I have worked as one of Adrian's agents for a number of years."

Jillian's cup rattled in her saucer. "But what you are doing now is treason."

"Well, I suppose that depends on one's point of view," Diana said.

Out of the corner of Jillian's eye, something moved beyond the large, rear window of the cabin. When she glanced in that direction, nothing was there. But she could have sworn she saw the top of someone's head. She turned back to Diana.

"Aren't you an English citizen?" she asked. "Working against England for another country is treason." As she took another sip of tea, she peeked at the window again and nearly choked. Her husband's face was clearly framed by one of the panes of glass. A thrill ran through her which she quickly hid.

Diana toyed with her cup. "I may not be an English citizen much longer. I might decide to become Mrs. Cooper Stone."

At Diana's announcement, Jillian dropped her cup and saucer. They shattered, and tea spilled onto the hem of Diana's dress. "Oh dear," Jillian said. "I am so sorry. How clumsy of me."

As Diana jerked her skirt away from the spill, the window crashed back on its hinges and Adrian jumped through. He landed with a wet thud. He was barefoot, dripping wet, and his shirt, transparent with seawater and open at the collar, clung to his chest. Jillian had never seen him look quite so dashing and masculine. Astounded that he should come to her rescue, she grinned idiotically.

"What—How—?" Diana stammered. "Oh, my goodness."

Jillian's grin died when her husband barely spared her a glance. After quickly running his gaze over her, his jaw clenched. Then his attention focused on Diana. Of course he would be more concerned with his mistress than his wife. Adrian despised her.

Jillian's heart shriveled.

Adrian was furious at finding Jillian bound to a chair. He was relieved at finding her unharmed, but the jolt of seeing his former mistress on the American's ship shook him.

"Diana?" he asked, confused.

Diana smiled. "I am keeping your lovely wife company, darling. We were just having tea. Won't you join us?"

Angry suspicion slithered through him. He scowled. "Why is my wife tied up? What are you doing on board Cooper Stone's ship?"

Diana shifted a bit uncomfortably. "Well, I do hope you're not going to be churlish about this, Adrian. I thought I might travel to America."

"Do you mean you have switched your allegiance to Cooper Stone?" Adrian demanded.

Diana fussed with a fold of her skirt. "Well, yes. I suppose you could say that."

Her betrayal stung. "I offered you enough reward to reopen Avingdon Hall," he ground out.

Diana laughed contemptuously. "That drafty old place? There is nothing there. I would die of boredom in the first week." She smiled sweetly. "You know how I hate to be bored, darling. And Mr. Cooper Stone is such an exciting man."

Adrian stared at her as he realized how he had been duped. Rage warred with disbelief. "*You* revealed the information about the lost correspondence."

Diana fluffed out the skirt of her gown. "I do apologize for that, darling. I truly meant no harm." She looked up at him, her eyes pleading. "Please, you must believe that. I only wanted some happiness and security for myself. And I warned you that I couldn't guarantee that I could discover any information about the letter."

"Because you already had the information I sought," he flung at her.

Diana shrugged and smiled.

"Then I wish you luck, Diana," Adrian said coldly. "Since my wife appears unharmed and I have the secret correspondence, I will be lenient with you. Soldiers will be arriving soon to arrest Cooper Stone. You might wish to disembark the ship and disappear. But if I ever see you again within England's borders, I will have you arrested."

Diana rose from her chair and approached him. "You are a dear, sweet man, Adrian." Standing on tiptoe, she placed a kiss on his check.

Adrian jerked away as if he had been burned. "I only do this because of our past friendship." He stressed the last word. "Leave before I change my mind."

With a sad smile, Diana collected her shawl and disappeared out the cabin door. Relief swept through him at her departure. He turned to his wife to untie her. But the stormy expression in her eyes made him consider leaving her bound, at least until he had a chance to explain himself.

Jillian was hurt and furious at her husband for letting Diana go free. The woman had betrayed him, had kept her prisoner, and would have allowed Cooper Stone to take her to America. But as the door closed behind Diana, Jillian heard a familiar voice from the deck above.

In surprise, she blurted, "You brought Kip with you?"

Adrian shrugged a shoulder and frowned as he concentrated on untying the ropes binding her. "I had no choice. He—um—convinced me."

Jillian wondered how Kip had *convinced* him.

He met her eyes. "You might have told me he was your brother, Jillian." Adrian's words accused, and hurt shadowed his eyes.

Guilt made her glance slide away. "I'm sorry. I never had the chance."

She felt Adrian's searching gaze, but a commotion above deck and the sound of many feet distracted him. "I think those will be our reinforcements," he said.

"She must be down here!" Lawrence shouted from above.

"You brought Lawrence, as well?" she asked.

"If I hadn't, I never would have heard the end of it," Adrian grumbled. He finished untying her and pulled her to her feet. "When we return home, I would like some truthful answers."

Jillian's chin rose. "I think we both need to exchange some truths."

"You are absolutely right," he agreed. He brushed a stray strand of hair back from her cheek. "I'm glad you're safe, Jillian."

A warm spot pulsed in her heart. "I'm glad to see you, Adrian."

Before Adrian could reply, the door crashed open. "There you are!" Lawrence exclaimed. "You've rescued her already. I always miss the excitement."

Adrian grinned. "He's referring to my meeting with Rystoke."

"More than a meeting," Lawrence corrected. "Why, Adrian knocked the bloke right on his arse."

Jillian laughed in delighted astonishment. "You hit him?"

"I'm afraid so," her husband admitted.

Kip appeared through the door. "Jillian! Are you all right? Are you hurt?"

"I'm fine," she assured him. She placed a hand on Adrian's arm. "Please, I just want to go home."

The three men escorted her above deck, where soldiers stood guard over Cooper Stone. He had the effrontery to smile at her. Anger surged through her. She strode over to the American and slapped him across the face.

"Go home to America, Mr. Cooper," she said, as she watched the imprint of her hand appear on his cheek.

"I'm afraid he won't be returning to those shores for quite a while, your grace," the captain of the guard said. "He's been arrested as a spy."

"Come, Jillian," Adrian said gently as he took her by the elbow. "It's time to go home."

Hearing Adrian utter those words brought a spark of warmth to her insides. Without a word, she allowed him to guide her down the gangway and into his coach. Lawrence and Kip climbed in after them and they set off for Adrian's house — their house.

Jillian listened to the men recount what each of them had done to rescue her. She was content just to have her husband hold firmly to her hand. She and Adrian had many things to discuss and work out, but the security of his presence and his apparent concern for her were all she needed at the moment.

Just as they reached the house, Adrian said with a smile, "I have a surprise waiting for you."

Intrigued, she glanced at Kip and Lawrence, but they merely grinned at her. As she stepped down from the coach, she felt she was where she belonged. She was home.

Boggs opened the door before she reached the top step. "Welcome home, your grace," he greeted her. "May I extend congratulations upon your safe return on behalf of myself and all the staff?"

Surprised and pleased at the majordomo's warm welcome, she thanked him, then Adrian led her into the drawing room. Duchess Matilda sat before the fire. Across from her sat a middle-aged man, who rose politely.

"Jillian," Adrian said, "may I introduce the Laird of Ayton?"

Politely, Jillian stepped forward and offered her hand. "Welcome to our home, sir."

"Jillian," Adrian said gently. "This is your father."

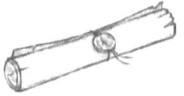

CHAPTER 24

"Oh, my." Jillian's knees buckled.

The laird grabbed her and helped her to a chair. Duchess Matilda poured a cup of tea and held it out to her. Jillian took it, but her hands shook so badly, the tea sloshed over the rim of the cup. The laird rescued it and placed it on the table.

"You're my father," she said as she looked into his kind, gray eyes. She could not catch her breath.

"Aye, lass." He smiled. "Y'r father."

"But why—? How—?" Confusion roiled inside her. She glanced at Kip, then at Adrian. Her husband would divorce her, now that he knew she was illegitimate. What a cruel surprise he had prepared. Did he hate her that much? He was smiling, looking quite pleased with himself.

Jillian turned her gaze back to the laird. "Why did it take you so long to find me?" Pain underscored her words.

He sat down across from her. "This is a wee bit of a long tale." He smiled as he reminisced. "I met Lilith, y'r mother, durin' her first season in London. She was a bonny lass with hair o' gold and eyes the color o' bluebells. I fell in love with her, and she with me. We wed late that summer.

"I dinna tell her I was already wed, to a woman who hadna' recovered from th' birth of her last son." He indicated Kip, who stood beside Jillian's chair. "She was ne'er th' same. Could barely feed herself. It was a poor thing I did, t' wed another woman, but I didna' think so then. I loved y'r mother, and I didna' think Lilith would ken why I couldna' marry her. But my wife was wife t' me no more, an' no' a mother to m' sons. I hired a kindly woman t' care for her." The laird's gray eyes grew sad.

"Then you were born. A bonny lassie you were." His eyes lit up. "Aye, a bonny lassie. But Lilith discovered m' lie when ye were but two years. She left me without a word t' anyone, and took ye with her. I searched for her. I hired men to search. We ne'er found a trace. Until just a wee while ago I received this." He pulled a wrinkled, much handled, folded letter from his coat and handed it to Jillian.

Jillian immediately recognized her mother's hand. It was dated just before Lilith died. Tears clouded Jillian's eyes. It was the letter Kip had told her about, the one that her mother had sent to her father explaining that she had fled to Ayton's enemy, the Earl of Rystoke, and that the earl was now Jillian's guardian. She had wrung the promise out of the earl to find a suitable husband for her daughter. The last line wrenched Jillian's heart: *I always loved you, Bryce, and I hope that someday you may forgive me for what I have done, as I long ago forgave you.*

"I didna' ken how much I had hurt her by not tellin' her th' truth," the laird said. "If only I had told her, she might ha' stayed. Ye see, Rystoke and I—our families—ha' been feudin' over our lands for generations, since th' Border Wars. There's nay love lost 'atween us. I hate th' man." The laird shook his head sadly. "If only she ha' stayed a wee bit longer. The boys' muther died a se'nnight after Lilith left." He drew a ragged breath and leaned forward in his chair. "I loved yer mother verra much, lass."

Jillian's throat closed on her words. Tears spilled over her lashes.

"I'm verra sorry for your pain, lass," he said. "I'll ken if you ne'er want t' see me agin."

She shook her head in bewilderment. "So much has happened." She sniffed. "I never expected to meet my father." Those words felt strange.

"Aye. I ne'er expected t' lay eyes on my bonnie lassie." He paused a moment. "I ne'er meant for ye t' be an outcast."

Jillian glanced at Adrian. He was staring out the window with his back to the room. He was probably scandalized by her origins. Now, she understood Rystoke's gloating.

"Why did my mother go to the Earl of Rystoke?" she asked.

The laird's expression turned grim. "Like I said, it's an old feud, goin' back generations. Ayton lies in th' Borders. Rystoke's title seat is in Northumberland. His family received their grant as a result of th' first earl being named a Warden of th' Marches. He was a mean one, and kept th' peace by raidin' and lootin' the homesteads in th' Borders. Th' clan didna' have th' means t' fight back. Me great-great-grandfather tried t' fight him off th' best he could, and he died tryin'. Land that should ha' gone t' good Scotsmen went t' th' English Warden instead. There isna' love lost between our families."

Jillian finished, "So when my mother decided to run away, she went to Rystoke, knowing he was your enemy and knowing it would hurt you more than anything to see her with him."

"Aye." The laird's single word held all his pain and regret.

"And she must have used Rystoke's hatred for you by threatening to leave him and go back to you," she surmised. "That's how she wrung the promise from him to launch me into society."

"Lilith was a verra smart woman." Ayton nodded.

Jillian glanced down at the letter in her hand. "I think she realized she had made a terrible mistake."

Her father shook his head sadly. "It doesna' matter nay more. She is gone to her Maker, and I forgave her long ago." He smiled then. "I have another wee surprise for you."

Jillian couldn't imagine what else he might have to tell her.

Ayton glanced down, as if uncertain about his words. "I've had my solicitor write up formal adoption papers."

Jillian caught her breath. "You wish to adopt me?" A thrill ran through her.

The laird smiled and took her hand. "Aye. If you dinna' mind this old devil for a pa, that would make m' heart glad."

"I would like nothing better." Jillian smiled back through her tears.

"Then it's settled." Her father beamed. "Ye must come to Ayton."

"Oh yes," Kip agreed. "That would be splendid."

Overwhelmed, Jillian shook her head. "I can't believe all this. Now I find I have a brother and a father."

Kip laughed. "So, when do you think you can come to Ayton?"

"I don't know." If she went to Ayton, her husband would not have to concern himself with her any more. She glanced around for Adrian, but he had slipped out of the room. "We are still in mourning for Adrian's mother. It may be several months before I can get away."

The laird turned to Adrian's grandmother. "Duchess Matilda, would ye be willing t' travel t' Ayton?"

"Only if your manor is not drafty and cold, Ayton" the lady said. "These old bones of mine cannot abide the damp."

Despite the duchess's peevish words, Jillian could see she was quite pleased with the invitation. Her father also extended the invitation to Lawrence, and Kip began describing the hunting around Ayton. Jillian murmured an excuse and slipped away in search of Adrian. She found him in his study. He was sitting behind his desk and staring out the window.

"Adrian?" She stepped hesitantly into the room.

He turned to her slowly. Those glorious topaz eyes held dark devastation in their depths. Closing the door to the study behind her, she advanced into the room. Uncertainty made her insides tremble. What did he think of her now? As she approached the desk, he placed a small, tightly rolled bit of parchment before her. She recognized it immediately.

Dumbfounded, she asked, "You didn't give the secret letter to Rystoke?"

He shook his head. "Lawrence, Kip, and I made up a forgery to get him to tell us where you were." He turned back to the window. "It's yours now. As you said before, finders, keepers."

Jillian picked up the tight little roll. All that had happened since that fateful night when it had bounced into her shoe flashed through her mind. All the misunderstandings, secrets, and deceptions loomed before her like great, hulking shadows. She wanted to banish those shadows into the darkness of oblivion. With a decisive movement, she placed the secret letter back on the desk.

"No," she said quietly. "This isn't mine. It never was. Use it as it should be used, Adrian."

He swung away from the window, and his eyes lit up. Then his lashes lowered, covering that light. He swept the tiny roll into the top drawer of his desk.

"Lord Castlereagh will be very appreciative," he murmured.

"I didn't do it for Lord Castlereagh." Her tone was dry.

Adrian looked up at her with narrowed eyes, then turned to the window again. "When will you be leaving for Ayton?"

"I'm not sure." She decided he must be very anxious to get rid of her.

He nodded. "You must be very pleased to finally meet your father." His voice was distant, yet it held an underlying edge.

"I can't believe after all these years I finally have a family." She kept her tone level, when all she wanted to do was shout with happiness. And she wanted to share that happiness with Adrian.

Adrian stilled at her words. "I'm sure it must be very confusing for you," he said stiffly.

An awkward silence fell between them.

Jillian decided that she must speak, to try to make peace between them. She took a deep breath. "Adrian, I know the circumstances of my birth have been somewhat of a shock, and I will not blame you if you wish to divorce me."

Adrian swung around to face her. "Is that what you want?"

Stunned at his intense response, she stuttered, "N-no, n-no, I don't."

"Then I don't, either."

"You don't?" Jillian did not think she heard him correctly.

"No." He stood and came around his desk. Those topaz eyes gleamed in the shadows of the room. "Why should it matter to me what the circumstances of your birth were? That happened years ago. It is an old scandal. Besides, my grandmother informed me that you are a baroness. Excellent bloodlines, particularly if we are to produce any children."

"But—" She gaped up at him.

"Why didn't you give the secret letter to Rystoke until he forced you?" he asked abruptly.

Jillian blinked at his sudden change of subject. "Because I never trusted him."

"Why did you give the ragdoll to Kip?" He took a step toward her.

"Because I was afraid von Heisburg would find it. I didn't trust him, either." Confused at his questions, she wondered where his questions were leading.

"Why were Kip and von Heisburg here together on the day I saw you?" He took another step forward.

Unnerved, Jillian retreated a step. "I had asked Kip to bring the doll with the letter back to me. Von Heisburg intruded on our meeting."

"Ah." He advanced again. "Why did you want the doll with the letter back on that day?"

She took another step back. Her brain turned sluggish with him so near, and his intensity was a bit alarming. "I was going to give it to you." She forced her words out of a tight throat.

"Why didn't you?"

"Because Kip had put it on his ship and it had already sailed to Ayton."

"His ship?" Adrian's brows rose and he halted.

"Yes, you see, he's…" She bit her lip. She could not divulge her brother's secret.

"He's what?"

"I can't tell you." Miserable at having to keep yet another secret from her husband, she hung her head.

"Jillian, unless he's murderer or a traitor, I don't see how I can bring charges against my own brother-in-law." His tone gently cajoled.

She looked up at him and saw he was telling the truth. After making the decision to banish secrets and deceptions to the nether world, she realized this was not the time for lies and hidden truths. She took a breath. "He's a smuggler."

Adrian burst out laughing. "You don't say? The devil. Well, I certainly can't fault him for that, can I? Not when my own ancestors indulged in the same activity. And if he doesn't involve me, I can't stop him."

She gasped. "You won't arrest him?"

Adrian shrugged. "If I don't catch him at it, how can I? Besides, smugglers don't concern me."

Confused and startled at his change in attitude, she mumbled, "That's very generous of you."

His brows drew together. "I would say it's more than generous. Considering I thought he was your lover, you are lucky I did not run him through when he arrived to tell me you had been taken prisoner."

"You have nothing to be angry about in that quarter," she said as her affronted pride reared its head. "I never had another man, while you ran to the lovely Lady Avingdon whenever you had the chance."

"Is that what you think?" he demanded as he advanced.

"It's what I know." She retreated despite her reluctance to do so.

"You are wrong," he said flatly.

Her brows snapped together. "I saw how you reacted when you saw her on Cooper Stone's ship. You even let her go, despite the fact that she had betrayed you." She backed away as he stalked toward her.

"I let her go because we are — were — friends. And that is all." He waved away her argument.

"But..." Jillian backed up against the door to the hall.

"No buts. She was my mistress once. That ended as soon as I met you." He reached around her and turned the key in the lock.

Jillian heard the decisive click of the bolt and felt a delicious shiver skip up her spine. Her husband's broad chest blocked out the room beyond and his overwhelming presence before her made her heart thump loudly. She couldn't think straight. Bracing the palms of her hands against the door behind her, she focused on his last words. "You gave up your mistress when you met me?" she asked in disbelief. "I find that difficult to believe. You escorted her to the theater and visited her several times after we returned from Dunbary. People saw you."

A single, dark brow quirked upward. "Did they, now? I wonder if these people knew that I visited her because she was working for me as an informant, that my visits were very brief, and that Diana always left the theater escorted by other gentlemen."

"Y-you did? She did?" she stammered.

"Yes." He gave a definite nod. "Do you know why?"

Speechless at what he had revealed, all she could do was shake her head.

"Because I love you, silly woman."

Jillian's mouth dropped open. "But-but-but — "

Adrian chuckled.

"This is nothing to laugh about," she huffed, affronted, even though his statement of love had started a warm glow within her. "Why didn't you tell me all this before?"

He sobered. "How could I? I thought you had your own lovers. I thought you were spying for Rystoke." That devastation entered his eyes again. "I can understand your anger. You believed I was betraying you. Maybe I was by not telling you what I was doing. For that, I'm truly sorry." He closed his eyes and turned away. "Let me know when you decide to leave for Ayton."

Jillian caught his arm, not prepared to let him get away that soon, not after he had just told her he loved her. "How can I go to Ayton when I will be going to Dunbary with you?"

He frowned. "I never said I was going to Dunbary."

She smiled. "I know, but I think it would be a perfect place to spend our period of mourning."

"I don't understand."

She grinned. "I love you, silly man."

Those wonderful, topaz eyes lit up. "Ah, now I understand." He placed his hands on the door on either side of her, blocking her in. "You plan to take me prisoner and abscond with me to some remote place."

"Something like that."

"There is just one problem."

Worry creased her brow. "What is that?"

"It seems I have taken you prisoner first." He leaned toward her, pressing his body against hers.

"So you have." The feel of him sent a flush through her.

"Do you know what I do to my prisoners?"

She shook her head as the blood pounded through her veins and her knees turned shaky.

"I kiss them senseless, then I ravage them until they cry for mercy."

"How shocking," she murmured as she watched that chiseled mouth descend toward her lips.

As their mouths came together, white heat exploded in her center, evaporating all the misunderstandings and hurt that had been between them. Her arms wrapped about his middle and she pressed herself against his hard length. As if starved, their lips sought each other hungrily. Their tongues tasted and tested, dueling and stroking.

His body pressed into her. She felt his need throb against her and a sweet ache curled low within her. He quickly undid her dress and pushed it from her shoulders. Dragging his lips from hers, he rained kisses down her throat. Her protest at losing his kiss turned to a whimper of pleasure as his mouth found the tip of her breast. Lightning flashed through her as he teased and sucked. Her husband's weight pinned her against the door. She was glad for the support, for her knees went weak. *He loves me, he loves me*, repeated itself inside her head like a litany, as she indulged in the glorious sensations he aroused.

Someone knocking on the other side of the door broke through their haze of passion. Boggs asked to be admitted. Adrian raised his head, but did not take his gaze from her face.

"What is it, Boggs?" he rapped out.

"Your pardon, your grace," Boggs answered, "but a message has just come from Lord Castlereagh."

As Jillian moved to unlock the door, he stopped her and gave her a wicked grin. "Push it under the door, Boggs," he said. "The lock seems to be jammed."

There was a moment's hesitation from the majordomo, then in his most formal voice, he answered, "Very good, your grace." A white square slid beneath the door.

"I have the message, Boggs, thank you," Adrian said as he bent to retrieve it.

"I will engage a locksmith to fix that lock as soon as possible, your grace," Boggs said.

"There is no hurry, Boggs." Adrian sent Jillian a sly, intimate smile. "Duchess Dunbary and I are discussing our plans for the rest of the day. We will be quite some time."

Jillian smothered her giggles, as Boggs acknowledged Adrian's comment and moved away.

"That was quite wicked of you," she said.

He threw her a grin and ripped open the message. His breath escaped in a silent whistle as he read.

"What is it?" Apprehension clutched at her.

He glanced at her. "It concerns your former guardian."

"I hope he rots in hell," she spat.

A wry smile twisted his lips. "He may do that. He has fled to his seat in Northumberland. Lord Winslow has been arrested for smuggling. Without their leadership, the opposition in Parliament to repealing the Orders in Council will fall apart."

"Then war with America can be averted?" she asked.

"I hope so." Adrian glanced down at the note again.

"But with the secret letter…" She waved a hand in the direction of the desk where it sat.

"That will definitely help." He smiled.

"Will Rystoke be arrested for treason?" she asked.

Adrian nodded. "If they can find him. But, if he has any conscience at all, he'll…"

Jillian drew a breath at her husband's incomplete statement. "Take his own life," she finished.

Adrian touched her cheek. "I'm sorry."

Jillian shook her head. "No. Don't be." She met his eyes. "If he takes his own life, it will be the only honorable thing he has ever done." She cupped her husband's cheek. "He is in the past, Adrian, part of something dark and secret. I want the rest of my life to be in the light."

He covered her hand and kissed her palm. A tingle swept up her arm and she smiled seductively.

"Hmm, I like that," she murmured.

His topaz eyes burned into her. "You are a wicked woman."

"I am *your* wicked woman." She grinned.

"My wicked wife," he agreed and tossed the letter from Lord Castlereagh over his shoulder. "Now, where were we?" He braced his hands on the door on either side of her and leaned into her. "Ah, yes, I remember now. We were discussing a trip to Dunbary."

Jillian blinked up at him. "We were?"

"Of course." One of his hands covered her breast. His head dipped down. "Don't you remember?" he whispered against her lips.

She never had a chance to answer, for all thought fled as she gave herself up to the truth of her husband's kiss and the reaction of her body and soul. No matter what happened between England

and America, no matter what secrets and lies occurred between the two nations, she knew she was done with deception. Her truth was her love for her husband, and his for her.

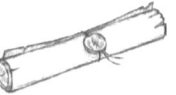

AUTHOR'S NOTE

After much debate in Parliament and discussion in the salons, clubs, taverns and streets concerning America's military threat and the seriousness of her Non-Importation Act of March, 1812, which forbade certain British products from being imported into America, the economic situation in England finally convinced the government that the Orders in Council should be repealed. Prime Minister Spencer Perceval saw the orders as a strong weapon against Napoleon and could not understand why the United States should complain. Yet, by April of 1812, members of Parliament who had supported the Orders began to oppose them, and the Prince Regent issued a formal statement which foreshadowed their repeal. Hundreds of prominent businessmen signed petitions for repeal and sent them along to Parliament.

However, the American chargé d'affairs in London, Jonathan Russell, had been transferred from Paris only a few months earlier and did not have the connections in British political circles to grasp the growing trend. All he had were the official documents from the Foreign Office which restated its unyielding position, and articles in the British press which were habitually insulting to the United States. His reports back to President Monroe in Washington as late as April, 1812 stated only that the Orders would not be repealed. Congress and the people of America were angry.

On May 11 of that year, a horrifying event occurred. As Prime Minister Spencer Perceval was entering the House of Commons, a man named Bellingham, who had lost all his wealth because of the war with Napoleon and had focused on the Prime Minister as the source of his troubles, pulled out a pistol and shot Perceval through the heart. The death of the Prime Minister threw Parliament into confusion. A new Prime Minister was not chosen until the beginning of June. The Orders in Council were finally repealed on June 23.

But it was too late. A fast ship could carry dispatches across the Atlantic in six weeks. President Monroe and Congress had heard nothing but bad news. When Russell, the American chargé d'affaires, sent out this latest, joyous news of the repeal of the Orders, he hoped it would reach America in time to avert disaster. Unfortunately, it did not. Annoyed beyond endurance, America had declared war on England by an Act of Congress on June 18, 1812. Parliament had repealed the Orders in Council five days too late. The War of 1812 would be fought and become part of history.

CONFESSIONS OF A DANGEROUS DUKE

(SNEAK PEEK)

Patricia Barletta

PROLOGUE

April, 1812, The Coast of France

The chill night breeze blew across the empty landscape as Arianne de Vouvret, her husband, Jean-Paul, and her father, François Chiasson, hurried across the uneven ground. Clouds ran before the wind and scudded across the moon, creating shadows that helped to hide the three in their flight.

Arianne halted as the sound of dislodged pebbles came from behind her. Was someone there? Or had it only been her imagination? All she could hear was the wind, toying with the branches of trees and sending loose leaves into giddy flights. She searched the moonlit darkness behind her, but she could see nothing as the silent, swift clouds moved far above them in their nighttime game.

"Arianne, what is it?" Jean-Paul stopped and turned back to her.

She listened a moment longer, then shook her head. "It is nothing." She smiled reassuringly at her husband, even though he probably could not see it. "Hurry along with Papa. I am coming."

She watched Jean-Paul take her father by the arm once more to guide him across the uneven ground. He had been ill, and was still weak, but they'd had to flee. Their hiding spot, a tiny farm not far from the northern coast, had been discovered. And so they had run.

Only a little farther, she thought, *and they would reach the beach where a boat waited to take them to safety.*

"Hurry, *chérie*," Jean-Paul urged.

She picked up her skirts and hastened after the two men in her life who were more dear to her than anything on earth. They wended their way through the woods that curved back from the shore. Beyond the edge of trees was an open, rocky plain, a small sandy cliff, and then the beach and the sea. As they cleared the woods, Arianne knew they were the most vulnerable, for then they were silhouetted against the expanse of water. Her spine tingled with the touch of imagined eyes watching. She linked her arm through her father's.

"We're almost there, Papa," she encouraged.

He did not waste breath on an answer, but patted her hand reassuringly. His labored breathing told her how much of a toll this flight had taken on him. She worried about his strength.

On her father's other side, Jean-Paul slowed and turned his head to listen. His hurried footsteps faltered. "We're being followed! Quickly! To the boat!"

As they broke into a run, the explosion of a gunshot swept to them on the night wind. Jean-Paul grunted and stumbled. Arianne cast a glance at him. He took four more steps, then collapsed on one knee.

"Jean-Paul!" she screamed and reached out to help him.

"Go on," he urged, pain lacing his voice. "Take your father and run."

Fear clutched at her as she knelt beside him. "I won't leave you."

"Arianne, you promised you would stay safe," Jean-Paul scolded gently, his words weaker than normal.

"You promised the same," she said, then turned to her father. "Papa, take the boat, cross the Channel. I will come to you when I can."

"What kind of father abandons his children?" her father demanded kindly. "Come, we will cross the Channel together." He took Jean-Paul's arm and tried to help him to his feet.

After an unsuccessful attempt to stand, Jean-Paul shook his head. As he coughed up blood, Arianne and her father gently laid him on the cold, rocky ground. She felt the warm wetness on his back and the rough-edged hole in his coat. The bullet had found its mark in her husband. She tried to staunch the flow of blood with her hand.

"I can't go on," he struggled to tell them. "You must leave while... you have...the chance."

"I'm not leaving you." Her arms tightened around him.

She looked up, across her husband's prone body, to the edge of the woods where five dark figures emerged. *Too late*, she thought.

Too late for escape. They would be taken together. She would plead for help for Jean-Paul.

Turning back to her husband, she smoothed his brow and brushed the hair from his face. "I will get help for you. They don't want your death, only our lives."

With a smile, he reached up and touched her cheek. "You are dearer to me than life, *ma chérie*," he whispered. A gurgling cough twisted his face in pain. A dark line of blood dribbled from the corner of his mouth. Delicately, Arianne wiped it away with her skirt. Again his words came, tortured and barely audible. "Run, my flower. Run and live. I love you."

His breath ended with his words. His eyes stared beyond her at something only he could now see. He was gone.

"No!" she denied. "No, no, no, no!" Arianne bent over him, hugged him, tried to love some life back into his body.

Her father knelt beside her and placed a comforting arm around her shoulders.

A heel grinding against stone announced the arrival of their pursuers. Their footsteps had been hidden by the wind and her own wailing. She knew who they were—one of them even by name.

"Madame de Vouvret, Monsieur Chiasson," Henri Pinard greeted them amiably. The black patch over his left eye gave him a rakish appearance, but beneath his debonair exterior lay a heart as cold as Hades. His single-eyed gaze swept over them. He smiled with chilly satisfaction. "We are well met. Were you planning a midnight sail, perhaps?"

Arianne heard the mocking words, and her grief turned into a cold, hard rage. Immediately, her tears dried up. Her lips drew back in a feral snarl.

"You killed him." Her low tone was more deadly than any screech of anger. "You killed him when he had done nothing more than try to save his family."

"A pity," Pinard acknowledged as if he were lamenting the lack of wine at a picnic. "A tragic accident, but then, he was of little use to us."

"Pig! Snake! Monster!" The words erupted in a growl from her deep, visceral hatred of the man. She would have gone on with her name-calling, but grief choked her and made her thoughts spin off into a void.

Arianne's father rose to his feet. "You will leave my daughter out of your scheming, Pinard. Take me and let her go."

Pinard crossed his arms. "I will certainly take you, François, but I have found that the lovely Madame de Vouvret has become rather valuable."

"You are vile, Pinard." Arianne spat onto his shiny boots.

Pinard's mouth twisted in distaste. "Fortunately, madame, I am not easily insulted, and both you and your papa are too valuable for me to do more than admonish you to mind your manners and keep a civil tongue," Pinard said.

A furtive movement from Arianne's father made Pinard's henchmen swing pistols and swords around in his direction.

"You are too wise to do something so foolish, Monsieur Chiasson." Pinard nodded at the knife in the man's hand. "And you should know after our long association that I do not tolerate insubordination from those in my employ." At his gesture, one of his men wrenched the knife away.

Arianne's father stiffened his spine. "I am not in your employ any longer, Pinard."

Pinard glared with his single eye. "You are in no position to refuse, François, unless you would care to see your daughter come to harm." Those pistols and swords swung in Arianne's direction.

"No!" Monsieur Chiasson's shoulders drooped. "I will go with you."

"Good. Now," Pinard went on, "presuming that neither one of you has any more objections or trinkets to show us, we'll be off. I do wish to be back at the inn by morning for croissants and hot chocolate." He swung about as he motioned for his henchmen to bring the prisoners.

"But my husband —" Arianne tried to twist free of the two men who had pulled her to her feet. "You cannot just leave him here."

Pinard turned back to her with an annoyed scowl. "Of course I can." One of his men whispered something to him. Pinard sighed with irritation. "Well, perhaps you are right. Questions are bound to be asked." He pointed at two of his men. "You and you. Bury him. The rest of us will be off."

Arianne realized it was useless to protest as she was hauled after Pinard. When she glanced at her father, he gave her an imperceptible shake of his head in warning. Pinard could turn cruel at the slightest provocation.

Too late, she thought again with a longing glance back at the dear form of Jean-Paul, now an indistinct, dark shape on the ground. Her heart twisted painfully. Too late to tell him her secret, the one she herself had just discovered. Instinctively, she placed her hand over her womb, then realized she should not make such an obvious, protective motion. She turned the motion into a nervous gesture. If she were very careful and very lucky, she would be able to keep her secret to herself, and Pinard would never discover it.

She went quietly with her captors. Wiping her husband's blood on her skirt, she knew that she would never wipe his memory from her heart, nor the man who so casually took his life. She stumbled along, passive now in Pinard's custody, tears a chilly stream down her cheeks. She vowed some day she would wreak her revenge. Glancing up at the sky, she called on the moon and clouds and the heavens themselves to witness what had occurred in their presence, and allowed the wind to entwine her heart in its cold embrace.

ABOUT THE AUTHOR

Patricia Barletta is a multi-published, award-winning author of historical and paranormal romance fiction. As a native of the Boston area, she has been inspired by its history, which influenced her stories, and probably had an impact on her decision to become a high school British Literature teacher so she could pay the bills. She received a Master of Fine Arts in Creative Writing degree at the fabulous Stonecoast program in Maine. She loves to travel, especially to do research for her stories. When she's not at a yoga class, gardening, or socializing with friends, she's writing about dark heroes, feisty heroines, magic, and other fantastical things in her historic old home in Boston.

Find out more about Patricia and her books at:
patriciabarletta.com

Follow Patricia Barletta on BookBub.

www.ingramcontent.com/pod-product-compliance
Lightning Source LLC
Chambersburg PA
CBHW030416180626
46812CB00005B/2037